# one

*Time present and time past*
*Are both perhaps present in time future,*
*And time future contained in time past.*
T.S. ELIOT, "BURNT NORTON,"
FOUR QUARTETS

I
–

For a person who was rather private, it was startling to hear her name in such a public place.

"Effie Gillis?"

The tone was tentative, bordering on disbelief. She could have ignored it, but she turned, out of curiosity or anxiety. She was in the St. George subway station, heading home, Christmas shopping finished. It was December 19, 1997, another detail she'd remember.

She knew him right away though she hadn't set eyes on him for decades. Campbell, JC Campbell. He was standing near the end of the east-west platform, a newspaper in his hand, smiling. She noted the glint of silver in the hair around his temples.

"My God," she said.

They shook hands.

"It's been, how long . . ."

"Twenty years, at least," he said.

They fell silent briefly. She remembered that he'd taken a job with a television network in the United States. Something about his passport, she recalled; American employers loved the Canadian passport. It travelled better than their own because it was less likely to provoke an inconvenient attitude at certain border crossings. She recalled a drunken farewell party at her house. It was in the Beaches, so yes, it would have been 1977. Twenty years ago, 1977, the year of raised voices, slamming doors, her child cowering underneath the kitchen table. The farewell celebration was a kind of respite.

She remembered him as being tall, but he was maybe five eleven, only slightly taller than she was. Still slim. She remembered black-framed glasses, longer hair, a mullet, maybe. Hockey player hair, they used to call it. Now the glasses were gone, presumably replaced by contact lenses. The hair was cropped short. He had the same emphatic hairline, with a hint of widow's peak. He had the look, she thought, of a sober single man.

He smiled, narrowed his eyes. "And yourself, you and Sextus . . ."

She felt the blush but didn't mind, knowing that it made her seem younger.

"Yes and no," she said. "One of those things. There's been a lot of water under the bridge since . . . when was it? Seventy-seven, I believe."

"Seventy-seven it was when I went off."

"We split up after that," she said. "But, miracle of miracles . . ." She laughed.

"I was glad to hear that you were back together," he said. The statement seemed cautious, speculative. "Sextus and I have stayed in touch, sporadically. I felt bad when he told me you two split, back then. But he's still—Sextus—living in Cape Breton?"

"For now. We're trying to come up with a plan."

"Your brother, Duncan. Still in the priesthood, I imagine?"

"Yes and no again," she said. "He's here in Toronto now. But still a priest. A rarity."

"I haven't seen Duncan since university," he said. "And yourself, still in academe, I gather? I think Sextus told me that you got a doctorate. Tenure and the whole nine yards. Would be kind of hard to give that up."

"And do what?" She laughed.

"Just look at you," he said, arms held wide. "You look fantastic." Now he blushed. Her eyes drifted to his left hand. He was wearing gloves.

"So you're back here now, are you? The last I heard, I think you were overseas or in the States, working in the news."

"Still in the news, but back home," he said. "Speaking of home, I'm just heading there. I bought a little place in lower Riverdale."

She could have told him that she lived just three blocks away from the St. George station. It would have been appropriate, reciprocal disclosure, but something stopped her. She felt a certain freedom here and she wanted to enjoy it for a moment.

She was living in a duplex she'd rented, the ground level and second floor of an old Victorian mansion close to everything. She'd sold the big house on the Kingsway, and the transaction left her relatively wealthy. She'd been able to complete the renovation of her old home in Cape Breton, and even after that she had a nest egg that would supplement the inevitable academic pension. Or buy another house. But she didn't want to go into that with him, how she lived or where or why. She felt oddly stimulated, talking to a stranger who was still familiar. The gloves, the haircut, the cashmere overcoat marked him as a man of style. He could have been from anywhere, the attractive man before her. She felt a mild excitement trying to recall their common past.

"So you were Christmas shopping, I imagine," he said. The easy smile was yet another feature that was unfamiliar.

"Just on my way home," she said. "I live nearby. So you've got all the shopping done already?"

"Well," he said, "my shopping is pretty limited."

"Yes. You reach a certain age."

They fell silent. He was nodding, thoughtfully it seemed. And it might have ended there, but he suddenly suggested going for a drink around the corner on Prince Arthur, and she couldn't think of a single reason to resist.

At the pub there was a Christmas party in full swing, old-timers getting plastered. He seemed to know most of them. Reporters, he confided. She had a glass of wine. He had a Guinness.

"So the man himself," he said. "I imagine he'll be coming up for Christmas. Or will you go down?"

"You mean Sextus?"

"Yes. Wasn't there talk of himself moving back to the city?" His brow was furrowed, eyes innocent.

"Neither of us likes to travel much this time of year," she said, not really answering what he was asking. "I think way too much is made of Christmas anyway. You know, it's a manufactured feast at best . . . to seduce the pagans from their superstitious rituals."

"New Year's was the time," he said. "*Oidhche Chaluinn.*"

"Ah. You know about it."

"Well, of course."

And when the waitress offered them a menu, he didn't answer, just stared at her, waiting.

"We might as well," she said.

———

JC Campbell was part of the clique from home when she and Sextus Gillis first came to Toronto, back in the early seventies. She was a fugitive. That was how she saw herself. She needed the distractions of the unfamiliar city and would have been much happier if she'd been able to blend into an entirely new society of total strangers. But Sextus was part of an odd assortment of construction workers, miners and newspaper reporters with nothing much in common except Cape Breton and what seemed to be a mutual belief that life would always be more or less the way it was just then, a serial ceilidh with brief interruptions for recovery and as much employment as was needed to sustain it. They all seemed to be in their mid- to late twenties, all prosperous enough to have sufficient money for the basic necessities and enough left over to nearly satisfy voracious appetites for fun. Some were single, all were childless, though she was pregnant at the time.

Maybe she'd begun to notice JC Campbell in those frantic early days because he, like her, seemed to be on the periphery of everything. He seemed to be just a little bit more serious about work, a little less inclined to be unconscious at the end of every social function. He often helped her with the cleanup after the other men had stumbled home or off to temporary sleeping arrangements. Back then she thought he was from Halifax. She'd suspected, for a while, that he was homosexual, that his remoteness came from a feeling of exclusion. But Sextus told her that he probably held himself a little apart because of fallout from an incident when he was still a student. JC had secrets, but he definitely wasn't gay.

———

That evening, December 19, 1997, they parted after dinner with a hug. It was almost fraternal, but it left a lingering sensation oddly similar to reassurance, and it stayed with her, as did certain moments in their conversation.

The next time she saw him he was on television. There was sunshine. He was talking to a camera. He had told her that he preferred to be the guy behind the scenes, the producer or the writer. But there he was, speaking to the world. She found herself staring without hearing what he had to say.

Effie Gillis had by then achieved just about as much as she aspired to in terms of her career and her life. She was into healthy middle age, she was a department head at a major university. She was published and looked forward to perhaps a peaceful decade contemplating parts of history she deemed to be important, conveying insight with poise and credibility to her students and her peers. She and Sextus were rebuilding a relationship that she'd convinced herself might now provide stability even if it fell short of the intimacy she still craved. It was easy in such circumstances to forget the fragility of expectations. The reminder, when it came, was brutal.

After the initial shock wore off, she would be able to recall with some amusement that it came on a Palm Sunday, a week before the end of Lent, when warm spring days and all the old familiar stories of redemption lift the spirits. Her brief encounter in the subway station months before had all but faded from her mind. Then her brother called. His words were blunt, especially from a priest: "The miserable quiff is having an affair with Stella Fortune."

"Who are you talking about?"

"You know who I'm talking about. That sleazebag Sextus."

In the background she could hear dishes rattling, human babble, raucous laughter.

"Are you there?" Duncan asked.

"Yes, I'm here," she said.

"Well, say something."

"What do you expect me to say? That I'm shocked? That after all the years I've known him, anything he could do would come as a surprise, especially involving women? Wake up, Duncan."

"Effie, I thought Stella had more sense than that. Sextus Gillis. Of all the goddamned people she could have——"

"You thought Stella had more sense than your sister," she said tightly, anger rising.

"I didn't mean that."

"No?"

"I feel like an idiot," he said. "I told her things . . ."

"Presuming you were dealing with some higher sensibility."

"I'm sorry I called," he said. "I should have left you in the bloody dark."

He hung up, and afterwards she felt sorry for the selfishness of her reaction. She could picture her brother standing there alone, slouched against the wall beside the pay phones, misery personified.

Duncan had moved to Toronto in the fall of 1997. He told her only that he'd been granted a sabbatical to work the streets in what he called a rescue mission. Saving lost street people while rescuing his ministry, he said. Trying to redefine his priesthood, to give it relevance, or, maybe, in the end, to give it up entirely. Effie hadn't been aware that Stella Fortune was a factor, though she'd known that they were friends when he was pastor in her parish in Cape Breton.

Duncan called later to apologize. "You're the one who should be pissed," he said.

"No," she said. "You didn't deserve me lashing out."

"I feel it's my fault," Duncan said. "If I'd been paying more attention . . . But I thought she had more . . . character."

"We don't know the whole story," Effie said. "One thing Stella has is character. But character sometimes gets trumped by needs."

"I don't think I want to know the whole story," he said, and laughed briefly. "You didn't have a clue?"

"I didn't. How did you find out?"

"Stella phoned. Apparently he just started dropping in on her. Then he made it clear to her that he wanted a more intimate relationship."

"So she came to you?"

"She wanted my advice."

"My God, Duncan," Effie said.

"What?"

"I can't believe how thick you are. Do you really think it was *advice* she wanted?"

She told herself she was too old for heartache, but not for embarrassment. Privately she knew it was her smugness she regretted most; it bothered her that she had let her guard down, as if past mistakes could ever immunize a fool from future foolishness. All the years she'd known Sextus, all the old betrayals, now weighed heavily upon her. She realized she didn't really mind the now inevitable solitude. She'd learned to think of it as independence. What bothered her was this reminder that there was, never far beneath the surface of her poise, a yearning (dare she call it loneliness).

It took about three days for the embarrassment to ripen into an unspeakable anger.

On day four, which was Holy Thursday, Sextus called her.

She hung up.

He phoned again that same day and left a message: they needed to talk; he'd made a huge mistake; he wanted to explain; he knew she'd understand if only he could have a moment. Nobody understood him better than Effie did.

She erased it.

Her smugness, she now realized, had come from the certainty that male behaviour could never catch her by surprise again. It was a small reward for all the years she'd spent coping with the turmoil men cause. Father. Brother. Husbands. Live-in partners. Even her neurotic male colleagues at the university. There was no excuse this time. It was entirely her own fault. She could and should have seen it coming. Her brother had disapproved of her renewed relationship with Sextus from the outset, but she really didn't need a warning. Sextus Gillis had been dazzling and disappointing her since childhood. She dumped a husband for him, eloped and married him, tried to raise a child with him, tried to rise above his infidelities—and eventually threw him out and got over him successfully.

She should have had the sense, based on past experience, to avoid another entanglement from which there could be no constructive disengagement. But she was home when they started up again, back in Cape Breton where, she concluded afterwards, most of her worst life lapses had occurred.

She was vulnerable (God, how she hated to admit that), but, it seemed, he was too. And it shouldn't have been totally far-fetched to think he'd changed a little at middle age, grown perhaps. Except it *was* too much to hope for and certainly too much to ask for. And here she was, messed up again.

Then it was day five, Good Friday, and JC Campbell was on her doorstep.

"Well, well, well," she said. "I didn't think I'd be seeing you again."

"I'm a reporter," he said. "I have ways of tracking people down. May I come in?"

She stepped back to let him in, then closed the door behind him. Stood there, mind blank.

"What a great spot," he said, hands on hips, taking in the room. He walked over to a bookcase and studied a shelf of Gaelic volumes, murmuring more compliments. She was at a loss. To ask abruptly what he wanted would sound unfriendly. He was an old friend of sorts, but then again he was a stranger and, more to the point, one of Sextus's friends. She felt vaguely threatened.

"I was going to pour a drink," she said.

"So, what are you having?"

"A Scotch," she said.

"Single malt or blend?"

"Single," she replied.

"No ice in mine, then." He was smiling.

He still had his coat on, sitting at the corner of her kitchen table, sipping his drink. "You probably don't realize that I am on a mission."

"It hadn't crossed my mind," she said.

"Well. It's awkward. And I make it a policy to stay away from personal . . . situations. But you know Sextus."

She stood, walked away from the table, then turned. Leaned back against the kitchen counter, arms folded. "What about him?"

He raised a protective hand. "I know, I know. But I said that I'd drop in on you to say what he hasn't had a chance to say himself."

"He hasn't had the chance because I don't want to hear it."

"Fair enough," he said. "I'll keep it real short. Whatever it was he got involved in—I don't know the other party, whatever her name is. It was a fling. He said you'd understand the difference: a 'fling' as opposed to an 'affair' or a 'relationship.' Personally I don't quite understand the difference. I'm just saying what he said."

"So you can report back. You said it. Mission accomplished."

"Sextus," JC said, shaking his head and smiling. "Sextus never changes. He actually thinks it was Duncan's fault. Really. Duncan left some woman dangling, the way Sextus sees it. She was lonely. He had no choice. He had to respond. Damsel in distress and all that. He actually blames Duncan."

"I don't think my brother should hear that part of the story. He'd tear Sextus's head off. Not that it would be any great loss." She laughed, for the first time in days, and felt a momentary ping of joy.

"I hear you," he said. "Yup. I hear you loud and clear." He drained his glass and stood. "That's not bad. What is it?"

"Highland Park," she said. "My brother turned me on to it."

"Well, I'd best be on my way," he said. "I've done my thing." For the first time he seemed to be embarrassed.

"I'm going to freshen mine," she said. "Do you have time for another?"

"If you twist my arm."

Before he left her place on Good Friday, even though she barely knew him, she invited him to dinner Easter Sunday, knowing that he'd stay the night. She also knew that she was motivated mostly by malice when she slept with him the first time. And because she assumed it would be the only time, she allowed her fury to explode.

*I'll show you what it feels like to be dominated, to be used.* And when she sensed his submission, she rose in primal majesty above him, and in her mind, assumed his body as her own and wildly thrust it back at him. *I want you to be hurt, hurt, hurt.* Her hands turned into fists, as if to strike him, and only then did she realize that he had firmly grasped her by the wrists, was fighting back, and everything she ever was or ever would be fused without warning in that all-consuming instant *now.*

And *now* he shouted back, and suddenly they both were laughing as they collapsed, entangled in absurdity.

She expected, looking back on it, that JC Campbell would have been severely daunted by her raw display of passion, a bit intimidated by her self-indulgence, her aggression. She didn't really care. But in the end she realized he hadn't even noticed what she thought of as perversity, was unbothered by her obvious emotional detachment.

When she woke up on that Easter Monday morning, he was making breakfast.

Reality intruded briefly just before he left that day. At the door, he said, "I'll call you later." She tried to smile. How many farewells begin that way? *Give me a shout. Have a nice day.* She felt the dead weight in her chest. At least he hadn't mentioned "love," the second most abused word in the English language, after "sorry." How many times had she lived this doorway scene?

She forced a smile. "Sure."

"I have to pop into the office for a bit," he said. He stood silent for a moment. "I *will* call."

"You don't even have my number." She felt the urge to laugh. His face was almost boyish.

"I do," he said. "I made a note of it, from your kitchen phone, on Friday. When you weren't looking. I didn't think you'd mind."

"That was sneaky. You only had to ask."

"I was afraid of the answer," he said. He turned and trotted down the doorstep, then stopped and waved.

And shortly after five o'clock that day he called.

She hadn't really been prepared for the anger that poured out of her in what passed for "making love." In the aftermath, she was surprised by his extraordinary calm, as if her provocative behaviour and her outburst had been commonplace in his experience. The last thing she expected was to ever hear from him again. In her own mind, it had been Effie's last one-night stand. But he was almost eager when he called on Monday evening. He thought they should have lunch on Wednesday, talk some more. Talk more? What had they talked about?

It was a polite lunch at an Italian place on College, a place she was surprised he knew. One of *her* favourite places, but he suggested it. The conversation was mostly about how she came to specialize in Celtic studies. He listened carefully, avoiding speculation or analysis, though he ventured one conclusive comment. "It makes sense," he said. "It's an area that needs examination by someone with a modern outlook. Someone who can connect the dots between then and now, maybe tell us something about ourselves."

"Well," she said.

"Well, what?"

"I couldn't have put it better myself."

There was very little discussion about him. That would come later, by way of mostly disconnected observations about other things, figuring out where he was at certain moments in her life.

By the end of lunch she wanted to know more: about Lebanon and Israel; about Russia and the Balkans and the Caucasus; about Spanish-sounding places that had been mentioned on the news. El Salvador.

Duncan had friends there, she said.

"Really?" He sounded surprised. "I'll have to ask him." Then, "I suppose you get back east quite a bit. Stay in touch."

She laughed. She told him she'd pretty well lost touch with Cape Breton after she and Sextus moved to the city in 1970. She'd only started going back in '94, started fixing up the old home. Before that, maybe once in God knows how many years. Not since about 1972.

He was surprised. "I would have thought Cape Breton was an ideal place for fieldwork, research."

"I kick myself all the time," she said, "especially now that I realize what was there and what I was missing. But no, I let it all slide. True tradition bearers are now few and far between. Unless you count the graveyards."

"Early seventies," he said. "I seem to recall something. Someone died. I remember Sextus talking about it."

"That would have been my father," she said, nodding. "He died around then."

"So that would have been your last trip for quite a while."

"Actually, I didn't even go home for that."

"Ahhh," he said. He was tracing circles on the tablecloth with the salt shaker. "We forget how travel was in those days. It was a big trip then."

"Yes," she said. "A very big trip."

He asked about the possibility of meeting up again on Friday evening. Drinks, maybe dinner. Talk some more?

"Give me a call," she said. "When you know your sched."

"The sched is pretty simple these days," he said. "I'm in editing."

"Something interesting?"

"Not really," he said. "A lot of hoohoraw about Y2K and the end of Western society as we know it. The millennium bug, wiping out computers everywhere at midnight, December 31, 1999. Mark the date."

"No great loss."

"I agree," he said. "A hundred percent."

They left in separate cabs. He held the door of hers for just a moment. "Our Easter dinner," he said. "I can't remember anything as . . . memorable." He blushed.

She smiled. "Memorable?"

"I'll try to think of a better word. How about Friday? It'll be my homework. I'll hand it in at dinner, poetry perhaps. I expect your standards are high. Regarding poetry."

"Merciless," she said.

He kissed her quickly on the forehead before she ducked into the back seat. And he stood there as the taxi drove away.

Only once had Sextus's name come up during the time they spent together after JC's visit on Good Friday. JC wanted to know how long she and Sextus had known each other.

"Oh my God," she said. "Forever." And she'd looked away, vaguely irritated. "We were children."

She changed the subject then, but later, as she stood alone in her kitchen, listening to the whisper of her kettle, the first time she met Sextus came back to her. It was a very precise memory.

—

*She and her father were standing in the barren yard at home. A car stopped near their gate. A man and a boy emerged. The boy was nine or ten years old, about Duncan's age. They walked toward the closed gate then stopped there. The man was heavy-set, with thinning hair. He stood, elbows resting on top of the gate, the boy beside him. Effie's father walked slowly toward them as she trailed behind, uncertain. He took the same position, forearms resting. Effie studied the boy, who was staring at her, his steady hazel eyes unblinking.*

*"Well, Angus," said the man. "So this is you. Back at square one, back home on the Long Stretch." He gestured widely with both arms, returned them to the top pole of the gate.*

*"Luckier than some," said Angus.*

*"There's that," the man replied. He extracted a package of cigarettes slowly from an inside pocket, poked it open, presented one to Angus.*

*Angus shook his head.*

*The stranger took one for himself, flicked a lighter, squinted at the flame and smoke.*

*"Sorry for your loss," he said, exhaling. "I heard about the missus when it happened. Last year it was, I think. I was still in East Malartic. So I couldn't even get in touch."*

*Angus nodded. "The TB got her. The place was rotten with it. There was nothing anyone could do. And where are you now?"*

*"Stirling, near Loch Lomond."*

*"What's there?"*

*"Zinc. Base metals."*

*"Right."*

*"They're hiring. I was wondering . . . you were an able man in the raise."*

*Angus laughed, placed a hand on Effie's head. The hand was heavy, seemed to grasp her skull for steadiness.*

"I'm kind of tied down just now," he said. "Got all the raise work I can handle right here, raisin' kids."

"I suppose," the stranger said.

"I hear there'll soon be lots of work right here. The new causeway to the mainland."

"So they say. I'm planning to move home for that myself," the man said. "Should be good for a few years' work. We can do some catching up then."

"You saw Sandy?"

"I did. He's doing okay, considering. You know Sandy. Doesn't say much anymore."

Angus laughed. "And who's the gentleman beside you?"

The man looked down.

"Another Sandy. The son and heir. Alexander Sextus."

"Sextus?" Angus said. "Quite the handle."

Effie thought the boy looked bold. "What's your name?" he asked.

She looked away. "Effie MacAskill," she said at last.

"We'll be seeing you," the man said to her father. He dropped his half-smoked cigarette, stepped on it and turned away. The boy looked back and waved; no longer bold, he now seemed shy.

"Who was that?" asked Duncan, who by then was sitting on the doorstep.

"That's Jack Gillis," Angus said. Then, to Effie, "What'd he say that boy's name was?"

"I don't know, I couldn't hear," she said. "Something sex."

Her father looked at her sharply, then laughed and walked away toward the barn.

———

The Friday night dinner date was at a trendy fusion place, reputed to be terrifyingly expensive. It was cold for early April, but the air was fresh with hints of spring. She'd read about the restaurant, but it was her first time there. The menu had no prices. "If you have to ask how much, you shouldn't be here," JC said. He seemed to know the menu and the staff.

A waiter appeared with a tray of small plates, each with a careful arrangement of bite-size foods in sauces, garnished with sprigs of green and red. With exaggerated flourishes, the waiter placed them at the centre of the table. Poured water. She watched JC eat, noted how he picked at food, more curious than hungry.

A slim, young Asian man who, Effie gathered, was the owner, appeared near the end of dinner to inquire about JC's health. There were none of the usual formalities, whether they enjoyed the food, the service—satisfaction was a given. He and JC seemed to have a well-established friendship.

"Great guy," JC commented later. And, as he prepared to pay the bill, a server appeared with a half-bottle of dessert wine that they just had to try. Compliments of Mr. Lee.

Before they left, she excused herself, went to the bathroom to inspect her makeup. She looked and felt clear-headed. She had cleverly avoided cocktails, stuck to wine. Now she felt that she was ready for whatever. But at her door he declined when she offered him a nightcap. He had a heavy day on Saturday, he said apologetically. But he wanted to see her again soon, to talk more about the summer and her plans.

The prospect of a summer holiday together had arisen over dinner in the context of a general discussion about weather. In the city you could sense the end of winter, the inevitability of summer. But summer came reluctantly and invariably late to the east coast. As a rule she stayed in Toronto until July, then she would fly to Halifax and rent a car. That year she said she thought she'd enjoy driving out on her own, all the way. Hadn't done that for a zillion years.

And that was when he told her it felt at least that long since he'd been back to Nova Scotia, the last time a visit in the sixties that he'd rather not remember, even now. He laughed, remembering. "You probably knew about the scandal?"

"Can't say that I did."

"Pretty tame by the standards of today. But I got someone, as we used to delicately put it, in trouble. I was starting out in university. She was from Cape Breton. We arrived at a kind of settlement, but it pretty well wiped me out financially."

"I see," she said. Waited through a long pause, then gambled: "So . . . you have a child."

"I suppose I do," he said.

"Boy or girl?"

"Girl," he said. "In her mid-thirties by now. I lost touch a long time ago."

"That's a shame," Effie said.

His frown tugged down the corners of his mouth. "Depends on how you look at it."

"So where did she end up?"

"Last I heard she was in your neck of the woods. Around the Strait somewhere. The mother was from Isle Madame. Petit-de-Grat. You ever been there?"

"She'd be French. *Acadienne.*"

"*Oui.*"

"I'm not sure what to say."

"It all worked out," he said. "It launched me into journalism."

She suppressed a laugh. "Really!"

"A long story, maybe for a long car drive."

"I suspect you have a lot of stories."

"A thousand and one," he said.

His handling of chopsticks, she'd noted, was masterful.

"And I could share the wheel. Those drives are killers."

"I wouldn't be averse to company," she said. "To share the driving. And, of course, the gas."

"And the accommodations."

"That too."

Everything about him was so easy, she told herself, settling at home that night with a small nightcap and a book she had no intention of even opening. He had no reluctance to disclose, but neither had there been the compulsive revelation she had heard so often, the self-mythologizing that can happen in the early going. His life was rich, as far as she could tell from his brief references to distant places and events. But such details always seemed subordinate to his avid curiosity about her. The overall impression he gave her was that nothing in his life, no prior time or place or individual, was as central to his consciousness as this one, here, with her.

She would, in later years, remember one event that would define JC Campbell and mercifully contradict so much that she would later struggle not to know. They were on the subway. It was shortly after that first Easter. The car was crowded. They were standing, swaying with the motion of the train. She smelled smoke. A man seated close to them had lit a cigarette. The people on the train were instantly uneasy, moving away, as if he'd lit a fuse. JC smiled, leaned down, said softly, "Put it out." The smoker just stared, cleared his throat as if to spit and turned away.

He was in the act of raising the cigarette to his lips again when JC caught his wrist, then squeezed the ember on the cigarette

between his naked thumb and forefinger. Then he broke the cigarette in two. Sparks fell to the man's lap and he tried instantly to
stand, but JC now had him firmly by the collar. Held him down.
Leaned over, whispered something.

The train was slowing for a station stop. JC released him. The
man stood and moved toward the door, muttering dark threats. JC
said to Effie, "Wait for me at Broadview." She said "No!" but JC and
the stranger were already gone. As the train pulled away, she could
see the man through the window, wild-faced, waving his arms while
JC stood rock-still, hands jammed into the side pockets of his jacket.

"What happened?" she asked later.

"Nothing," he replied.

"You frightened me."

"Why? How?"

"What you did."

"Sometimes you have to do what you have to do."

———

It would be May before she'd have the confidence to talk about
him, to share her feelings with another. May 31, to be exact, a
Sunday. She called her brother, Duncan, and invited him to dinner.

"I might have news," she said.

"News. It's a perfect day for news. Good news, I presume?"

"I hope so," she said. "What's the day?"

"Pentecost," he said. "It's Pentecost Sunday."

"Sorry, Father, I've been missing Mass lately."

"You're forgiven," he said. "For your penance, a good act of contrition and three fingers of Balvenie for your confessor."

"You're on," she said.

———

"So is it anyone I know?" Duncan asked. He was sitting on her sofa now, studying his drink with a pastoral expression on his face.

"I think so," she replied from the kitchen. "I think you'll like him," she said, and was instantly disappointed by the lack of originality.

He raised an eyebrow. "They're all likeable at first, aren't they?"

"You know what I mean," she said.

"Tell me one good thing about him."

"How about three: he's intelligent; he's worldly; he's a grown-up." Now she was standing in the archway between the kitchen and the larger space that served as dining room and den, hands concealed beneath the apron she was wearing. "And he's very good-looking. That's four."

He made a grimace of approval.

"He says he remembers you from university."

"That's going back a bit," he said. "So what's his name?"

"JC Campbell. He was part of the gang, back in the seventies."

"Hmmm. That rings a bell. JC. Yes, I remember. Serious, he was."

Now he was engaged, studying her face with new intensity. "How much has he told you about himself that's real?"

"Everything I need to know," she said.

"I see," he said, resuming his examination of the drink. "So what's he been doing with himself all this time?"

"He went off to the States. Worked in television all over the world. Now he's back."

"Baggage?"

"What do you mean?"

"Wives, kids, war wounds—you know what I mean."

"None of the above as far as I can tell. Well, almost none. A child he never knew, maybe."

Duncan sighed. "So how did this come about?"

And she explained. The accidental meeting in the subway station; the peculiar visit on Good Friday, pleading Sextus's case. Dinner on Easter Sunday (censored for her brother). She emphasized the cautious management of expectations.

But over dinner, perhaps enthused by wine, she released a torrent of previously unspoken thoughts and feelings: the renewal of her confidence; how time they spent together seemed to linger in her memory like the aftertaste of something special; the spontaneity of their laughter.

"I'd quite forgotten how great it feels to laugh. So much I'd forgotten about just getting up in the morning and imagining another person, and knowing that you're in their thoughts and that there's a place where you're more than the sum of what you are in your own mind . . . even if it's only in someone's imagination."

"Yes," he said. He seemed distracted.

"I don't know if I'm making any sense. I'm sorry to be going on like this." She picked up her fork, then put it down again, realizing that the dinner had gone cold.

"You're making sense," he said.

"We've actually talked about a trip home together this summer. What are your plans?"

"I'll be staying here," he said. "You'd go to the old place?"

"Yes," she said.

"Well, it must be serious," he said and smiled. "Has he told you how we met, in university?"

"No," she said. "Nothing specific."

"Near the end of his first year. He came to my room, said he'd heard that I was seminary bound. Word of something like that would get around in those days. The old priests would single you out if they thought . . . Anyway. He asked me straight out. Then he told me that it was something he was thinking about."

"Go away," she said. "Get out."

"I thought he was serious. But then early in year two, around October I think, he disappeared. There were rumours of a scandal. I never heard of him again, till now."

He stood then, folded his napkin and walked into the kitchen. She leaned back to see what he was doing there.

"I'm going to mark your calendar," he said. "Yes . . . on the last page. January 1999. I'm going to mark the date, January . . . sixth."

"What's January sixth?"

"The Epiphany," he said.

"What's special about the Epiphany?"

"My three favourite feast days. Easter. Pentecost. Epiphany."

Then he was back at the table, and he had the bottle of Balvenie.

"We'll toast this happy development in your life. And if he's still around at the Epiphany . . ." He compressed his lips into what seemed to her to be a cautious smile. "Who knows?"

He poured for both of them. "So when does the big trip take place?"

"We're hoping in July. But it's still in the planning stage. His work is unpredictable."

"Home," he said. "My God, that'll be the test for a relationship."

———

*It was summer. She was, maybe, twelve years old. They were swimming— Effie, Duncan, John and Sextus—in the little cove on the edge of the village. The water there was warmer than the strait that fed it, less saline on account of the forest streams that ran down into it from the hills behind it. She was huddling alone on shore, goose-pimpled, pale. She'd* been feeling fluish since the night before. Sextus was just emerging from the water and suddenly was laughing hysterically. She thought he was pointing at the ground until she heard him shout, "Effie's bleeding!"

And when she looked down, she saw the watery trickle on the inside of her thigh.

"Effie's got the rag on," Sextus crowed, leaping from one foot to the other as she stared down at herself, dumbfounded, as if looking at someone else's body. "Effie's got the rag on, hoo hoo."

She was only partially aware that her brother, Duncan, was lunging through the water, shouting, "You shut your dirty mouth!" until he was upon him, lifting, heaving, and Sextus, long, bony limbs flailing, went sailing through the air and disappeared into the depths, leaving only foam and ripples on the surface of the water.

"You go home," said Duncan quietly. "Just go." And it was the breathless anger in his voice that cut her loose from them. Sextus resurfaced, gasping, choking in half-drowned indignation; John stood silent, tragic-faced. She backed off then, fighting the humiliating tears, isolated for the first time in her life.

"Go see Mrs. Gillis," Duncan ordered. "Go now."

Mary Gillis was their nearest neighbour, John's mother. Mrs. Sandy Gillis was her public name, a fact that in her earliest remembering, Effie found disturbing. The submission, as she would later understand it, the submergence of the woman's own identity. But even in their later life, when they were adults, family, Effie found it difficult, if not impossible, to call her Mary. She was always Mrs. Gillis, and always would be, an existential circumstance over which neither woman had control.

Mary's husband, Sandy, had grown up with Effie's father, and they'd gone away together, fought in the Second World War and come home damaged by something sinister that happened overseas. Both Sandy and *her father seemed to have been permanently infected by the wickedness of war, inhabited by violence. When they were together, anything could happen. But she was afraid of Mrs. Gillis too, for the sorrow she carried in her, the traces of the misery that seemed, in Effie's mind, to originate somewhere deep within the gender they shared.*

*"You'll get used to it," was all Mrs. Gillis had to say when Effie told her what had happened at the cove. Then she turned her face away. "You'll have to be more careful now."*

*"Careful of what?"*

*"They're all animals, you know. Nothing but animals. Don't you forget that."*

———

She would remember 1998, especially the summer and its golden autumn, as the beginning of a conversation she assumed would last forever. There was so much she had to know—about JC, about the world he'd travelled, where he started, where he wanted life to end.

Her simplest but most important insight was that he was different from all the men she'd known before him. And yet, somehow, he reminded her of all of them, embodied what was best and worst in all of them. She realized that the male traits that had once left her feeling bitter and abused were but distortions of the qualities she recognized and liked in JC Campbell. Men, she now cautiously considered, weren't *essentially* perverse. The perversions were, for the most part, situational, and therefore fixable. This revision of her understanding was restorative, and therapeutic for the memory. Even inevitable disappointments folded easily into what she saw as fresh insight into JC Campbell and men in general.

He was comfortable with questions, and she realized it was because he had no fear of answers or of the dark places he sometimes revisited to find them. This was new in her experience.

"Where did you grow up, exactly?" she asked him once.

He seemed puzzled. "In Halifax. You knew that."

"I heard you telling someone once, years and years ago, that you came from Bornish, in Cape Breton."

"Well, that's true, too."

She laughed. "Nobody is from Bornish. Nobody's lived there in a century. It's another word for Nowhere."

"Well," he said, "that's me, Nobody from Nowhere. Bornish happens to be the first place I remember."

She listened closely as he gave her spare details that described a mother who once worked in a lumber camp in the middle of Nowhere and how he lived there with her as a toddler.

"Your dad?"

"What about him?"

"He was there?"

He laughed. "No. Just us."

For him it was a place of sensory impressions now imprinted in the deepest part of memory, the mingled scents of spruce and pine and fresh sawdust, of machinery and gasoline and sweat; and the sounds of men laughing, the clatter of their eating, the menace and the reassurance of their presence.

She noted that he was blinking rapidly.

"What are you looking at?"

"I'm just listening," she said.


On a Wednesday evening early in September her doorbell rang and it was Duncan. "I was in the neighbourhood," he said.

She'd been calling him since she'd returned from her summer visit to Cape Breton, but he never seemed to be available.

"I signed up for an evening Gaelic class at the university."

"You," she said. "You're as fluent as I am."

"*Bu choir dhuin a bhith bruidhinn Gaidhlig* . . . See, I can't remember how to say 'more often.'"

"*Nas trice,*" she said. "I promise we'll try to speak it more often. Now come in and have a drink. It'll bring the Gaelic back in a flash."

"I can only stay for a moment," he said, walking past her. "You came back early this year. Was the house okay?"

"The house was perfect. A little lonely, though, which was why I came back."

"I thought you had company."

"Just for a week. It was a last-minute thing for him. He came late, after me."

"And how did that work out?"

"Exquisitely," she said. "You're sure you don't have time to visit?"

"I have a meeting," he said. "But there'll be another time. The Epiphany, if not before."

"Ah yes, the Epiphany," she said. "But I think I've had enough epiphanies to last a lifetime." She knew that she was blushing as she said it.

"That's good," he said. "It isn't always easy to distinguish between an epiphany and a catharsis." He stood to leave.

"Get out of here," she said, slapping him playfully.

But when she closed the door behind him she just stood there, hands clasped before her, trying to process what seemed to be a vague presentiment of sadness.

## 2

She knew that she was late, and her anxiety increased as she read the notice on the window of the pub: "Closing early. Christmas Eve. Have a wonderful holiday!" It was December 24, 1998, and that morning JC had called and asked her to meet him for a drink at Dora's at five.

She knew Christmas Eve would be quiet at the university, so she'd gone to the office to confront a backlog of administrative paperwork, then lost track of time.

JC was waiting at the bar, the pint in front of him half finished. She placed a hand on the back of his neck, and when he turned, kissed him quickly on the cheek. "Sorry I'm late."

"No urgency," he said. Then he ordered each of them a double single malt.

"Doubles?"

"We're celebrating. Isn't it close to our first anniversary?"

"How so?"

"We missed it, actually. It was on the nineteenth, one whole year since our encounter on the subway platform."

"I think more of the encounter Easter Sunday," she said.

"Well, yes. But I still remember that first time. The innocence, maybe?" He grinned. "I'm probably more sentimental than you are. Something clicked on the subway platform."

"True," she said.

As they sipped their drinks, they turned to generalities. He asked her about Cassie. And she told him her daughter was up north with the new man in her life, meeting family. They planned to stay in Sudbury until after New Year's.

"Sounds serious," he said. "Who's the guy?"

"His name is Ray."

More than that she didn't know. He frowned.

Her daughter was, like him, a journalist, and they had hit it off the moment Effie introduced them. In fact, Cassie was unsubtle in her hints that her mother and JC should live together. Maybe more. Effie would just smile and swat the notion down, suggesting that Cassie should focus more on her own love life. They were like that, mother and daughter, having grown up together, as Cassie liked to say.

"You'll turn into an old maid soon enough yourself if you're not careful," she told her only child the last time they spoke about it.

"Use him or lose him," Cassie answered. "One of these days I just might grab the yummy Mr. Campbell for myself."

"Feel free," her mother said. "But don't you think he's a little old for you?"

Cassie blushed.

Just a few days later, Cassie declared that they should have a chat. Mom and daughter, heart to heart. Not right away, but soon. Her face was solemn.

"Oh my," said Effie.

"Just keep an open mind," said Cassie.

———

At Dora's JC was relaxed, a pleasant change, she thought. For weeks he'd been on edge whenever the subject of work came up, obviously troubled by the story he'd been working on since early summer, the case of a condemned man awaiting execution in a Texas prison.

"When will it be on?"

"Last week," he said.

"Sorry. I haven't been following the news," Effie said.

"You aren't missing much," he said.

"Remind me. I know he got in the way of our summer and that he's been haunting you all fall."

"He writes to me, quite an intelligent guy. Sam Williams. From Alberta, originally. Was in on a gruesome murder in east Texas, years back."

"But you don't think he did it."

He shrugged.

"It's coming back to me," she said. "But he writes to you?"

"We stay in touch."

"Is that advisable?" she asked.

"He doesn't have anybody," he said. "He's needy, but he's hardly any burden where he is. Plus, I'm quite convinced that he got shafted by the system."

"Aren't you setting yourself up for grief?"

He laughed. "Me? Grief?"

"He's going to die. We're talking about Texas."

"It isn't quite that simple," JC said. "But let's not worry about Sam."

She studied her drink. "What is it about him, then?" she asked at last. "Why would you stay in touch?"

He shrugged. "It's nothing, really." He smiled at her. "What about tomorrow?"

"Ah yes," she said, returning to the safety of her glass. "Tomorrow. Christmas Day."

They left Dora's just after seven and decided to walk to his place on Walden Avenue. The night was cold, with a penetrating dampness. Across the Don Valley to the west, the city loomed, glittering and silent as if abandoned for the holiday. They walked hand in hand, shoulders touching. The sky was dull with amber streaks.

"Christmas should be in the country," she said. "I miss stars and snow."

"Maybe someday."

She was looking at him, waiting for elaboration, but he kept walking, staring at the ground. So they didn't see the young man approaching, didn't notice the aggressive, shambling gait. The blow caught her by surprise, the shoulder slamming into her shoulder as the stranger hurried by. She knew it was deliberate, or at least an act of boorish carelessness.

"Asshole!" she called out.

It was only when the stranger stopped and turned to face them, fury blazing from his hoodie, that she felt afraid. JC moved between them.

"Sorry, brother," he said softly. And there was something in his tone, the way he'd turned and placed himself, both hands now raised, palms turned outward. "Let's all just keep on having a nice Christmas."

The young man wavered. "Fuck you, man," he said, but he turned quickly and strutted away, shoulders lurching in his haste.

"Well done," she said.

JC shrugged. "Who knows what's going on in that poor bugger's life."

Just inside the door, the floor was littered with envelopes, mostly Christmas cards. He scooped them up and dropped them in a large bowl, which was already full of keys and change. Their cat trotted down the stairs, meowing urgently.

"You aren't going to open them?" she asked.

"Another time," he said. "They make me feel guilty. I never sent any."

He squatted to receive his greeting from the cat.

"Who do you get them from?" she asked, poking through the envelopes. "Here's one from the States."

"That'll be from Sam," he said, and stood.

Then he was kissing her. And she nestled into the embrace and kissed him back, with a sudden yearning that dispelled all of her anxieties.

"I think I'll stay awhile," she said, shrugging off her coat.

"I was hoping you'd say that."

"Something just came over me."

"What'll you have?" he asked.

"I've had enough to drink for now. I'll make some tea."

"Make it a one-bagger," he said. "I'm going to indulge myself some more."

They were settled at the kitchen table, she sipping an herbal tea, he savouring a small puddle of old whisky, when the phone rang.

"Let it ring," she said.

"I'd better get it." He reached for the receiver, said "Hello," listened for a moment. "When did you blow in?"

She knew immediately from his tone who was on the line. She waved a hand to get his attention, mouthed, "Don't tell him I'm here."

"We're having Christmas dinner here tomorrow," he said. "Why don't you come? It'll just be me, Effie and Duncan." He winked at her. "Noooo. Don't be foolish. They'll be thrilled to see you. That's all water under the bridge."

He laughed. "I can guarantee it," he said. "You'll be perfectly safe here."

Then, after a long pause, "Well, bring her with you. I have a massive turkey. Is it anyone we know?"

Another pause. "I see. You're a hard man to get ahead of."

He looked at Effie. "Well, actually this isn't a good time. I'm going to have a nap, then go to midnight Mass. Maybe we could meet up there."

Another wink at Effie. "Understood. We'll see you tomorrow. Call when you're ready to come over. I'll give you the directions then."

He put the phone down, drained the last of his drink, then stood and poured another. "He's got a new girlfriend," he said. "A student."

"A mature student, I assume."

"Oh, I doubt that. I doubt that very much."

Early Christmas morning Effie went home to change, wrap the gifts and prepare mentally for a long and complex day. The city seemed empty. There was a bitter chill. She flagged a solitary cab on Broadview, and the silent driver made her nervous with furtive eye contact in the rear-view mirror. She thought about how much simpler life might be if she and JC just lived together. But she quickly felt the stirring of anxiety that always came when she contemplated any loss of independence. She'd lived with three men, had grown with each of them but had also paid a psychic price that made cohabitation something she wasn't eager to repeat.

At home she sorted through her mail. A clutch of flyers promising unprecedented bargains on Boxing Day, a Christmas card from her life insurance company and another with her name and address written in a hand she recognized immediately—John Gillis's.

She sat slowly, with her coat still on, and opened it. It was a simple, rustic scene: a small, snowbound house by an untracked country lane, wisps of smoke rising from a chimney, a festive wreath hanging on the door. Inside the card, the simplest of messages: "Seasons Greetings." And below it, handwritten: "Sincerely, J.G."

She felt a flash of grief, and in its wake, confusion. In the twenty-eight years since she'd abandoned him he'd never written. Not once. No letter of recrimination. No questions. All the practical inquiries involved in ending their marriage came from lawyers. There had been no acknowledgement of birthdays. When her father died, there was no sympathy, but that was understandable, given what he knew about their history. For a long time she found comfort in John's resolute indifference. It seemed to be a silent confirmation of what she wanted to believe: he never really cared for her; she had been a temporary refuge in a storm of personal disintegration, grasped the way a drowning man would grab at flotsam. His father had killed himself and he had needed her, but only for a while. But isn't that the way with all relationships? They're really only for a while. The story of her life.

This seasonal greeting was exceptional. She slipped the card back in its envelope and stood. Enough.

The afternoon of Christmas Day they worked together in JC's tiny kitchen, both wearing aprons. There was music playing. Candles flickered. By three o'clock the bird was stuffed and in the oven.

Sitting with a drink, she was surprised when, after what seemed like a long silence, JC proclaimed, "My problem is that I was always basically *in favour* of the death penalty."

"Did you say death penalty?"

"Sorry," he said. "I was thinking about poor Sam. Where he is on Christmas Day, that it could be his last Christmas."

The phone rang and he stood.

"That'll be himself, looking for directions."

The doorbell startled her even though she'd been bracing for the gong. She stole a glance at her reflection in the window of the microwave. She smoothed her skirt but then rebuked herself for caring what the bastard thought, remembered all the treachery and settled down to what she believed was a level of calm objectivity.

Sextus looked, for lack of a better adjective, happy. She'd seen him briefly in Cape Breton in the summer looking haggard and needy, probably from guilt. She'd kept her distance. Now she told him he looked fit, that he'd obviously been taking care of himself for a change. He revealed that he'd taken up jogging.

She suppressed a bitter comment, turning to the young woman who was with him.

"I'm Effie."

"Sorry," Sextus said. "I'm slow with the introductions. Susan Fougere. This is the famous Dr. MacAskill-Gillis I've been telling you about."

A jolt of anger. Smile. Extend the hand. Susan seemed to be no more than twenty-two years old. Pretty face, nice figure, cleavage likely all the way up to just below her creamy throat.

"Welcome," Effie said. "We're thrilled that you could come." Savoured the "we."

Susan smiled as Sextus turned to struggle out of his coat. When he turned back, Effie asked, "And how is our John?"

Sextus frowned. "To tell the truth, I haven't seen him lately. Saw him at the mall about three weeks ago. He was in the distance, but I didn't think he looked well. Skinnier than usual. Face kind of sunken. He's fanatic about the running, John."

"You didn't talk to him?"

"I lost sight of him. I called later, but there was no answer. I tried to get in touch before I left to come here, but again . . . no answer. You know the way he is."

"I had a Christmas card," she said.

He twitched with surprise. "No shit?"

Susan's eyes flicked back and forth between them in perplexed curiosity.

"I'm sure you've met his cousin John," Effie said to her. "My other ex-husband."

"I'm afraid I haven't," Susan said. "But I've heard about him."

Effie couldn't discern from her tone just how much she might have heard. The wily Sextus had likely been creative with the details of their peculiar history and all the intermingling that might have been off-putting to one of tender years and limited experience.

Then JC was asking for instructions regarding drinks.

Duncan arrived during the second round, accepted a Scotch and insisted that he wasn't hungry. He'd spent the day working at a homeless shelter, had handed out 479 plates of turkey and felt like he had sampled some from every plate.

Effie put Sextus beside Susan, Duncan directly across. She and JC, at either end of the table, kept busy with the carving and the serving, he liberally pouring wine. Duncan accepted a small plate of vegetables so as not to seem unsociable but insisted that he couldn't stomach another bite of turkey. He managed to extract from Susan that she was a journalism student at Ryerson; Sextus volunteered that he'd met her at a weekly paper in Cape Breton. He was an occasional contributor. He encouraged her to raise her sights, consider journalism school. She had a gift. She was clearly flattered.

"I became a kind of mentor," Sextus said.

There's another word for that, Effie thought as she exchanged a discreet smile with JC.

Susan had grown up near the causeway and was looking forward to moving back home. She found the city edgy in a good way, but she missed her friends. Effie, now up and standing by the stove, saw Sextus squeeze her thigh.

"By the way," he said to Duncan, "Stella says hello."

Duncan reddened instantly and stared down at his plate. "Does she now."

"You should give her a call," Sextus said. "Check in."

"Maybe I will," said Duncan.

Then Sextus asked JC if he was working on any interesting stories.

"The odd one," said JC.

Duncan wondered out loud if he'd had any news from Texas.

"We've been corresponding," JC said.

Effie was surprised. "You know about this Texas stuff?"

Duncan and JC exchanged what seemed like nervous glances.

"I filled him in on some of the basics," JC said. "Old Sam is pretty religious. I thought maybe Duncan could drop a line sometime."

"Who are we talking about?" Sextus asked.

"Nobody you'd know," said Duncan, coldly. He turned to JC. "This petition you were mentioning. It's quite likely that the Vatican will take a position. It wouldn't be the first time. I've spoken to the office of the nuncio."

JC was nodding.

"Is this about that Canadian guy on death row in the States?" Susan asked. "The guy they're going to execute?"

"JC's in the media," Duncan said. "He's done stories on that case. I did a little research on canon law, about the death penalty."

"I've been following it," said Susan. "But what's your involvement with canon law?"

"Duncan here is a sky pilot," Sextus said, smiling.

"A what?"

"A priest," Sextus said. "From back home, as a matter of fact."

"Oh," said Susan.

Duncan suddenly seemed uncomfortable. "So where are you from, exactly?" he asked.

"Havre Boucher," Susan replied.

JC inquired about the drinks. Did anybody want a refill?

"So you'd have been in Father Allan's parish," Duncan said.

"Well," said Susan. "We actually left the church. Because of him. I don't know the whole story, though. I think there was something about my younger brother." She blushed. "They say that Father Allan was . . . different."

"I'd be surprised if he wasn't one of yours," Sextus said to Duncan.

Duncan flashed a warning glance his way, but Sextus didn't notice.

"Duncan was the guy who put a stop to all that shit. Weren't you, Duncan? He was the guy the bishop would send out—"

"Dessert's ready," Effie announced.

———

After dinner they made small talk about home. Safe gossip, old stories that were mostly funny. Effie realized that she was drinking too much wine too quickly. She calculated that she'd consumed three stiff Scotches before the wine. *Fuck it,* she thought. It was one way to cope, not to care about the reefs and shoals so near the surface of every subject that came up.

JC proposed a toast: "To the second-last Christmas of the millennium."

They all murmured excitement at the vastness of the thought.

"Here's lookin' at 1999," he said. "A last great year."

"Speak for yourself," said Sextus. "Every year is a great year."

"You know what I mean," JC said.

"Nooo," everybody said in chorus. "We don't know what you mean!"

"Whatever," he said. And they clinked glasses merrily.

"So how long do you plan to be around?" Effie asked Sextus.

"Who knows," he said. "I'm playing it by ear. We should get together for a coffee, or a drink. Catch up."

*Right,* she thought. *As if.* But she said, "Absolutely. Give me a call. I assume you still have my office number."

"Know it off by heart," said Sextus.

"Have you been talking to our daughter lately?"

Sextus looked at her, pointedly, it seemed. "Ahhh, the darling daughter. On the phone, before I left. She said she was going to be away. Probably just saying that so she could avoid me."

Susan caught his hand, squeezed it loyally and said, "I doubt that."

"She's away but back a week tomorrow," Effie said. "Did she mention anything about the new guy in her life? This Ray?"

Sextus looked surprised. "Not a boo. Who is he?"

"Haven't met him yet. But it seems serious."

"Well, there's another reason to stick around," he said. He was clasping Susan's hand in his.

Effie's head was buzzing. Thoughts and words were scrambling to be heard, but she knew it would be prudent to keep most of them inside. JC was overgenerous with his booze, she noted. She'd speak to him. *Hospitality isn't entirely about how shit-faced everybody gets.*

She smiled at "shit-faced," a word her students liked to use. Her father would say "pissed to the gills," and that too was apt. She was just about to offer coffee when, in the babble of words and laughter at the table, she heard a word that sounded like "fidelity."

"Fidelity," she said. "Now there's a topic I could write a book about."

There was a sudden silence, but she didn't really care. Everyone was piss-gill-shit-faced. "I have one basic rule about fidelity," she added merrily. "JC can sleep with anyone he wants to as long as she's older than I am."

She was the only one who laughed. She turned toward the kitchen counter, lined up the coffee mugs, turned again. Saw four round, blank faces staring at her.

"One rule only, that's all," she repeated. "Older than me . . . she has to be. That's the bottom line."

"Well, that kind of narrows it down," Sextus said.

Susan giggled.

The room was suddenly and overwhelmingly hot.

"Excuse me," Effie said.

In the bathroom she studied her face in the mirror but saw a stranger looking back. Older woman, well turned out but plain. Face pale, hair needing care. *Maybe I should cut it,* she thought. She squinted and the image became sharper. *Maybe I need glasses.* Then she told herself, *Stop fretting about your looks. Think of aging as maturing, growing wiser. What did Daddy used to say? No point getting older if it doesn't make you smarter.* But still she wondered. With an extended finger, she stretched the skin below an eye. *What else did Daddy say?*

Overwhelmed, she dove toward the toilet.

She rinsed her face, restored her lipstick, then went to sit for a while on the edge of JC's bed, head light but stomach feeling better. Loud laughter came from downstairs.

She sighed and stood. Her head spun, then stabilized.

In the darkened hallway near the top of the stairs, she saw Sextus standing, hands in pockets, a concerned look on his face. When she tried to brush by, he blocked her with a suddenly extended arm.

"Please," he said. Then placed his forehead on her shoulder. "I'm so, so sorry."

"About what, exactly?" she replied.

"Everything," he said. "Tonight. Last year. Nineteen seventy-seven. My screw-ups, one and all."

Then he was facing her, hands gripping her shoulders. She just stared at him. At that moment her entire life seemed to occupy one clear, sharp quadrant of her brain, like a Mozart composition, one of Einstein's theories. Fully formed and ready for articulation.

"I just wish I could explain," he said. "There was nothing—"

"Move, please," she said.

He dropped his arms and she brushed by him and walked downstairs steadily, suddenly dead sober.

The next day being Boxing Day, she spent the night.

—

*The battering wind seemed to scream, flattening the high brown grass in the marsh of Tantramar—the tantric marshes, Sextus called them, laughing wickedly. The wind pushed their small car onward and away from yesterday and toward tomorrow, a force as reassuring as the grass they'd smoked in a service station toilet back in sober Amherst, dispelling fear and purging all misgivings. She was singing farewell to Nova Scotia, the sea-bound coast, with the brown marsh grass undulating all around them and the sky dipping and swirling and clouds racing head-long with them toward an unseen finish line, the future. Laughter throbbed in her veins, the fear and anger falling far behind; faster, faster, through the Isthmus of Chignecto. "Isthmus be love!" she screamed, and wrapped her arms around his head so he could hardly see to drive, and the Chignecto wind now hurried them on, now tried to turn them back, as if it knew the future.*

## 3

It was the eve of the beginning of the last year of a millennium, and Effie Gillis was alone. She hardly ever answered the telephone at home. "That's why God invented answering machines," she would tell her friends. But that night she was waiting for a special call, and she picked up quickly when it rang.

The phone call was not the one she'd hoped for, but from the former husband whose name remained a hyphenated adjunct to her own (because he was the first and because she liked the Gaelic form of Gillis). John was calling for no apparent reason, which was, for her, another cause for some alarm. He didn't even mention that it was New Year's Eve. No "Happy New Year," none of the traditional formalities.

John had an aversion to telephones not unlike her own, and even when he was in the darkest depths of the suffering she and Sextus had inflicted on him many years before, he had never called her or anyone else she knew to share his misery. So what was this about?

"I'm surprised you're home," he said. "I'm not interrupting anything, am I?"

"No, no," she said. "I was just sitting here. How are you, John?"

"Ach, I'm okay."

And then he was silent.

Her first assumption was that he was drinking again, but he sounded completely sober. She thought she could eliminate lone-liness and boredom: she knew he suffered both, but she also knew how well he could suppress them. Which left the probabil-ity of illness.

"You're sure you're all right? You know Sextus is in town?"

"I heard he was going up. And did you see him, then?"

"Yes," she said. "We all had Christmas dinner."

"You did?" He laughed. "That's just great." He sounded as if he meant it. "I hear he has a new girlfriend."

"Yes, she was here too. I was worried about giving her a drink."

"Oh?"

"She looked like she was underage."

"Hah," he said.

"So what about yourself, John?"

"Ah well," he said. "Look. I was just wondering. Are you going to be around in the new year?"

"Of course," she said. "Are you planning a trip?"

"Ah no," he said. "No plans. But a fella never knows. I've been doing some thinking."

"It's good to hear from you at any time," she said.

"All right, then."

Another long pause.

"I hope 1999 is good to you, John. You deserve it."

"Ah well, I'm not so sure. But thanks. I hope you have a good one too."

And he was gone, as enigmatic as ever.

She thought of calling him back, digging deeper. But it was almost midnight in Cape Breton, almost 1999, so she let the impulse fade. And she was wondering about JC. She knew he planned to visit, but he had said he'd call first. According to the Hogmanay traditions he'd learned about while based in London years before, his arrival would be shortly after midnight. He'd bring gifts. He was a dark-haired man, a harbinger of good luck in the year ahead.

She'd just been getting out of the shower when John called. After that, she had dressed in something casually flattering—slim grey sweats and a black cotton turtleneck—and settled down for what she expected would be a short wait for JC's call or, more likely, his inebriated arrival.

It was 12:43 when the phone rang again.

"Is this Dr. Gillis?"

The caller's formality persuaded her to answer yes. He then identified himself as Sergeant something with the Metro Toronto Police Service.

"I'm calling about James Charles Campbell," he said, as if he was reading the name from a document.

Her mind instantly processed the unfamiliar James Charles. "JC," she said. "Yes. What about him?"

"There's been an accident," said the policeman. "Mr. Campbell gave your name. Or rather, he had your business card in his wallet. Are you by chance his . . . doctor?"

"Not that kind of doctor. I'm a friend," she said. "What happened?"

"We aren't exactly sure. We're looking into it. It seems he fell, or got knocked down. On his street. Walden Avenue."

"Where is he?"

"Toronto General. He's under observation."

When she got to the hospital, she found him asleep. She sat at his bedside for an hour, watching as he slept. There was a bandage on his head. A tube running from a plastic bag hanging on a pole delivered a clear liquid to his arm. He was pale.

*What a way to start the year,* she thought. She struggled to suppress her fears. With him, she had what seemed to be an open-ended future. He had banished a nagging feeling of finality that had started after she'd turned fifty. Now his vulnerability had been revealed. She placed a hand on his, and the warmth was reassuring. His face, in sleep, was firm, his mouth firmly shut. His sleep was still and silent. The hospital shirt was open at the chest, and the curled hair she could see there stirred her, as did the snugness of the plastic band around his sturdy wrist.

"He'll be fine," the doctor said to her when he came in to check on JC. "By tomorrow you'll see a big change. Give us twenty-four hours. Right now, he's heavily sedated. We're going to keep him that way for a while."

So she went home.

January 2 was a Saturday. The hospital was quiet, the normal stream of visitors and staff reduced by the holidays. Perhaps it was the unnatural heat and humidity of the place that made her nervous, or the distracting sounds and smells of steamed food, biochemistry and crisis; the whispered private conversations in darkened rooms and the harsh impersonal announcements on an intercom; awkward visitors with coats on, solitary patients attached to IV poles or shapeless under sheets. By the time she reached his room, she was feeling vaguely miserable.

He was propped up slightly on the bed, eyes closed. She touched his hand.

He smiled a brief, thin greeting. "I was just thinking," he said, "what it must be like to be stuck here with some chronic illness."

He looked away, toward the window. "I wouldn't have blamed you for finding an excuse to stay away. Hospitals. Christ, deliver me."

"Come on," she said. "A hospital is a hopeful place. I was here yesterday, but you were sleeping."

"They told me. Maybe I'm just antsy because I see a lot of hospital in the future."

"What the hell are you talking about?" she said, forcing a laugh.

"Look at me, flat on my back. And because of some teenage punk . . ."

"Please," she said. "There was an accident. You got conked on the head."

"I don't know," he said, examining his hands. "I don't know—there was a day."

"What happened?" she asked.

He grimaced. "Actually, it was the cat's fault."

"The cat?"

The story came out in fragments. The cat had bolted just before midnight on New Year's Eve. JC was placing an empty wine bottle in his recycling box on the back deck before setting out for her place. The cat slipped between his legs and vanished up a fence and a tree and onto the roof. JC followed, up the fence, from the top of which, by stretching, he could reach a fire escape.

The cat, being long-haired and snow white, shouldn't have been all that hard to find in the darkness. Effie had named him Sorley, after a white-haired Scottish poet whose work she taught to under-graduates. She could easily imagine it: JC up on the roof, prowling, swearing quietly, angry mostly at himself for the momentary carelessness that enabled the cat to dash for the deck while the patio door was open.

JC's roof was part of a continuum of rooftops on Walden, which though called an avenue was more like a narrow one-way lane between two rows of old, mostly semi-detached houses in what had once been a factory area but was now a second Chinatown. JC lived in number 14.

He stood on the roof for a long time, watching for movement. On an earlier visit to the rooftops he'd learned to avoid skylights, of which there were four, having once inadvertently peered down and caught sight of two naked men struggling in what seemed to be an act of intimacy.

He finally spotted the cat about four units along, on the roof of number 20, he estimated. Being an indoor cat, Sorley had the kind of confidence that apparently diminished as the surroundings lost familiarity. To proceed farther, he'd have to leap a gap between number 20 and 22, so he'd settled down to await the inevitable recapture, eyes serenely shut, his thick tail tucked tidily along a silky flank. JC gathered him up without a word and was about to make his way back in the direction of his own place when he heard a shout from the street below.

"Hey, asshole! Get fucking down here, right now."

He'd found the hostile tone to be perfectly understandable in the circumstances and had no intention other than to oblige. He would have reacted the same way had he seen a stealthy figure on the rooftops any night, let alone the eve of the brand-new first day of the last year in a millennium.

It might have turned out differently if he'd gone straight to the street, carrying the cat in the crook of his arm to confirm what any normal person would have probably considered an unlikely explanation. But after descending from the roof, he tossed the cat through the sliding patio door through which he'd fled originally, and quickly closed it.

There were three men waiting in the street, and they had obviously been celebrating. They were young and full of righteous certainty, and they had no interest in listening to his explanation.

To be precise is difficult. There was, on JC's part, some genuine confusion about whether he had insulted one of the aggressors with a crude homophobic slur. That was what the young men told the police afterwards. He clearly recalled being shoved from behind, but nothing after that. The fact that all three claimed to have a clear recollection of the epithet left him at a disadvantage. Charges were unlikely. And in any case, while the young men told their version of events, JC was on his way to the hospital, unconscious in an ambulance.

When he heard what he'd been accused of, he vehemently denied their story. "It's a word I never used in my life," he told the investigating officer. "I'm not saying they made it up. But I know I'd never have said something like that. It isn't in me."

"They're also saying you're a pervert," the policeman said. "Up on the roof, looking down the skylights."

"That's pure bullshit too."

He was watching Effie closely for her reaction. "Pathetic, eh?" he said.

"It was a misunderstanding," she said.

"Yup," he said. "Life's just full of misunderstandings."

There were a hundred things she could have said to comfort him. But she realized that he wasn't in the mood for comforting.

Then Sextus spoke. "Well, look at this," he said. "The mighty oak has fallen."

She turned and he was in the doorway. "I could come back," he said, then walked in and threw his overcoat on the foot of the hospital bed.

JC moved stiffly to raise himself. "Christ, they'll let anybody in." Sextus leaned to clasp his hand.

"If you don't mind," Effie said, "I'm going to Walden now to check on the cat."

JC waved. She knew that Sextus was waiting for a greeting from her, some signal, but she ignored him.

"You'll have to forgive the mess," JC warned her.

She nodded, blew a kiss and left.

Effie was almost at Yonge Street when she heard the clank of the streetcar lumbering behind her. She had to run to catch it at the stop and cursed the dirty wetness now inside the low-cut boots she'd carelessly selected for the visit to the hospital. Once settled, she watched the city turn seedy as the tram proceeded eastward. It was snowing, and the swirling flakes were gathering velocity.

Sorley, a blue point Himalayan with eyes like icebergs, was really hers, a birthday gift from JC. But the long hair seemed to activate some dormant allergies, so she'd had to give him back. During Christmas dinner, Sextus had noted with his customary sensitivity that in all likelihood her problem wasn't really about cat hair, but about tomcats in general. Nobody laughed, least of all JC, who later made the sympathetic observation that if Sextus wasn't such an asshole, she'd still be with him.

The cat stood just inside the door, bushy tail straight out behind him, and yowled accusingly. But by the time she was removing her second boot, he was making friendly rumbling sounds and tight figure eights around her ankles. She could feel the pungency of the litter box in her eyes but went straight to the sink and filled the cat's metal drinking bowl with water. She found the cans of cat food neatly stacked in the usual cupboard. Sorley was on the counter in a bound and eating even as she spooned the food into his dish, so she left him there and turned her attention to the soggy litter box. When that was done, she poured a Scotch and sat.

JC's place was a reno from the late seventies, gutted out, dry-walled and painted white. It was sparse but comfortable. His only alteration had been to replace the industrial carpeting, which had been fashionable during the eighties, with hardwood floor-ing. On the walls were three large, well-executed photographs from home. Mabou Harbour, thick with lobster boats. Port Hood Island, backlit by a sunset that was almost equatorial. An old black-and-white of the Canso Causeway, presumably a day or so before they finished it; foaming water surged through a narrow gap as four men crouched to jump the distance and be first across. Propped here and there on tables and the TV set were smaller photos from the places he had been for work, ruined buildings, hostile-looking brown men with machine guns, important people he'd known. There was one of him and Arafat. Another with Pierre Trudeau and Castro. Gorbachev and a smiling bearded man with a television camera on his shoulder. On his dresser in the bedroom, there was a photograph of her, though she was not particularly fond of it. Her hair was too unkempt, she had protested, her face too slack, her eyes half-open, making her look weary. JC insisted the net effect was one of wantonness and that was why he claimed it and kept it by his bed.

The cat, his immediate needs accommodated, had vanished. She tried to sink into the silence of the little house but was unable to ignore the rising shrieks of wind outside. She stood, went to the front window and peered out. The snow now streaked horizontally down Walden, the parked cars already turning into shapeless hummocks. She remembered the open cat food tin on the kitchen counter and went back to cover it with plastic wrap and put it in the fridge, which she noted badly needed cleaning. JC's mail was scattered on the kitchen table, and she couldn't resist quickly flipping through it. Among the cards was the envelope from Texas. She saw, in the upper left-hand corner, a return address. *Ellis I, E13—1—14, Huntsville, TX 77343*. She recognized the careful printing and she sighed.

Eventually, she switched on the radio. JC had the tuner set on an AM all-news station, and they were telling people to stay off the streets. A good idea, she concluded after one more look outside. She decided she would stay there for the night.

She dozed awhile on the couch and when she checked his kitchen clock she was surprised that it was nine. She turned on the television and there was a movie halfway finished. She flicked it off, wandered into the kitchen and decided to tidy the table, where, buried under newspapers, she found his laptop. On top of the closed lid he'd left a small square disk. His carelessness surprised her. How easily the disk might have been swept up with the newspapers, tossed and lost, and with it whatever information he'd stored on it.

Briefly she examined it. On the label he had written "Huntsville, TX, '98." Curiosity aroused, she again picked up the envelope from Texas, opened it and examined the Christmas card. It was a traditional religious greeting card: the manger scene, the swaddled baby in the straw. Inside, in careful handwriting, this message: "Hope you enjoy a peaceful holiday. Thanks for the poems. I'm looking forward to 1999. I expect good things. God bless, Sam."

Poems? What poems? She'd already warned JC about getting close to Sam. Now it seemed she had sound reasons for concern. Her hand was trembling. And suddenly she wanted to be in his bed, even if alone.

The cat was on the bed, a splash of sprawled purity against the navy blue duvet. Effie shooed him from the room and closed the door behind him. Then she picked up the bedside photo of herself, searching once again for what made it special to JC. It had been taken about five years earlier, during a time of emotional drift when even the university had become a source of insecurity and disappointment, mostly because of the mental collapse of the man who headed her department. But Effie, at the time, was also being noticed for her study of Celtic antiquity interpreted through art forms, *The Penannular Circle and the Celtic Ethos of Uncertainty*. Her work had been well received, not just by the Celtic crowd, but by Sociology as well. And when the head of her department died, she got his job. She had the doctorate in history, but it helped that she was female, an attractive redhead who could have stepped straight out of a Georgian lithograph, a fluent native speaker of the Gaelic language and Canadian to boot.

There was a chill in the bedroom. She found a pair of JC's sweatpants in a bottom drawer. Then a T-shirt. Before undressing, she leaned close to the full-length mirror on the closet door and, again, studied her face for signs of the deterioration that she dreaded now that she'd begun the headlong sprint toward sixty.

The thin, soft skin below her eyes was only mildly crinkled. Her neck was smooth, with only the slightest sagging between her chin and throat. She stripped quickly, then clambered into the sweatpants and noted with some satisfaction that her legs were just as long as his; there was noticeable thickening at waist and hips, but her thighs were still compact from her energetic daily walks to class. Sliding the T-shirt over her head, she paused for just a moment to observe that, with upraised arms, her breasts were those of someone half her age, well formed and still relatively firm. Many years before, when she had made a self-deprecating comment to Sextus about their size, he'd laughed and reassured her that one day she'd be grateful. "They're long-term assets," he had told her. "They'll be outstanding over the long haul, not sitting on your lap like sleepy puppies when you're old and fat."

Crude, she now thought, though she still smiled at the memory.

And then she was in JC's bed, but it was terrible Sextus on her mind as she drifted off to sleep.

—

*They stopped somewhere in Quebec because Sextus said he was hungry. He needed a sit-down meal. They'd been living on soda pop and chips and chocolate bars all day and were a little edgy. They were in Rivière-du-Loup. The waitress couldn't speak English, and Sextus struggled unimpressively in French. "You must be Lou," he joked. The waitress was confused. "Lou from River du Lou." She didn't get it, so he ordered. "Deux Cinquante," he said, holding up two fingers. "Et deux poulet chaud." Effie wasn't sure what he'd asked for, but they got hot chicken sandwiches and beer.*

*Looking out the window, he said, "I don't think I could handle it if I thought that you were feeling guilty about anything."*

*"What's wrong with guilt?" she asked.*

*"Guilt is poison," he said.*

*"Guilt is normal," she replied. "Bitterness is poison."*

*He dredged a french fry through congealing gravy. "I wonder what your father thinks," he said.*

*"I don't want to talk about it."*

———

She woke up vaguely angry, a half-remembered dream producing acid in her gut like the half-absorbed heavy nightcap she now frequently consumed, against her better judgment, to help her sleep. Sleep had become an issue. Also dreams that left her troubled. Lying there in JC's bed, she said aloud, "Come on. Don't kid yourself."

She'd considered telling JC about the latter part of Christmas night, Sextus's clumsy effort to engage after she had left the dinner table; then the aggressive second try, three days after Christmas, when he showed up on her doorstep unannounced.

"You gave me the address last year, if you recall," he said. "May I come in?"

There was a taxi driving off. She stepped aside.

"I know I should have called in advance," he said. He shrugged, taking in the room. "May I look around?"

In the kitchen, he said, "This is kind of painful, thinking that I might have lived here."

"What do you want?"

He stayed for an hour. The conversation, one-sided though it was, still might have mattered if it hadn't been a replay of a dozen other conversations.

There was nothing between them, him and Stella. He found a dozen ways to say it. She marvelled at the creativity. She'd known forever that he was a liar, but it was the creativity that fascinated her. When she thought about it afterwards, she was impressed.

It wasn't his visit that left her feeling stained, or anything he said, or anything that happened. It was the insanity that nibbled at the edges of her reason as he spoke. She'd poured drinks, which was probably the first mistake. At one point, he'd placed a gentle hand upon her hand, and she'd left it there. And when he touched her cheek, she failed to pull away. But it wasn't those tiny infidelities that frightened her. It was an odd, disorienting impulse, an almost uncontrollable compulsion to first subdue and then humiliate him, to degrade him by degrading his idealism, his claim to know exactly who she was. Who she was *supposed* to be.

Of all the men she knew, he was the one who had known her from her days of innocence. He thought he knew her best, and thus would find his disillusionment most painful. *He's a sentimental sitting duck,* she'd thought. She had simply to lay a hand on his. Allow a tear to slip. And then to take him down, down, down. She had a hundred memories to draw from to find the keys to his humiliation. But in the end she realized it would be like jumping in front of a car to harm the driver.

When he asked, "This thing with JC, when did that get serious?" she stared for a moment, then told him, "You'd better leave, right now."

He nodded.

She watched him walking down the street, shoulders hunched, head bare, and loathed him for the pity she felt—loathed him for all the questions that perplexed her. Where had that compulsion come from? Was it perversity or was it anger? Or was it weakness, masquerading as a virtue? She loathed herself for the fear that, once again, had given her the clarity and strength to throw him out. Why couldn't it have been pure principle, or courage?

She knew JC would understand. She knew she could even shape the narrative to make it comical. She could make him laugh about it. But she didn't tell him, and she wouldn't tell him now. And the reason why she wouldn't tell him frightened and depressed her, because it was such stark evidence of weakness in her character.

She brushed her teeth and then remembered Sorley. The cat was nowhere to be found, but cats are like that. They seem to have the power to go invisible. *Lucky things,* she thought. She missed her daughter then, but was elated to remember that Cassie would be back in town that evening. Back from her extended holiday with the new relationship. She peered out the front window onto a street that was vague with snow.

That Sunday, after the blizzard, the city was paralyzed. There was chaos in slow motion, people wading through the drifts as though through deep water. Distressed cars with fuming exhausts and spinning wheels, barely creeping. She struggled along an uncleared sidewalk to a nearby Chinese grocery for milk. People everywhere were digging, effusive in their greetings, full of manic camaraderie.

When she was a girl, she dreaded days like this. But on a Sunday morning in the nation's largest city with a mug of coffee in her hand, the isolation was a comfortable shelter. Later on this day she'd see her daughter, maybe meet the new man in her life. She thought briefly of what it might be like to be a grandmother. It was, she realized, a distressing notion. Then the cat was in the room, stretching and yawning and reminding her of food. Peeling plastic off the opened can, she prayed that Cassie wasn't stranded somewhere in the wilds of Northern Ontario.

Once upon a time, winter was a prison, viewed through windows blind from furry frost, a passing car or truck a living highlight in a landscape flattened by violent winds and waves of snow. Fantasy was her religion and the prospect of escape was her salvation. Her memory was full of silences, broken only by the creak of her father's rocking chair, the rattle of an unruly newspaper, the snap of fire in the ancient woodstove. And the wind, of course. Always the wind, blustering in the stovepipe, rattling a damper. Small sounds, but sufficient evidence of life to accentuate her solitude.

There was a radio, but her father only turned it on to hear the weather. Sometimes the news, but information always left her father agitated. Storm warnings, politics and conflict, people in distress, he'd shake his head and mutter. Click. Silence reigned again.

*And suddenly she was thirteen and he was there, standing in the middle of the dingy room, reeking with the smells of town, of booze, stale smoke and cold. The radio was blaring, filling the house with the warm fluid of music on waves of air from far away. Boston. New York. West Virginia. Places, in her fantasies, full of light and life. He swore at her, turned off the radio, raised his right hand as if to strike.*

*But Duncan was before him. Duncan, still a boy.*

*"That'll be enough." His boy voice was husky, his boy face suddenly dark and full of danger.*

It was all he said. But it was sufficient in that fleeting moment and, in her mind, it was the moment when the boy became a man and, for a long time after that, it was what a man must be. A rescue.

"What's it doing out?" JC asked.

"Snow up the yingyang," she said. "Hardly anything moving."

"How did you get here?"

"Hey," she said. "Did you really think a little snow would stop a country girl?"

"You never know," he said.

"I spent the night at Walden," she said. "Just me and Sorley. He says hello."

He smiled.

"I'll be going home to Huron from here," she said. "I'm expecting Cassie."

He shrugged. "Did I tell you the cop thought it was significant that they were queers?"

"Who are you talking about?" she asked, even though she knew precisely.

"Those guys, the other night. The cop says it's a new twist on gay bashing. Now jazzed-up gays are bashing guys like us. The cop and me. I thought he was going to say 'normal' people. But maybe he's right. He figures they're just getting back for all the historical prejudice and fear and bullying. Mr. Cop thinks it's kind of funny. The shoe on the other foot now."

"As far as I'm concerned," Effie said, "the cop was trying to draw you into some kind of an admission."

"Maybe."

He looked off toward the window. "What got me was when he told me how old they were. The guy that knocked me down was born in 1980."

"Well, that would make him——"

"I was thinking back to '80. What I was like back then." He laughed. "According to the cop, I tried to take them on. Can you believe it?" He shook his head.

She said nothing.

"You know, there was a time when I'd either have had more sense or I could have made mincemeat out of somebody like him. The moral of the story is, I guess those days are gone."

"You're overreacting," she said. "We're going to have to talk to someone about that concussion."

"You get vulnerable eventually. I guess that's the downside of getting old."

"According to George Burns, getting old is better than the alternative."

He didn't laugh. "Sometimes I wonder."

Sextus was at the nursing station as she was leaving. She hoped he wouldn't notice her, but he called out. "Hey!"

"Ah," she said, as if she hadn't seen him there.

"How's the invalid?"

"I wouldn't use that particular word," she said.

"I was thinking, Christmas Day, that JC is getting harder to figure out. Getting mystical . . . this Texas business. Phew."

"What about it?"

"He's getting too involved."

"What do you know about it?"

"We talked. Briefly. It's something deep," he said. "This guy at the end of his life and knowing it, something most of us try not to think about. It's morbid, if you ask me." He grinned. "JC is starting to show his age."

"Maybe some people should start to act their age," she said and instantly regretted it.

He only laughed.

"Don't get me wrong," she said. "I don't begrudge you one second of whatever happiness you have in your life. Or judge how you find it. Or where." She waved a hand as if to leave.

"You're as old as you feel," he said, "and I feel twenty-five."

"Excellent," she said and turned.

"About the other day," he said, placing a hand on her arm to stop her. "It was presumptuous, going to your place. But I guess that's no surprise to you."

She stood, her back to him, words rushing but unsaid.

"I was supposed to go home tonight," he said. "But I'm staying on a few more days. I want to meet Cassie's new boyfriend."

"Good," she said. "I'll be interested in hearing what you think."

"She sounds pretty serious about this Ray."

"We'll see. 'Serious' is relative."

"I wouldn't know anything about that."

She didn't have to turn to know that he was smiling again. She could always hear the smile.


Cassie's voice was merry when she called. They'd try to be there by seven, and they were starved. The drive down from Sudbury had been hellish, but Ray couldn't wait to meet her.

"You never told me what Ray does for a living," Effie said.

"He's a doctor."

"A doctor!"

"Didn't I tell you? Oh well, a small detail. We'll be there by seven thirty at the latest. You can do your own assessment."

She tidied, but it would be more accurate to say she just shifted things around. She repositioned books that might shape subtle insights about character or serve as conversational connections. She left a volume of modern Gaelic poetry open on a coffee table. It was mostly love poetry, but only she would know that. He might ask about it, and his reaction to her explanation would tell her something about him. It was a poet after whom she'd named a cat, she'd tell him, a possible diversion into other, lighter, places. She set out her own academic tome, always guaranteed to stir at least a superficial interest. Penannular circles. Destiny.

She had planned to order pizza. Young people are always happy to be stuffed with pizza. She had beer and wine. But because they were "starved," she worried that pizza wouldn't be enough. Ray the doctor was probably health-conscious, watching the sodium and fat. Pasta, she decided, checking her diminished cupboards to reassure herself that she had all the ingredients she needed. There was still time to acquire some salad fixings from the small twenty-four-hour grocery on Bloor.

Ray wouldn't be the first of Cassie's men she'd met. But there was an amusing tension in her daughter whenever she mentioned him. Cassie, after all, was twenty-eight, established in her career. She felt a vague maternal pride—her daughter married to a doctor—but quickly felt ashamed at such pedestrian ambition. If Ray was right for Cassie, it wouldn't matter if he was a miner or a taxi driver. The only thing that mattered in the long run was Cassie's happiness. And she was, again, embarrassed by the superficiality.

*Piss off,* she told herself. *Chances are you'll meet the bugger once or twice before he vanishes like all the others into the legions of the Unremembered and the Never-more-referred-to.*

She was tempted to pour a drink, thought better of it. Poured one anyway. Sat for a moment, legs crossed, studying her bobbing foot. Then stood, drink untouched, to fill a pot with water. She remembered the mess in the spare room, where she'd left the litter from her Christmas wrapping. The bed was covered in festive paper, twine, tape and scissors. Maybe they planned to stay.

Cassie's gift was on the bed too. Effie had splurged on a Vuitton overnight bag. As a business writer, Cassie travelled frequently, mostly short trips to Ottawa, New York, Washington. Effie had also wrapped a modest gift for Ray. A book. A le Carré novel that she liked a lot. *A Perfect Spy.* But now she was having second thoughts.

Ray, the doctor, might have already read it. Or might find it trite. She rebuked herself again. *What am I thinking? He's no more literary than I am. Less so, depending on how you look at it.* But still, she changed her mind about the book. She picked it up and carried it to her bedroom, found herself downstairs again, distracted.

If they stayed, she thought, it would surely be a sign of something substantial. Possibly commitment. If he was a doctor, he must be in his thirties, depending on what kind of doctor. Even a GP would be nearly thirty, a perfect time to settle down.

She had a new CD, a gift from JC, Celtic music played in the Baroque style that originally inspired it. Cape Breton music, local, insular and, until just a few years earlier, considered primitive. Just like the language of the old people. Passé. But now in fashion, studied for its classical connections, its origins in ancient cultures. It made her smile. Where was all the scholarship when it might have nourished and perhaps restored a dying world to relevance?

She put the CD on, and the music warmed the room. She wondered who Ray was, really. What did he look like? Did he have siblings? Would she get to know his parents? She hadn't heard a surname yet. Maybe he had connections with home. Sudbury, she knew, was a vast and rowdy diaspora of people from her part of the east coast. Or maybe he was a foreigner. A Pakistani. She chuckled, imagining the look on Sextus's face when he found out. "A Paki? Jesus Christ!" She could actually hear him, the irrational distress. Then again, who knows? He might surprise her. He often did.

She had retrieved her drink and was sipping it when the doorbell rang. Then she heard the key, and the door opened. Cassie stood there, kicking snow from her boots. Effie rose quickly and rushed toward her, and they embraced.

"Ray is getting something from the car," Cassie said.

"You found a place to park."

"Half a block away."

"You're lucky," Effie said. "The snow."

Cassie stared at her. "You call this snow? Mother, we just came from Sudbury."

She saw a man moving quickly up the walkway, carrying a shopping bag. He was bulky in a zipped-up leather jacket, collar up, and a baseball cap pulled down. He was of average height, built athletically.

Cassie, whose back was to the street, was whispering, "Mom, Ray isn't what——"

"Well, you must be Ray," said Effie.

She saw a broad smile. He put the bag down. "Dr. Gillis," he said. There was something seasoned in the voice that caught her by surprise. Maturity, she thought. Then he removed the ball cap. His close-cropped hair was grey. And, as he moved toward her and into the light, extending a cold, firm hand for her to shake, she saw the deep lines in his face. For a moment, she thought, *They've brought Ray's dad along!*

But she knew that this was Ray. Prematurely aged by the pressures of his work? Or just plain old.

"Let me introduce you properly," said Cassie, gamely. "This is Mom——call her Effie. No more Dr. or Mrs. Gillis. And this is Ray. Ray Cameron."

"Cameron," said Effie. "There's a familiar name."

"I'm not sure where it's from," Ray said. "Dad was born in the north of England. I was born in Quebec, the Abitibi. Dad followed the mining. We ended up in Sudbury. More than that, I haven't got a clue."

"Your dad is . . . ?"

"Going on ninety-four," he said. "Mom is just a year younger. I've got the genes, if nothing else."

The obvious question was, of course, suppressed.

"Well, come in and close the door, and make yourself at home. I was just going to whip up something simple. Cassie, get yourself and Ray something to drink."

Cassie was already at the hutch that served as Effie's bar, examining the labels. Effie realized her hand was shaking. A chill, she told herself, from standing at the door.

"Ray," Cassie said. "What about you?"

"I'll just have a ginger ale or juice. Whatever's there."

*My God,* thought Effie. *Along with everything else, a non-drinker.*

Ray was now sitting. He'd picked up the book of poetry from the coffee table. "This is . . ."

"Gaelic," she said. "The language of your ancestors."

He laughed and put it down.

Cassie was perched on the arm of his chair, a languid arm across his shoulder, left hand glinting.

"I see you've acquired some new bling," Effie said.

"Nothing fancy," Cassie said, raising the hand.

"Nothing fancy?" said Ray, in mock surprise.

"So when should we expect . . ."

"We aren't in a rush," said Cassie.

"But probably at Easter," said Ray.

"By the way," said Cassie. "Where's the lovely Mr. Campbell? I half-expected he'd be here."

"Not to alarm you, but JC's in the hospital. He had a fall on the street, hit his head. They've kept him in for a few days. Observation, mostly."

Ray looked concerned. "Which hospital?"

"The General, but look, it's really nothing."

Ray and Cassie suddenly seemed grave.

"Come on," said Effie. "JC would be appalled if he could see your faces. Ray, surely to God you'll join us in a real drink."

"What the hell," Ray said.

At the dinner table, it was Ray who brought the subject to the fore. "I suppose we shouldn't let too much time go by before dealing with the elephant."

He smiled and Effie put her fork down, refilled her wineglass and reached for Cassie's glass, but Cassie stopped her.

"Well," she said. "The elephant, eh?"

"I'm sure it's on your mind. It's a question I get a lot."

"Right," she said. "It really doesn't mean anything anymore . . ."

"Exactly," he said. "So when I'm asked by some nosy person, 'How come you aren't married at your age?' I just laugh."

"There seems to be an assumption," said Cassie, "that if you aren't married at a certain age there's something wrong with you."

Effie's eyes darted from one to the other, waiting. "Okay," she said.

"Fact is, I've been married twice," Ray said.

Effie exhaled. "Is that all?"

Ray laughed. "Thank you. Twice is a lot, to some people. Like my parents."

"I mean, is that the elephant you had in mind?" said Effie.

"Well . . . What else do you want to know?"

She paused for a moment, then asked, "How old are you, Ray?"

He seemed surprised. "Fifty-eight."

"Fifty-eight," she repeated. "I must say, you don't look it."

"I get that a lot. But that's my age. I have proof." His smile made him look half that.

"You have family?"

"Boy and a girl. We spent Christmas together."

"I'm assuming they live with their mother," Effie said.

He laughed. His daughter worked in public relations for Inco. The boy was in his third year at med school. Following in the old man's footsteps. The daughter was the elder. Her mother died when she was only three. Ray remarried, a family friend, mostly because he needed help. Then the boy came along. When his son started university, Ray and his second wife had a long chat about life in general. Talked about their time together and concluded that, with the boy gone, the marriage had lost its rationale. That was the word he used, "rationale." They agreed to live apart and to actively consider restarting their lives, with other people—an unlikely prospect, they thought, considering their ages.

She was remarried within a year. He lost himself in work. No regrets. Then Cassie came along. His daughter had introduced them, as a matter of fact. Cassie was writing something about Inco and had met Inco's PR lady in a restaurant. Ray walked in. The Inco PR lady introduced her dad.

As the narrative unfolded, Cassie watched him, smiling.

It was all so goddamned orderly. All so rational. Effie looked toward her glass, picked it up and swirled. She could see John's ravaged face. She felt cold again remembering his pain. Just a flash of memory, but it conjured John and Sextus and the demons. Loud voices. Flight. Guilt. Slow recovery.

"Well," she said at last. "I'd like to propose a toast."

———

Later, at the door, she asked, "So, Cassie, dear, when do you plan to tell your father?"

"We're seeing him for lunch tomorrow."

Once she had asked JC straight out, "Back then, how much did you and the others know about what I was putting up with?"

"It was the seventies," he replied. "Everyone was kind of haywire."

"You know what I mean."

"Sextus and the women, you mean?"

She nodded. "You were different. I knew you weren't like the rest of them. There was a time when I thought that you were gay."

"I was considered kind of slow around the girls, I guess."

"How bad was he?"

"You mean Sextus?"

"Who do you think I mean?"

"It's ancient history."

"I want to know how big a fool I was."

"You were never a fool. We all thought you were a saint."

"Great. You all pitied me."

"We admired you," he said, teeth clenched slightly. "And never more than when you threw the bugger out. The only mystery for us was how you got mixed up with him in the first place."

She walked to work on Monday morning, feet crunching on the salted sidewalks along Bloor Street. It was cold, the sunlight sharp and brittle, the city still limping from the battering of the storm. *A wild beginning for the last year of a wretched century,* she thought. *Hard to believe it's 1999.*

She recalled how unsettling it once was to think ahead to 1984, the Orwellian year, and realize that the harsh dystopia imagined by the pessimistic author was not entirely fanciful. Pessimism, she recalled, was very stylish at the time. Channelling Hobbes, not Orwell, she told someone. Benevolent dictatorship could be the answer. Clans and chiefs. People thought she was odd. *That Effie, there she goes again.* Now 1984 was fifteen years ago and the world was more or less the same. Except that people listened to her now.

After Cassie and Ray had gone, she'd sat for a long time in semi-darkness, her mind adrift in the uncertainty their visit had created. It seemed they would be married in the spring, but there were no specifics. It was unlikely that there would be children, considering Ray's history and his age. Cassie was, in a very real way, the end of a biological limb on a family tree about which Effie knew very little. Duncan, as far as she could tell, was celibate and seemed inclined to stay that way. Their father had no siblings, barely knew his mother, had no knowledge of his father. And Effie had no concrete memory of the mother who had died when she was three.

Until now, the unlikelihood of grandchildren had seemed a sort of comfort. The century ahead was an uninviting place, offering a more extreme version of the century behind—unimaginable progress in technology, miracles in human health and comfort, all offset by epic self-annihilation. A gruesome prospect, shattered peoples and their cultures, vanished nations, the relentless devastation of the human habitat. Not the kind of world that any moral person should ever wish on progeny.

And yet, the prospect of biological extinction was unsettling now that it was real. It was irrational, she knew. But it was there. She frowned at fuming, mindless, hissing cars as they passed by.

At ten that morning she had a seminar on the songs of an eighteenth-century bard whose nature poetry became immortal despite the fact that he couldn't read or write.

At noon she lunched with a doctoral candidate who was bogged down on a thesis about feminism in tribal societies.

After lunch there was a message in her mailbox to call a certain Mr. Gillis, who claimed to be her former husband.

The hospital was only a short walk from her office. JC's mood was improved when she visited him mid-afternoon.

"I'm getting out in the morning," he told her. "Do you think you could pick me up?"

"Sure," she said. "You should come and stay at my place for the first few days."

He smiled. "Thanks. But what about his nibs?"

"Sorley too. The cat hair didn't bother me as long as I kept him off the bed. Maybe it was just a passing thing."

"Ah well," he said, looking away. "I think I need to be in my own space for a while. Maybe you could come to Walden?"

She noticed that he'd gone unusually pale. "Sure," she said. "What's the doctor saying?"

"He says I'm ready to go home, but that I should have someone with me." He smiled. "I'm not used to this."

"Consider yourself lucky."

"I had a dream last night. I was standing on a roof, and down on the street a bunch of guys were putting the boots to somebody. And I was standing there, trying to shout at them to make them stop. But there was no sound coming out of me."

"I've had it too, being on a roof," she said. "I usually end up falling off the roof, but I always wake up before I hit the ground."

She grasped his hand.

"It was the silence," he said. "Nobody noticing. About becoming invisible."

"Tell me about it," she said, then smiled. "You're talking to a middle-aged woman. What time do you want to be picked up?"

"Ten-ish," he said. "Have you talked to himself since yesterday?" he asked. "He was a bit uptight when he was here. I guess about meeting the new man in Cassie's life."

"He left a message. I haven't called him back yet."

"He seems to think everybody's keeping something from him. He was interrogating me to find out how much I knew about this Ray."

"He's a doctor," she said.

"Great. Just what we need. So you met him, finally?"

"I did," she said.

"So?"

"Well, the good news is that he'll make us all feel young again."

"And the bad news is?"

"I didn't say there was bad news. You didn't ask what it is about him that makes me feel young."

He shrugged.

"He's older than all of us," she said. "Practically a senior citizen. Not that there's anything wrong with that."

"So how old is he, anyway?"

"He says he's fifty-eight. I told him he looks younger. But he actually looks more like he's in his sixties."

JC shook his head. "How will Sextus take it?"

"Jesus Christ, you could have told me. I nearly fuckin' dropped—"

"Calm down, for God's sake," she said.

She hadn't intended to talk to him at all, but he called her again from the airport.

"It's ridiculous. He's older than I am."

She decided to say nothing.

"And did he tell you what kind of doctor he is, for Christ's sake?"

"It didn't come up."

"Ob-gyn. He's a gynecologist, is what he is."

"I don't think that should—"

"It's disgusting. I have half a mind to complain to the licensing authorities."

"Complain about what?"

"She probably went to him with some female problem and he took advantage."

"You're sick."

"Me? Sick?"

"In any case, you'd better get used to him; they'll be married by the summer."

"Married, my arse."

"Your arse won't have anything to do with it."

"They'll be married over my dead body."

The phone was suddenly dead.

Tuesday was overcast and cold. She drove to Walden first, let herself in. Fed the cat. Cleaned the litter box. Found a warm coat and stocking cap in a closet, then headed for the hospital.

JC was sitting on the side of his bed, obviously impatient.

"What a waste of time this was," he said, as he struggled into the coat. He stuffed the stocking cap into a pocket. "I won't need that," he said.

On the drive home he chuckled briefly as she described Sextus's furious reaction to Ray.

Then, minutes later, he said, "I can see where he's coming from."

"You can?"

He shrugged and looked out the window. Cars crept, trailed by clouds of vapour. Barely upright people minced gingerly through narrow gaps in mounds of dirty sidewalk snow, cringing at the filthy splashing of the passing cars.

"Winter," he grunted. "To think I used to miss this."

At home he sat silently on the chesterfield, the cat curled beside him, purring gently with his eyes closed as JC explored his neck and the space between his ears. "I suppose you've got lots on today," he said eventually.

"Meetings most of the afternoon. You'll be okay?"

"A hundred percent," he said.

Just before she left, the telephone rang. "Let it ring," he said.

Then there was a voice from the answering machine. "Hi. It's Sandra. Call me when you can."

She smiled at him. "Sandra?"

"Sam's lawyer," he said. "I'll call her later."

"So Sam's into poetry," she said.

"Poetry?"

"I read the card. I didn't think you'd mind. He thanked you for the poems."

"Ahh," he said. "'Burnt Norton.' T.S. Eliot."

"'Burnt Norton'?"

"'What might have been is an abstraction / Remaining a perpetual possibility / Only in a world of speculation.'"

"I didn't know you were into poetry."

"I had to look it up. Sam quoted it the second time we met. I photocopied the whole thing for him, and another one of the quartets. He impresses you like that, Sam does."

From the office she called Duncan.

"Why don't you drop by JC's place for dinner," she said. "He needs some cheering up." Then she braced herself for the parade of needy students.


Normally, she'd have been intrigued. The doctoral student was attempting to explain how Queen Maeve of Connacht could have been the prototype for Wonder Woman, but how, on a closer reading of the *Táin,* it becomes obvious that the ancient Celtic icon was a nymphomaniac. The scholar needed guidance. Was the link between the two a product of sly humour on the part of some druidic storyteller? Did Dr. Effie think of nymphomania as an assertion or a contradiction of feminist empowerment? And how could it be that Wonder Woman, if a nymphomaniac, has become a lesbian archetype? And where does this leave Queen Maeve?

Dr. Effie, the advisor, fought the urge to yawn.

Suddenly they all seemed so young. She found herself distracted by the taut clarity of their faces, the sheen of their hair, the fussy carelessness of their dress. Expensive clothing cleverly designed to look fashionably cheap.

It wasn't the simple self-consciousness of age. She'd been through all that, back just before her fiftieth. That was also, maybe not coincidentally, when she'd come to terms with the hormonal changes. The letting go, she called it. At that point she'd felt something almost like hostility in the way she responded to them, along with the textbook biological resentment, the longing and waves of sadness as she remembered her own stumbling transitions, the youthful struggles she'd endured.

This was different. She now felt sorry for the younger women—a deep compassion. She felt the need to warn them, but she would have had no idea where to start. And even if she did, they wouldn't listen. The more generous would have heard their mothers in her voice, and the more shallow would have spread the word that Dr. Effie had become a bore.

She knew that it was all about JC. The sudden manifestation of his fragility was a challenge to the image she had nurtured. She knew the image was a product of her needs, but she had considered it sustainable. He'd materialized at precisely the right time in her life, when her sense of personal irrelevance had been exacerbated by betrayal. Stella Fortune wasn't all that much younger than she was. Maybe a few years. Maybe more attractive. That wasn't the point. The brief reconciliation with Sextus had represented a recovery. Of what, she wasn't sure. But for those months of harmony she'd felt on top of things.

When he'd betrayed her again, she had slipped into the limbo that her nagging inner voice called middle age. A euphemism. In reality she was over the hill and halfway down the other side. And then there was JC, as if out of nowhere. Handsome, funny, youthful, seasoned JC Campbell, an undiscovered treasure from the past, unburdened by whatever baggage he'd accumulated in what had apparently been a hectic journey. Now JC, through no fault of his own, was weakened and suffering. She didn't have a clue what she could do to help.

"According to *The Book of Leinster,* Queen Maeve needed seven men to satisfy her. Only Fergus could do it for her all by himself," the student said.

They both laughed.

"What's become of all the Ferguses?" the fresh-faced younger woman wondered.

*What,* Effie thought, *becomes of Maeve and women like her?*

Duncan had a small crescent bruise on his cheekbone, just below the eye. She noticed it the minute he came through the door. First he lied, said he'd slipped in snow, bumped his head on a parking meter.

"Those parking meters—you gotta keep an eye on them," JC said.

"That's what I did," Duncan said. "That's why the eye is black. I had my eye on a parking meter."

JC clucked his tongue. "Good thing the parking meter was wearing mittens."

"What do you mean?"

Gingerly, he brushed at Duncan's cheekbone. "A little hash mark here. Looks like it's from a knitted mitten."

Duncan blushed, went to a hallway mirror to look at his face. "You're observant," he said. "Actually, it was some big guy, just off the reserve. Took a poke at me. He was wearing homemade mitts, and they were wet from crawling around in the snow."

He touched the eye cautiously. Laughed.

"So what really happened?" Effie asked.

"We had a little rassle. Then the cops came and tried to make a big deal out of it. Wanted to charge the guy. 'Charge him with what?' I asked. 'Unless you want to charge him with pissing on me.' And it was true. When he was on top of me, he pissed his pants. The cops thought that was a scream and let the poor fellow go. Said I was lucky. Said the last time they tried taking someone out of the shelter, the guy shat himself, then threw up in the back of the cop car. They said I got off easy."

"Christ," Effie said. "I can't imagine you in that place. At the very least, you should wear the collar, let them know—"

"You think they'd respect the collar?" Duncan was smiling. "Half of them blame their shit on people like me, men in collars."

"Give me a frigging break," Effie said.

"Actually, I'm considering moving in."

"Into what?" Effie asked. "The shelter?"

"The board thinks it would be a good idea. I'd be a stabilizing influence."

"You're out of your mind," Effie said. "I mean, if you're stuck for a place to live . . ."

Duncan stared at her, but the look was gentle. "Blessed are they that hunger and thirst after justice——"

"Blessed are the peacemakers," JC interrupted.

"Where does it say anything about getting hit and shat and pissed on for trying to make peace?" Effie said.

"Let me get you something to drink," JC said, standing.

Later, JC seasoned steaks for the broiler. There were stories about the early days. Effie knew them all.

"So Big Danny MacKay says out of the blue, 'Why don't you take your separatism and shove it up your arse,'" JC recounted. "And the guy from Quebec says, 'You got a lot of mout' on you,' and Danny says, 'And I got a lot to back it up with too.' And the war was on."

JC was laughing, and it sounded like music to Effie. "I think it was in '71 or '72. I remember Danny and me crawling on our hands and knees out a side door as the cops were coming in the front. Laughing our asses off."

He was leaning back against the counter, face flushed, eyes shining. Liveliest he'd been since Christmas, Effie thought.

"I don't know if you were ever at the place," he said to Duncan.

"Maybe on a visit," Duncan said.

"That joint near where Roncesvalles intersects with Dundas. What was it, Effie?"

"The Rondun," Effie said.

"Yes, yes. The old Rondun. We used to hang out there, me and Sextus, when we were at the *Sun,* after the *Tely* died. It was a great place for picking up the gossip from the big construction sites. We got a tip there once that the ironworkers were going to stop the pour for the CN Tower. You imagine." He was shaking his head. "Sixteen hundred guys pouring 50,000 cubic yards of concrete.

Nonstop, it had to be, and there's this table full of ironworkers at the Rondun pounding back the beer and planning to abort it. You must remember, Effie. The fight I had with Sextus over that? It was in your living room. He was all for running with the story. I told him they were making us a part of the blackmail against the bosses. I was on the desk. We never ran it. Sextus was savage."

"Sextus went back, I guess," said Duncan. "When did he go, Effie?"

"He left last night," Effie said.

"None too happy about the new son-in-law, I gather," JC said.

Duncan raised an eyebrow.

"Aha," JC said. "You haven't heard about Ray."

"Let's leave it for Cassie," Effie said, more sharply than she intended. "Let her make the introductions."

"But you've met him?" Duncan asked.

"Yes," she said.

"Sounds like he's going to fit right in," JC said. "The demographics are perfect."

"Enough," said Effie, as the phone rang.

"Leave it," JC said.

They could hear the answering machine cut in. "It's Sandra. I'm not sure where you are. But it's Tuesday night, and if you get this, please call me back as soon as you can. It's kind of important."

"You'd better call her," Effie said.

"I don't want to talk to her just now," JC said.

"Who's Sandra?" Duncan asked.

"A lawyer," JC said. "For that guy in Texas."

Dinner was more reminiscence. Who was in the city when they built the subway, TD Centre, CN Tower. Who worked where. A pointless argument of surprising intensity about what year Big Danny MacKay moved back home; how often he came back again to work. And how was Danny, anyway? In a wheelchair now, with the MS. Sun rises and sets on Danny Ban. They laughed about exploits that were once considered life-deforming but were now understood to have been an essential part of growing up, part of leaving innocence behind, becoming hardened for the hard times coming.

"You've got to get in touch," JC said. "When we saw him last summer, Effie and I, when we were down there, you could tell. Time is running out for old Danny Bad."

The cat wandered into the kitchen. Duncan picked him up. "This would be the culprit," he said. "The New Year's Eve fugitive."

JC smiled. "Time is running out for a lot of people. Right?"

Duncan shrugged, caught Effie's eye, then looked away. Stroked the cat.

Over brandy, after the dishes were cleared away, Duncan said, "The guy in Texas—where is death row, exactly?"

"It's about a twenty-minute drive from Huntsville. A godawful place. In December they had a plastic Santa in the yard, just outside the visiting centre. And plastic fucking reindeer."

There was a silence that felt long.

"I saw the story you guys did before Christmas," Duncan said. "You're pretty convinced that he's innocent."

"I don't know," said JC. "He says he's been found guilty by the people of Texas. Whether he did it or not is beside the point. That's the way the system works."

"I understand what he's saying," Duncan said.

"You do?"

Duncan looked at his watch. "It's getting late."

"Here's my problem," JC said. "I don't know what he wants from me. Certainly not sympathy. I'd have a hard time sympathizing, anyway. Society reserves the right to weed out evildoers."

"Evil?"

"You know what I mean. People who reveal a real capacity for doing evil things."

Duncan stood and stretched, reached down, mussed the top of JC's head. "In that case, I can think of a lot of people who should have been put down—real early."

"Name one."

"My father."

He turned to his sister, who was gaping at him. "*De do bharail, a'ghraidh?* Huh? What do *you* think, Effie girl?"

"I'll get your coat," she said.

At the door she told him, "I'm not sure which of you is harder on the nerves."

On the phone with her mother, Cassie tried to play her father's outrage for its hypocrisy. "How old did you say his girlfriend is?"

Effie laughed. "Age is just a number. I don't have to tell you that."

"Well, I wish he'd thought of that before he sounded off at me."

"What did he say?"

"That I was throwing my life away. Can you believe it? Some line from black-and-white TV. I almost laughed in his face."

"He'll get over it."

"Who fucking cares."

"Clearly you do."

"I don't think he's my father, anyway. We have absolutely nothing in common."

"Now you're out of line, girl."

"Really? You've done the DNA?"

"I'm not going to listen to this. Call me when you aren't hysterical."

She hung up.

Friday morning Effie decided to go back to her own apartment. She told JC at breakfast. He lowered the newspaper, studied her for a moment.

"Okay," he said.

"So I'll head there after class. You'll be okay?"

"I'll be fine," he said. Then smiled awkwardly. "Last night . . . ?"

"Don't worry about it," she said.

He shrugged. "An excellent reason to go home."

"This is exactly the discussion I don't want to have."

"Well, if there's something that should be discussed . . ."

"There's nothing to discuss. Unless you want to exorcise some dark masculine hobgoblin about virility, in which case I'm the wrong person to talk to."

"I recall we've talked quite a bit about your hobgoblins when you were going through the change . . ."

"That was different. That was clinical. This is your imagination playing games."

"We'll see."

He went back to the newspaper.

"By the way," he said before she left. "I talked to Sandra last night. They've set an execution date."

"What are you supposed to do about it?"

"He wants to see me."

*Texas,* she thought. *He has Texas on his mind.* The night before, she'd finally had to put an end to his hopeless struggle. "Just hold me," she said at last. "Just put your arms around me and relax. We need some sleep."

But he turned angrily away.

She understood the anger. She knew all about the insecurity, the pride. But to tell him that she understood would only have complicated an already stressful moment by bringing strangers into it. Bad idea to remind him at this point that she had seen his personal dilemma manifest before in vulnerable men. A handful, really, but enough to understand the phenomenon when it arose (or, more to the point, didn't).

She was smiling when she turned to check out a sporty-looking car that pulled alongside her at a red light. The young driver smiled back at her, raised his hand, a casual salute. She turned away, but her smile remained. She checked her makeup in the rear-view mirror.

In any event, it was the call from Sandra and the doomed man in Texas that were on his mind. It all made sense. The lapse was temporary. The tenderness would not be gone for long. It defined him, and it always had, even many years before. When you're young and strong and permanent, evidence of sensitivity can easily be misunderstood.

She remembered him sitting at a kitchen table somewhere long ago. Suddenly he blurted, "I sure do hope the man in there appreciates what he has going for him."

Sextus was asleep on a couch in the next room. JC had helped her wash and dry and store the dishes. He was sipping a beer, and there was smoky music from a radio. His hand, she realized, was gently on hers, palm down across her knuckles. She was shocked by the comment. She'd never thought of him as feeling anything. Even when he brawled, there was no sign of malice or even anger.

"You don't wear a ring," he said.

"We're not officially married yet," she said. "I was once, but . . ."

And she realized it was all too complicated and he probably didn't care, and it was none of his business, anyway. She removed her hand and held it up for examination. She imagined she could still see the faint impression her wedding ring had made in the two years she had worn it.

The ring, she remembered, was hidden in a drawer. Why hidden?

He stood, so she did too. The song on the radio was "A Whiter Shade of Pale," and they danced as the music filled the sudden silence of the kitchen.

"What does JC stand for?"

He stopped. "I think I hear something," he said.

"The baby," she whispered, stepping back. "I must . . ."

"Yes," he said.

And now, as she drove to her office in a city she had mastered in the last trimester of a life that finally seemed to have a shape and content of her own designing, it seemed so odd that she'd forgotten such a moment, and so many moments like it.

In her effort to impose coherence on the subsequent events, she would recall a Friday evening sometime in mid-January. They'd eaten in a little Chinese place not far from Walden and were returning home. The meal had been subdued, as Friday evenings sometimes were. She'd had a busy week. JC seemed bored.

She recognized the set and sway of the young man's shoulders as he hobbled toward them along Broadview, baggy pants slung low. The fear she'd felt on Christmas Eve was instantaneous. She didn't hear what JC said to him, but she heard the response.

"Go fuck yourself," the young man snarled.

They stopped. JC and the young man eyed each other for a moment.

"Fuck myself?" JC said softly, as if confiding. "When there's a cunt like you?"

The young man stiffened, hesitated, then turned and walked away. JC followed him for two paces, then stopped and watched him go. Effie felt weak. It wasn't just the shocking word. It was the tone, the sudden menace she saw in him.

———

*Sandy Gillis stood back, breathing heavily, though she could remember only an instant of his fury. Everything before the fury was fading quickly, a settling darkness filling in a hole where she knew there had been a paralyzing terror. Now she saw the menace prostrate on the barn floor. She wanted to go to her father, to comfort him, to reassure herself, but she knew that Sandy Gillis wouldn't let her.*

*"You're a sick fuckin' man," Sandy was saying, breathing in short gasps.*

*Her father's choking turned into sobs.*

*And then Sandy turned to Effie. "You go in the house . . . I'll get someone to come over. Go now."*

*"Don't hurt Daddy," she was saying.*

*"You just go."*

*And as she left, he said, "You don't mention this to anybody. Remember. Not a word."*

———

Much later on that Friday evening, after the second nightcap and just before he returned to his sullen silence, he advised her, coldly, as she would remember it, "Just so you know, they're like animals— they can smell fear. So, like, from now on . . ."

"What the hell are you talking about?"

"I could feel your tension, and he could too. I saw the way you looked at him."

"You're saying that I caused—"

"Maybe it's time you thought about doing something to get rid of some of the baggage you're carrying around. You've got more hang-ups than a cloakroom."

He was so far over the foul line that she knew he had to be aware of his absurdity. And she knew how dangerous that made him.

"If you wanted a fight tonight, you should have had it on the street. Don't pick on me."

"Bullshit."

She stood and put her glass down. "I'll call you in the morning," she said.

He looked away.

She didn't call him in the morning or on the Sunday morning either. And then it was Monday again. There was more snow in the forecast. Another major blizzard moving in from somewhere, deepening the endless winter. The numbness she felt wasn't even close to the misery she had known from past misunderstandings. She could reflect objectively on other winters in a life that was defined by isolation. A word she feared.

She wrote it down, drew a box around it. "Isolation." Under it she wrote: "The difference between solitude and isolation is . . ."

She remembered from her childhood the constant wondering

about her father. When will he leave? When will he return? Two simple questions, always burdened with unbearable anxiety. That was isolation. And it was isolation when she lived with John, imprisoned in his yearning and her own. And, in a way, Toronto had been her greatest isolation, because it was impossible to understand. How could she have been so isolated while living with a million people, the whole world passing through, surrounded by her friends, her life enriched by a baby who was of her substance, dependent on her, and a man who loved and needed her? And yet she was, in those early days, more isolated than she'd ever been at home.

It came to her as she sat there in her office, in the largest city in the country, the head of a department in the country's largest university. The difference between solitude and isolation is autonomy. And she wrote that word down and drew two boxes around it so she'd be able to remember its uncompromising challenge.

—

*She was sitting at her kitchen table with a book. It was a school book, and it was called* Beckoning Trails. *It had a blue cover, and on it there was a man skiing. She stared through the kitchen window, imagining that the road outside was beckoning.*

*Mrs. Gillis was suddenly across from her, in her father's place. She had her coat on. She placed a hand on Effie's hand. Effie stared at it, surprised by its warmth and softness.*

*"Where do you keep the tea, dear?" Mrs. Gillis asked.*

*Effie pointed to a cupboard.*

*Mrs. Gillis poked inside the wood stove, moved the kettle to the front. The kettle rumbled.*

*"Please stand up. I want to check your clothes," she said.*

*Effie stood.*

*Mrs. Gillis knelt before her, passed a hand over the front of Effie's skirt, lifted the skirt quickly, looked under and let it fall.*

*"Okay," she said. "You can sit now."*

*"Where's Daddy?" Effie asked.*

*"They went to town." Then, when the teacups were filled, Mrs. Gillis said, "Will you read something for me?"*

*Effie stared at the page, but the words were gone, replaced by ugly scratches that were meaningless. "'The day is done . . . '" she managed. But she could read no more.*

*Mrs. Gillis took the book. Read slowly. "'The day is done, and the darkness / Falls from the wings of Night, / As a feather is wafted downward / From an eagle in his flight.'"*

*"That's nice," she said. "John loves that one."*

*"Where's John?"*

*"He isn't home yet."*

*"Read more."*

*"'I see the lights of the village / Gleam through the rain and the mist, / And a feeling of sadness comes o'er me / That my soul cannot resist: / A feeling of sadness and longing, / That is not akin to pain, / And resembles sorrow only / As the mist resembles the rain.'"*

*The wetness on Effie's cheeks caught her by surprise.*

*"That's enough reading," Mrs. Gillis said. "You come with me now. I have the supper on."*

*"I have to wait for Duncan."*

*"We'll leave a note for Duncan."*

———

The second major snowstorm of 1999 moved in on Wednesday night. By noon on Thursday, media reports of chaos in the streets had generated hysteria at city hall. The mayor of Toronto asked the federal government for help. The federal government, with tongue in cheek, Effie was convinced, sent in the army: four hundred soldiers armed with brooms and shovels, backed up by a mechanized brigade of snowploughs. Effie found it all hysterically funny, but she was also grateful that she was able to stay home, marking exams, while the less fortunate were forced to flounder to their dreary offices.

JC called her on the Friday night. His voice was subdued. He wasn't feeling well, he said. A bit of flu. He was lying low, but he wanted her to know that he planned to go away on Monday for a while. Heading south.

It was a great idea, she thought, and she told him so. Cuba or Barbados would be lovely. Even just the Keys. She envied him. He corrected her: he didn't plan to go quite that far south. He'd asked the office for a leave of absence, and they'd consented to four months. He was going to go to Texas for a week. Hang out in Huntsville, spend some time with Sam. He was going to try to get his head around what was really happening there.

"At the very least, it might be healthy to get a little perspective, spend some time with someone worse off than I am."

She choked off the logical response: "How can you compare your life with his?" Once upon a time she would have said it, spontaneously. But she also knew that she would quickly have regretted saying it, and that the injury inflicted by her words would far exceed the insult that she felt.

She asked if he'd be coming by before he left. He didn't think it would be wise, he said, to risk passing on whatever bug he had.

"I was out of line the other night," he mumbled.

"I understand," she said.

"Sometimes I'm a bit—I don't know."

"It'll be okay."

Saturday night she attended the symphony. She wasn't particularly fond of classical music but found a deep resonance in the musical themes and rhythms of certain serious performers and composers. The program on Saturday featured violin concertos by Antonio Vivaldi, and he was one of those composers who, at times, evoked a rare serenity and memories of her father seemingly transported to a place of harmony as he listened to the local fiddle players.

The invitation had come from a history professor whose husband was down with the flu and who didn't want to waste expensive tickets. After the performance, they had a quiet drink on King Street, not far from the concert hall, then she dropped her colleague at her condo near St. Lawrence Market.

Driving up Jarvis on her way home, Effie noticed a man standing at the corner of Carlton, waiting for the light to change. Even before his face confirmed it, she knew it was JC. He'd said he was preparing to leave town, to go to Texas. He wasn't well. Why was he there on a seedy part of Jarvis? He was a long walk from where he lived, but maybe not for a man who was working through the challenge of a mid-life crisis. She decided not to think about it any further.

But at home she felt restless. The post-concert glass of wine sat like a sour scum upon her tongue. She plugged in the kettle to boil water for a cup of tea, resolving to cut back on the alcohol intake, at least until Easter.

Suddenly she ached for Easter and the springtime. As she waited for the kettle, her gaze shifted to a calendar on the kitchen wall. December. *Long gone,* she thought. She removed the page and stared at January 1999, trying to remember why there was a circle drawn in ink around the sixth, a Wednesday. What about the sixth? Then it came to her. Duncan had made that mark in May. The Epiphany, he said, a benchmark of some kind, a reference to her and JC Campbell.

They had made it through the summer, the ecstasy of summer, and through the blissful fall all the way to the Epiphany and then beyond. There were challenges, of course, but the basics were intact. She found great comfort in the small gestures, his sorrowful apologies, all the signals that he needed her.

She felt reassured, but she couldn't shake a feeling that was close to dread, and she remembered Duncan's words when he briefly visited in September—epiphany or catharsis, and that sometimes it's easy to confuse them. The kettle squealed.

The mug was hot, the fragrance of the tea refreshing, but she couldn't get the sight of JC Campbell off her mind. It was how forlorn he seemed. She was well aware of how defeat reshapes a man, restructures neck and shoulders, tips the face. And she saw it in the lonely-looking man on Jarvis Street, only slightly less pathetic than the spectacle she'd seen just south of there, moments earlier: a woman, or maybe just a girl, huddled in a cheap imitation leather jacket, thighs and knees pressed together below a foolishly short skirt, a hungry face lit briefly by the futile ember of a cigarette.

She listened to the silence of her home. She told herself again that there was comfort in the silence. The nurturing silence of a hard-won solitude. Autonomy. She raised the slowly cooling mug.

# two

*But to what purpose*
*Disturbing the dust on a bowl of rose-leaves*
*I do not know.*
T.S. ELIOT, "BURNT NORTON,"
FOUR QUARTETS

## 5

Monday morning she was up with the dawn, quickly lost in essays, once again lamenting how the carelessness of language can devalue creative insights and original ideas. She found the sloppy spelling, the lazy syntax, to be deeply irritating. But it was, she acknowledged, an improvement over when she also had to deal with almost indecipherable handwriting.

She stared out a window, momentarily transported back to a shabby little schoolhouse, felt the ache of isolation, the craving for escape, and reminded herself: *This is it, this is the escape.*

"*Huh???*" she underlined with three firm strokes of the red pen. She scratched another cryptic marginal comment and then reviewed it guiltily, wondering how much of her criticism was a projection of a mood that had nothing to do with students, scholarship or literacy.

Her workspace was a small bedroom that overlooked the street, and she was accustomed to early-morning traffic, especially on a Monday. But the taxi slowing down as it approached was unusual. She watched as the driver studied numbers on the houses. Then the taxi stopped at her front step and a rear door swung wide.

There was a long pause before JC emerged. He stood as if briefly unsure, carrying the travel case they'd purchased for the cat.

When she opened the door, she smiled bleakly. "Oh. You." The taxi was idling at the curb, vapour swirling in the frosty air.

"I know," he said. "I should have phoned. There was half a plan that Duncan would look after him, but he called late to say he didn't think it would be such a good idea where he's living now. With the street people. A bit rough there for a well-bred cat."

He smiled. "To be truthful, I didn't have the guts to call. Me all over, right?"

This diffidence was new, she thought, and disconcerting, as was the long scratch running down his cheek, starting just below his eye.

"What happened to your face?"

"Ah," he said. "Mr. Sorley got me. I was taking out some tangles. I trimmed his claws . . . I guess I should have done it sooner." He was blushing, uncomfortably.

"You should put something . . ."

"I did. A smear of Mecca. The miracle balm, you claim."

He held out the cat case. "You don't mind?" Through air holes she could see two intense blue eyes.

"No," she said. "He's mine anyway. He'll be company."

"I hope he doesn't cause an allergic reaction."

"I'm over that," she said. "How long will you be gone?"

"The week," he said. "I fly to Houston this morning. I'll pick up a rental and drive to Huntsville."

"Is this a good idea?"

"I don't know. Maybe not. I didn't tell anyone in Huntsville that I'm coming. I can always change my mind. In which case, I'll be back tomorrow night."

"I'll be here," she said.

"I hope."

"I have coffee on."

"I'd better carry on. You know how the Americans can be at immigration. I'll call or email. Or something."

"If you get a chance." Then she said, "I saw you Saturday night. Out walking. I'd have stopped, but I was by before I noticed."

"Saw me?" He seemed confused.

"Yes. On Jarvis."

"It couldn't have been me. I never left the house all weekend."

He produced a can of cat food from the pocket of his overcoat and presented it to her. Something about the gesture almost made her sob. He leaned close, kissed her cheek, held the contact for a moment. His cheek was warm and smooth. Under a strong aroma of shaving lotion and a sharp undertone of Listerine, there were traces of stale whisky. A fading musk of old cigarette smoke on the overcoat.

After he was gone, she retrieved a plastic pan from a storage closet, lined it with a garbage bag and half filled it with cat litter, then placed it in a discreet but accessible alcove. Then she released Sorley from the cage. He stepped out stiffly, blinking, stretched and yawned and wandered off, but returned shortly, stepped into the litter and, studying her with what she imagined was distaste, vigorously pissed.

In the kitchen she opened the tin and spooned food into a dish. She felt him at her ankles, and when she picked him up, he purred in fond appreciation. She scratched his ears and he closed his eyes. When she fluffed his fur, she realized that it was seriously matted, had been neglected for quite some time. She examined his paws, pressing back the furry flesh buds to reveal long, curved talons that were razor sharp, untrimmed. She lifted him, held his punched-in pug face close to her own, looked into the glacial eyes. He yawned again. His breath was foul.

"Dear, dear," she said quietly. "Why is Daddy lying to us?"

Her eyes were watery.

Cassie called just before she left for class. They'd picked a date, decided to get married on April 10, the Saturday just after Easter. They planned to keep it small, but she was open to suggestions regarding guests.

"You'll have to help me with the Cape Breton crowd," Cassie said. "The only one that's obvious to me is Uncle John. Dad, of course. I'm not sure about that girlfriend."

Before hanging up, Cassie told her that Ray had been putting together some information on concussions, how people with even mild head injuries react over the short and the long term. "It isn't his specialty, exactly, but he's asked some colleagues for input."

Effie said that she was looking forward to reading anything he came up with, and she meant it.

At four thirty Tuesday afternoon, as she prepared to leave for home, she noticed the blue call slip in her mailbox.

"Mr. Gillis, 3:45. Your ex again?"

There was a telephone number, with the 902 area code.

"Shit," she said. She balled up the paper, dropped it in a wastebasket and turned out the lights.

When the phone rang late that night, she ran to answer it, surprised by the instant wave of joy it caused.

"Effie?"

There was a long pause, filled by a babble of voices.

"Effie? It's John Gillis here."

Oh God. "John—this is a surprise."

"Yes," he said. "Drove in today."

John was in a bar, she guessed, judging from the voices and the clatter.

"So where are you, for God's sake?"

"Haven't got a clue," he said. He could see the CN Tower through a window, though, which didn't tell her anything except that he was in Toronto.

"Walk outside and check for a street sign," she instructed.

"I was just leaving anyway," he said.

"Were you calling this afternoon?" she asked. "At the office?"

"I spoke to someone there. Said I was your ex. Hope you didn't mind."

She laughed. "I thought . . ." but caught herself. "They didn't get your name."

"Looks like I'm on King Street. And . . . the other one is Simcoe."

"Can you see Roy Thomson Hall?"

"Is that the round thing?"

"Yes. Where are you parked?"

"I'm not sure."

"Well, get in a taxi, then."

And she gave him her street address. Then she dressed quickly and poured a large drink. And sat back, mind racing.

John was standing, watching the taxi drive away, when she opened the door.

He turned, removed his hat.

"Well, this is a nice area."

He seemed to stiffen when, thoughtlessly, she kissed his cheek. The alcohol aroma was overwhelming. She fanned it away, theatrically.

"Whew," she said.

"I've had a few, but don't you worry."

"I'm having one myself," she said. "Would you join me?"

"Well. I suppose."

Over his drink he said he'd started driving Monday morning without a plan but with the remote idea that he might end up in Sudbury. He'd been there once, years before, with Uncle Jack. She vaguely remembered. It was back in the sixties, just after his father's death. They could never forget the date. November 22, 1963. Sandy Gillis killed himself the day they killed the president of the United States. John and his uncle Jack wound up wandering Ontario, in search of work. In Sudbury John was offered a job, but they turned Jack down. Something about his lungs they didn't like. Probably the beginning of the cancer that brought him down a few years later. All in all it had been a great trip, though. Released him from the fog of horror that imprisoned him after his father shot himself.

"You'd remember all that, though you were pretty young. Me going away with Uncle Jack."

"I'm the same age as yourself," she said.

"You always seemed younger. You seem younger now."

"You're obviously looking for something, with the compliments."

He blushed. "You don't have to worry about that."

There was a long silence.

"Your mother, Mrs. Gillis . . . how is she, anyway?" she asked, knowing the likely response.

"Ah well," he said, then sipped. "You know she's in the nursing home?"

"I heard that. But she's well?"

"Good days, bad days. Most days she doesn't know who or where she is."

After Sudbury, he and Jack had spent a couple of days in Toronto. Met a lot of guys from home at some little bar they all hung out in.

"The Rondun, probably," Effie said.

"I think that was it," he said. "A queer name like that."

On a whim he'd tried to relocate the bar. Just for old time's sake. He'd been thinking a lot about Jack recently. No special reason, just that it was creeping up to thirty years since he passed away, poor Jack. He drove all over the west end. Didn't recognize a thing.

"Haven't you been here since then?" she asked. "Since the sixties?"

"Managed not to have a reason," he said. He had almost visited in '93, when Toronto still had a decent ball team. But there was something that prevented it. There was always something.

But now there was something in particular motivating him, he said. He needed time alone, time to think about life changes. And he also thought best in a car, behind the wheel. No phones, except the mobile, which he kept turned off. Figured he'd revisit the places he and Uncle Jack had toured through all those years before. Get perspective on his life, or what passed for life.

He'd come as far as Ottawa, and it was while sitting in a Tim Hortons there that he remembered the little bar from years ago in Toronto and decided on the spot that driving all the way to Sudbury in the wintertime was probably a bad idea. So he changed course.

"A roundabout trip, but here you are," she said. "So you slept in Ottawa?"

"No. Just carried on."

"You haven't slept?"

"I have a lot on my mind."

And suddenly the call on New Year's Eve came back to her. The pauses and unfinished sentences. The nervous laughter. And now he sat in front of her.

"You don't mind me having a few drinks?" he said.

"You know yourself," she said. "You'll have to be the judge."

"Ahhh. But you didn't know the way I was, after you . . . back in the bad old days. When I was on my own. Not too proud of what I can remember about that."

"I feel bad," she said. It was spontaneous, as was the sudden grief.

"No, no, no," he said. "It all worked out for the best. Don't you go . . ." And he laughed again and tilted back. "Your man, who was down with you last summer. I was sorry afterwards I didn't get to meet him."

"There'll be another time," she said. "He's away just now."

"You didn't say what line of work he's in."

"He works in television."

"Interesting."

"I was worried about you, at New Year's, when you called. It was great hearing from you. But phone calls out of the blue at this point in life often bring bad news."

"There was news, all right. But I couldn't get the words out. I can't imagine what you thought, so."

"You're okay, are you, John? There's nothing wrong?"

"Ah yes," he said. He turned and studied the kitchen counter. "Do you have any more of that good stuff?"

"Help yourself," she said.

He was pouring with his back to her. "The news, such as it is . . . is that I'm getting married."

"Jesus," she said. "Bring that bottle over here."

———

The story emerged in fragments. He'd met someone at his AA meetings. She was in her thirties. Struggling with drugs as he struggled with alcohol. Something between them seemed to make the struggle easier. He'd actually fallen off the wagon once or twice since he met her, with no permanent consequences. Like now. He'd be fine in the morning. No more binges.

"When?" she asked.

"Could be any day," he said. "We're just going to go off and see a judge. Have a few people, mostly from the program. Real low-key. She's a lovely woman. You'd like her."

"Well, that's just wonderful. What's her name?"

"Janice, but you wouldn't have known her. She came to the area with her family after you were gone. The family eventually moved on, but Janice stayed behind."

Janice had a good job at the mill but lost it after missing work for days on end. Now she had a job at the Superstore. Worked her way up to managing a department. Solid woman. Never a slip.

She raised her glass. "I wish you both all the happiness in the world. I mean that, John. I really do."

"I know you do," he said, staring at the table. "And the same to yourself and . . . what's his name?"

"Campbell. JC Campbell."

"Here's to yourself and JC Campbell. But you haven't asked me why I'm getting married, after all this time."

"It seems like a pretty normal thing to do when you love somebody. And, oh yes, you'll probably be getting an invitation to another wedding before long."

"Not . . ."

"No, no. Not me. No fear. Cassie is getting married. Maybe at Easter."

"Little Cassie?"

"Not so little anymore."

"Well, well."

"She's marrying a doctor," Effie said.

"A doctor! You think. Little Cassie. You'll give her my best."

"I will. So tell me, then, what persuaded you to take the plunge again?"

"Ah," he said. "There's a good question. Why do you think?"

"Well, I'm assuming that you're in love."

"I suppose so."

"And we all need companionship."

"I'm not so sure about that part. I got kind of fond of my own company over the years."

"Okay," she said. "There are loads of reasons, I'm sure."

"What would you think if I told you I have to get married?"

"Have to? What do you mean, you have to?"

"Exactly that. I have to."

"Meaning what?"

"Well . . . meaning she got knocked up."

"What?"

"Pregnant is probably a nicer way of putting it."

Effie was laughing then, eyes glistening. "You must be thrilled," she said.

"Thrilled? Not exactly."

"I couldn't imagine a better parent than you."

His face was sorrowful.

"What's wrong, John? This is brilliant news."

"It's just that it never occurred to me that I was able. You must remember back when we were . . . how much I wanted to have a family. But couldn't. Surely you remember that? And then, when

Cassie came, I knew for sure it wasn't you who was the problem. For the longest time I thought it was why you left. Because I couldn't give you what you needed."

"Oh, John," she said.

"I eventually understood all the reasons. But that one was the easiest to live with. At the time. Me sterile."

Then they sat in the timeless silence, where there was no longer past or future, just the frozen moment.

In the morning he was gone. He'd spent the night, snoring loudly on her chesterfield—she could hear him from her bedroom. But by morning it was as if he'd never been there, as if their conversation, so deep and in so many ways so deeply sad, had never happened. Where did he go from her place? How did he find his car? What had drawn him to the relative turmoil of the city, into a vortex of unhappy memories that almost all began and ended with her? Effie. MacAskill. Gillis.

## 6

JC didn't call or send the promised email. She never really thought he would. By Wednesday evening she allowed herself to miss him. The night was long and sleepless in the bed they'd shared. She tried to count the times but fell asleep. Then woke, imagining she heard a sound. Fell asleep again, channelled vague scenes from a movie she remembered. *Dead Man Walking.* Woke up again. JC told her once that she reminded him of Susan Sarandon. She'd laughed. Susan Sarandon with tiny titties. Tiny? I don't think so. You're a liar, she accused. They wrestled. Now the word kept her awake: Liar.

*Where is he?*

He'd been the first to share this room, this bed—the one she'd bought for Sextus. It was Easter Sunday night, not quite a year ago. JC had shown surprising confidence for a first visit to a lady's bedroom. A lady of some standing, a lady of a certain age. She'd been thinking, *He's as casual as if he's here to buy the place and I'm his realtor.* Except they were holding hands. They'd both had a considerable amount to drink, but she was clear in mind and purpose.

"I'm surprised," she'd said, while they were in the kitchen, cleaning up. "That in all those late-night cleanup sessions years ago, when you and I would be the last ones standing . . . you never tried anything."

"I could say the same thing," he said.

"Really, though. We could have got away with murder."

That was how it started.

Later, "So tell me, Mr. Campbell. Back then, when a guy like you *did* decide to make a move, how would you begin?"

He smiled, loosened his necktie, folded his dish towel neatly, set it down, patted it gently. "I remember once . . . we danced, you and me," he said. "You probably don't even remember."

She nodded.

"I even remember the tune," he said. "'A Whiter Shade of Pale,' I'm pretty sure. Up till that moment, I always associated it with people smoking dope. Ever after, any time I heard it playing, it was us slow dancing in your kitchen. Your husband comatose in the next room. I'm sure you don't remember."

"And what prevented you from taking advantage of the situation?"

"Well, for openers, it never crossed my mind that you'd have been even slightly interested. But also, if I recall correctly, there was a baby somewhere."

She laughed. "Very good."

"And I suppose I was afraid of disappointing you."

"How would you disappoint me?"

"Men are almost always disappointing women."

"Almost always? There are exceptions?"

"Yes. Bad guys. Bad guys never disappoint. Maybe that's why girls like the bad guys."

She walked to the stove, conscious of his eyes on her back. "Coffee?"

"How about another small brandy?"

She turned, the brandy in her hand, swirling it. "And if there was no baby . . . and no drunk husband in the next room?"

He stood. "And we're dancing to that tune?" Then he was in front of her, head tilted slightly, hands on her hips, body swaying as he shifted from foot to foot, a kind of shuffle dance to silent music. "I don't know for sure." He seemed to concentrate. There was moisture on his upper lip. "Maybe," he said finally, stopping the movement, now staring straight into her eyes. "Maybe I'd have . . ." With a nimble thumb and forefinger he undid two buttons on her blouse. She raised an automatic hand, placed it just below her throat. He removed the glass of brandy from her other hand. "And you'd have done exactly that," he said. And sipped.

"And what would that have told you?"

"Nothing." He sipped again, the music clearly playing in his head. "Ah."

"The revelation would follow, in due course. You'd ask me, or tell me, to leave. I wouldn't expect you to hit me. Or you might have been . . . subtly . . . positive."

"Subtly?"

"I've always had you figured for a subtle kind of . . . woman."

"Girl, you almost said."

"Woman."

"Okay. How subtle?"

"You would have kept your hand upon your throat for maybe a minute, looking a bit confused."

"Yes."

He leaned closer, until their foreheads almost touched, eyes studying the hand still lightly clutching the loose fabric of her open shirt. A strand of hair had fallen across her brow. He gently brushed it back, then placed his hand on her neck, thumb resting on her cheek. He put the glass of brandy down behind her on the counter.

"Tell me something. You're the Gaelic scholar. Why are tits . . . I should say breasts . . . always masculine in Gaelic?"

"My, my," she said. "Aren't you full of small surprises? Where did you hear that?"

"I studied the language of Eden during my brief time at the university."

"I didn't realize they taught those kinds of things."

"Actually, there was a native speaker in the class. One day he asked how come."

"And the professor said?"

"He said we'd get to grammar in the second semester. Of course, by the second semester I was long gone."

"Gone where?"

"Ah. That's a whole other story. So why masculine?"

"I think your native speaker and the prof were out to lunch."

"Really. So yours are . . . feminine?"

"What do you think?"

"Umm. I'd have to agree with you."

"So you've opened buttons. *Mo chiochan* half-exposed and we're dancing . . . kind of."

"Yes, we've resumed dancing as if you've forgotten the buttons, and then, near the end of the song, I'd probably have kissed you."

And with his thumb now beneath her chin, he tilted her head slightly and was kissing her, first lightly, then with an intensity that, even though she was prepared for it, still caught her by surprise.

Ray had written a brief note and enclosed it with the articles he photocopied. According to the doctor who had assessed JC, he'd shown signs of mild TBI (traumatic brain injury) on the Glasgow Coma Scale. She felt her stomach lurch. Ray's note was reassuring, though. He explained that a high number on the Glasgow scale was a good thing, and JC had been rated at 13 out of a possible 15. His MRI was normal. So there was nothing to worry about. Just give him time. Headaches, mood swings and mild episodes of frustration related to difficulty thinking clearly were to be expected. She was not to be unduly worried if he showed fatigue, mild depression, slight staggers, olfactory impairment. She should be prepared for small surprises for, perhaps, a year. Barring a repeat performance, JC would be good as new. Ray said he was dying to meet him, that he sounded like a fascinating man.

"Bear in mind," he wrote, "this prognosis is second-hand, from friends in neurology. I'm a gynecologist. My expertise is on the other end of a different kind of patient."

By Thursday night she gave in to a gnawing loneliness. Fought it briefly, remembering John's visit. John *had* to get married. John was going to be a father. She admitted that she had conflicted feelings about the news. JC said he was going to Texas for "a week"—or was it for "the week." Did that mean seven days, or five?

She called Cassie. "Valentine's Day," she said. "I want you to keep it open. I want to have a little party, for you and Ray. Invite some friends. We can tell people then about April tenth."

"Valentine's Day?"

"Yes. Is there a problem?"

"Not really, but it's Ray's birthday, too."

"No kidding. Then we can tell people it's a small birthday party, and then spring the real news."

"Did you tell JC yet?" Cassie asked.

"No. Actually, I haven't seen much of him for the past . . . while."

"Oh."

"He went to Texas for the week. That fellow Sam. I don't know what to call him—friend, project. Whatever. He went down to see him. But he'll be back. Certainly by Valentine's."

"Mother. You don't sound—"

"Oh, stop it. It's the third week of January, for God's sake. The *faoilteach*. It's always like this."

"What is?"

"The *faoilteach*."

"The what?"

"It's from the word for "wolf." It was when the wolves . . . oh, Christ. Never mind. I have to go. I have the kettle on."

"Mother?"

"Bye."

Her hand was shaking. *Sonofabitch bastard,* she thought. *I can't believe I let this happen again. How old do you have to be before you're immune to this bullshit? Why didn't I tell Cassie about John's visit, that he'd been here? What am I afraid of?*

To visit Duncan at the shelter was an impulsive thing to do and, sitting in the cab on Sherbourne, she had growing reservations. Duncan never liked surprises, unannounced intrusions into his private life. She went anyway. The Epiphany was past. The Epiphany was her excuse.

The image of JC wandering on Jarvis Street returned, and she struggled with the questions that were lingering like the fumes of booze and cigarettes he'd left behind. She knew from personal experience that everyone has secrets. We keep secrets mostly for the benefit of others. What about lies? Why do we lie?

When they stopped in front of the shelter, the cab driver smiled and said, "You must be a social worker."

"No," she said, as she stuffed her wallet into her coat pocket and opened the car door. "I'm not a social worker."

The street was shabby: abandoned-looking brick buildings with commercial frontage; large, blank windows, some papered over; faded signage from long ago relevance, perhaps prosperity.

There were four men near an entranceway, and she looked above them for the sign. "Hope Is Refuge," it said, and she walked toward them, nodding as she approached. They stared back silently.

The door was locked. She scanned for a buzzer, doorbell, intercom. She felt stranded, nervous. And still she was shocked when someone said, "Big feeling twat." The voice was too close.

Then Duncan spoke. "You guys move along. It'll be another hour." His face was flushed, eyes hard. "You'd better come in," her brother said.

The place seemed empty, tidy. There was an overpowering odour of antiseptic detergent. Somewhere, a radio or stereo was playing "I Guess That's Why They Call It the Blues." She walked behind her brother toward a door and waited while he selected a key from a bundle that he had taken from his pocket, then she followed him into an office that was austere, furnished with a small desk, an office chair and a vinyl-covered couch. There was a wooden crucifix prominent on the wall behind the desk.

He waved her to the couch and went behind the desk and sat there on a creaky chair with wheels, elbows on the desktop. Briefly, he covered his face with his hands and sighed, and when he looked at her, his face seemed sad. In the harsh light of the office, she noticed dark crescents below his eyes.

"You shouldn't have come here, or you should have told me."

"I'm sorry," she said. "I didn't think—"

"It isn't that," he said. "That was unusual. They tend to be polite."

Suddenly she felt ashamed, coming to this place to talk about herself and her anxieties. Pathetic. Duncan was sitting back now, elbow cradled in the palm of one hand, the other cupping his chin and cheek. "You're okay?"

"I'm okay," she said.

He was studying her face. She had intended to ask him to come out for coffee and a chat. Now she was uncertain how to even start a conversation. She considered speaking Gaelic but realized she lacked the fluency, perhaps in English, too, for deciphering the nuances of the love and lies and loss that now distracted her.

"I was thinking of volunteering," she said impulsively, shocked by her unconsidered words.

"Here?"

"Yes," she said, emboldened. "It would be a relief from the ivory tower."

He stood. "I don't think so," he said. "One of us is enough."

She stared, waiting. Finally she asked, "What do you mean by that?"

"It's going to get pretty hectic here in a few minutes. We can talk another time."

He walked to the office door and opened it, stood there waiting. "How is JC, anyway?"

"He's fine," she said, then stood. "He's away just now."

"Right," he said. "So I heard."

"You heard?"

She could hear voices somewhere and the clatter of dishes, and she could smell steam and food aromas.

"*Bidh mi gad fhaicinn,*" she said.

"Yes," he said, distracted. "See you around."

She decided to walk to the subway station on Bloor, at least a mile away.

*I lied,* she thought, waiting for the light at Wellesley. And she almost laughed aloud at the irony. She went to see her brother seeking insight about lies, then lied about the reason for her visit. But she had to admit she felt better. Everybody lies.

At home in bed, she tried to think of someone in her life who hadn't lied at one time or another for some momentarily important reason.

And for the first time in a long time she thought of Conor Ferguson. Conor, who had told her up front there are always necessary lies—benevolent deceptions, he would call them. "Everybody has the capacity to lie," he said. "But the biggest lie is always why we lie."

"So tell me, why do we lie?"

"Ask your brother," he said. "He'll know all about the Noble Lie."

"Have you ever been married, Conor?"

"No."

On Friday afternoon when she got home, there was a message on the answering machine. It was rambling, disjointed, the musings of someone who'd been drinking heavily. JC said he was still in Huntsville. He had called at one o'clock, when he knew she wouldn't be there. Touching base without the peril of engagement. Still, she felt mildly grateful for the call.

He had just returned from the Ellis unit, had seen Sam there. On Tuesday afternoon, someone from the prison PR staff had given

him a tour of what he called the Walls facility, which she gathered
was a different part of the establishment. There was nothing ambigu-
ous about "death chamber," "gurney," "isolation cells." He said he'd
seen the old electric chair, which was on display for tourists.

When he spoke of Sam, there was a quaver in his voice. He said
their conversations were surreal. But he didn't say when he'd be
back home, or even when she'd hear from him again.

She called his place on Walden, because she felt compelled to
talk to him, even if he wasn't there. The friendly voice on his
answering machine was reassuring. She told him to make a note
about February 14. She hoped he'd be available; she could use the
help. A valentine was optional.

Then she poured a drink, watched a bit of television, ate a sandwich. Poured another drink and listened, again, to the recorded
voice from some unimaginable town in Texas where you could
tour facilities for killing people.

She fell asleep curled up in a chair, fourth whisky barely touched.

———

*"Effie, dear," the teacher said. "Would you come here for a moment?" The
tone was ominous with kindness. "A gentleman would like a word with you."*

*The gentleman was smiling, just outside the classroom door. First she
noticed that his eyes were brown, then she registered the wide brown belt,
the holster and the gun—the yellow stripe along the trouser leg.*

*"Hey there," he said. Touched her shoulder. "Do you think you could
spare a moment for a little chat? Just you and me?"*

*She looked back, saw John watching from his desk but knew he couldn't
see the cop. "Yes," she said.*

*They sat in the front seat of his car.*

*"Effie," he said. "How old are you?"*

"Thirteen."

"Effie," he repeated, sighing. "I'm going to ask you a couple of questions. I want you to think before you answer. Okay?"

He seemed young, radiated kindness. He was handsome in a cowboy kind of way.

"What questions?"

He frowned through the windshield for what seemed like a long time. "You're old enough to know that boys and girls—or rather, men and women—have . . . relations. Do things, like, together."

He was studying her face. She was confused. Said nothing.

"I think you know what I mean."

She shrugged.

"Sometimes a guy . . . a man will try to do things with a girl or woman, and it's okay. And sometimes it isn't okay. You know that, right?"

"I think so."

"It's okay, for instance, when it's your mom and dad together."

"I don't have a mom."

"I know. I'm just saying. When you're older, there will be boyfriends. And it'll be okay."

"Okay."

"But there are certain people that it's never okay for. Never okay for them to try to do things with you. Ever. And when you're only thirteen—obviously a very grown-up, pretty thirteen . . . but it's never okay, for anybody."

"I know."

"So, Effie." He sighed again. "I have to ask you. Did anybody, ever, anytime . . . try to do anything?"

There was a peculiar movement in her stomach, part nervousness, part nausea. And in her brain there was a silhouette but nothing else that she could see. But she could remember sound and smell. A revolting smell she was unable to identify. And the sounds were frightening and sorrowful.

"No," she said.

"You're shaking," the policeman said.

She stared at her trembling hands as if they belonged to someone else. She looked straight into the policeman's eyes. "No," she said. "I don't think so."

"You're absolutely sure?"

"Yes."

He seemed perplexed, but he also looked relieved. "Okay, Effie, you can go back in now. Anybody asks what we were talking about, tell them I'm looking for a lost dog. Out your way. Okay?"

"Okay."

"I already talked to your brother."

"You did?"

"About the dog."

———

John phoned on Saturday morning.

"We did it," he said. "Tied the knot, yesterday afternoon. Went to see the old judge at his house. Short and simple. I recommend it, if you ever do it again yourself."

She offered heartfelt congratulations.

"Queer time for a wedding, January," John said. "But it keeps the guest list down."

"How many did you have?" she asked.

"Just us and the witnesses," he said. "Best way to go. Short and sweet and simple."

She felt a sudden wistfulness. She told him that he and Janice would receive an invitation to Cassie's wedding. Keep April tenth available. He laughed. Janice hated to travel, but he'd try to talk her into it. A little honeymoon, he'd call it and maybe tempt her that way. Effie remembered an awkward night in a motel room years ago. What year was it? The year Duncan was ordained—1968. He'd married them. John seemed to drive forever afterwards.

"Cassie will be devastated if you don't show up," she said. "You know she calls you Uncle John."

There was a long, uncomfortable silence.

"Great girl, Cassie," John said finally. "I have her graduation picture on the mantel. And what about himself, her father? Have you talked to him?"

"Not lately."

"Saw him in town a week ago," John said. "His nose is definitely out of joint about something. When I mentioned Cassie getting married, he just snorted and walked away."

"Take it with a grain of salt."

"He's starting to look his age, that fellow is. I felt like telling him."

"Sextus?"

John laughed. "Yes. Hard to imagine, isn't it? Sextus aging like the rest of us."

"So how is Janice?"

"Oh, she's great. Aren't you, Janice?"

There was a voice in the background.

"I don't think you told me the due date."

"Well, that depends, doesn't it?"

"Depends on what?" Effie asked.

"Depends on who the father is. Right, Janice?"

She could hear a woman's voice raised in the background, then he was laughing too.

"I'm dying to meet her," Effie said.

"I tried to introduce you last summer," John said. "One morning when she and I were out for our run, we saw you on the road."

## 7

The summer had remained a regular topic of discussion all
through their first spring together. JC's enthusiasm was infectious. He wanted to explore Cape Breton, a place about which
he had very distant, mostly pleasant childhood memories.

The mother of his child was dead. A car accident in the mid-
1970s. After that, his daughter had been raised by her mother's
relatives and JC lost touch, except for the cheques that he continued sending until 1985, when she turned twenty-one. He
admitted writing the last batch with a feeling of relief that, when
he'd mailed them, turned to loss.

"So through the seventies," she said, "you were dealing with
that. And nobody knew what you were going through? The mother
of your child killed . . ."

"Actually, I wasn't going through much of anything."

"But you must have—"

"No. Not really."

"Do you know her name? The daughter?"

"Her first name. Sylvia. I don't know what last name she ended
up with. You have to remember, once I got on the Amnet treadmill,
that was pretty well my life. Till '96, when I came back."

"Amnet?"

"American networks."

"And what was it that brought you back in '96?"

"What brought me back?" He seemed to think. "Fatigue, I guess it was. Yes. A certain kind of fatigue."

He smiled.

"But here I am, right? All rested up. Ready for the unknown."

———

On Saturday she wandered to a coffee shop on Bloor. She bought a newspaper, scanning it for even a small reference to Texas, what might be going on there. She found nothing that enlightened her. She sat, sipping at her coffee, trying to imagine JC in that place.

Fed up with dark probabilities, she forced herself to contemplate the word she'd been savouring—"autonomy." The essence of autonomy is independence, something she had struggled to recognize as being paramount among her considerable achievements— the silver lining in the black cloud of abandonment. *Conditioning,* she thought. *I'm in training for another disappointment.*

"Is there anybody sitting here?"

She shook her head, mustered a weak smile, moved her newspaper so the man had room to put his mug down and resumed her meditation.

"May I?" he said, nodding toward the front section of the heavy weekend paper.

"Be my guest." She looked away, aware she was being inspected. She had the irrational urge to light a cigarette. It's odd how the old impulse returns, even decades after the last smoke. How many of our urges last so long? Cigarettes had once been perfect social moderators. "Would you care for one?" she'd have asked. And he'd have said, "No, thank you," or conversely, "Why not?" And probably have lit both cigarettes, a brief engagement that could have dissipated like the smoke or evolved into a genuine encounter.

The man now reading her newspaper was decent-looking, she thought, maybe early forties. He wore no rings. He had a fashionable whisker shadow, his hair clipped short; no ear stud, no visible tattoos. He was wearing a scuffed leather jacket and a yellow turtleneck with a polo player logo on the breast, which she didn't like but could overlook because the shirt was faded, obviously old. She opened her purse, checked her cellphone. It was turned off. Perhaps he'd called. She turned it on, but there were no messages. She placed it on the table anyway, beside her coffee.

He put the paper down. "Thanks," he said. "I just wanted to check something. I'll pick one up."

"You can take that one."

"I'll gladly pay for it . . ."

"Don't be foolish," she said.

"I love your accent," he said. "You're Irish."

"No," she said with a quick laugh. "Far from it."

"Newfoundland, then."

"No, not quite." There was a moment of eye contact, and she looked away. Imagined the cigarette, imagined exhaling away from him. Simply having something to do to hide the nervousness in hands and face.

He reached into a pocket and plucked out a card. "I must be off," he said. "Thanks for the paper. If I can ever return the favour." He put the card on the table, then stood up. "You don't have a card, I suppose."

She shook her head.

"I'm Paul," he said, holding out a hand.

She hesitated for a moment, then briefly shook his hand.

He stood silent, but the expression on his face was eloquent. He wanted to know more.

"I'm Faye," she said.

"Yes," he said, then smiled and walked away. She watched his back, the easy, athletic stride. The card said Paul Campion. There was an address that could have been an office or a residence, and there was a telephone number.

Walking home, she noted that her spirits were improved. She knew it was the brief speculation she'd noticed in a stranger's face. For a moment she allowed herself to be what she presumed he had observed: a younger, more attractive and interesting package than the one she lived in.

It was a flight of self-indulgence, she knew that. But it felt good and it was a welcome interruption.


When the doorbell rang Sunday night, she considered ignoring it. She was wearing sweatpants and a T-shirt, fresh from a bath, looking forward to bed. She knew it would be JC, and she felt angry and disappointed. *So now he's back from Texas. At least the asshole could have called.*

He was leaning with one hand propped against the doorframe, head hanging. When she opened the door, he looked up and stepped back, swaying dangerously near the top step. Instinctively, she reached for him. She'd rehearsed a short, sharp greeting, but she was speechless. JC spread his arms, palms toward her as if in supplication.

"You'd better come in," she said at last.

He stumbled almost imperceptibly on the threshold but recovered quickly. "Sorry," he said. "I know it's late. I came as soon as I could, to get the lad. I hope he hasn't been a problem. With the allergy."

"The cat is the least of my problems," she said.

Then he wrapped his arms around her and held her so tightly she could hardly breathe. He said nothing, but rocked gently from side to side. He reeked of smoke and alcohol and sweat. "I need to be with you tonight," he whispered. "I need to stay here with you."

"It's okay," she said. "Let me get you something. I'll make tea."

"No," he said. "No tea."

"Okay," she said softly. "You go on up. I'll shut things down."

He walked slowly and with what seemed like great deliberation toward the stairway, still wearing his overcoat. He paused briefly at the bottom step, as if measuring the distance he had to climb, then slowly mounted.

She watched him go. Then sat and waited.


The overcoat was tossed aside. He was on the bed, face down, unconscious.

Gently, she removed his shoes. She undressed herself, then retreated to a spare bedroom. The night was endless.


She called Walden at eleven the next morning, not expecting him to answer. But he did. His voice was husky.

"I hope I didn't wake you," she said quickly.

"No problem," he said. "I was just going to call you."

"You were sound asleep when I left for the office. I thought you needed the rest. But you seem to have got home okay."

"Yes," he said. "But I'm afraid I forgot something at your place."

"Ahh," she said.

"The cat."

She laughed. "Well, the shape you were in last night, I shouldn't be surprised."

"Sorry about that," he said. "I hope I didn't make too much—"

"Don't mention it," she said. "I've seen far worse."

"I'll come and get him this evening."

"Sure," she said. "I'll fix some supper for us."

"That won't be necessary," he said.

"Well, we have to eat, anyway. I promise I won't harass you."

"I'm not worried about that. It's just that the appetite hasn't been the best lately."

"I'll keep it simple."

"What time?"

"Whenever you get there."

She bought two T-bones and a bag of premixed greens on the way home. She made an olive oil and vinegar dressing. She tidied. In her bedroom, she could still see the imprint of his body on the duvet. As she was about to leave the room, she noticed a small red object on the floor beside the bed. She picked it up and examined it. It was a small cutting tool with a retractable blade. Something tradesmen used. A utility knife. Yes, that was what they called it. She slipped the tool into her jacket pocket.

By eight she was convinced JC wasn't coming and was contemplating an even simpler dinner for herself. Then she heard the doorbell.

He seemed refreshed and almost cheerful. "What's on the menu?" he asked.

"Steak and a salad. You like yours rare, right?"

"Medium-rare."

"You'll excuse a lack of starch," she said.

"I'll appreciate a lack of starch," he replied. And they laughed together for what felt like the first time in ages.

She didn't offer alcohol, and he didn't ask for it. She made a pot of mint tea. They spoke about Cassie's wedding plans. She told him that Ray had researched head injuries and sent some background information, which she'd left at the office. He thanked her, said he'd been briefed by a specialist at the hospital. He wasn't worried. He was no stranger to concussions. "Not that it's something to be proud of."

"Life is full of small concussions," she replied.

"But you don't anticipate them at my age," he said. "This should be when life calms down."

She remembered the cutting tool, removed it from her pocket. "I found this on the floor, upstairs."

He seemed startled. "Oh," he said, reaching for it.

"What's it for?" she asked.

He shrugged. "Opening packages. Cutting twine."

"Someone I once knew told me it could also be a weapon."

"Really?" He laughed. "What kind of person was that?"

"Just someone I knew. I was considering a course in self-defence at his gym. He said if I was worried I should carry one of those. He said 'the most effective weapon is the one the other fellow doesn't know you have.'"

"Old flame?" he asked.

"You could call him that. I must have mentioned Conor?"

"Can't say you have." He studied her face, waiting.

"We lived together for a while. After Sextus. I'm surprised Sextus never mentioned Conor. Anyway . . . it didn't end well."

"Ah," he said. "Conor bailed on you."

"No—Conor died on me."

"I'm sorry."

"That's okay. It was a long time ago."

He put the tool in his pocket. His eyes were troubled.

She asked about Texas. He checked his wristwatch. He said there wasn't much to tell her about Texas. Sam had a new execution date and, by coincidence, it was right around Cassie's wedding. They planned to put him down on April eighth.

"Put him down?" She was frowning.

"That's how he refers to it," he said. "He's full of black irony. Said he was going to try to persuade them to do it on Good Friday. They're kind of religious down there."

"I can't imagine any irony in his situation."

"What else is there?"

"So what do you talk about with someone who's going to die?"

"We're all going to die."

"You know what I mean."

"We talk about life. Plus, Sam's a big believer in God and heaven, a literal afterlife. So it's kind of like talking to someone who's getting ready for a big trip to some exotic place. A holiday that's never going to end." He laughed and looked away. "It helps, looking at it like that."

"What about you? Do you believe?"

"Not a chance." He yawned and stretched. "I'm thinking of writing a book," he said.

"A book?"

"Why not? You wrote one."

"Mine wasn't really a book," she said. "So you'll write a book about the death penalty?"

"Not exactly." He raised his eyebrows.

"What, then?"

He studied her intently for what felt like a long time. "Impotence," he said.

"Impotence?"

"I'm becoming an expert on the subject. We talked a lot about that too. Me and Sam."

She studied the face, so familiar, but now impenetrable. "You can spend the night," she said.

"Two in a row. That's almost cohabitation."

"Suit yourself." She stood and started gathering the dishes.

"Hey," he said. "Look at me."

She looked.

"I love you," he said.

She stared, the swift reciprocal response on her tongue. But she closed her mouth around it. Finally she said, "I know that."

He stood then.

"Please stay," she said again.

"I can't."

Now it was another Saturday and the silence was suffocating. Mid-afternoon she poured a drink and nursed it for an hour. As darkness settled, she refreshed it, then called his number. There was no answer, and she set the receiver down before the machine cut in. During her solitary dinner, in spite of all her better instincts, she uncorked some wine.

Returning from the bathroom, she staggered slightly and reproached herself, then laughed. Reproached herself for what? She could stagger without any social consequences. She was alone. But wasn't that the problem, drinking alone? She drew back a drape and peered toward the street, but it was gone, lost in the inevitable night. *Another day has disappeared,* she thought, *another piece of my existence. And I sit here waiting, inflaming apathy with Scotch and wine. The story of my life, waiting for some man to intervene.* And they always do, but always for their own ends. John rescued her from home. Sextus rescued her from John. Conor rescued her from Sextus, but at least he left her with an education and a home. That was progress, of a sort. JC Campbell rescued her from . . . nothing. Well, perhaps self-loathing.

Then she felt the familiar bolt of anger, the pre-emption of the building sorrow, stood straighter, turned and walked steadily toward her kitchen. On the cupboard she saw the business card. *How did that get there?* It had been in her purse. It was wet now, splashed at some point in the afternoon or evening. She laughed. And for a fleeting moment, giddy recklessness dispelled the sense of isolation. What if? We only live once.

She pressed the buttons on the telephone, and it was only when it started ringing that she felt the panic. But it rang and rang and slowly she relaxed. And when no one answered, she felt enveloping relief.

*My God,* she thought. *What on earth is coming over you?* She poured the last of the wine down the sink. Sanity restored, she undressed quickly, donned pyjamas, splashed water on her face, applied a cleansing cream, rinsed it off and brushed her teeth.

When the phone rang in the morning, she was so sure it was him she simply murmured, "Hey, you," when she picked it up.

There was silence. Then the unfamiliar voice. "Is this Faye?"

She paused, recalibrating. "Who's calling, please?"

"It's Paul," he said. "I hope I'm not getting you at a bad time."

Her head was throbbing, her mouth dry. *Paul. Who is Paul?* Then she remembered.

"I didn't realize I'd given you this number," she said.

"My phone rang last night. I was waiting for the machine to pick up . . . you know the way the phone is. The solicitations. I forgot the machine was turned off. So I did the star-sixty-nine thing . . . and this is what I got. Serendipity, I guess."

"Right," she said. "I did call . . . umm. I misplaced my cellphone and thought I might have left it at the coffee shop. I'd dialled your number before I realized you left before I did. I'm sorry."

"No apology necessary," he said. "I believe in serendipity."

"Anyway, I found the phone, buried in my purse, just after I called your number—"

"Why don't we meet up for another coffee . . . later today?"

"Maybe some other time. I'm actually getting ready to leave town."

"Lucky you," he said. "Back east, I suppose."

Now she was fully alert. Just hang up, a small voice urged.

"Are you still there?"

"Yes. Look. I must go. I have a lot to do."

"Of course. But maybe I'll bug you again about that coffee. A drink, maybe."

"We'll see," she said.

"Right." He laughed. "Actually, I prefer Effie."

"Pardon me?"

"You also go by Effie, right?"

"How do you know that?"

"I've done my homework," he said. "I hope you're impressed."

She was sure she heard him laughing as she put the phone down.

—

In the darker moments, she could, and always would, return to the summer months of 1998 for comfort. All through May and June she and JC had discussed driving through the United States, through New York and Maine, to get to the east coast. Then they decided that the journey would be simpler through Canada, even when they factored in the chaos of traversing Montreal. He mentioned camping. She thought the notion was absurd. They were going to stay in all the best motels, she said, and she'd pay the tab. Growing up, she'd had enough bugs to last a lifetime. A deal, he said, but only if she'd let him cover the gas. The pleasure of anticipation was exquisite, almost to the point of dread. Somehow she knew that this was real. But weren't they always real when they were only plans?

They were to leave on Saturday, July 4. He called the night before.

"You aren't going to believe this," he said.

And she knew. It was as if she'd known all along.

"You're going to kill me."

"What's the crime?" she asked.

"Actually, a criminal," he said. "They want me to go to see a criminal."

"When?"

"Um. As soon as possible, I'm afraid."

"You can't get out of it?"

"I tried. They want me to approach this guy we've discovered who happens to be in a bit of a pickle down in Texas. He hates the media, has never given an interview. The boss thinks I can talk him into one."

"Pickle?"

"He's in a prison, on death row. They're going to execute him soon."

"Why you?"

"Who knows? My boss calls me the Reverend. Maybe that's a clue." He laughed. "She thinks I can talk him into it."

"Maybe she's right."

"I hope she's wrong, in which case it'll be back to Plan A. You and me and the open road. Let's hope. But I wanted to give you a heads-up."

"Thanks," she said.

"Maybe you could come with me. You ever been to Texas?"

"I don't think so."

"I'll call," he said.

And she said, "Sure," knowing that he would, but maybe not.

———

*She'd been at the window, near the landing halfway up the stairs, since early morning. They'd told her to be ready to leave by nine. By ten she'd given up, resigned herself.*

*The car horn tooted at the gate. It was just past noon. She saw Sextus darting through the gate and up to the front door. She heard Duncan call her name. She sat on the stairs, fighting tears. Duncan started up the stairs.*

*"They're here," he said. "Finally."*

*Her decision was spontaneous and irreversible. "I can't go," she said. It was, she knew, a refusal born of disappointment.*

*"What do you mean you can't go? You've been talking about it all week."*

*"I don't feel well."*

*"You were fine at breakfast."*

*"I'm not now."*

*"Come on," he pleaded. "We've never been around the Cabot Trail. It's overnight. We'll get to eat in restaurants."*

*"You go," she said. "I'm staying here."*

*"Goddamn."*

*"Don't swear."*

*His face was dark with worry. "What will you do?"*

*"What will I do? I'm thirteen. I'll think of something."*

*"What will I tell Sextus and his father?"*

*"I'm sick," she said. "Tell them that."*

*"Where's the old man?"*

*"I have no idea."*

And she was sick, as she would be many times thereafter. Sick of promises. Sick of the seductive hope that followed promises too lightly made. Sick of expectations, the shallow giddy joy that people cultivate in others to harvest their approval or their favours; sick of what, even then, she knew to be self-interested kindness. Sick, sick, sick, until she recognized the foolishness of joy derived from the conditional: might, could, would. Even the future tense was loaded with the likelihood of disappointment.

*From the window on the landing she could see them talking by the car, looking toward the house, looking toward her window, knowing she was watching them. She saw Sextus shrug, say something to his father. Duncan looked back again, his face bereft, then opened the rear car door and disappeared inside. The car moved off, dust lingering. She wept.*

—

Saturday, July 4, was sunless after an early morning drizzle. *Two days,* she calculated. *It will take two days.* Traffic on the parkway was grim, Willie Nelson blaring on the stereo. *On the road again . . . Insisting that the world keep turning our way . . .* She felt a sudden surge of love for Willie and then an unexpected dampness on her cheek. Or was it for Conor? Willie had been his favourite. Willie Nelson and Van Morrison—he thought the sun rose and set on them. Now Conor was a ghost. Little things like songs would bring him back in times of insecurity, a moment in her past when everything seemed stable.

"*Don't expect too much,*" he'd warned her. "*Love, friendship, loyalty aren't real. They're only qualities.*"

"*What's real?*" she asked.

"*Our solitude,*" he said. "*The moment.*"

She wiped her eyes, checked the rear-view, remembering Conor. Conor, the one who never let her down. Except by dying.

"*Love and friendship are only temporary absences from solitude. Sunny days. You can't keep sunshine in a jar. Remember.*"

Right you are.

And then she was singing along with Willie.

In a service centre washroom mirror she spied on three young Muslim women, niqabs set aside as they shared their lipstick, passed around magenta eyeshadow, then retreated back into their costumes, walking out in single file like nuns.

Afterwards she wasn't sure how long she stood there, water running, staring down the drain.

———

*The old barn had been her secret place, a kind of cloak that she could pull around her for security. It was always warm there, and the musk of old hay and long-departed animals created a sensuous space that was as far away as she could ever hope to get from home, from school, from disappointment.*

*There were always new discoveries, discarded artifacts from other times. Once there were kittens, suddenly present and just as quickly gone, but the softness and the innocence remained. Dry and dusty bottles without labels, pieces of machinery with wooden wheels, cobwebs laced among the spokes. And a maze of secret spaces, hiding places—impenetrable.*

*"Are you in there?"*

*The small internal voice would answer no.*

*"I know you're in there somewhere."*

———

Inching through Montreal, she remembered stopping there in 1970 to see a friend, someone Sextus knew in university. Big Ed. He was tall and blond, handsome in a way. A college football player, Sextus told her. A tackle, whatever that was. A standout at Dalhousie, which wasn't saying much, Sextus joked. She felt vaguely attracted to Big Ed. Attracted, she would later realize, to the idea of being someone new to someone new, unburdened by a history. Attracted to the future, in a way.

The traffic crawled along the tangled bypass, a maze of sudden ramps and exits, intimidating trucks and darting cars. JC had warned her about Highway 40. Keep to the centre lane. You can't go wrong. Highway 40 was aggression in slow motion, her own aggression mitigated by the glow of recollection. Smoked meat. Pizza. Names flipped up in memory. Dunn's. NDG. Snowdon. Ma Heller's. The Hunter's Horn. And with them came thin strands of ecstasy that led her through to the other side of pandemonium.

Near Rivière-du-Loup she stopped at a small motel just off the highway, near a service station. It was only seven o'clock. She could have carried on. People often used to stop there. It sounded musical, the way they used to say it. Riverduloo. A long day away

WHY MEN LIE    141

from home. A day or two away from Elliott Lake or Sudbury, or
Detroit, or Wawa. Or Toronto. Some other destination of necessity.

The motel room was flimsy. Thin covers on the bed, a chair that
sagged and squeaked, a TV set bolted to the dresser. Settled in, she
flicked the TV on, went to the washroom, brushed her teeth.
Conditioning instructed her to eat, but she felt no hunger. She'd
packed a bottle. Balvenie single malt, her brother's choice, purchased days earlier for the special nightcap with JC at the end of
what would have been their first day on the road. She thought it
might relax her, then realized she didn't want to be relaxed.
Returning to the bedroom, she heard the sound of someone
gasping. On the television screen a man and a woman, backsides
to the camera, were performing lurid, feral sex. Massive penis in
the cutaway, sliding, glistening. She stared in shock. The woman
looked back toward the man behind her, hair draping half her face.
She slowly licked her lips. Effie felt a sudden, involuntary tingle
of arousal, quickly followed by disgust.

———

*"They only want one thing, and they're dangerous when they don't get
that one thing they're always after."*

*"Yes, Mrs. Gillis."*

*"You can call me Mary."*

*"Yes, Mrs. Gillis."*

*"Your daddy always has a knife on him."*

*"I don't know."*

*"Be careful."*

*"Yes."*

———

Close-up of repellent penis; vagina like a passive, bestial eye, uglier than sin. *The thing they're always after.* She spied a knob on the wall near the television set, crossed the room and studied it. "A" and "B." Next to "A," Scotch-taped in clumsy letters, the word "*adulte.*" Adult. Adultery. Was there a common root? Adultery, exclusively for grown-ups. She shivered, remembering another motel just down the road from here. Labatt's 50, hot chicken sandwiches and a side order of adultery. She turned the knob to "B," and Molly Blue, JC's television colleague, surfaced on the screen, telling her of some atrocity in some unlucky place. She turned back to "A." Now the woman was on top, breasts like squash suspended. Effie quashed the television picture, rummaged in the small bag she'd packed and found sweatpants, T-shirt and a book.

She couldn't read, gave up and turned out the bedside light.

—

*Sandy Gillis said, "You tell me if anyone comes near you. Do you hear me?"*

*"Yes."*

*"You come straight to me."*

—

In the dark, she tried to picture Toronto as she remembered it when she arrived in 1970. Cop cars were, for some peculiar reason, yellow—taxis for Cape Bretoners, the boys would joke. Bouncing jingles on the radio. "C.h.U.m. 10.50 ta.RON.ta." Ancient brick and granite buildings with new black towers reflecting cloudy skies. Thrilling smoky bars. Food aromas jostling the senses, competing for her hunger. Fat ducks shinier than patent leather on display in steamy Chinese diners on teeming Dundas West. The Greek place where the kitchen seemed to be an extension of the dining room, where she simply pointed at submerged selections in oily liquids. Just as well that she could point: she didn't have a clue what she was ordering. Nor did Sextus.

She asked herself how she would avoid encountering Sextus at home. Tomorrow or the next day. And the day after that. JC would have been her shield, her triumph. She felt a spurt of irritation. *You can't depend on anyone.*

She slept in semi-conscious episodes, part dream, part memory.

———

*"Effie, what are you doing, hiding in there?"*

*She stared back at him. He squatted down in front of her.*

*"You didn't go with the others . . ."*

*"I didn't feel well."*

*His hand was on her brow. "You're warm."*

*She turned her head away.*

*"I have to go to town," he said. "You'll be all right?"*

*She heard the truck pull up outside.*

*He stood, turned and walked away.*

*She watched him go, watched him walk toward Sandy's truck, climb in and slam the door.*

*Exhaled slowly.*

———

From Rivière-du-Loup to the New Brunswick border, the road was basically unchanged from 1970, so the memories came flooding back intact, fully shaped sequential scenes from the movie of her life, strung together on the frame of retrospect. They were in his father's car because his father was dead. At first, Jack had died slowly, with the cancer in his lungs, but then death had become impatient. Jack's great, kind heart just stopped. Did Sextus use the sorrow they all shared to take advantage of her? She was suspicious at the time, but her suspicion vanished in a flame of guilt. It was just too cynical—even Sextus would not manipulate such a situation, cloak the raw seduction in the cloth of grief. His dad was dead and she was in his bed. Guilt reduced to doggerel.

She remembered the cheap, intoxicating drama of it all. Was it really all his fault? Did he really have to try so hard, to lie so hard? Was she really such a challenge, her virtue such an obstacle? Or was it simple exploitation of the willing? She imagined a small green Volkswagen on a long hill, labouring westward, the direction of the future, and the eastward road to yesterday blurred briefly.

And now the trees pressed closer on the potholed two-lane highway. Maybe that's why thoughts of home were looming like the spruce and pine and juniper, full of menace. Eastern Ontario and most of Quebec had been wide open, free of small constraints, bound only by an oceanic lake, a river long and broad as history, eternal towns of stone huddling around their spiky churches, indifferent to time and passing strangers. She remembered the intoxicating freedom she'd felt years before, driving westward, in her sinful liberation from those dark and gloomy trees. *Fhuair mi'n t'aite so'n agaidh naduir.* The despairing words of the long-dead bard from Nova Scotia flooded her with gloom. "My place, at war with nature," was how he saw it. The suffocating truth.

———

*The silhouette was at her bedroom door again. She followed the glow of the cigarette, the ember moving, a tiny point of light from the unseen hand to where she knew his face would be. The truck had returned in darkness, but she knew.*

*From behind him, in the kitchen, the disembodied alcoholic growl.*
*"Hey, Angus, come away from there."*

*Silence, ember moving upward, flaring again.*

*"I said, get away from her door."*

*Chair legs scraped on the floor. The silhouette turned, revealed the*
*familiar profile and was gone.*

*"Hey, Angus, what's your fuckin' problem, anyway?"*

———

Sunday at noon she called home from a pay phone in a coffee shop
in Fredericton, New Brunswick. There was one message.

"Hey . . . guess where I am. Davy Crockett country, but only
for a day or two. Be well. Drive safe. Don't let the bedbugs bite."

She was suddenly hungry, ordered a burger and a coffee,
bought a paper from the day before. Fires in Florida. Clinton
and Lewinsky—did they or didn't they? Where there's smoke,
there's fire. The Oval Office. Clinton should be fired, they were
saying. *Who cares?* Tampa Bay was scheduled to play the Jays on
Sunday at the SkyDome. And now it was Sunday. Staring out the
window of the coffee shop, she was trying to remember why he
went to Texas.

The voice on her answering machine was untroubled. He was
working, that was all. That was the way he was. She felt a glow, and
the newsprint disappeared. JC Campbell. After so much disappointment, decades of disillusionment, could she now believe
in someone?

Even Conor, precious though his memory might be, had been a
mystery. He told her at the outset that he'd be honest about the
need for some dishonesty. And somehow she understood. Dishev-
elled Conor with the slept-in face; Conor of deceptive softness, in

his body, in his voice; Conor of the contradictions. Except in appearance, they were so alike, Conor and JC, and she was, at once, warmed and frightened by the recognition.

She re-engaged with the broad page of the paper, resumed the Clinton story, the travails of power. The president of the United States had been alone with this young woman, this intern. Frequently. Something had happened. Some exchange of favours. A story old as human nature. It was in the book that Conor gave her once. *The Book of Leinster.* The *Táin Bó Cúalainge*—the Cattle Raid of Cooley. The book that sent her back to school, launched her down the road to scholarship. "What caused the pangs of the men of Ulster. It is soon told." That was how the book began. Sex caused the pangs of Ulster. Sex was the cause of everything.

*"I'm Conor Ferguson. And what would your name be?"*

*"You can call me . . . Faye. Faye Gillis."*

The story in the newspaper was accompanied by a photograph of Clinton and his wife, Hillary, loyal and defiant. There was an inset of Lewinsky, smiling, big-haired, more than slightly stunned. Effie tried to imagine the scene in the Oval Office: Lewinsky on her knees, Clinton talking business on the telephone, this mountain of hair concealing mischief in his lap, Clinton trying not to gasp while setting the world's agenda. Kings and queens and mistresses. Power and sex and dreams of immortality. Moral authority blown away, for what?

She carefully examined the photograph of Hillary for evidence of pain as she studied Bill's for signs of deceit. It takes a psychopath to hide deceit completely. Bill Clinton was no psycho. You could see it clearly, fear in his eyes, though he seemed serene enough in contrast to the brittle indignation of the faithful wife.

Maybe he was innocent. Maybe it was exactly what Hillary called it: a right-wing plot. She wouldn't put it past them. But in the end, she felt for both of them. She'd been there. Been everywhere and every one of them. She'd been Monica. She'd been Bill. She'd been Hillary. She'd boxed the compass of emotional entanglement, circumnavigated every possible betrayal. Now, at middle age, liberated and alone, she could freely calculate the benefits and costs. What role was worse? Betrayer or betrayed? Her brother wasn't any help, the priest, the comforter of strangers.

"If you're having a personal problem, just spit it out," he'd said impatiently. "I don't have time for metaphors."

That was the end of that. But now, on July 5, 1998, sitting alone in a coffee shop in Fredericton, she could with confidence declare a preference. She'd rather be betrayed than betray.

But at the end of the day, who really cares? In the long run it's the dustbin for us all. Conor Ferguson's philosophy, again.

———

Sextus had probably begun his infidelities when she was immensely pregnant—1971. "As early as that? Because of that?"

JC was guarded, obviously sorry to have obliged her with his insight. "It's ancient history now," he said. Why would she insist on revisiting something that could only be a source of pain? She reminded him that she was a historian. She wanted to approach her own past with the objectivity she'd bring to any scholarship. History was only painful for the amateurs. And there were things he deserved to know about her.

He scoffed. "You can't investigate yourself objectively. It's a fundamental rule in journalism. The same applies to history."

"Okay," she said. "You tell me. You were there for most of it. You were a reporter then. Give me the cold hard facts."

He knew he was trapped.

Sextus's first betrayal was with someone they all knew, someone so unlikely that the knowledge made her laugh.

"You find it funny?" JC said in disbelief. "I thought it was pathetic at the time."

The philandering became so commonplace that it was no longer interesting, even to the gossips in their crowd, as it was only peripherally interesting to her now, a lifetime later. Still, he told her what he knew.

"You know the way it was back then, in the seventies?"

"I hear a lot about it now," she said. "The zipless encounters and free love horseshit. As if anything is free."

"But back then, it was pretty meaningless. Casual entanglements, often triggered by booze or dope and kind of sanctioned by a lot of junk sociology—the age of Aquarius and all that garbage. I'd have thought you knew about it."

"I was a homebody. Remember? I was becoming a mom. My so-called husband worked all hours. He travelled. I took fidelity for granted. I was naive."

"So when did you twig?"

"When he joined the gym."

JC laughed. "Ah yes. The gym."

"You all knew?"

He nodded.

And maybe she'd known too, long before she first admitted it. The thing about knowledge is that you can have it without knowing what it is. Wilful ignorance, they call it.

"So what was the final clue?" JC asked.

"There was no final clue. I just felt something. I don't know how long I felt it before I put a name to it."

———

Except for the gym, nothing about him had changed. He was attentive and consistent in his moods. Loved their child and doted on her. Shared his work frustrations, which were mostly minor. She told herself it was loneliness that made her look for him one evening. Not an actual surveillance, really, but more a yearning to be close. She went to the gym wearing her happiest face. She told the girl at the front desk that she was supposed to meet her husband there. He was a member.

The girl checked. "Ah yes. Mr. Gillis." But he wasn't there that evening.

There was a little office that she hadn't noticed, and a man standing in the doorway. He seemed to sense distress. He was the owner-manager, he said. How could he help?

Oh, not at all. She'd hoped to meet her husband there, but there had clearly been a mix-up.

"His name?"

"Sextus Gillis."

He picked up a small box of file cards from the desk, walked his fingers through them. "Sextus. Gillis. Now there's an interesting name. It doesn't ring a bell, but . . . ah, there it is. And what would your name be? I'm Conor Ferguson."

She hesitated. And then said, "You can call me Faye. Faye Gillis."

"Ah, Faye," he said. "Lovely."

He held out a hand. It was a soft hand, like the rest of him, like the accent with the slight uptick at the end of sentences, like the smile. He was slightly shorter than she was, and he had a paunch that was exaggerated by a turtleneck sweater that was half a size too small. His hair was unruly and thinning at the front, curling around his ears and collar. But his eyes were the feature she remembered later. They were blue and businesslike, almost cold in contrast to the warmth that seemed to radiate from the rest of him. The eyes were managerial. The rest of him, the body and the manner, spoke of service.

"Here's my card," he said. "If you ever consider gettin' into shape yourself. Maybe a little cardio for the long haul."

"Cardio" with the stone-hard *r* and the soft, soft uptick *o*.

She smiled. "The heart's in pretty solid shape already."

"Ah, of that I'm sure," he said. "But then again, the heart is full of little secrets."

"You're Irish."

He hesitated. "In a manner of speakin'. Yes."

A week later she called and asked if he would meet her at a coffee shop across the street from the gym. She wanted to talk about fitness, the possibility of a personalized training plan.

She got there early, found a discreet table near a window.

After some brief discussion, he asked her what was really on her mind.

"I want to know whether or not my husband *ever* goes to your gym, Mr. Ferguson. Frankly, I think he's using it as a front for something else."

He pursed his lips, raised the coffee cup, looked intently at her across the rim. "I really wouldn't know anythin' about that," he said. "Actually, I have three gyms in the city."

"He said he goes to this one."

"You don't say." He sipped. Sighed. "You think he's cheatin'?"

She wasn't really ready for the question. She was silent.

"All I can say truthfully, and respectin' people's privacy, is that I know all my regulars. I'm sorry to say I don't know yer man."

"Thank you," she said.

The feeling wasn't unfamiliar, the emotional void that suddenly surrounded her. But she surprised herself. She felt no pain. And though she was in a strange city, among strangers, she was unafraid. She felt a mild humiliation, but it was offset by the sense of power that comes from secret knowledge, the measure of control it gives. And there was Conor. He was easy to be with. He was a private place where she could go to hide, to fantasize. They didn't talk about the reason they got to know each other in the first place. He never tried to take advantage of what he might correctly have assumed to be a period of vulnerability. Hard to believe, after knowing Sextus, who saw vulnerability as opportunity. Conor was gentle in his manners, but there was a directness in his speech, even in the way he looked at her. The conversations over coffee grew longer and more frequent. He had a deep knowledge of his country's folklore and seemed fascinated that she could speak a language in which so much of his mythology was rooted. He'd grown up in a place she'd never heard of. Armagh.

Their growing friendship was enriched by irony. He should have been Sextus's friend, another part of the diverse band of strangers Sextus frequently brought home, usually unannounced. Conor and Sextus would have got on famously, for a while, at least. Sextus knew about the world, about its afflictions. He knew the history of the troubles in the north of Ireland, the Catholics and Protestants and all their animosities. They both loved alcohol, and both seemed to have a remarkable capacity for controlling its effects.

The closest thing to intimacy in those early days was in one brief, impulsive moment when she touched Conor's hand and declared, "I'm glad you're here to listen . . . it's a comfort."

He blushed and turned away. "Ah well," he said. Then, "Thanks for sayin' that."

When they were parting that day, he hugged her briefly, his face close to hers. On her temple she felt the whisper of a kiss. But still she told herself their bond was virtuous, and it gave her moral confidence.

She'd pretend to be asleep.

Sextus would ask softly, "You awake?"

She'd feign a murmur. "No." Then, "Your hair is wet."

"I showered at the gym . . . didn't want to wake you."

"Good night."

"Good night."

And she'd lie there in the void, composing the rough draft of what she knew would be her future.

———

The causeway was in shadow when she crossed, the sun already tucking in behind the mainland. But the light still caught the Creignish hills and flickered on the bay, dancing on the northern reaches of the Strait of Canso. It was July 5, but there was a chill. She noted with dismay that Cape Porcupine, once a looming barricade against the world, now seemed to have become a gravel pit. Had it really been so totally diminished, torn apart and humbled for the sake of a few demeaning local jobs and fat profits for the owners of some foreign corporation? Or was it ever quite the eminence she remembered from long, dull days of staring at it through a schoolhouse window?

Cape Porcupine resembled an environmental crime scene. A noble mountain, turned into a quarry, hacked and torn apart and, as far as she could tell, unlamented by any local individual or group. She made a mental note: JC should bring a crew down, frighten local politicians and their corporate accomplices with the spectre of exposure on national television. Wake people up.

She carried on to town, bought provisions. Bread, milk, tea, cereal. A box of fried chicken would simplify the arrival at the old house on the Long Stretch. She realized that she was stalling. Her anticipation was underscored by dread with hints of sadness. JC would have been a brand-new factor in the going-home equation.

She stopped at the gate, unlocked it, swung it wide, propped it open with a stick. The grass was tall and thick with hardy weeds. Farther along the road, through the grove of poplars that obscured the Gillis place, she could see a glow of light. She wondered briefly what it looked like now.

Over the years, she and Duncan had, quite independently, transformed their old place. There was vinyl siding, a hefty propane tank, new windows all around. New doors. New wiring with a 200-amp service panel. There was even a dishwasher, of which Duncan disapproved. She had hired a contractor to bulldoze what was left of the old barn. Duncan hadn't commented.

She hesitated only briefly.

———

*"Daddy?"*

*"What are you doing, hiding in there? Let me see you."*

———

The kitchen was now ablaze with light, her suitcase near the door, bags of groceries on the kitchen counter. The stereo blared in what had been her bedroom and was now her office. *Chiquitita, tell me what's wrong* . . .

She once dared JC to confess his greatest flaw. He hesitated for a moment. "I love ABBA," he said finally.

"Oh . . . my . . . God," she replied.

"What's wrong with ABBA?"

*You're enchained by your own sorrow / In your eyes there's no hope for tomorrow.* She walked to the door of the office, pointed the remote toward the stereo, turned it off. Poured a drink and sat at the kitchen table.

———

*Conor had warned her to be ready. The movies lead us to anticipate a dramatic buildup, background music to prepare us for the shock. But there never is background music, just the normal sounds. In retrospect, they always seem banal. And the end is always bitter.*

*When the moment came, the soundtrack was from the television, the hollow chatter of a quiz show about stories in the news. They always watched it. An old man was struggling in the middle of a long question. Cassie was in bed. The dishes were washed and in the cupboard. His late nights had become ludicrously later. Last night it had been near three a.m. But now he was home, looking pale, struggling to stay awake. She'd had enough.*

*She heard the words, much as he did, as if someone else was speaking them.*

*"One of us is going to have to do something," she said without looking at him.*

*"Do what?" he said wearily. Then he stood, walked to the television*

set and turned up the sound. When he turned back, he smiled at her, then came and sat beside her. Squeezed her knee.

"I want you to move out for a while," she said.

"What?"

"You heard me."

"Where's this coming from?"

She sighed. "I don't want to have to spell it out. I just want you to go away for a while so I can think."

"Go away where?"

"That's up to you. I suspect . . ." For a moment her voice was gone, and she could feel the pressure of tears. She took a deep breath. "I'm talking about a trial separation," she said.

"Separation . . ."

"Like the Trudeaus."

"The Trudeaus! Give me a friggin' break."

"I need time. You can decide when——"

"When!" he shouted. "When? How about right fucking now."

The door slammed. She knew that the child's eyes had briefly opened, the bony little body stirred, hand found face, thumb found mouth. Effie held her breath. Silence broken only by a spatter of applause and people talking in a television box, oblivious behind a television window.

The next day, at the coffee shop across from Conor's Gym, she told him, "He left last night."

"Ahhh, Jeesus now," Conor said, his large, soft hand gently covering hers. "Are ye all right, then?"

———

She stayed up too late and drank too much, and in the morning she tried to tell herself the creeping sadness was just a symptom of a hangover, something to remember if she was to spend the summer here alone. Keep the liquor down to a dull roar. She realized that she was slamming things—cupboard drawers, the coffee urn, the coffee can, the refrigerator door—muttering vile obscenities at inanimate objects. She paused for a moment, then sat at the corner of the kitchen table, took a deep breath. There was an ashtray with a single crumpled butt. *Where did that come from?* She examined it, trying to summon specific details from the evening before. She remembered a senseless impulse to call Sextus. She was sure she hadn't. It was at that point, she was now certain, that she'd staggered off to bed.

Pouring coffee, she noticed her cellphone where she'd left it. The message light was blinking. The battery was almost dead, but the message was brief: "Hey, I'm at the airport. I get to Halifax at—oops, they're about to close the gate. Gotta run. I'll call you when I get there."

She was laughing as she fumbled for the charger in her purse, briefly flirting with the notion of a splash of whisky in her coffee.

She spent the morning cleaning. There was epidermal grime throughout the house, coating unexpected surfaces. She vacuumed dead fly clusters from the corners of the windows. There was a mouldy teabag fixed as if by glue to the inside of the teapot. She changed the bedding. After noon she napped. She woke up refreshed, showered and, shortly after three, began to watch the road. She wished she'd bought flowers when she was at the superstore in town.

By four o'clock she'd redressed. She'd been wearing shorts but imagined cellulite and selected a flimsy cotton skirt and sandals, a navy V-neck sweater. The sweater was flattering in a modest way.

She considered a quick trip to town to buy some flowers and, while she was there, to replenish the liquor supply, but she dismissed the impulse. There'd be lots of time for flowers. Maybe he'd *bring* flowers. There was a half a bottle of Balvenie. That would do. She alternated between dismay and pride as she surveyed the house, so burdened with her history and yet emerging gradually to become a statement of her taste, her future.

In some detail she imagined the reunion scene: where they'd sit, what they'd talk about. She'd walk with him around the property, summoning pristine memories of childhood, briefly mentioning where the barn had been, pointing out the Gillis place. For dinner, she'd suggest a restaurant across the causeway, on the mainland. She'd never been there but had heard reports that it was passable. Someone had told her Ethan Hawke was spotted there once, eating supper just like everybody else.

And later, after darkness fell, she'd light a fire to dispel the dampness, create a cozy atmosphere. And then . . . who knows? She hoped he'd be tender.

At five, she heard the sound of a car stopping. He was driving a black Mustang convertible. She met him in the yard, just inside the gate. She knew she was flying at him like a hen, awkwardly. She didn't care. He caught her as if she were a child, and she clung to him, arms around his neck. He staggered but quickly found his balance and his strength. She felt the sudden sting of tears, but happily, they didn't overflow.

When finally she spoke, she said, "My God. The car!"

He laughed. "It seemed to suit the mission."

"Come in," she said. "You look like you could use a drink."

"Well, then, I've created an incomplete impression," he said.

"You're hungry," she joked.

"That too."


Later she asked him, "How was the trip?"

He was vague. Something about a man who had been sentenced to death years and years before, but because there were so many of them in that situation, he got lost in the population of the doomed. Until recently. He'd demanded action on his case. "Turn me loose or put me down," was how he told it. Did she have any idea how many people were sitting around in the U.S. prison system waiting for the call to oblivion? Dead men sitting.

"We want to do his story. That's why I went down there."

"And he said . . . ?"

"No way. He hates the media."

"So it was a wasted trip?"

"Not really. He's thinking about it."

"How did you pull that off?"

JC sat up. The blankets fell away as he swung his legs over the side of the bed. "It was brilliant," he said. "Sam says to me . . . his name is Sam . . . he says, 'Give me one good reason why I should talk to you.'"

"And you said?"

"I looked him in the eye and said, 'Because they don't want you to.'"

She was confused. "Don't they listen in on your conversations?"

"Maybe."

He slid into a pair of jeans. She thought, *From behind he looks like a teenager.* "Turn around," she said.

He turned. "What?"

"That's better. I need for you to look grown-up. You have a little belly."

He sucked it in. "I do not. Why don't we drive to town and get a bite to eat? I'm friggin' starved."

"There isn't much in town," she said.

"Okay. Why don't we drive into town and get a couple of big fat T-bones and a couple of bottles of their best plonk. I'll whip you up a piece of red meat, Texas-style."

"Do that and anything could happen," she said.

"I thought that anything that could just did. Do you have more surprises?"

"Maybe."

She was walking out of the liquor store when she spotted JC talking to another man, who had his back to her, near the entrance to the Sobeys. There was familiarity before the recognition. Sextus. She felt a brief temptation to step back into the liquor store and wait. But JC saw her, waved, continued talking. Sextus turned, and now he, too, knew that she was there. She walked briskly to where they stood, slipped a proprietary arm around JC's waist. Said nothing.

"I believe you two know each other," JC said with an irritating smirk.

"We've met," said Effie.

Sextus, by outward appearances, was in distress. His face was flushed, his smile tight. "If I didn't know better I'd say you two were a number." He forced a kind of laugh.

"Nah," said JC. "Just a couple of old-timers catching up. Effie thought it was time for me to come home."

"I didn't realize this was home—for you."

"You'll have to drop by," said JC.

She pinched the soft part of his waist, just below the ribs.

"How long are you around for?" Sextus asked.

"God knows," said JC. "I'm reconnecting."

"Well, that was awkward," she said when they were in the car.

"How so?"

"Come on."

"I wish I had a photograph of the look on his face when you walked up. It isn't often you see him rattled."

"You actually asked him to drop by."

"Don't worry," he said. "It ain't going to happen."

"Don't be so sure."

"Trust me."

"How long *are* you here for?"

"I could only get a week," he said.

"Then back to Texas?"

"No, back to working on the Y2K piece. They want it for the fall launch. Then Texas, if he agrees."

"I'm not sure why that convict would even consider talking to you," she said.

"It boils down to one word. Autonomy. "

"Autonomy?"

"He'll agree to talk to me because the system doesn't want him to. A rare act of autonomy, something he hasn't felt for ages. Also, if he talks to me, at least he'll be leaving his voice behind."

"So what were you talking to the other criminal about?"

"Sextus? We were talking about this guy we used to know . . . you remember him, I'm sure. Danny MacKay."

"I know Danny."

"Sextus says he isn't doing so well, says he'd probably appreciate a visit. What do you think?"

"I'm supposed to go to see him anyway," she said. "To check on Duncan's boat."

"Duncan has a boat?"

"Yes. Danny MacKay looks after it. I think he used to own it. Duncan bought it from him a while back."

They drove in silence. Then JC said, "When he heard I'd been to the States, he asked if I was doing anything on the Clinton-Lewinsky business." He chuckled. "Sextus has a one-track mind."

"So that was it? Danny Ban and Bill Clinton?"

"Well, there was a little bit of maaan stuff."

"What kind of maaan stuff?"

There was another silence before he asked, "When was it that you found out about his affair with Stella?"

"You said it wasn't an affair."

"Whatever you want to call it."

"It was in April, shortly before you showed up. Why?"

"Well, I was just trying to assure him that I did my best to set the record straight, back before Easter. I'd given you his side of things."

"Yes. You were a big help." She looked at him and smiled, but he was staring straight ahead and frowning.

"He said he was planning a trip to Toronto. He's thinking of coming up for Christmas. Hasn't seen your daughter for quite a while, I gather."

"Great," she said. "I suppose you invited him to stay at Walden?"

He laughed and patted her knee as he turned the Mustang onto the narrow road they called the Long Stretch.

## 8

They would, in a yet unimaginable time, argue over small details of that summer week in 1998, he remembering rain, she uninterrupted sunshine; it was hot and dry, cold and wet, windy, calm. They would be able to agree that the feelings were exquisite, their compatibility astonishing for two exclusive personalities. The days were spent in exploration, in the awkward merging of divergent memories; long nights and mornings spent in bed, in deep talk and adolescent play, and always subtle curiosity, deft disclosure. There was one day they were mostly lost, hopelessly exploring rutted back roads, looking for a place he more imagined than remembered—that long-lost place called Bornish.

"Somewhere back of Glencoe," was the most he could offer, and at the first bump of stone on the low belly of the Mustang, he surrendered. "I'm told there's nothing out there anyway," he said, backing carefully into a grove of juniper and pine to turn around.

"Just stop for a minute," she said. "Let's just sit and breathe."

She sank back in the leather car seat, eyes shut. All around them, the whispering of trees; somewhere near, the specific gurgle of a brook.

"It felt like this," he said.

"Yes," she murmured. "This was what it felt like."

On the way back, she remembered that she'd passed this way several years earlier, to visit an old relative in Hawthorne, Aunt Peggy Beaton.

"We could go that way," she said. "Stop in and see Danny Ban, get that over with."

"Danny Ban?"

"Danny MacKay," she said. "We always called him Danny Ban. Fair-haired Danny."

"Right. Danny. I think we used to call him Danny Bad."

She laughed. "But Danny wasn't the only bad one, I recall."

"No," he said, brow furrowed as he focused on the dusty, rocky road.

The MacKay place was set back, past a grove of poplars, on a slight rise. Soft hayfields fell away, ripe for cutting, rippling in the gentle summer breeze. Near the house, there was an old, tilted barn and a propped-up fishing boat partly swaddled in a tarp. A dog emerged from beneath the deck and trotted toward the car, barking. JC got out, squatted down before the dog, offering the back of his hand. The dog sniffed, licked, waved his bushy tail, then turned and dashed toward the house, announcing the arrival.

Jessie MacKay met them at the door. Effie made the introductions. JC Campbell, an old friend of Danny's.

"I remember," Jessie said, gripping JC's hand. "He isn't great," she whispered. "But he'll be thrilled. Come in."

The last time she'd seen Danny was at Aunt Peggy's funeral, eighteen months earlier. He'd been moving slowly then, with the help of a walker, his once-large frame ravaged by the multiple sclerosis.

"Well, Holy Jesus," he said, instantly recognizing JC. "Will you get a load of who just walked in? My God Almighty. JC Campbell."

"'Fraid so," JC said, face flushed, his smile contorted by dismay.

Danny was in a wheelchair, pulled up tight to the kitchen table. There was a mug and a small plate, the remnants of a sandwich in front of him. "Jessie," he shouted. "Do you remember this renegade?" She was standing back, smiling and rubbing her hands together.

"*De ghabhas sibh?*" he said to Effie. "*Deoch bhuat?*"

"*Chaneil,*" said Effie. "We're okay. We're driving."

"Well, that never stopped this fellow before. Jessie, get that bottle of rum I've been saving."

"I didn't know you could talk Gaelic," JC said.

"I can't," said Danny. "But a fella gets old and the goddamnedest things come back to you."


The rum was poured. Jessie, Effie and JC took seats around the kitchen table, the reminiscence gathering velocity with every sip. The two men alternated anecdotes, the women tolerantly smiling, laughing, holding back whatever memories they had of all the wildness. Inevitably the interstitial silences grew longer. Then there was the sound of a car. The dog barked twice outside.

"That'll be Stella," Danny said.

Jessie stood. Effie felt a sudden tension in her stomach.

"And how is Father Duncan, anyway?" said Danny.

Effie wasn't certain how to answer, wasn't clear about the meaning of the question. "Duncan," she said. "Ah, he's great. Working with the homeless in the city."

"God love him," Jessie said, leaning toward the window. "That would be him for sure. The man's a living saint."

"He was awful good to us," said Danny, "the time when we lost the young fellow. I suppose Effie's told you about that."

JC seemed confused. "I'm not sure."

Jessie walked toward the kitchen door. Danny made a face behind her back and shook his head, a private warning, something not to be discussed aloud. "Ah well," he said. "It's a long story anyway."

"Danny and Jessie lost their boy," said Effie carefully.

"I'm sorry to hear that," said JC, the formality in his tone a reminder that the friendship that once bonded him and Danny had been hollowed out by time, drained of intimacy. There were slow footsteps on the wooden deck.

"We felt bad for Father Duncan. You could tell the young fellow looked up to him. I think it bothered Duncan real bad that he never said a thing when they'd be around the boat together. Never let on that he . . . So. Then again, I guess it bothered all of us. The never letting on. We'll have another little sip, then?"

"No, no," Effie said, standing quickly. "We just dropped in for a minute. I was going to call ahead, but we were in the area. JC was trying to find his way to Bornish."

"Bornish?"

Jessie opened the kitchen door and stepped outside.

"Come on," said Danny. "There's no need to run off. You'll stay for supper. It's only us and Stella. Effie, you know Stella. Just sit down. The two of youse can catch up."

JC stood. "We'll come back another time. I promise."

"Ah, you don't have to promise," Danny said, looking toward the door. "I know you're all busy." He seemed to slump into the wheelchair, moving the shot glass from which he'd sipped his rum in small circles on the surface of the table. "I'm sorry to be like this," he said. "But there isn't much a fellow can do, is there."

Effie heard the women's voices at the kitchen door, the hand upon the doorknob, and she was desperate to leave. The women burst into the room.

"Effie," said Stella in mock surprise. "Jessie was making me guess who the visitors were. I'd never have imagined. And the car! I'd have guessed Burt Reynolds!"

She turned toward JC, smiling. "JC Campbell," he said, extending his hand.

Knowing Sextus as Effie did, it didn't require a lot of imagination to see the two of them involved. Stella's honey-blond hair seemed more sun-bleached than Effie remembered. The grey-blue eyes seemed over-cautious; tanned skin over a strong bone structure; a pinch of cleavage showing where a button was undone; subtly beautiful, in a substantial way. Effie felt a momentary anger, then a rare uncertainty.

Stella was shaking hands with JC, lingeringly, Effie thought.

"I don't think we've met before," Stella said.

"I've been away for years," JC said.

"You're from Toronto?"

"Yes," he said. "And a lot of other places."

She laughed lightly, let go of his hand, then turned to Effie, her smile tentative.

"And how is Toronto, anyway?"

"Toronto is Toronto," Effie said. "Hard to describe, as you well know."

"It is that," she said. "I often regret leaving the place. But . . ." She shrugged.

"So when did you live in Toronto?" JC asked.

"Years ago now," she said. "I kept a pretty low profile. Married then."

"Ah," said JC.

Effie observed his poise, his curiosity direct but somehow inno-cent. Suddenly she understood his peculiar interaction with the condemned man in Texas.

Stella asked her, "How long are you around?"

"Pretty well the summer," Effie said.

"I'd love to get together," Stella said. "We could meet in town, maybe. Have a coffee."

"I'd love that," Effie said. She leaned in then, kissed Danny's forehead softly, swiftly hugged Jessie. "We must be off. We left something thawing." Emphasized "we" for clarity.

Danny wheeled out to the deck, JC walking alongside, his hand on Danny's shoulder. The three women walked behind. Stella looped an arm through Effie's and kept it there as they walked across the deck.

At the head of the deck stairs, as Danny and JC professed their determination to have another, longer visit, Stella leaned close to Effie. "The man worships you," she said.

"What man?" said Effie tightly.

"Sextus," Stella said. "You know that."

"Sextus worships Sextus."

"We really should talk."

Effie studied the searching eyes, in the daylight a deep, compel-ling blue, no hint of sorrow, just what seemed to be a genuine regret. "Okay," she said. "But don't get me wrong. You did me a favour."

Stella swiftly hugged her and stepped away. "And how is . . . Father Duncan?"

"He's well."

"Will you tell him I was asking?"

"I will."

"You tell Father Duncan, if he's ever around," said Danny, "it would be great to catch up."

"I'll be seeing him," she said. "I'll tell him."

Through the trees they could see the sun low on a patch of distant water. The late daylight was murky, the air damp and heavy with a chill. The Mustang rumbled down the Hawthorne road, big tires crunching gravel. They were silent, privately processing.

Then JC said, "You didn't ask about the boat."

Effie didn't seem to hear him.

Finally on pavement, JC said, "I assume that was the other woman." She didn't answer.

"That was tough," JC said. "Seeing Danny MacKay in that condition. Jesus Murphy."

Passing through Judique, he spoke again. "That Jessie. There's one impressive woman. Danny's a lucky man. You say she and Stella are sisters?"

Effie sighed. "Yes."

"I remember," JC said. "Jessie was one friggin' witch when we were young. A little wildcat." He laughed. "She was into throwing things when they were first married. We'd get gassed up at the Rondun or some place, and Danny would invite half the pub to come back home, if it wasn't Sextus first, dragging us to your place. We'd arrive there and Jessie would go through the roof. More than once she chased us out."

There was another long silence.

He reached across and placed a hand upon her thigh. "Of course, it was different at your place. You were what we always imagined the perfect wife should be."

She stared through the car window. They were in Creignish,

where Stella and her brother had met when he was pastor there. St. George's Bay sprawled off to the horizon, flat and black, the first lights twinkling on a distant mainland.

"So how come *you* never settled down?" she asked, still staring at the empty bay.

He seemed surprised. "I don't know."

"You struck me as someone who needed that. Needed somebody and a place of your own. I never really saw you as part of that gang."

"Possibly," he said.

"So why not? Ever. I'm sure there were lots of chances."

"Fear, I guess."

There was another long silence. They passed the Creignish church, and she noted with surprise that he raised a hand and made what seemed to be a small cross on his forehead.

"Did you just make the sign of the cross?"

"Maybe," he said. "Old habits die hard."

She laughed, reached across and grabbed his free hand in both of hers. "So tell me, really, what you were afraid of."

"Women change," he said. "Or, at least, evolve. It's a good thing. But it makes life unpredictable."

"And men don't change?"

"Men don't change."

"I've seen men change."

"You've seen behaviour change. Men don't change, essentially."

"And women do?"

"It's a known fact. Scientific. A little witch like Jessie turns into Mother Teresa. Danny stays Danny, MS or no MS. Trust me."

"Trust you?"

"Well . . . maybe not."

———

At the roundabout, where the causeway joined the island to the mainland, he asked: "So what happened to their boy? I gather he died."

"He killed himself," she said.

"Jesus."

"It was a tough time. It was hard on everybody."

"What did Duncan have to do with it?"

"They were friends," she said. "He bought their boat. That's all."

Preparing dinner, she wondered privately about the silences. Surely they weren't out of things to talk about already. She noted that he drank more than she did, kept topping up his glass with rum.

"I didn't know you were a rum drinker," she said.

He just smiled at her, as if through a glass doorway.

She was alone when she awoke. She peered quickly through the bedroom window. The car was where they'd left it. She put on a housecoat and went downstairs. The house was empty. She boiled water for coffee.

She was pouring when he returned, wearing rubber boots that were wet and flecked with grass.

"Went for a walk," he explained.

"And did you see anybody interesting?"

"Just a jogger."

"Did you talk to him?"

He came to her and wrapped his arms around her, kissed her forehead. "You don't talk to joggers. But he waved."

"That would be John," she said.

"John who?"

"John Gillis. My ex. One of them."

"Right," he said. "Remind me. How many are there?"

"Two. No, three. Counting Conor."

"Conor. Right. You haven't told me much about Conor."

"There isn't much to tell."

"What's for breakfast?"

"What do you want for breakfast?"

"Do you serve it in bed?"

"That depends."

They left for town near noon. She needed house supplies, said that she could get anything she needed at the Walmart.

"The Walmart?" he replied. "I don't do the Walmart."

"There's a bookstore at the mall," she said.

"Good," he said. "I'll check it out. And I assume there's a coffee shop?"

"Yes," she said. "It's near the Walmart. We can meet there."

She entered the mall from the Walmart, searching for the café where they'd agreed to meet. Then she saw it, a space that was more an alcove than a coffee shop. He was sitting at a small table, a book beside his coffee cup, intently listening to the woman facing him. Effie couldn't see her face, just the back of a blond head, and for an instant she thought it was Stella. But it clearly wasn't. The woman was smoking a cigarette. Whatever vices Stella had, smoking wasn't one of them. Then JC reached across and placed a hand on the woman's hand, which she turned palm up so that their fingers were interlocked. The woman leaned toward him, and they kissed in what seemed to be a friendly way, cheek to cheek. She stood, and Effie changed directions quickly, flustered.

The woman was young, maybe in her mid-thirties. JC stood. They embraced. The woman stepped back, brushed her cheek or perhaps a stray strand of hair. They were still holding hands. Another kiss, this time lightly on the lips, and the woman walked away. Effie could only think of one word to describe the look on JC's face. Bereft.

JC sat. Effie turned and walked quickly back to the Walmart, where she knew there was a washroom.


He was sitting in the same position when she returned, now leafing through his book. He smiled broadly when she walked up to him. "Hey," he said. "How was Mr. Walton's mart?"

"The usual," she said, looking for evidence of deceit in his expression but finding only clarity.

"Look what I found," he said. "What a great bookstore."

It was a red book, *The Breed of Manly Men,* a regimental history of the Cape Breton Highlanders.

"How do you pronounce that?" he asked, pointing to a motto on a crest. She said it for him, swiftly. *Siol na Fear Fearail.* A Breed of Manly Men.

"I didn't know you were a military buff."

"I'm not," he said. "But back at the house, I saw a photograph of some soldiers, and on the back it said they were Cape Breton Highlanders, in Italy, I think."

"My father was in that outfit," she said. Then sat and folded her arms, waiting.

"I'll get you a coffee," he said.

"No, thanks."

"Is there something wrong?"

"I don't know."

He seemed to hesitate. "The damnedest thing just happened," he said. "I'm in the bookstore. I see this book. They only have one copy. On an impulse I decide to buy it. Forty bucks. Highway robbery, but what the hell. I take it to the cash, present my credit card. The woman goes away, comes back and asks me where I'm from. I tell her. Then she asks if I ever knew anyone from Isle Madame. I say maybe. And . . . if she doesn't burst into tears . . ."

"Not . . ."

"Sylvia," he said. "My kid." Suddenly his eyes were full.

"Oh my God," said Effie.

"I thought I told you about her," he said.

"Oh my God," she repeated. "I'm so sorry . . ."

"Sorry?"

"I mean, I'm so happy . . ."

"I brought her here, hoping you'd come back in time to meet her, but she had to get back to the shop."

"We can go there now," Effie said.

He hesitated. "No," he said at last. "There'll be another time. My head is kind of screwed up now. I've had enough emotional drama for today."

"Okay," she said.

Driving back from town, he said, "You'll have to forgive me."

She caught his hand. "You're forgiven."

"I knew there was a remote chance that I'd bump in to her. But I never really expected . . ."

"Just let it filter in," she said. "It'll take time."

"I asked her for a phone number," he said. "She told me I could reach her through the shop. Do you think that's strange?"

"Perhaps her life is complicated."

"Yes," he said.

He seemed to withdraw then. She felt no resentment for his sudden melancholy. His visit had created an archive of new memories that would, in time—she was sure of this—renew the old place and make it unambiguously hers. They'd walked it and talked it, eaten it and drunk it, and saturated it with an uninhibited abandon neither would easily forget, if ever.

"When we come back next year . . ."

"Next year," he'd said, continuing her thought. "Let's try to make a trip in early June, or even May. Put some plants in the ground."

At home, she said, "I think I'll take a walk. You interested?"

"No," he said. "I think I'll put my head down for a bit. A little nap to freshen up. Okay?"

"Okay."

She heard the chainsaw before she realized the sound was from the Gillis place. Walking up the lane, she calculated that she hadn't been there in nearly thirty years. John didn't see her coming, so she stood and watched him, trying to remember the boy she married so long ago, the man she fled. In 1968, in that field, Duncan, newly minted as a priest, had solemnly pronounced the terrible finality of their commitment, till death. Sextus had come home from somewhere and stood by, smiling. At the end, he kissed both cheeks lightly, like a foreigner, squeezed her hand.

From behind, John had the shape and posture of an old man, shoulders rounded, back bent slightly. She could imagine skinny legs inside the baggy work pants. The sawdust flew; the noise was horrifying. Then it stopped suddenly, and the silence startled her. If he was surprised to see her, he managed not to show it. He slowly removed his work gloves, whacked his pants legs, then ambled toward her. She held out a hand. He hesitated, then touched her fingertips.

"I meant to go over," he said. "But you have company."

"A friend," she said.

"It's been a while since you've been."

"Yes."

"Will you come in?" He spread his arms, smiled shyly.

"If it's okay. Sure. I suppose the place is all changed."

"I suppose it is," he said. "A bit of a mess, though."

There was a teacup and a bowl in the kitchen sink, newspapers and unopened mail strewn on the table, a jacket hanging on a chair. The kitchen seemed larger than she remembered.

"I took out a wall," he said, responding to her thought.

"Where did that come from?" she asked, pointing toward a massive sandstone fireplace.

"It was there all along," he said. "That's where the stove used to be."

She remembered that much.

"I always suspected there was something behind that wall. I could tell from the shape of the chimney that it was probably part of a fireplace."

"The table?"

"Found it at a yard sale."

"It's beautiful."

"A bit battered."

"Now that I remember, it's all changed, isn't it?"

"I suppose. Being here day in, day out, it's hard to tell the new from the old."

"The old table was over there."

"I guess it was."

Face to face, she was suddenly surprised by how little he had changed. The hair, though prematurely white, was thick; the face was lined but healthy; the eyes were clear and interested. She knew that she, too, was being carefully inspected, and it felt, somehow, reassuring.

"I could make tea," he said.

"No, don't bother."

"It wouldn't be a bother."

"So when did you discover the fireplace?"

"Oh, Christ. It's hard to remember. There were a few lost years there." He laughed. "Yup. A few lost years, for sure. After you."

"You know why I ran away, John?"

She was surprised at having said it and by his easy acknowledgement.

"I often meant to talk to you about that," he said. "It was on my mind. But anyway, here we are." He shrugged. They stared at each other and past each other, into time. "It's a hard word, 'sorry,' sometimes."

"Yes," she said. "Especially when you really mean it."

"I did. I mean it now. I don't know what got into me, the night you ran away. I thought for a long time it was the old man coming out in me. I blamed him. But eventually I had to face the fact. Even if there's some of him in me, I'm my own person."

"I never blamed you," she said. "I was way, way out of line, and we both know it."

"Still, there's no excuse."

Into the silence then, she said, "You're looking awfully well, John."

"You're looking pretty good yourself. You're sure you won't have a cup?"

"Not this time. I left the company by himself over home."

"I see."

"He's from Toronto. I think his mother was from around here someplace, but he grew up in Halifax."

"I see."

"How about yourself? Is there anybody?"

"Well . . . yes and no."

She laughed. It was, she thought, the perfect answer—the safest answer. She placed a hand on his forearm. "You should come by," she said. "Maybe later. Meet him before he goes."

"How long is he here for?"

"He'll be leaving tomorrow."

"Ah well," he said. "Maybe the next time."

"I hope."


JC was in her office reading when she returned. "What's happening in the world?"

"I dropped in on John," she said.

"Ah. How was that?"

"It felt weird," she said. "I see him each summer, but I haven't been inside that house since I . . . left. We had a good chat."

He was studying her face.

"I'll tell you sometime."

"Your call."

She sat beside him. "How's the book?" she asked.

"Kind of dry," he said. "But interesting. Lots of anecdotes. You say your dad was in it?"

She walked to a bookcase, retrieved a photograph. Three men, two in army uniforms, one in work clothes, standing at the front of a truck. The civilian was holding a rifle in one hand and, with the other, propping up the antlered head of a deer that was draped across a fender.

"Duncan gave me this before he went away. I didn't know he had it. That's my father there," she said. "And that's John's father, Sandy. It was just before they went overseas."

"And the guy with the rifle?"

"That's Jack, Sextus's dad."

"Well, well. So this Sandy . . . he's the one who was shot. In the war."

"In Holland. Yes."

"I think I heard something."

"It isn't a very pretty story."

"They rarely are."

"Would you care for a drink?"

"Why not."

She was up early, to maximize the day, she told herself. His flight was in the evening. He'd have to leave by mid-afternoon. She was already resigned to the reality of his absence, resolved to keep the morning busy.

Over coffee, he told her he'd like to revisit the bookstore, see if Sylvia was there. "Would you come with me?"

"Of course."

"You're sure?"

"Absolutely. And curious."

"Good," he said.

But it was a stranger at the cash. "Sylvia's not in today," she explained. "She phoned in earlier. Anything I can do to help?"

"Give her this," said JC, dropping a business card on the glass-topped counter.

The woman squinted at it. "Sure," she said.

"Wait," he said. Retrieved the card and scribbled quickly. "There," he said, and slid it back across the counter. Then he turned to Effie. "I put down your number too. I hope that's okay."

She nodded.

"That's the cemetery over there," Effie said as they drove away.

"Is that where your dad is?" he asked, peering through the passing trees.

"All three," she said. "The men in the photograph. They're all there."

"Can we see?" he said.

She was surprised. "I suppose, but it's been so long I'm not sure I can find them."

"Two Gillises over here," he called out. "Alexander and Jack."

"Then my father isn't far away," she said.

He was holding her hand. Then he put an arm around her shoulder. "You're trembling."

"Chilled," she said.

She studied the simple headstone, wondering who had made the effort. Then she realized it was a basic military marker. "Cpl. Angus A. MacAskill. 2nd Batt., N.S. Highlanders." And some dates. She hadn't realized he'd been a corporal.

She leaned her head on JC's shoulder. She wanted to say, "Please don't go," but suppressed the impulse. "He was a very bad man, in many ways," she said, and suddenly regretted saying it.

He wrapped an arm around her and squeezed. "People aren't bad," he said. "They just do bad things sometimes."

"Maybe," she said. She could feel the ground below her feet shifting, as if she was about to slide away. She placed her arm around his waist, held on. "I always blamed him for what happened to Sandy Gillis."

"I heard Sandy Gillis killed himself," JC said. "Why blame your father?"

"My father pushed him over the edge."

"How so?"

"Sandy had no memory of the war or what happened there before he got shot. What they did—to the girl that shot him."

"A girl?"

"Yes."

"I heard it was a sniper."

"It was a girl."

"What happened to the girl?"

"My father killed her. With a knife. After she shot Sandy."

She imagined that his arm had slackened slightly, that a tiny space had opened where their shoulders touched.

"How do you know all this?"

"Sextus. He worked it out. Years later."

"So when was it that your father broke the news to Sandy, finally?"

"November 1963."

"An eventful month, for sure."

"Sandy couldn't handle it, and he killed himself right after-wards. November twenty-second."

He grunted. "The day Kennedy was shot."

"Makes it even harder to forget," she said.

There was a long silence, broken only by the whine of traffic on the nearby highway.

"Does anybody know what made your father lay that on Sandy, after all those years?"

"I do," she said. "I know."

"Do you want to tell me?"

She shook her head. "Yes. No," she said.

And suddenly she was running through the gravestones, throat burning from the rising bile, stomach churning as the acid formed a vacuum in her throat. She flung herself against the cemetery fence, choking on the remnants of her breakfast.

Then he was beside her.

"I'm not crying!" she shouted. "Just leave me alone."

He stepped back but kept one firm hand on her heaving shoulders. The sun was filtered by low-hanging cloud, but the day was warm, the air around them motionless. She thought she heard a robin in a nearby tree.

# three

*Go, go, go, said the bird: human kind*
*Cannot bear very much reality.*
T.S. ELIOT, "BURNT NORTON,"
FOUR QUARTETS

## 9

By early February she'd convinced herself it was because she cared so much that she'd begun to spy on him. She no longer walked to class. She would take her car so that afterwards she could drive past Walden. JC had stopped answering his telephone. She would mention Sorley whenever she left a message on the answering machine: "Hi, stranger. Hope everything is okay. I was just wondering about my cat, if he needs anything. Tell him I miss him. You too."

Once, after dark, she parked on Broadview and walked along his street, past the little house. She walked briskly so that it seemed she had a respectable reason for being there. There was a light, but it was dim. She calculated that it was in the kitchen, the swag that hung above his table. It had a dimmer switch. Driving home, she felt a torrent of reproach.

There was something foreign in JC's manner since he'd returned from Texas. The anger was replaced by something darker. Or maybe he had found a deeper place within himself, a place where he could go for privacy, unconscious of the distance it would open up between them. She'd abandoned any expectation that he would show up for the party she was organizing for Valentine's Day, even though he'd promised. There now seemed to be two JC Campbells. The one she would visit briefly or who would show up unannounced at her place, warm and interested, happily reliving happy times: the early days; their chance encounter in a subway station; his farcical attempt at reconciliation on behalf of Sextus; their summer holiday back home last year—an idyll that became more sacred as it faded. Then there was the other, the one in her imagination, the dark and silent shapeless absence, fortified inside the little house on Walden. Her only consolation was that a part of her still lived there with him.

Maybe it was the time of year. February was always bad. The weather, the irritated weariness in all the faces—friends, faculty and students equally. Or maybe it was time to just move on. Again.

And she thought, *My God, where are you now?*

*The book,* she thought. He'd mentioned something about writing a book. What was the subject? Impotence, he'd said. She knew exactly what he meant.

She needed him and, in particular, she needed his advice and the firm decisiveness she had started to rely on. He was direct, sometimes impulsive, but his instincts were reliable. He would know exactly what to do about the phone calls, about the stranger who had begun to insinuate familiarity.

She knew that in a moment of vulnerable carelessness she had exposed herself. But self-reproach soon turned to irritation and now approached a kind of dread each time the phone rang. And it rang a lot, day and night.

There would be pleading: "Hello. Please call. You have my number."

Then remorse: "Hey, this is Paul. Just to say I can't imagine what you think . . . me bugging you. You won't hear from me again. I promise. Have a nice life."

Hours later: "Faye? I really want to talk to you. Call me when you get this."

The last one left her shaken: "Hey, I'm not sure what kind of game you're playing, but I'm getting really, really sick of it. Call me."

It seemed that every time she walked through the door of her apartment, she'd see, again, that winking light. And when there was no one there, just living silence, it was always worse.

"Sorley sends his love," JC said merrily as he kissed her cheek.

He was the last one to arrive, and now that he was here, he seemed to fill the room. Cassie almost ran to him, eyes glistening. "I'm so glad you came," she said.

"I wouldn't have missed it," he said. He hugged her and turned to Ray, pulled a bottle of Balvenie from a bag. "Something for the birthday boy," he said. "And a bouquet of roses for my Valentine." He handed them to Effie.

He shook hands with Duncan. "Father," he said, nodding with mock gravity.

"It's been a while," said Duncan.

"Indeed it has. So, what's on?"

Effie made brief introductions. It was a small gathering. A young woman whose name was well known from her byline in a daily newspaper; three men of diverse ages who seemed to be doctors. There was music, a nostalgia disc from the seventies; there was much light chatter. Effie noted that he had two longer conversations, one with Ray and one with Duncan, and seemed subdued in both. But over dinner he was dominant. He laughed the loudest, was first to launch the sharp responses, teasing and laconic.

He gave a long and rambling account of a letter he and Sam were writing to the governor of Texas. "Sam figures they're executing all the wrong people," he declared. "He figures since it's a form of human sacrifice to appease the pagan gods, they should be doing as the pagans did. Execute the pure, the innocent. Babies, virgins. That's the way to win divine approval. Not by sacrificing human garbage."

The table fell silent for a while. She noted he wasn't really eating, just pushing bits of food around his plate.

"Interesting theory," Duncan finally said.

"He's serious. He's really going to send it."

"Is that wise?" Cassie said. "That Bush guy is his only hope."

JC laughed. "Well, in that case, there's nothing left to lose."

Gathering the dishes, Effie whispered to him, "Can we talk later?"

"Sure," he said. "What's up?"

"I might have a little problem."

"Oh?" He seemed engaged. "What kind of problem?"

"I'm being harassed," she said. "Some man keeps calling."

"Some man?" He was smiling. "How did he get your number?"

For just a heartbeat, she was unable to respond.

"Okay, later," he said, and squeezed her arm. "When we get a moment to ourselves."

After the cake, Effie called for their attention. And there was applause when Cassie told them of their plan. She and Ray were getting married just after Easter. She glowed as she spoke. Ray listened, sombre, Effie thought, his bearing more that of a proud father than a groom to be. JC was smiling, staring at his hands.

The young woman, whose name was Moira, spoke briefly. She and Cassie had been friends since journalism school. Cassie blushed as Moira hinted at possibly indelicate disclosures about her appetites, Ray's masculinity. When everybody laughed, JC laughed loudest. Effie's brief discomfort passed.

When the general conversations revived, Effie overheard her brother comment, as he handed a drink to JC, "I didn't realize that you were a friend of Tammy's."

"Who?" JC frowned, flushing.

"Tammy."

"Who's Tammy?"

"Tammy's a little street girl, hangs out around Jarvis and Gerrard. I thought I saw you talking to her. But I guess I was mistaken."

"I have no idea who you're talking about," JC said. Effie wondered if anybody else was conscious of the aggression in his tone.

"I think it's pathetic," Cassie said. "I don't know who's worse. Those poor girls or the creeps who take advantage of them." There was a murmur of agreement. Then, "By the way, *Father,* how do *you* happen to know her? Huh?"

Duncan laughed. "On the really cold nights, she comes to the shelter to get warm. Helps out sometimes, so I got to know her a bit. She's from some small place back east, but she gets vague when I ask too many questions. I kind of keep an eye on her."

"I think I know the one you're talking about," Cassie said. "You can see them from the window of the Thai restaurant on the corner. Remember the one I pointed out that night, Ray? It must have been twenty-five below, and she's out there in this cheap little leather jacket and a skirt up to here."

"Sounds like her," said Duncan.

JC was listening, his expression now dark. "People do desperate things to survive," he said, finally.

"She's far from stupid," Duncan said. "I keep trying to talk her into going back to school. There's hope for her."

"Don't count on it," said JC.

Duncan shook his head sadly. "Last time I saw her, she'd been beaten up. By her pimp, I gather, though she calls him her boyfriend."

There was another long, thoughtful silence.

"Well, I sure wouldn't mind getting my hands on the cock-sucker," JC said. "Just for five minutes."

Everyone stared at him, startled.

"I think it's time for beddie-bye," he said, standing suddenly. "I have a doctor's appointment in the morning."

Effie was speechless.

"I'll call you tomorrow," he said. "After the doctor."

"Please do," she said. Should she walk to the door with him? He'd promised her they'd talk.

He held Cassie's hand for a moment. "Honey, I wish you all the best things in the world. I hope I'll be there for the wedding, but I might not be able to make it."

"Awww," she said. "What could be so important that you'd miss my wedding?"

He kissed her cheek lightly.

"Duncan," he said. "Can I talk to you for a second?"

After about ten minutes by the front door with JC, Duncan returned to a silent room, seven staring faces. "He's okay," he said.

Effie began to gather plates.

"There's a lot going on in his life just now," Duncan whispered to her. "He just needs space."

"Space we'll give him," Effie said, working to contain the fury she now felt.

Cassie and Ray lingered until after Duncan and the other guests were gone, Cassie busy with dishes. Finally she asked, "You okay, Mom?"

"Just dandy," Effie said. "It's ironic. He has this theory: women change, but men don't." She laughed. "He should look in the mirror." Then she asked Ray, "How long did you say the after-effects of a head injury last?"

"I wouldn't be too concerned about the head injury," Ray said. "But has anybody talked to him about the incident that caused the injury?"

"What about it?"

"A certain kind of man can suffer psychological trauma that's far worse than the physical damage from an assault like that."

"I don't know what you mean."

"I put myself through med school working underground in Sudbury. I knew younger versions of JC. Serious men, hard as rock. The problem is that, when subjected to a superior force, rock shatters."

"Come on."

"It's true. You say he's changed. I didn't know him before the incident on New Year's Day. What's different? Maybe his theory is right. Maybe he hasn't changed, isn't capable of change. Maybe his problem is the inability to cope with change. What do you think?"

She didn't know how to answer.

She stood with them as they donned their coats to leave. Cassie stooped. "What's this?" she asked. Then, "Somebody lost a floppy disk. There's no name on it, just—"

Effie took it from her, looked at it briefly. "I'll hang on to it," she said.

"What was that word?" Cassie asked, smiling oddly. "Impo—?"

"It belongs to JC," Effie said. "Some notes about stuff he considers to be important. I think he's writing something."

"Let's hope so," Cassie said. "It often helps to write things down."

Standing at the closed door, Effie examined the disk she'd last seen just after New Year's. Above where he had written "Huntsville, TX, '98," he'd printed in bold capitals the word "impotence."


The light on the answering machine was blinking, and she snatched the phone receiver from the cradle. There was no sound, just breathing. She slammed the phone down, ran to the kitchen, rifled through a drawer until she found the stained business card. She punched in his number.

"Listen, you fucking bastard," she hissed when he picked up. "You call here again and I promise . . . you'll be sorry. Do you hear me?"

She almost screamed the last part.

"No problem," he said softly, almost sadly.

She slammed the phone down and stood there shaking, a feeling like elation coursing through her veins.

## 10

After JC had gone back to the city, that blissful summer of 1998, he'd called her every night while she was in Cape Breton. The ringing telephone, usually at ten o'clock, became the highlight of each solitary day. He was working hard, couldn't remember a more productive time in his life. She was a distraction, but a good one. He was inspired by her, even found himself writing small snatches of poetry, he said.

"I can hardly wait to see some."

"You'll be waiting," he said with a laugh.

"That isn't fair," she replied sulkily. Then realized she sounded like a girl. She accused herself of trying to be cute, resolved to be more conscious of her age, of her maturity. But then she'd tell herself, *There's nothing wrong with feeling young. There's nothing wrong with feeling happy.*

She remembered how she cursed her father as they stumbled past his grave on that last day of his visit. "You've done it again," she whispered.

But it was different this time. She could feel it in the arm around her shoulder, but also in the quality of the silence following her unexpected breakdown. It was not, she realized, the fearful silence that follows some unexpected revelation of vulnerability or the resentful silence that gathers over interrupted pleasure. This was the silence of trust, the silence of unquestioning accommodation, the silence of the strong. And she knew that, one day, she'd tell him everything, in spite of all her reservations.

She rarely left the Long Stretch, driving to town only when she needed to replenish groceries or to buy wine, though she rarely felt an inclination to drink alcohol. She was, she admitted to herself, worried about the places it would take her. On one trip she visited the bookstore in search of reading material. She needed more escapism. Or maybe it was reality she sought, remembering who worked there.

She bought a novel by a famous local author who, hitherto, had written only short stories. The publication had been widely discussed by people in the English department who'd assumed that she knew the writer personally, being from the same small place.

"I spent years away from there," she said. "I'm almost a stranger there myself."

She was surprised by the lack of resemblance between JC and his daughter. Sylvia was slightly overweight, had soft features and none of the taut planes and angles that defined her father's face. Her voice was also soft, but Effie noticed that her smile was easy and authentic and, with mild alarm, that her eyes had the colour and directness that revealed so much of JC's character. She offered a compliment about the bookstore, and Sylvia seemed pleased.

"You aren't from here, then," she said.

"Well, I grew up here," Effie said. "But that was a long time ago."

Sylvia smiled. "It couldn't have been all that long ago." They both laughed.

She wanted to say, "I know your father." But she didn't, because she had no idea what that simple message would convey. She knew from personal experience the potential turmoil in those enigmatic words, coming from a stranger. "I know your father."

"Is this your shop?" she asked.

"No," Sylvia replied. "I just work here."

"Well, it's a great store. I'm impressed."

"Thank you."

Walking away from the store, the words came back to her, "I'm almost a stranger here," and it felt true. She tried to imagine a future conversation, and whether she'd feel awkward for having failed to be forthright at their first encounter. Would Sylvia even remember her?

She spotted Stella in the parking lot. She thought she could avoid her, but Stella called out cheerfully, "Hey, stranger!"

When she got close, Stella said, "I've been meaning to come out for a visit. But . . ." She shrugged. "I think you probably know how I feel. Guilty, sad, helpless in a way. Have you talked to Sextus?"

Effie shook her head. "There really isn't much to talk about."

She was torn. She wanted to say, "Yes, I know exactly how you feel." But she also wanted to say no, emphatically, to extract some possibly original disclosure from this woman who projected so much strength but who was, at the same time, so obviously needful. And was there really such a contradiction there? Couldn't the strong be driven sometimes by their needs?

"Duncan says hello," she lied.

The smile was spontaneous. "Say hello back for me," Stella said. "He hasn't been home since, has he?"

"He's pretty tied up with his street people."

"I can imagine. I was a social worker in Toronto years ago. It was different then, not so many homeless. But I can imagine what he's dealing with."

They were standing in the parking lot. Effie was conscious of appraising stares from passing men. What is it they look for when they stare? What is it they need? She had a pretty good idea of what men want, and the sudden bitterness was like a chill. She thought of Sextus, and how she had mistakenly believed that his needs had finally aligned with hers; that his nervous heat had been replaced by warmth, the superficial urges set aside for something deeper. She'd sensed solicitation: What did *she* want? What did *she* need? At first she was suspicious. It was nothing more, she thought, than a more mature seduction, but self-interested nonetheless.

Now she studied Stella's face, trying to estimate her age. Forty-five, she thought. Could that have made the difference? Did the biological divide lie somewhere in that narrow corridor, mid-forties to mid-fifties? Was that where primal magnetism started to wane?

"Well, I suppose I should get going."

"Yes," said Stella. "I won't keep you. Danny asks about Duncan all the time. If I'm hearing anything."

"It was sad, seeing Danny," Effie said.

"Even just a phone call from Duncan would make a big difference."

"To Danny?"

Stella laughed. "Of course. Or . . . to me. I could be the messenger."

The directness was startling.

"I suppose you'll be around for a while longer," Stella said, as she turned away.

"A bit longer," Effie said.

"You know where I am in Creignish. Up on the mountain road. Don't be a stranger."

She rose early and took long walks, savouring the damp dawn air. She studied the rising sun for clues about the coming day. "Red sky in the morning, sailors take warning," the old saying went. And it was perversely true. The most dramatically beautiful mornings were announcements of a grim day to follow. Returning from one early walk, she was startled by the soft thud of footsteps behind her and wheeled in fright. It was John. He was running, and a woman was running beside him. They were dressed identically, in tight spandex pants, T-shirts and baseball caps, as they cantered lightly by. She noted that they were similarly built: strong legs with bulging calves and quadriceps, flat chests and narrow shoulders. A ponytail protruded from the back of the woman's ball cap.

John shouted breathlessly, "Hey! Come and join us." But she wasn't sure if he was teasing her, inviting her to run with them, or if he meant she should join them at the house. She stopped and watched them go. The distance opened, and she saw the last of them as they jogged up the lane to the old Gillis place.

Boiling water for her tea one evening, she heard a car slowing near her gate. She moved the curtain imperceptibly and saw that it was Sextus. The car came almost to a complete stop, then accelerated suddenly and was quickly gone.

She was sitting in the darkness, on the small deck at the front of her house. She noted that July was almost over. Sudden bats swooped past. She hated bats, but tolerated them since discovering their massive appetite for bugs. A car drove by, music thumping. Silence quickly filled the space behind it. It was near midnight.

"Do you think that women eventually stop changing?" she had asked him that night during their phone call.

"Yes," JC said. "Eventually."

"When, do you think?"

"Depends on the woman, I guess."

"I bumped into Stella in town the other day."

"And how did that go?" he asked.

"It was nothing special. I think she'd love to hear from Duncan, if you happen to be talking to him."

"If I see him. And how is Stella, anyway?"

"Sad and gorgeous. Don't go getting interested."

He just laughed.

Now, alone again, she wanted to have told him, "Maybe what you see isn't so much change as adaptation. Women adapting to the needs they see around them, or feel within. We are the original first responders."

She'd try to remember that thought for next time; maybe she should make a note of it. But she didn't feel like standing up, opening the screen door, fetching pen and paper, investing so much effort to capture what was just another moment of transient self-consciousness. Maybe she should get a drink. But she didn't have the energy to do that, either.

Sitting in the darkness in the place where her conscious life began, she realized that he was right: women do change. And she thought of all the people she had been. The solitary girl, so burdened by her isolation, her awkward circumstances; then, suddenly, a woman, something she discovered in the strange appraisal of her older friend, her almost brother, Sextus Gillis, the new awareness in his eyes, the new purpose in his smile.

"My God, you've changed," he said. He was smiling, but it was a smile she'd never seen before. She was fifteen, and his sudden strangeness was frightening because of where she'd seen it first.

"You've turned into a stranger," John told her sadly near the end. "What's come over you?"

"It's called growth," she said. "You should try it sometime."

She sighed, remembering her casual cruelties. And then reflected on the greatest changes of all, the frequency of those internal signals she'd read about, discussed with women friends.

"The changes can be mitigated," someone offered.

"By what," she laughed. "Death?"

"It's called hormone replacement."

"Hormones? I can't count the pickles hormones got me into. Hormones, the last things I need."

Everybody laughed at that.

"Don't be a stranger," Stella had said, and Effie had been unexpectedly moved by the longing in her voice.

She'd asked JC, "So, what if you thought some old broad you were interested in had finished changing? Would she tempt you then?"

"Well, that depends," JC said.

"Depends on what?"

"Depends on what kind of an old broad she's . . . become."

"You know," she said, "you're insufferably condescending."

"You're absolutely right. You're always right."

"Now that I think of it, as long as I've known you, you've been insufferably condescending."

"Kind of proves what I've been saying. Men don't change." He was laughing.

"So change can be a good thing, in your feeble mind."

"Of course."

"At least we agree on that much."

"Good night, my sweet."

"Night."

A dog barked somewhere. Something scurried in the darkness. Another darting bat flipped through a pool of light. She imagined she could see the ugly little face, the pin-toothed mouth, a stream of insects flowing down the tunnel throat, turning into shit bombs to be dropped in people's attics. She felt a sudden spasm of anxiety. She was weary of changing, fed up with the process of becoming, the spinning wheel of evanescence, the endless fading. Afraid that, from now on, with each new incarnation she would be reduced, until, finally, she reached complete invisibility.

In the darkness she was startled to see the outline of the barn, then realized that she was looking at a grove of trees. But for a moment it was there again and so was he, the ghost man she'd escaped, eventually exorcised by growing up and growing wiser.

*"Daddy, you're scaring me."*

*"Don't call me Daddy."*

She shuddered. And at that precise moment she decided. *Pack your bags, babe—you're out of here, heading back to the city, first thing in the frigging morning. You can't do this alone.*

She left the Long Stretch shortly after dawn. She felt a giddy kind of joy standing at the gate, staring at the empty, silent house. *Next time I stand here,* she vowed, *he'll be standing with me. We'll arrive together, stay together, leave together. We will live like adults. I'll make sure of that.*

The rising sun, a scarlet slit between the layered banks of cloud, promised favourable weather. She knew the joy was also from the freedom of an undetected flight, and this time she wasn't weighed down by the guilt she'd felt at previous departures. She told herself that this was not so much a flight as a constructive retreat. She had business in the city. She had a life to furnish.

She'd got up in darkness, made her bed and quickly packed. She'd briefly considered staying one more day, to visit John, perhaps to talk. But why? To talk about what? She'd meant to ask about his mother, who was living in the seniors' residence in town. But Mrs. Gillis had no memory, probably wouldn't even know who Effie was. Her mind was gone, someone said. A blessing, in a way. She was the widow of Sandy Gillis. "The things that she put up with when Sandy was around—best forgotten," someone said.

"Sandy's been dead for thirty-five years," she had answered.

"Yeah, but you didn't know the real Sandy."

She wanted to reply, "Oh, but I did. I truly did." And she wondered about memory. Sometimes when the mind "goes," memory and truth are reconciled. But she checked herself, as she always did. Who could understand how much Mrs. Gillis knew and why? And what did she, Effie Gillis, really know?

*"Do you know that or are you just rememberin'?" Conor had asked.*

*"Is there a difference?"*

*"Rememberin's for the poets and the martyrs. It's only what we know that matters."*

At the causeway she saw the flashing red lights, heard the warning clang and felt the instant surge of aggravation. The bridge was swinging, blocking her escape. She slammed the steering wheel with her fist. "Shit, shit, shit," she said, then felt silly for swearing. A hulking tugboat inched through the canal before her, dragging a barge, probably full of gravel from the quarry that was devastating old Cape Porcupine. She wished that it would sink, then quickly realized that, should her baleful wish be realized, she'd never get away.

It had been even earlier when she and Sextus made their unimpeded getaway in 1970, the dawn still distant, over the Atlantic Ocean somewhere, slower than the barge, hauling daylight to an unsuspecting world.

The tug crept by, barge lingering behind, a lifetime in ten minutes.

Sextus had phoned her once, a few days after JC left. "How is it going out there?" he asked.

"Just fine," she said. "I've been sticking close to home."

"Still have your company?"

She considered saying yes, but told the truth. "He's gone back."

"Too bad," he said. "I was kind of hoping we could get together while he was around. Chew the fat about the old days. You don't think he'll be back?"

"Not this summer," she said.

There was a long pause.

"Can I tell you about a dream I had? It was kind of sweet. You were in it."

She decided not to answer.

"It seemed to be a long time back. We were still kids . . . but teens, I think. You, for some reason, had to sleep over at our place, in the village. And we were short of beds. So Ma said, 'You two can share a bed.' And I was a bit taken aback by that. We were almost grown-ups, in that sense. Anyway, we went to bed, wearing our pyjamas." He chuckled softly. "So you were way over on one side of the bed, and I was way over on the other side. Eventually I said, 'Do you think it would be okay if we held hands?' And you said, 'I don't see any harm in that.' And you reached across and we just lay there, on opposite sides of this big bed, holding hands. That was it. Innocence, eh?"

There was the sound of a passing car.

"Are you still there?" he asked.

"Yes," she said. "Good night, Sextus."

"Look," he said. "I have something I want you to read some-time . . . something I've meant to show you but never had the nerve."

"Hmmm."

"Something I wrote a few years ago. John and I spent a fair bit of time hashing through the family secrets. It was going to be a kind of memoir. But when I finished, I realized I could never publish it. I think you're the one person who could read it, objectively. You might find it helpful."

"Helpful?"

"I think you know what I mean. Stuff I learned about your father, and Uncle Sandy. And about us."

"I have to get some sleep."

"Good night," he said. "I'm sorry, bringing that up."

At a truck stop just past the New Brunswick border, she filled her car with gas. On an impulse she bought two cans of Red Bull.

Near Florenceville, she was startled by an aggressive whoop behind her. When she looked in her rear-view mirror, there was a police car almost on her bumper, headlights and roof lights flashing furiously. She had the presence of mind to signal as she pulled to the shoulder of the road, heart pounding.

She lowered her window. The policeman seemed to hesitate by the rear door until he saw that she was a woman travelling alone. He stepped forward, bent and peered inside.

"In a bit of a hurry, are we?"

"Oh, God," she said. "How fast was I going?"

"I clocked you at 125," he said.

"And what's the limit?"

He looked at her skeptically. "It's usually a hundred."

"Oh, man. I'm so sorry. I don't know where my head was."

"I'll need your driver's licence, registration and proof of insurance."

"I'm sorry," she said again as she fished through the assorted debris of purse and glove compartment, looking for the documents.

After she handed them over, the policeman was gone for about five minutes, then returned with a stern expression on his face.

"I'm going to let you go with a warning," he said, giving her back the documents. "But pay attention to the speed limit. When you're in Quebec, they might be a bit stickier."

"I can't thank you enough," she said.

He pointed at the cans of Red Bull on the passenger seat. "You planning on driving right through?"

"I was hoping to," she said.

"Well, don't put too much faith in that stuff." And just before he turned away, he added, "Whoever he is, I doubt if he's worth dying for."

She was driving westward, driving fast. The sun, behind her when she left, was soon above and then in front of her, inviting her to stop before it disappeared. But she ignored it, the insistent glare before the darkness, the seductive urge to stop, relax and rest. Mind racing forward, then back, reviewing what had been revealed, enumerating small evasions, elaborating the disclosures yet unmade, heart swelling at the prospect of unfettered honesty, intimacy unqualified.

In Drummondville she stopped for gas and coffee and almost called JC from the restaurant. Then she thought, *No*. But in the car, before she drove away, she rang and got his answering machine, left a brief message, "Expecting to arrive in the wee hours . . . will call you in the morning."

She thought afterwards she might have added a casual "love ya." But she felt a quiet satisfaction that she hadn't.

"Emotional boundaries are important," he'd told her. "Wisest advice I ever got from anyone."

"And who was the wise advisor?" she had asked, not expecting an answer.

"A woman friend," he said. "I foolishly blurted out some adolescent nonsense one day, and she told me that."

Effie laughed. "Let me guess," she said. "You were having a risky affair with somebody. You got sloppy. She reminded you the risk was mostly on her head because she was married."

"How did you figure that out?" he said, scowling slightly.

"Am I wrong?"

"No."

She caught his hand. "So now the ending?" she said. "You can't just leave me hanging."

"She left him."

"She left him for you?"

"She left him."

There was a long silence.

"I know what you're thinking," he said at last. "It was a long time ago. I've grown up since then. I think."

"I hope," she said.

———

*Conor said, "Well, if you can't bring yourself to marry me, can I make another kind of proposal?"*

*"Proposal?"*

*"Consider it a business proposition. I want to put the house in your name. And I want to set up a separate company that'll own one of the gyms. You'll be the president of the company, and own all the shares."*

*She was laughing. "Me? President of a company? Own the house. Why?"*

*"It'll be helpful to me, businesswise. Plus, you need some security in your life. I think it's about time for that."*

*"I'm working on a Ph.D. Won't that be security enough?"*

*"Trust me on this," he said.*

———

It had rained. The Don Valley Parkway had a scrubbed emptiness that seemed to deepen her exhaustion. She felt numb, leaned stiffly into the steering wheel, studying the road.

There was a solitary bicycle weaving along Bloor, a small red light flashing on a backpack. Someone young, she thought, giving him a wide berth, wondering where he could be coming from at that hour. Then she saw that it was a girl, and was briefly anxious. The rain resumed, softly.

Approaching her house on Huron, she could see a small, dim light glowing somewhere inside and felt a faint revival.

He was asleep on the chesterfield, wearing a dark T-shirt and shorts. He was on his back, hands folded on his stomach, one sandaled foot resting on the floor. She stood and watched, keys in hand. Then she walked softly to the kitchen, poured a glass of water. When he placed his arms around her from behind, she was not surprised and leaned her head back into his shoulder.

"I was getting worried," he said.

They nuzzled briefly. Then, standing there in her kitchen, he slowly undressed her. She shivered. He removed his T-shirt and, after slowly unfastening her bra, slid it off, slipped the T-shirt over her head and arms, then picked her up and carried her upstairs. She woke briefly when he leaned down, pulled back the duvet and placed her gently on the sheets. Then he covered her and sat. She briefly rubbed his back, and then was gone again, into a darkness that was warm and welcoming and soft.

12
—

The day after Valentine's JC phoned to say the doctor had given him a clean bill of health. There was nothing in the outcomes of all the scans and tests to cause continuing alarm. Pressure on the low side, prostate enviably flat.

"This is great news," Effie said.

"He thinks maybe I need a shrink," JC said.

"A shrink? Why do you think he suggested that?"

"I told him I wasn't sleeping much."

"Oh."

"He thinks I'm depressed."

"And what do you think?"

"I don't get depressed."

"Lucky you."

"You know what I mean."

"Yes."

"What did you think about Ray and Cassie?"

"What about them? I'm thrilled for them," she said.

"Okay."

"What about you? You don't sound too thrilled."

"I'm not sure."

"Not sure of what?"

"Oh, somebody told me once that marriage is the mother of disappointment."

She laughed. "What somebody was that?"

"Just somebody."

"Sounds like somebody depressed."

"Somebody with a lot of experience, that's all."

"You really think you'll miss the wedding?"

"It's possible. Sam's date is the eighth."

"But why does Sam's date matter to you? I thought you'd finished with that story."

There was a long pause. She thought briefly that he was gone, but she could hear him swallow and what sounded like the bump of a mug set down on a table. Or a glass.

"I don't know. They want me to be there."

"To be there."

"He wants me to be a witness. For him. They have media witnesses and witnesses from the victim's side. And witnesses for the inmate. Sam doesn't have anybody. Just Sandra. And me."

"Jesus, JC. I think that's a really bad idea."

"I've seen worse."

"Well, maybe that's half of your bloody problem."

"We can talk about it some more," he conceded.

"I can't imagine a worse idea," she said. "By the way," she added, before he could hang up. "You left something here last night. Your Texas computer disc."

"Ahhh, Christ," he said. "I was wondering what I did with it. You hang on to it for now."

"I will. Think about what I said. Texas is a bad idea."

"I'll think about it. Oh," he said. "You wanted to talk. Some guy."

"Yes. I've been getting harassing phone calls."

"Do you know who from?"

"I have a name."

"You have a name?"

"I have his business card."

JC laughed. "He gave you his card? Can't be all that sinister, then."

"Maybe."

"Just tell him straight . . . tell him you're engaged."

"Am I?"

"Well, what do you think?"

"Yes," she said. "I guess so." But it was only after he had hung up that she admitted to herself she no longer really knew what to think.

That day at work, the receptionist on her floor reported that a man had come to see her. He didn't leave a name. But he was casually handsome and very friendly, had a lovely smile and warm, engaging eyes, wore jeans and leather jacket.

"He said he'd try to get in touch with you at home," she said. "He called you Faye." She smiled. "Faye," she said. "I didn't realize."

Effie didn't know Molly Blue, but JC often mentioned her; they'd been colleagues for decades, working overseas. Molly read the local evening news, so when she called unexpectedly in early March, Effie could imagine a familiar face at the other end of the telephone.

Molly was hoping they could meet. It was ridiculous, she said, that they hadn't ever crossed paths. She'd listened to JC go on about Effie like a schoolboy ever since . . . when was it? . . . Easter 1998, wasn't it?

"And, God, you should have seen him mope around last summer, after he came back from that trip to Cape Breton. I never saw him look so good and seem so low!"

Then Molly sounded serious. "I'll be honest with you. I'm worried about our guy. This Texas thing. I think we should talk."

Effie agreed.

She'd passed by his house on two occasions, observed the same dim light inside. The contacts were now entirely on the basis of his initiative. He'd call her, at the office or at home. His tone was so "normal" as to seem unusual; they'd talk of weather, world events. Once he lapsed. "I know I'm being an asshole," he said. "But please, hang in."

"You aren't being—" she began before she realized the line was dead.

Hang in? No longer. She snatched a coat and her car keys, her mind made up. She'd had enough. He would either get control of himself, with or without professional help, or she was gone. There was a fire truck blocking traffic, so, in her impatience, she revised her route and turned down Jarvis. Near Gerrard she saw two women huddled, sharing a cigarette. She realized that one of them was the girl named Tammy. She pulled to the side of the street, then reconsidered and drove on.

His house was dark. She rang the doorbell and listened for sounds of movement, but the internal silence had a quality of abandonment. She returned to the car. Crossing the Don Valley on the Dundas overpass, heading home again, she saw him walking toward her, head down. There was no place to safely stop. On the west side of the valley, she considered turning back. Something prevented it, fear perhaps. So she carried on.

On Jarvis, she saw the girl again and pulled over.

"Hey," she shouted, clambering out of her car. "Just a minute."

The girl was hurrying away from her.

"Hey, Tammy. Wait." The girl paused and turned. Effie hurried up to her.

"What do you want?"

She couldn't have been more than eighteen. Effie saw immediately that it wasn't Tammy. The girl was black.

"I'm not Tammy," she said. "I don't know no Tammy."

"You were talking to her before."

"I wasn't talking to nobody. And I don't want to be seen talking to you. Who are you anyway? Are you a cop?"

"No, no," Effie said. "My brother is Tammy's friend. My brother. The priest. His name is Duncan. Father Duncan."

The girl paused. "The priest?"

"Yes."

"Father Duncan," she said. "At the shelter. You're his sister?"

"Yes," said Effie. And she lied, "I met Tammy there once."

"Tammy went home," the girl said.

"Where does she live?"

"She lives with my brother. In St. Jamestown."

"Where in St. Jamestown?"

"I don't know. It's a big place."

"What's your brother's name?"

"Robert. Why do you want to know? Everybody interested in Robert all of a sudden."

"What everybody?"

"I don't know. That priest, for one."

"Duncan."

"I just know he's a priest. But I gotta go. I can't be seen talking to you. You look like a fuckin' cop."

Effie laughed. "I'm a teacher."

The girl hurried away.

"When did you last see JC?" she called.

The girl kept going.

She met Molly Blue at Dora's on the Danforth. The place was almost empty. There was a fireplace and a small table close to it. They sat there. "I'm going to have a Scotch," Molly announced. Effie ordered a glass of wine. She estimated Molly Blue to be in her late forties. She was shorter than she appeared to be on television. Effie appraised the lean body and guessed that she was a regular in some Pilates class. She had frank grey eyes and a smile that made engagement easy.

They exchanged elemental biographical details. Molly had grown up in Willowdale, in north Toronto, studied journalism in Ottawa, worked for newspapers for a couple of years, then moved to TV. In the early eighties there was a big demand in the U.S. for Canadian talent, especially to work in foreign places, so she went to ABC, and that was how she first met JC Campbell.

Effie asked about the name Blue.

"My grandfather came from somewhere out east," Molly said. "Cape Breton, actually. I remember someone saying there's a place named after us." She laughed. "Hard to imagine."

"Blue's Mills," Effie said. "It isn't far from where I grew up."

"No way," said Molly, and laughed again.

Effie loved the laugh, spontaneous and careless. She found it hard to believe that a woman whose livelihood depended to such a large extent on looks could be so unselfconscious.

"And you've never been?"

"No," said Molly. "Grandpa married someone from the west. Actually lived in Winnipeg. That was the place I always identified with. Mom and Dad were both from there. But I remember talk. Blue's Mills, just think. A thriving metropolis, I imagine."

"Not exactly."

"Are there still Blues there?"

"I don't know," said Effie.

Molly went to the bar to order another round. When she returned, she said, "JC goes on about Cape Breton—you'd think he grew up there. He used to talk about some little place. I forget the name. Borneo or something."

"Bornish," Effie said. "We tried to find it last summer. It seems to mean something special to him. But there's nothing there."

"I thought he and his mom lived there once," said Molly.

"In a lumber camp," said Effie. "His mom was the cook. But there's no village or anything."

"Well, well," said Molly. And seemed to drift. Then she said brightly, "And here we are, talking about him like two high-school girls. Here's to his health."

They touched glasses, but Effie was suddenly uneasy. "So how well do you know JC?"

"There was a time when I wanted to know him a lot better, I'll admit. I have to say, first time we were introduced, I felt the buzz. I'm sure you know what I'm talking about."

"When was that?"

"Oh, I think it was the summer of '82. The Israelis invaded Lebanon. We were in the London bureau. He went out with Jennings. Then, when things calmed down a bit, they sent me. We covered quite a bit of ground together after that."

She felt the heat in her face, but couldn't resist asking. "And what happened to the buzz?"

"Ah, the buzz. You work together a lot. You fight. You learn too much about each other, and at the same time, not enough. You each construct a practical persona and that's what you exchange. Superficialities. For the most part, you leave out the emotional stuff that might have turned the buzz into something more . . . melodic." She seemed to be aware of the sadness that had crept into their midst. She drained her glass quickly and set it down. "I'm going to tell you, girl to girl . . . exactly when the buzz disappeared."

She looked around, then brought her head close to Effie's. "We were in the middle of nowhere and I was feeling like shit. Ugh. I could hardly hold my head up. He noticed, kept asking if there was anything he could do. Said he could arrange to have me escorted back. So I finally told him. Just to get him to back off. I told him I was having a really bad period, which was the truth. Cramps, fever, the whole damn thing. Figuring he'd run a mile. But not our JC."

She waved to a young waiter. "Daniel, bring us another round." Then she resumed. "He asked me if I was *clotting.* I nearly fainted. He was dead serious. He really wanted to know, seemed to know what he was talking about."

"Charming," Effie said.

Molly nodded. "That was when I realized that we'd gone from buzz to intimacy without passing through the romance that makes intimacy tolerable. Not that we ever could have had a future. We're too much alike."

She moved her glass around in front of her, smearing a puddle that had formed from condensation. "He got in touch three years ago, and I could tell that he was kind of burned out. He'd just covered Chechnya, and before that it was Bosnia. Rwanda. El Salvador. You name the misery, and JC was in the middle of it. We were talking on the phone, and I could tell he was a mess. I asked him, if I could line up something for him here, would he come home? And he broke down." Her eyes were suddenly wet. "Ahhh, shit," she said, wiping. "The poor guy." She sniffed and sighed. "But he bounced back. He was the old JC again. Seemed happy. Met you, told me all about you. Then . . ."

"Then what?" Effie asked.

"That's what I was hoping you could tell me."

Effie shrugged, grew cautious. "He had a fall," she said. "Early New Year's Day. Some little confrontation in the street turned into a pushing match, as I understand it, and he fell and hit his head. My son-in . . . my daughter's boyfriend, or fiancé, is a doctor, and he says even a mild concussion can lead to changes in behaviour for a while."

"That could be. But frankly, I'm worried about this Texas business. I wasn't happy about him getting into it in the first place. The intensity—it's too close to what he had to leave, what burned him out before."

"I'm afraid I can't be much help," Effie said. "We haven't had much contact lately. I've tried to tell him that Texas is a bad idea. This witness thing . . ."

"What witness thing?"

"Witnessing the execution. That Sam guy has asked him to—"

"Oh, for Christ's sake." Molly slammed her glass down on the table.

Effie said, "I'd have thought you'd be the first person he'd talk to about it."

"So he's agreed to watch some asshole's execution. It'll be the end of him. It'll bring back every ghost of every stinking corpse he's ever seen. And he's seen a lot of them. You have to stop this."

"Me?" Effie said. "I can't even get him to discuss it. I think he wants to write a book about it."

"Right," Molly said. "A book. A two-minute news story is about all it's worth. He thinks there's a book in it? He really is cracking up."

"He says the story is about impotence."

Molly snorted. "Impotence, my ass. The story is about the crisis everybody has to go through at middle age."

Effie suddenly felt overwhelmed. "Maybe it should be you."

"No, sweetie. Not me. You're just going to have to put your foot down. You want another drink?"

"I don't think so."

Parking on Walden, she felt exposed. It was awkward because Walden was one-way running east. He knew her car, so she had to park well past his house, facing east when he invariably walked west. And in any case, following on foot was tricky. He was a journalist. They were like cops, expert in following and being followed. Eventually she resorted to logic: her primary interest was Jarvis Street and learning why he sought out women who were little more than children. Prostitutes. Maybe he was working on a story. She considered asking Molly to find out, but if he wasn't, what then?

She drove up Jarvis, turned west and circled back, then drove along Gerrard and stopped. It occurred to her that Ryerson University wasn't far from there. They had a journalism program. Maybe it was as simple as JC going there to lecture students.

Ryerson used a lot of working journalists as part-time teachers. Maybe that was it. She sighed, remembering the scene in January, the girl named Tammy, standing, waiting, just over there. JC hurrying toward her. But maybe he didn't even know this Tammy. Maybe he'd just walked on by. But Duncan had actually seen him talking to her once. Or maybe he hadn't. Maybe it was someone else. *But why did JC seem so damned defensive when Duncan mentioned her? Why am I sitting here, getting chilled?*

She turned her mind back to last August, after she'd returned to what felt like tropical Toronto, and the relative serenity that followed in the autumn. The ball games at the SkyDome. Hot dogs and beer. She'd never gone to a ball game, though she'd wanted to since the city got the franchise in '77. Conor wouldn't even consider it. "Fat-arsed millionaires standing around chewing gum," he'd complained. "Makin' up their minds whether or not to put some effort into winnin'." Hockey he could understand, the speed, the contact. But JC loved baseball, and it turned out she did too. They'd sip their beers and chat, interrupted periodically by the crack of a ball against a bat, the relaxed excitement of the crowd's reaction. They'd watch the play momentarily, then resume the conversation, which was usually about nothing. Until the next bat crack and crowd wow, the next fan-rouser from the PA system.

But it wasn't all frivolity. She had resolved never to divert a happy moment by raising questions that were troubling. And she had also decided that she'd stick to fact, avoiding places in the memory that were clouded by uncertainty. So she talked about her mother, of whom she had no memory. And of Mrs. Gillis, who had tried to fill the role, and of the wounded warrior, Sandy Gillis, and of John. She was bluntly honest about John, about his goodness and his weakness and his usefulness. She even wept for him, and JC held her close.

"Everybody came through okay in the end," he said softly.

"Not exactly," she replied.

"It was the war that ruined those guys," he said. "John's father, yours. Thousands like them. The evil infects people, and the infection migrates through the generations. Violence changes DNA. That's the way I see it, anyway. And I think memory is the same as eye colour or pigmentation—it travels in the genes. We just don't know how to extract the bad stuff or to change it. That's what we're up against. The permanence of violence."

That made sense to her. Her father had suffered and because of that became an agent of suffering. JC enabled her to see that, had framed the subject of violence so that there could be no moral judgment of the victims of it and therefore no betrayal of the man who, after all, had given her the life she now enjoyed, had given her experience that shaped her and made her strong. *We're all the victims of past violence,* she realized. *We all have that in common.*

"You never thought of moving out?"

"Of course. I did, eventually," she said.

"It started when you were what? Twelve or thirteen?"

"That was when I noticed."

"The knife should have been enough—you were in danger."

"It was never like he was going to do anything with it. It was just there. I was terrified of the knife, but not of him. Of course, it was later that I understood. It wasn't about me at all. It was about that girl, in Holland. The one he killed. He had to kill her, you know. Or she'd have killed him."

"Why do you think she tried to kill them in the first place?"

"I don't know. I don't want to think about that. You said your-self, about war."

"Yes."

"The poor girl. I often think of her."

And then she realized the girl was standing there, a hundred feet away. Just standing on the corner, smoking. Effie couldn't see her face but knew it was Tammy. In the glow of the street light, she could see the flimsy jacket made of imitation leather, the knee-high boots.

A car approached, slowed, then stopped. The girl spoke briefly to someone in the car. The car drove off.

Then Effie saw JC.

"Just keep walking," she pleaded. "Just walk on by. Don't even notice her."

And it seemed as if he would. He didn't appear to be aware of where he was, seemed lost in some distant memory, maybe men-tally preparing for a class at Ryerson.

"Keep on going," she whispered. "Please."

He slowed. The girl on the corner noticed him. She turned away. For a moment Effie thought she was about to flee, but she turned back to face him. Then they were speaking, separated by a space of about ten feet. Even from where she sat, huddled in the darkness of the car, Effie couldn't miss the familiarity in how they stood, how they gestured as they spoke.

And then he came closer to her, hands shoved into his jacket pockets. She produced another cigarette. He lit it for her. Then he reached into his jeans and extracted something, handed it to her. She accepted it and shoved it in a pocket. Then she turned. JC looked around. For a moment Effie was certain he'd seen her car, seen her sitting there behind the steering wheel. But then he walked over to the girl and grasped her by the elbow; she yanked her arm away from him. Effie could see that clearly. Then they walked together down Gerrard Street. Effie watched them go until they disappeared into the darkness of the winter night.

It surprised her when she realized that what she felt was pity. A younger woman might have felt insulted, even frightened to discover such darkness in one she believed to be the mirror image of herself. But Effie had learned that one must never assume that she knows anybody. The human personality is like a wardrobe, with varied ensembles of expression to produce reactions in another, or a slew of others. Love me, need me, fear me, laugh or cry with me, obey me. We rarely see another human in his moral nakedness. But that, she realized, was what had been revealed on Jarvis Street. She'd seen JC Campbell stripped of all his qualities, and the effect was not what she expected. Not that pity was less distressing than anger would have been, or jealousy. She understood that pity causes distance and distance is the cause of loneliness. She'd already known enough of loneliness.

———

*Only one of the three strangers in her living room stood when Conor introduced her. Faye Ferguson, he called her, which was strange. The "Faye," she thought, was private. The man who stood was slim, of medium height, with thinning hair. His smile was warm, his accent the same as Conor's. Mr. Harrison, Conor called him. He was wearing a sports coat. The other two were burly, wearing bulky leather jackets. "And this is Mr. Megahey, and Mr. Cahill." They nodded but remained seated, their expressions frozen in whatever moment she had interrupted. Old friends from home, Conor explained.*

*"Conor says you're becomin' an expert in Celtic history," said Harrison, whose interest seemed to be authentic, except that he pronounced the "Celtic" with an s. Seltic history. "And you're a Canadian, born and raised."*

*She nodded.*

*"You're a lucky woman," he said. "Canada is a grand country."*

*"Yes," she said. Then added, "But I've never considered nationality to be much of an asset."*

*Cahill smiled thinly. "Maybe that's because your nationality has never been a liability."*

*"The boys won't be stayin' for dinner," Conor interrupted. "The four of us are goin' for a pint, and we'll probably grab a bite to eat. You're all right, then?"*

*"That's fine," she said. "I have a lot of work to do."*

*They all stood. Harrison shook her hand and nodded. "It was a pleasure, Faye."*

*When they were gone, she wondered where and why she'd felt such loneliness before.*

———

Cassie's marriage was a wonderful distraction—a local anesthetic was how Effie thought of it—and she embraced the project as if it were her own. She'd become extremely fond of Ray. She saw him as a rare example of stable adulthood in a time defined by error and despair.

Screw it, she would say in her mind. Screw it, screw it, in a kind of sing-song mantra. She forced herself to laugh at all her new ironic insights, which were not, upon reflection, really new at all, being as they were about the darkness of male sexuality. Which made them seem that much more laughable.

The phone rang and she picked up, knowing it was probably a mistake. She said nothing, just waited.

"Faye?"

Silence.

"I saw you on the street today, on St. George. I had a class there. You were at the light, waiting. You seemed down. I almost crossed over to talk to you, but I kept my promise. You looked like you could use a friend. I can't stop thinking about you . . ."

She gently pressed the hang-up button, realizing that it was sadness she felt.

JC called and left a message, wondering if there was anything wrong. She almost called him back: "Anything wrong? What fucking planet are you living on, you idiot?" It was almost funny enough to have authorized a reengagement. But no. There were worse conditions than isolation. Loneliness doesn't have to be the end of the world.

On April seventh there was an urgent message from Molly Blue. Effie returned the call immediately.

"You know about Texas?" Molly said.

"What about it?"

"That character has lost what seems to be his last appeal. It'll be on the news tonight. A circuit court in New Orleans has turned him down. And our hero is packing his bag."

Effie sighed.

"You heard what I said?"

"Yes. I heard."

"I know you two are kind of estranged . . ."

"He told you that?"

"Not in so many words. But he asked me to look after the frigging cat for a few days. Effie, you have to intervene. This is serious. This could be the end of him."

"What makes you think I can influence him?"

"You're the only one who can."

"I'm busy with my daughter's wedding. I don't have the time, and I don't have the energy for a lost cause."

"A wedding . . ."

"Look," said Effie. "He isn't the only one who's had miserable experiences."

Molly's voice was shaky. "Forget yourself for a moment. Think of him as sick. He's sick. I don't know if it's from the knock on the head or from a whole life of hard knocks. But he's not normal. I know the man better than you do. Trust me. This is not JC. This is a composite of the wickedness he's witnessed. And now he seems to think that he can make sense of it all by watching one specific wicked moment up close, actually knowing the victim for once, really understanding the nature of what he's witnessing by allowing himself to be a part of it."

Effie, exhausted, said, "I have no idea what you're talking about."

"You don't have to understand," Molly said. "Just let your feeling for the man you think he is take over. Because that's who he really is. And you were one lucky broad the day you connected with that man. Don't blow it now."

Effie couldn't trust herself to survive another sentence. "I'll try," she said.

"You have to."

His phone rang and rang. And then she realized he'd disconnected his answering machine.

When Sextus called her at the office, he offered her two options: lunch or dinner. "I tried you at home a bunch of times, but nobody answers."

"What do you want?" she asked.

"Simple," he replied. "Lunch or dinner. Say dinner and I'll consider it a date and arrive with all kinds of expectations. Lunch? No strings attached."

For a moment she actually considered dinner. "Lunch," she said.

"I'm having lunch with your father tomorrow," she told Cassie.

"Lovely," said Cassie. "When did he arrive?"

"I'm surprised he hasn't been in touch."

"He hasn't been in touch for ages. I wasn't even sure if he was going to turn up for the tenth."

"He wouldn't miss your wedding."

"He's probably just here to get his oil changed with that silly Susan."

"Cassie, for God's sake . . ."

"In any case, when you see him, tell him I want you both to walk me down the aisle, if you think you're up to that."

"Of course I'm up to that. We're actually on quite good terms."

Sextus winced when she mentioned Stella even before the waiter came to take their order. She'd planned it that way. There would be no pussy-footing, no wasting time. Just get it out in the open and get it over with.

"I thought we were here to discuss Cassie's wedding."

"Indulge me," she said. "What was that about, anyway?"

"I have no idea what that was about," he said. "That's as much as I can tell you."

He was staring around the restaurant, his face a study in unhappiness. "Stella is one of two or three women I've met in my lifetime who actually impressed me."

"Impressed?"

"I don't know how to explain it."

"How did she impress you?"

He stared at her for about half a minute. "She reminded me of you."

"Oh, come on," Effie laughed. "Spare me."

"It's true," he said. "Your personalities are similar. I was attracted to her. Met her in town. Had coffee. Talked. Decided to meet again. Anyway, it was never going to be any kind of a relationship."

"So what prevented a *relationship?*"

"I didn't impress Stella as much as she impressed me."

"And what does it take to impress Stella?"

"I wish I knew."

They stared at each other for a while as Effie tried to maintain a rational perspective.

"So what about this young Susan?"

"Jesus."

"Come on. Lighten up." She summoned up her warmest smile. "Was she impressed?"

He hesitated. "Yes. As a matter of fact, she was quite impressed."

"I suppose she'll be coming to the wedding."

"No."

"Oh?"

"I haven't talked to her since I went back."

"Well, well."

"I realized when I looked at Cassie and what's his name—Ray whatever—how . . . what it must have looked like, me and Susan. Kind of indecent, I thought at the time."

"Indecent?"

"I don't think that anymore—not about them. I wish them well. But for myself . . . I know what I want in my life, and it isn't someone who still has Barbie dolls."

Effie laughed, and this time it wasn't the managed mirth that she'd been deploying to control the conversation but a spontaneous explosion of glee.

He shook his head. "This guy Ray, does he know what he's getting into?"

"Cassie, in case you haven't noticed, is way beyond the Barbie dolls. She's nearly thirty years old."

"Still. How old is Ray?"

"Late fifties, early sixties."

"You mark my words. He's going to turn you into a grandmother. You can tell by the gleam in his eye," Sextus said. "He's a baby-making machine. I've known old rams like that."

"She wants both of us to walk her down the aisle."

"So there's going to be an aisle?"

"Yes. Duncan will officiate. We give her away?"

"Sure," he said.

A waiter took their orders. He decided to have a whisky, double. She had a glass of wine. He had made her laugh, and it reminded her of what she'd missed in the long aftermath of their breakup, years ago. Humourless Conor. A series of brainy, insightful, tender, sentimental, macho, stupid—you name it—flings, relationships, one-night stands, not one of whom could make her laugh the way Sextus Gillis could. It was the laughter that came out of . . . *Oh my God,* she thought. *Compatibility?* It was a terrible thought, but it was true.

Then he ordered a second double.

Near the end of lunch he produced a briefcase and extracted from it a large package. He placed it between them on the table.

"I want you to take this with you," he said. "Keep it. If you ever get around to reading it, feel free to burn it afterwards."

"What is it?"

"I told you about it. It was going to be a memoir."

"A memoir."

"It started after a weekend I spent with John in '83. We talked through our difficulties, explored a lot of places that had always been off limits. It became a serial thing. We'd talk from time to time. Pooled a lot of understanding and came up with what I thought was a new appreciation of what made us the way we were. Are. All of us. You included. Duncan. Our whole confused generation, in a way. The mutant spawn of a rotten century."

"Those had to be some conversations."

"Whatever. I did a lot of research. Phoned people, wrote to people. Old war veterans, etcetera. A few years back I started putting together quite a yarn about this interesting character, namely me."

"I'm not sure I want to read it."

"Seriously," he said.

"If it's about you, why were you interested in the war? Your father wasn't in the war."

"But yours was, and Uncle Sandy was. And it affected you and

Duncan. It affected John big time. And I assume it will have affected your daughter."

Effie shrugged. "None of this should come as a surprise. We don't come out of nothing when we're born."

"Right." He stared at her for what seemed like a long time. "I'm tempted to order another drink," he said.

She put her hand on his. "Bad idea. And I have a meeting this afternoon."

"I want to give you a heads-up," he said suddenly. "If you read this thing."

She stiffened. His face was flushed and he was sitting poker straight. He looked away from her.

"You get particular about small details when you write something autobiographical. So I started getting particular about us, when we did what, where, etcetera. If you follow me."

She frowned. "Why on earth does that matter for a goddamn book?"

"It doesn't really," he said. "I just started obsessing about Cassie. Was there a chance that—"

"Jesus," she said. "I can't believe—"

"So I went to a doctor."

"You did what?"

"I had a test, and do you know what?"

She looked at her watch, suddenly desperate to leave.

"I was borderline," he said, almost angrily. "I was just above the threshold of sterility."

"So why bring this up now?" She was half angry, half full of pity for him. "This was what? Nearly thirty years ago. So even if you weren't class-A breeding stock, obviously I am. The outcome was okay, wouldn't you agree?"

He nodded.

"How come you never mentioned this when we got back together a couple of years ago?"

"Because I persuaded myself that my weak, watery sperm had been enough to do the job. The evidence was there. She's the picture of a Gillis. There was an old photograph of my Gillis grandmother at home, when Grandma was a little girl. They're identical. So I put it out of my head."

"Okay. So?"

"She was also John's grandmother."

"Oh, for Christ's sake."

"You know John got married."

"Yes."

"You probably don't know that his wife is knocked up."

"So what?"

"She was up the stump *before* the wedding. The word is that's why they got married at all. Makes it kind of hard for me to continue my delusion."

"Sextus," she said. "What the hell difference does it make?"

"Well, you tell me. Who is Cassie's real father?"

She stared at him for a long time, weighing possible answers. And there were many. But then there was a voice: *It's only what we know that matters . . .*

"You are," she said quietly.

"I don't believe you," he said.

"That's up to you."

"I didn't mean to let this get away from me like that. I'm sorry. I spoiled your lunch."

"You didn't," she said. "You made me laugh. I haven't laughed for ages."

"Oh?" he said. "Don't tell me that you and Jesus are having problems."

"Jesus?"

"That's what we used to call JC years ago. Because of the JC thing. But also because he'd be the last of us to get in trouble. But when he did, he had a miraculous way of getting out of it."

And she laughed again. They'd called him Jesus. And she laughed some more as she walked up University to her meeting.

## 14

She stared at the manila envelope for a long time before she opened it and extracted the first few pages. *Why Men Lie,* he'd called it. She smiled, wanted to ask, "Where's the punctuation mark?" Or was it a statement, something he was now prepared to disclose to someone he had lied to. She doubted that. She stuffed the pages back inside the envelope, then placed it back in her briefcase. *This belongs at home,* she thought. It wasn't something for a nosy student or colleague or janitor to find. She surveyed the tiny office, books and manuscripts piled everywhere, promising the truth of one thing or another; truthful revelations about human history.

She loved her books as she loved the knowledge they bestowed. But she was afraid of what he'd written; afraid of what he knew; afraid of why and what he wanted her to know—the power his knowledge gave him. *What is the point,* she asked herself, *of knowing all the generalities if we are in the dark about our own particulars? Life is but an aggregation of particulars. But must we know them all? Is forgetfulness not merciful?* She well knew how one particular of a forgotten part of life, suddenly remembered, can ruin everything.

On her desk there was a photograph of Duncan, standing on the bow of his boat. He was smiling broadly, dressed in jeans and T-shirt, arms folded. She thought of all the photos that litter people's lives, stored in envelopes, inside boxes. No names or dates. People captured in moments that seemed important at the time. Moments of transient happiness, recorded as specific images, particulars of life that someone thought should be indelible; but without the words, the images are only mortal, as fragile as the subjects and the living memory.

She picked up the photograph of her brother and realized that she couldn't precisely remember why or when she'd taken it—or if, in fact, she had taken it herself. Then it came back to her: Stella had given it to her. But when had Stella taken it? And what might explain that smile, a smile she knew—because she knew her brother well—to be unusual? Would there come a day when someone would invest a lot of energy and time to discover who this man was, where he was and when, and whom he was smiling at?

*I could do it now,* she thought. She could inscribe that enigmatic photograph so that blind posterity would know at least that it was Duncan, perhaps that he was *Father* Duncan; that the boat was called *Jacinta,* for reasons he'd never shared with her; that the moment was recorded by a woman whose name was Stella Fortune; that she was his friend, and maybe more than that; and that she wounded him. But now Effie was in the realm of speculation, and speculation is the mother of exaggeration and untruth and suffering.

She opened the briefcase again, studied the package that contained a manuscript, said the word out loud. "Speculation." Then she snapped the briefcase shut.

The wedding celebration was to be in the house that Ray and Cassie shared in Riverdale. It was on a quiet street not far from Walden. A Thursday night, two evenings before the marriage, Effie and Cassie were busily preparing. It would be a small event, twenty special guests, all coming to the house after the ceremony for a gathering of close friends and family.

Ray was in his den, watching television. He called out, "Effie, you should come and see this."

It was the evening newscast, and Molly Blue was reporting on a new development in a death-row story in Huntsville, Texas. As Effie arrived in the doorway, she heard a reference to the Texas governor, who seemed to be expressing disappointment in the action of a judge somewhere. There was a photo in the corner of the TV screen, a white-haired man with a kind face, the name Sam Williams superimposed. Then a picture of a small room, not unlike a doctor's examining room. The only furniture in the pale green room was an imposing gurney. Molly said, "The stay came through just minutes before the scheduled execution."

Then there was a slender woman, pretty in an earnest way, talking about another effort to get the Williams case before the United States Supreme Court. The woman was identified as Sandra Bowers, attorney for the condemned man. Then JC appeared. He was smiling broadly as if, in a way, the reprieve had been for him.

Molly asked him questions and he was objective in the answers, betraying no personal concern about the killer at the centre of the drama. He spoke of "process," alleged irregularities at trial and certain ambiguities that raised disturbing questions in the minds of many people about the legitimacy of the death penalty. Effie remembered that "legitimacy" was a word he used frequently. Then he was gone, replaced by a group of protesters waving placards in the darkness outside what she presumed was the prison.

And then Molly was reporting something else, and Effie's anger crystallized. She had watched him talking on the television screen as if he were a stranger, extracted from reality by the distancing effect of the technology. But now he was real again, as was the pain and disappointment he had created.

"He looks great on TV," Cassie said behind her.

She couldn't think of a reply.

"I wonder if that means he'll be here Saturday."

"I wouldn't count on it," Effie said.

"Not sure if you heard the news from here," the message said. "In any case, I'll fill you in when I see you. There's a lot to talk about. I'll be getting in late Friday, so I guess it'll be at the church Saturday. Night, hon."

She listened to the message twice as she sat with her coffee in the morning. Her kitchen looked out over the backyards of her neighbourhood. Artificial ponds and porches, back decks littered with the evidence of normal lives: bicycles, toboggans, skis. In her head she rehearsed what she felt would be their final conversation. She would be calm. She would be resolute. She studied the backyards, imagining the interlocking lives behind brick walls, beneath tight rooftops. Kids grumbling; couples cuddling or laying out quotidian arrangements; dogs and cats yearning for outdoors. She wondered why he'd called her "hon." It wasn't a word she'd heard him use before.

She stood, poured more coffee. The sadness thickened, threatening to metastasize to full-blown sorrow. For her own protection she revisited the scene on Jarvis Street. That a man could be so

totally undone was shocking to her. It made Sextus's serial trans-
gressions seemed profoundly trivial. At least he channelled his
infantile fantasies in directions that were, dare she think it, healthy.
At least she could identify with them.

She thought of Stella: Who could blame him?


"I think I owe you an apology," Duncan said when he called.

"Oh?" Effie was confused.

"I never followed up, after your visit to the shelter. We were
going to talk."

"It wasn't anything important," she said.

"The Epiphany came and went. Are we any more enlightened
now?"

"Not really."

"Will he be back for the wedding?"

"It's tomorrow," she said.

"Aren't you two celebrating an anniversary yourselves?"

"How so?"

"Wasn't it last Easter, you and JC—"

"I'd forgotten," she replied.


Saturday, April tenth, she rose early. The house was silent, and she
sat for a moment, relishing the stillness. She wasn't looking
forward to the day. Even though this was her daughter getting
married, she was prepared for the discomfort she always felt at
weddings, all the rituals of happiness that were, no matter how
communal, essentially exclusive. She was always happy *for* the
couple, but was never able to rise above the sense of failure she
felt when reminded of the false beginnings and unhappy endings
in her life. She knew that she'd be spending time with all of them

today: John, Sextus, Conor, JC Campbell. They'd be with her even if she didn't go.

She dressed carefully. Her appearance, she thought when she made her final survey, was deliciously seductive. She called a cab.

The church was small. St. Martin's was a place that Ray remembered from his student days. There had been a Mass in Latin and a choir that was exceptional, so he'd go there for the peacefulness he felt revisiting a liturgy he remembered from his boyhood. Ray had a sentimental streak, Effie had realized with some amusement. Duncan consulted with the chancery and was assured that the use of Latin had been authorized, that the church was "kosher," as the deacon he had spoken with described it.

She was early, but Sextus was waiting in the vestibule. The dark suit made him taller, slimmer, younger. He hugged her, pressed his cheek to hers. "You look edible," he whispered. She hugged him back, shushing him.

"Are we the only ones here?" she asked.

"Most of them are inside," he said. "Maybe fifteen people."

She realized that he had placed an arm casually around her waist. She would normally have moved away, but she felt stabilized by the loose comfort of his strength. She'd long, long ago ceased to think of him as strong.

The church door opened and JC entered. If he was surprised to see them, he managed to suppress it. She instinctively moved closer to Sextus, felt his hip firm against her own.

"Hey," said JC smiling.

"Well, look who's here," she said, and instantly regretted it. "When did you get back?"

"I got in late," he said. "I left a message, but you've probably been busy."

His smile was weary. He extended a hand, and Sextus grasped it warmly. "You're looking jet-lagged," he said.

JC seemed surprised. "Slept like a log." Then, nodding toward the interior of the church, "I'd better go in. I'll catch you later."

Walking past them, he brushed Effie's hand. The gesture was too casual, she thought, and the anger flared, but the church door opened again and it was Cassie, with Ray and his son, the best man, close behind.

At the climax of the service she realized that Sextus had grasped her hand and was holding it firmly. And when Ray placed the ring on Cassie's finger, she felt what seemed to be a shudder passing through him.

JC was near the back of the church. She fought an urge to look around.

As the celebration unfolded around her, she resisted a powerful longing to be somewhere else, alone. It was a feeling of irrelevance, she realized, or maybe it was simply isolation. She wanted to just slip away. Wave down a taxi, retreat homeward. Surely anyone who mattered to her would understand her reasons, but she knew she had to stay. Simple courtesy dictated that she be there. She resolved to avoid the alcohol, except for mandatory toasts.

JC made it easy by appointing himself bartender. She couldn't imagine engaging with him, even for the simple purpose of acquiring a glass of wine. She remembered she had brought a bottle of expensive single malt Scotch for Ray and had stashed it in Cassie's office upstairs.

*I'll crack the bottle and have one,* she thought. *I can replace the bottle later. No harm in one.* Then she hesitated, remembering her father.

*He never stops with one.*

A familiar wave of anxiety increased her need for a stiff drink and at the same time made her feel vulnerable and weak. She went upstairs with a water glass from the kitchen cupboard.

The little office was peaceful. She savoured the privacy and the sharp, smoky sting of whisky on her tongue. She felt removed from, but at the same time part of, the happy chatter she could hear spooling out below her, the strands of celebration like ribbons. She smiled at the ripples and, sometimes, small explosions of laughter. This quiet moment couldn't last. There would have to be a reckoning. She drained the glass and walked downstairs.

JC was drinking cola. She watched him pour, squeeze a wedge of lemon, sip distractedly. He was smiling, easily engaging with the guests, pouring liquor liberally, frowning at the upraised hands of moderation. She could almost hear him: *Let your hair down . . . this is Cassie's special day.*

The longing almost choked her. How she wished she could reverse their lives, rewind to the summer and the autumn of '98, the spontaneity, emotional transparency, the feeling of security and confidence. All gone now.

Then Sextus was beside her. He leaned close, face flushed, drink in hand. "I plan to scoop tonight," he whispered.

"Scoop?" she laughed. "I haven't heard that in thirty years."

"What about it?" he said. "Come home with me."

"Home! What home?"

"I have a hotel room for the night. Then I'll be staying here, after they leave for their little holiday or honeymoon . . . whatever they call it these days."

"Thanks anyway," she said. And walked toward the bar.

———

"I guess we should talk," she said, forcing a smile.

Then they were sitting facing each other in Cassie's office. She had turned away from his embrace, only a simple gesture of familiarity on his part, she felt. A hug exchanged by friends who haven't seen each other for a while. Her reaction had set the mood.

"So," he said. "I suppose you heard what happened in Huntsville."

"You know what I think about Huntsville."

"Yes." He was studying his hands, twirling his thumbs around each other. "It was quite a moment. I went to see him yesterday morning."

He nodded toward the whisky bottle. "Do you think she'd mind?"

"Go ahead," said Effie.

He poured into the water glass she had used. "What about you?"

"I'm fine," she said.

"Here's to us," he said, with a questioning expression.

"Yes," she said. "We should talk about us."

"Where do you want to start?"

She wanted to reply, "Let's start a year ago, at Easter. Let's relive every day and maybe find the moment when this awkwardness began." But instead she said, "Let's start on Jarvis Street."

He seemed confused. He looked away. "Jarvis Street?"

She waited, then repeated, "Jarvis Street."

He sipped his drink. "Okay. What do you want to know about Jarvis Street?"

"We could start with Tammy."

"Ah," he said. "Tammy."

"I just don't understand you," she said. "Exposing yourself and, I suppose, us to the likes of that Tammy and her pimp—"

"What pimp?" he interrupted.

"Robert or whatever his name is . . . in St. Jamestown."

"How the hell do you know that?"

He was standing, drink forgotten. "You'd better explain," he said.

"Me explain?" she said, outrage rising.

"I want to know where you got that name."

She'd never seen this look, this colour in his face. She looked away, suddenly afraid and sad. "It doesn't matter."

"Believe me," he said, "it matters. Where did you get the name Robert? And St. Jamestown?"

"His sister told me," she said wearily.

"Whose sister?"

"That Robert."

"His sister?" Now he laughed, and sat down. "You're good," he said. "I've been trying to track that motherfucker down for months. And now you tell me what his name is and where he lives. You know his sister!" He laughed again. "His sister! Jesus Christ, I can't believe it." He drained the glass. "I've gotta go," he said. And he stood again.

"Wait."

But he was gone. She heard his footfall on the stairs, then heard the front door closing.

———

*The door slammed behind her, but Conor quickly yanked it open.*

*"And where do you think you're goin' now?" he asked softly. Once she'd considered it charming, how he pronounced "now." "Where you're goin' nye?" But the charm was gone.*

*"I need to be alone," she said. "I need to think."*

*The conversation had veered out of control quite unexpectedly. He'd been examining the business card with what she thought was amusement. "And what do ye think the RCMP security lads would want to talk to me about?"*

*"You tell me," she said. "He wasn't here long enough to tell me anything."*

*"He didn't mention any names at all?"*

"*Mr. Cahill,*" *she said, hoping that the ironic use of* "*mister*" *registered.*

"*Ah. Cahill. That poor fella has been a cop magnet all his life.*" *He sighed.* "*And did they say anythin' else?*"

"*He called me Faye.*"

"*The Mountie did?*"

"*Don't you think that's odd?*"

"*It's your name, isn't it?*"

"*You're the only one who calls me Faye.*"

"*Well, now.*" *An odd expression crossed his face, almost fear, and it empowered her.*

"*I don't want you bringing whatever it is you're up to into my house,*" *she said, more loudly than she'd intended.*

*He smiled, fear now past.* "'*My house,*' *is it now?*" *His eyes were dark, with an unfamiliar glint.* "*Let's not get too carried away with the technicalities of legal ownership.*"

*And perhaps it was the tone that made her feel the stirring of something she hadn't known for years, the dark presence of danger.*

*She stood and walked resolutely out the door.*

———

Now the paralysis of dread set in, the disorienting doubt. The integrity of his reaction left her baffled.

"Did JC just leave?" It was Duncan, his face perplexed.

She nodded.

"What happened?"

She shrugged, distrustful of her voice.

Duncan sat.

"I asked him about that Tammy," she said finally.

Duncan sighed, folded his hands across his stomach. "And what did he tell you?"

"Nothing."

Duncan reached for the whisky bottle and the now well-used water glass, poured a modest drink. Sighed again.

"I've known about her for months," Effie said. "At first it never crossed my mind that he'd be so irresponsible . . ."

"You said he told you nothing," Duncan said.

She struggled not to shout. "For God's sake, he didn't have to. I'm not a child. I know what men want from people like that. But Jesus, some child prostitute in an alleyway on Gerrard Street? You'd think he could do better than that."

"Stop, stop, stop," Duncan said. "People will hear you. And you don't know what you're talking about."

"Well, if you know so much, you tell me," she said, tears threatening.

Duncan shook his head slowly, then sipped his drink. "He made me promise not to tell anybody."

"Tell anybody what?" she said.

"How about if I track him down and talk him into telling you himself?" He leaned close to her, put a hand on her arm.

"Am I interrupting something?" Sextus said from the doorway.

Duncan looked up sharply. "Come back later."

Sextus backed off.

"No," Effie said. "You have to tell me now. Later won't matter. Consider it a moral compromise for a higher cause."

Duncan smiled. "Right. Moral compromise. My specialty."

"I didn't mean that," she said.

"Secrets are funny," he said. "They demand fidelity regardless of their worth. Even an unworthy secret is a test of character. That's why I've never messed with your secrets." He drank.

She studied his face, meeting his searching eyes. "I don't need a priest just now," she said. "I need a brother. More than that, I need a friend."

He stood. "He's looking for somebody. He's kind of desperate."

"Who could he be looking for that would make him that desperate?" she asked.

Duncan sat again. "I'm surprised he didn't tell you. I don't know why he wouldn't. He cares a lot about you, you know. Maybe he wanted to protect you."

"From what?" she said.

"You didn't know that he has a granddaughter?"

"A what?"

"A granddaughter."

"Not that Tammy?"

"No, not Tammy. I understand you met the girl's mother last summer. She lives in Port Hawkesbury."

Effie nodded.

"Anyway, his daughter grew up in Isle Madame. And years ago she—I think her name is Sylvia—had a daughter that she never told JC about, until recently. I don't know why he didn't let you in on it."

"And she's in Toronto?"

"We think. She was last seen in Halifax. She had a black boyfriend, which the mother found . . . alarming. The mother did some checking, learned some unsavoury details about the guy, who's more than ten years older than the kid. Anyway, she heard that this boyfriend was a pimp, running girls from Halifax in Toronto. It isn't an implausible story."

"Black boyfriends don't have to be pimps," Effie said tartly.

"You think I don't know that?" he said. "In any case, JC asked me to help find her, to make some inquiries around the shelter. I didn't know he'd launched his own investigation . . . until I saw him talking to Tammy one night a few months ago. But that's the story."

"You're right," she said sorrowfully. "I don't know why he didn't tell me."

"He's always been a complicated guy."

"And guys never change."

"I don't know about that," said Duncan. "Now why don't you come downstairs with me, mingle a bit. It's a big day for your daughter."

"I think I'll go home," she said.

## 15

After Cassie's wedding there was a week of silence. Finally she called him, got the answering machine, apologized. She didn't try to qualify or evade. She'd been wrong. She had given it a lot of thought. Her grotesque suspicion had been unforgivable. But by offering an apology, she might at least recover a small measure of her self-respect.

The waves of self-reproach had been cleansing, in a way. Taken as a whole, her lives with men, for all the grief, had immunized her to a very real extent. Finally she understood that self-reproach was just another opportunity for self-improvement. It was, really, diagnostic. And after a long night of anger, loneliness, sorrow, self-pity, fear of growing old alone and, finally, the flood of tears, she felt a transformation. Failure was, she realized, a form of therapy.

Sextus called on April twentieth. She hadn't heard from him in ten days. He seemed subdued.

"Just wondering how you are," he said.

"I'm okay," she said. "And you?"

"I'm good. Look, I'm sorry if I seemed to be hitting on you at the wedding. But you know me."

"Don't worry about it."

"I don't think I'll be sticking around," he said. "Think I'll head back. Maybe you can check their place now and then while they're away, honeymooning or whatever. I find it creepy, being here with all their stuff. Every time I open a drawer, I'm afraid of what I'll find." His laugh was humourless.

She felt an impulse to offer comfort, but she resisted it.

"I'll be down probably in July," she volunteered. "John's baby must be due about then."

"That's what I hear," he said. "I don't suppose you got around to reading the great memoir yet."

"Not yet," she said. Again she resisted offering the reassurance that might comfort. A white lie would have been appropriate: "I've only started" or "I'll give you my reaction when I've had time to read a bit more." Her new protocol: words reserved for comprehension, stripped of sentimental purpose.

"So we'll probably see you down there," he said.

"*Ma bhios mi beo,*" she said.

"Whatever that means."

"Your dad would say that anytime he was referring to some possible future happening. 'If I'm alive.'"

He laughed. "That was the old man being the optimist."

"Bye for now," she said.

"Bye."

She'd hardly put the phone down when it rang again. He had an afterthought, perhaps.

"Yes?" she said.

But there was only silence.

———

Three days after she had left the apology on JC's answering machine, he called back and asked if they could get together. Maybe for a drink or dinner.

"Would that be wise?" she wondered.

Wise or not, he said, there was a lot to be explained. By both. "I was surprised to hear you apologize," he said. "I wasn't sure why."

"I jumped to some dire conclusions. I was wrong."

"Well," he said, "not necessarily. Not in the circumstances."

"What circumstances?"

"I realized afterwards, when I thought it through. You don't know me very well. Blind trust is a lot to expect from someone who doesn't really know you."

"I wonder if it's too late to correct that," she said.

"Let's see," he said.

They had lunch and, on the Friday, dinner. And she went home with him and stayed the weekend. They mostly talked, but in the intervals the physical intensity obliterated doubt.

The girl he was looking for had always been a problem for her mother, her teachers, the entire community. She was barely sixteen, but she'd been missing for months. There had always been, it seemed, conflict with her mom, so when she'd asked to spend a weekend with some friends in Halifax last fall, her mother welcomed the prospect of her absence. She began to worry, though, when days passed with no contact from the girl.

Her name was Marguerite. She had told her mother that she would stay with some university students she knew from high school. She'd always been advanced in school, doubled up some grades, and as a consequence she ran with an older crowd of kids.

Her mother speculated that it would have been a strain on her, always trying to keep up, that it explained why she was so resentful of anything that drew attention to her immaturity.

By mid-week Sylvia had contacted the Halifax police, who, in the manner of policemen everywhere, declined to take the matter seriously. She was probably a runaway. There were legions of them out there, teenagers on the lam from parents, boredom and authority. Eventually they surfaced somewhere—most of them, at least.

But they'd obviously gone looking. A week after her first call, they were able to inform her that the kid had been seen in the company of a black man whose name they hadn't yet been able to obtain. They'd been spotted in a dense complex of downtown drinking establishments known to the young in Halifax as the Liquor Dome. The girl didn't look unhappy, according to the bouncer who had recognized her photograph.

Further independent inquiries by her mother produced the worrying intelligence that a number of young black men were recruiting prostitutes in Halifax and moving them to Toronto. Sylvia convinced herself that this had been her daughter's fate and begged JC for help.

"When did she bring you into it?" Effie asked.

"In January sometime."

"And you never thought of telling me?"

He shrugged. "I guess I wasn't thinking straight."

"But now . . . ?"

"Let's hope."

JC had eventually discussed the problem with Duncan, who promised to make some inquiries: his homeless friends might have noticed someone new among the hookers on the street.

Effie interrupted, "I hope you aren't angry at Duncan for telling me."

"I should have told you myself. I don't know why I didn't."

"She matters to you, doesn't she?"

"She matters. I don't know why."

He had immediately started making casual inquiries in places frequented by men in search of sex that was quick, anonymous and cheap. He met Tammy. He'd heard a rumour that she had a black boyfriend who came from Halifax. She brushed him off, even attacked him once. It only made him more persistent. Eventually she agreed to help him. "I figured it was just to get rid of me," he said. "But I gave her my business card, just in case."

"When was that?" she asked. "The card."

He shrugged. "I forget. A month or so ago. On Jarvis."

"You've heard nothing more?"

"Nothing."

She fought a wave of remorse. "I can't imagine how you feel."

"Feel? I'm impressed. You managed to find out more than I could without really trying. How did you pull that off?"

"I was spying on you," she said. "I just didn't know what to think. I know it was . . . I saw you with this Tammy once. I just happened to be driving along Jarvis, and there you were. Sometime later, I saw her again, and she was with another girl. By the time I stopped, she was gone, but—"

"Another girl?"

"She was a black girl. I told her I was Father Duncan's sister, and that was when she mentioned her brother, Robert—Tammy's boyfriend, I think. And St. Jamestown."

He shook his head. "A needle in a haystack. Some hustler named Robert in St. Jamestown."

"You've been there looking, though?"

He nodded. "Now I can't find Tammy either. But at the end of the day, it doesn't matter, does it? The world is full of Tammys and Roberts and Marguerites. Lost people, all of them. Just getting by. Trying not to think of where they're heading. Every one of them a product of some other loss."

She placed a hand on his. "At the end of the day, it does matter." She smiled at him. "I never thought I'd hear either of us using that tired expression. 'At the end of the day.' Somebody I knew used it till I thought I'd lose my mind."

"Your Conor."

"How did you guess?"

"The Irish love it. 'At the end of the day.' It suits their outlook perfectly." His accent was a perfect imitation of a Belfast lilt. "Whatever became of that fellow, anyway?"

"He died suddenly," she said.

"You said once that you suspected he was a terrorist."

"I said that?" She shrugged. "I suppose he was."

"Was it . . . ?"

"No," she said. "Nothing like that. He owned some gyms. One day he was jogging on a treadmill, and that was when it happened."

JC laughed. "Sorry. But that's kind of weird."

"It was at the time of all the hunger strikers, and he was all worked up over that."

"I covered the hunger strikers," he said.

"I suppose you did."

"You realize that he was probably a gunrunner. The IRA had them planted all over the world, set up as legitimate businessmen. There was even a banker here in Toronto."

"Conor was getting out of it. He promised me."

"Men promise all sorts of things." He was smiling.

"Conor always told the truth. He told me he'd only lied to me once. And that was about Sextus."

JC was frowning. "What about Sextus?"

"Shortly before he died, he told me Sextus probably wasn't as bad as he'd made him out to be. Conor didn't like reporters much."

"You're kidding. He told you that?" He laughed abruptly. "You're sure he died on a treadmill?"

"He died on a treadmill. It was a heart attack. I saw the death certificate."

"I can't imagine—"

"I hate it when you go away," she interrupted.

"I hate to go away," he said.

"I know you do."

On May 19, Molly Blue phoned to let her know that she'd just seen the story on the AP wire: the stay of execution for Sam Williams had been vacated by a U.S. circuit court in New Orleans. Effie didn't understand what she was being told. "Does this mean he's been reprieved again?" she asked.

"No. The opposite," Molly said. "It means he'll be getting another execution date any day now, and we'd better get ready for it."

"Does JC know?"

"I'd be surprised if he didn't," Molly said. "I expect he heard the news straight from the guy's lawyer."

Effie thanked her for the call.

JC called five minutes later. "There'll probably be something in the papers about Sam tomorrow," he said. "It's my guess they'll be setting a new execution date fairly soon." He sounded weary.

"Have you heard from him?"

"I had a letter the other day. He actually told me in April, right afterwards, that he regarded the stay as a technicality—postponing the inevitable, I think he said."

"What will you do?"

"Whatever he wants me to do."

"Yes," she said. "But can I ask one question?"

"Fire away."

"Why?"

It was a long pause, but she knew that he was still there. Finally he said, "I want to see if dignity can survive impotence."

"Dear man," she said. "You, of all people, don't have to worry about impotence—or dignity."

"We all have to worry about impotence," he said.

The campus was subdued in June. There were summer students, but they seemed older, more dedicated to their studies. Effie had always enjoyed the post-graduation serenity of the place, the anticlimactic lull that follows the spasmodic intensity of finals, marks and the infectious ecstasy of students in the moment of relief that they can pretend briefly to be a permanent condition of their lives. The place was almost deserted as she walked away toward home.

She would remember June of 1999 as a blur of drink and food and talk. At first it was his narrative: romances that became relationships and died from distance or disinterest; exotic travel in a bubble of American and media entitlement; awful conflicts sparsely told. He described the final burnout, and she listened carefully for evidence of Molly's truthfulness.

Her own disclosures became more structured through his gentle questioning.

"Why don't you just start at the beginning?" he began. "Your mum died. It was just you and Duncan and your father."

"There's just so much I don't remember," she said. "And a lot of the things I do remember seem like bad dreams. Don't you have the same problem? Separating the real from the nightmares? You must."

"No," he said.

"Lucky you," she said miserably. "But you, of all people, must know that it isn't useful and it isn't fair to speak of things as fact when you aren't sure, when dreams and fantasies pollute your memory. Conor never trusted memory."

"Why don't you work back? Tell me how you got involved with this guy Conor."

"He just materialized at the right time. I felt betrayed by Sextus. I was alone in a strange place. I had a little girl. I had no job, no prospects. He was kind."

"Kindness is an asset, but . . ."

"Kindness is better than nothing."

"Okay. You needed kindness. What did he need from you?"

"I don't know. He had his cause. He didn't need a lot from me."

"That sounds hellish. Maybe you were window dressing. Part of his disguise."

She turned away. He caught her shoulder. She shook free. "Conor made me what I am."

"You made you what you are."

"Conor taught me that the most effective form of therapy is self-improvement. He nagged me into a master's program, then a Ph.D. He left me well off, materially. Years after he was gone, the head of Celtic at the university called out of the blue and offered me a contract. He'd been a friend of Conor's."

"And how much did you tell this fellow, the mysterious Conor?"

She shrugged.

"And did you feel better after that?"

"Not really."

He put an arm around her shoulder. "Whenever you feel up to it, maybe you can have a go at it again."

She nodded.

———

*"That knife," Conor said. "Can you describe it now?" His voice was soft, his eyes intense.*

*"It was just a knife."*

*"What did it look like?"*

*"It was long. It looked sharp."*

*"And where did he keep it? When he'd bring it out, where would he take it from?"*

*"From in his pants, I think."*

*"From his pants?"*

*"Or it was in his boot. Why does it matter?"*

*"How old were you when you first felt threatened?"*

*"I think I was about thirteen. I don't remember exactly."*

*"Can you describe the knife?"*

*"Sort of. Maybe like a hunting knife."*

*"A huntin' knife?"*

*"Something like that."*

*"Can you tell me how he held the knife?"*

*"What do you mean, how he held it?"*

*"Did he hold it in a fist? Or maybe like this? Like you would a small knife?" He held up a hand, thumb and forefinger together.*

*"I don't remember, really. He held it in front of him."*

*"In front of him? Where in front of him?"*

*"Christ, how am I supposed to remember where in front of him? I mostly just remember the knife being there, in his hand."*

*Conor sighed. "It's all right, love."*

*"I remember getting sick."*

*"You got sick?"*

*"I threw up afterwards."*

*His arms were around her then. "They're all gone now. The whole lot of them, poor bastards."*

*"Yes," she said. "All gone."*

————

It was a Friday night, July 2, 1999. They were at JC's kitchen table, the cat, Sorley, curled up on his lap. They were discussing a plan to revisit Cape Breton that summer, perhaps recover some of the magic of the year before and, in the process, exorcise some demons.

"You said something in the cemetery, the day we visited the graves last summer. It stayed with me."

He frowned. "I don't remember."

"You said that people aren't bad, they just do bad things sometimes."

"Okay."

"You really think that?"

"It's what got me through a lot of pretty depressing stuff."

"But do you think it's really true?"

"Yes," he said. "I believe it's true. It's the closest thing I have to a religious belief. If I thought for a moment that people are as wicked as the things they do, I'd be living in . . . Bornish."

She laughed. "You'd be the only one there."

"Exactly."

"I think I did a wicked thing once," she said. He waited, watching her face.

———

*She was racing through the field toward the Gillis place. The ground was rough, but it was quicker than the road. Through weeds and brambles, across a barbed wire fence, through a brook.*

*Sandy Gillis ran to meet her. "What's the matter with you?" His eyes were wild.*

*"I want Mrs. Gillis."*

*"She went to town. What's the matter?"*

*She backed away. "Nothing."*

*"Is he still there?"*

*"No."*

*"Where did he go?"*

*"I don't know."*

*"I'll find him."*

*"Please, no . . . don't hurt him. Please."*

———

"And when exactly was this?"

"It was just before Remembrance Day, 1963."

"So, go on."

She shook her head. "Another time. There's something else I need to talk about."

"Oh?" His smile was thinly spread.

"This guy . . . the stalker who keeps calling me—I want to tell you how he got my phone number. I did something stupid."

The telephone rang. "I should get it," he said.

She watched him as he listened intently. Then he said, "Keep an eye on her. Try to keep her there." He was silent for about thirty more seconds. "Sorry to hear that. I suppose you knew him pretty well."

He put the phone down. "That was Duncan."

"I see," she said.

"I have to go out," he said.

"That Tammy?" She felt a combination of fatigue, relief, despair.

"Duncan said she's hanging around in a crowd in front of the shelter. I'm going to grab a cab and go down."

"I'll drive you."

"No. I want you to stay here. I'll be back shortly. I have to hear the rest."

"She's already brushed you off more than once . . ."

"Duncan says she seems to be with a black guy."

At the door he turned. "I almost forgot. Duncan says he has to go to Nova Scotia for a funeral tomorrow. His bishop died. He says he might be gone for a few days. Maybe visit people. Said to tell you that."

JC was gone all night. Day was breaking when she finally went home. The city traffic was moving quickly, flowing on the caffeinated urgency of early risers. She was worried, but whatever apprehension she might have felt during the long night was ragged now.

At home she undressed slowly, showered, lay in her bed and waited. He would call and explain.

She had fallen into a deep sleep, and for a moment the ringing of the telephone seemed to be part of a dream that she would never, afterwards, be able to recall.

She sat up quickly, fumbled for the phone. It was ten o'clock.

"My God, you had me worried," she said.

But it was Molly she was talking to. "We have to meet."

"What about?"

"Dooney's," she said. "Be there in twenty minutes."

"What's happened?"

"I'll tell you when I see you."

Molly's producer had called her at home and asked her to come to the office as soon as possible. It was supposed to be her day off. She was not to be disturbed by anything less urgent than, say, final settlement of the Palestinian–Israeli conflict. That or World War Three.

When she'd arrived at the boss's office, there were two strangers waiting for her, both in suits. They were policemen. They wanted to know when she had last seen JC Campbell.

"Yesterday," she told them.

Had he been in touch the night before?

"No," she said.

They would appreciate her discretion, they told her. And obviously anything discussed would be strictly off the record. Had Mr. Campbell ever spoken of a Robert Borden?

Molly answered no. She'd never heard the name. Well, other than the former prime minister.

Effie was staring at her. Prime minister? "That's the look I got from the cops," said Molly.

The cops had informed Molly that the Robert they were interested in was no prime minister. He was a well-known street hustler, into dope and the sex trade. His body had been found in a dumpster off Gerrard Street just after midnight. No big loss, really. But murder, clearly.

"So what's your relationship with Mr. Campbell?" one man had asked, notebook now in hand.

"We work together," Molly had told him tersely.

They wanted to know for how long, and what she thought of JC Campbell's character, his temperament, and that was when she lost it. "Now what the hell would JC have to do with some dead drug dealer?" she asked.

Maybe nothing, the second policeman said. And that was when they told her they'd picked up Mr. Campbell near his home at three a.m., hoping he could be of some assistance in their investigation. "Would you have any idea where he might have been coming from?"

"I have no idea. What's he telling you?"

At this point they became cautious. They could only say that there was credible information that Mr. Campbell had been tracking Borden for quite some time, that his interest was not professional, that it was something personal.

"Then," said Molly, "they asked about you. *Dr. Gillis.* They seemed to be reading your name from one of your business cards. You can expect a call."

Effie, speechless, shrugged and looked away.

"For Christ's sake, Effie. Do you know *anything* about this?"

But Effie didn't really hear the question. The roar of the city and the clatter of the mid-morning coffee shop were merging in her head, shattering the words, reducing thought to mental spasms.

# four

❧❧❧

*Time past and time future*
*What might have been and what has been*
*Point to one end, which is always present.*
T.S. ELIOT, "BURNT NORTON,"
*FOUR QUARTETS*

## 16

For a millisecond she considered lying. The cop was asking when she had last seen him. Her impulse was to say two thirty that morning, to tell him that JC Campbell had been at her place until then and that he'd been on his way home from there when they picked him up. But a viable lie has to be at least close to the truth, and the truth was that she had been at *his* place until dawn.

"It was about nine o'clock," she said.

"Last night?"

"Yes."

The policeman made a note, then probed his ear with the sharp end of his ballpoint, a thoughtful expression on his face.

"That's dangerous," she said.

"What is?"

"The only thing you can safely put in your ear is your elbow." She smiled, disarmingly she hoped.

He flicked something from the end of the ballpoint. "Do you have any idea where he was going when he left you?"

"I know where he was going."

"Oh?"

"I assume he told you where he was going."

"You tell me."

"He was going to see my brother."

"Your brother?"

"Yes. My brother is a priest."

"Your brother is a priest."

"He is."

He nodded and wrote something in the notebook.

"What parish, your brother?"

"He doesn't have a parish. He works with the homeless."

"I assume *he* has a home."

"He lives at a shelter for homeless young people."

"The one on Sherbourne, near Dundas?"

"I think so."

"That's interesting," he said.

"Why is it interesting?"

"Our victim was in a dumpster just about a block away from there, in an alley off Gerrard."

"What happened to him?"

The policeman stared, rolling the pen between his thumb and forefinger.

"I doubt if that's significant, where you found him," she said. "In any case, I'd bet my life that JC doesn't know anything about it. What's he telling you?"

"Not much, actually."

"I'm sure he told you about Duncan."

"Who's Duncan?"

"My brother."

"The priest."

"Yes."

"What's your brother's other name?"

"MacAskill. Father Duncan MacAskill."

"Spell that."

"M-a-c-capital A-s-k-i-l-l."

"Do you have a phone number for your brother?"

"Yes, but he isn't there right now. He went away this morning."

"Went away where?"

"To Nova Scotia. His bishop died. Today is the funeral."

"Too bad."

"He was old. JC told you nothing about this?"

"I mean, too bad your brother isn't here. I don't think your friend understands how serious this is. I think he's playing games."

"How serious is it?"

"There's a witness."

"A witness?"

"There's a witness."

It was like a dream sequence. The surreal conversation with the cop had ended, but she knew it had only been the start of a longer dialogue. Then, as if by some magical transition, she was walking along College Street, approaching University. It was one p.m. when she left the police station. It was hot. There was a haze of moisture, heated gases and microscopic particles trapped beneath the pale blue dome of sky, the air as exhausted as the empty city faces blurring by her. They had declined to let her speak to him.

They had called her at eleven. Would she be good enough to come to the offices at College and Bay? Or they could send an officer around to take her statement. She said she'd go to them. She was there at eleven thirty. She'd somehow anticipated a reception commensurate with the gravity of the situation. But she was met at the front desk by a thin middle-aged man in jeans and a cheap sports jacket. He seemed tired. She noted he was overdue for a haircut.

They sat in a small room furnished with a table and two chairs. He fumbled for a pen, patting all his pockets before finally locating one pinned inside the pages of his notebook. The thickness of the notebook suggested to her that this was but one of many small atrocities competing for his time, neither crime nor victim of particular significance to him. The thought was reassuring, in a way. He asked for some personal details. Full name, date of birth, address, where she worked, relationship to Mr. Campbell.

As the interview progressed, she became more cautious. She remembered, from a television show, that affability and diffidence from the police are often calculated to disarm, that a conversation is more likely to be rich with unintended disclosure than an interview tightened by fear and paranoia. Stories of police misconduct came back to her, and the voices of the wrongfully accused and the wrongfully convicted. She'd heard somewhere that a police investigation was essentially an exercise in speculation. The larger questions of truth and innocence and guilt would be decided elsewhere, by people at a higher pay grade.

But the officer seemed decent, too hot and tired for guile. When she was leaving, he apologized for taking up her time, shook her hand, studied her with what she thought was masculine appraisal.

Now that she was on the street, one question kept repeating in her mind. It was one asked early and answered quickly, almost glibly: "How long have you known James Charles Campbell?"

"Practically all my life. Since the early seventies. I can safely say I know him as well as I know myself."

The policeman made no comment. He wrote slowly, face elastic, brow wrinkled and lips pursed in what might have been the effort of transcription or the suppression of a smile. The expression was, she realized, provocative. It was the kind of look that, in social circumstances, might have made her blurt out, "*What?* What, what, what?"

*How long have you known James Charles Campbell? Truthfully.*

There was sweat under her arms and on her back. Her clothing felt tight. Her body felt balloonish, bloated. *How well do I know anybody? How well does anyone know me?*

She showered, but the effort of drying herself only produced more perspiration. She donned a gauzy shift, considered wearing underwear but, remembering the depressing tension at her waistline, opted not to. She turned on an air conditioner even though she hated the noise and artificial chill. At three o'clock she poured a glass of Chardonnay.

It was a struggle to keep doubt at bay, and the awareness that her loyalty, her faith in him, was shaken brought on a distressing sense of emptiness. She thought, *This must be what depression feels like, an invasive presence that is autonomous and deaf to reason.* She sipped the wine and realized time had halted somewhere.

The policeman had said they would probably allow him to leave by dinnertime, and that they'd be attempting to track down Father Duncan. This detail was *important,* he had told her by way of reassurance. And by the end of the interview, it seemed to her that he was trying to be kind. And she was tempted to respond with courtesy. Then Conor's voice reminded her, *Don't be fooled by friendliness; they aren't your friends.*

But who was Conor? Really? She'd believed everything he told her, even though he'd cautioned her that truth is sometimes shifty, sometimes circumstantial. He didn't lie, he said. But he'd confessed to what he called benevolent deceptions. She'd loved him, she was sure of that. But had she known him?

And Sextus. Once she'd thought there was no one in this life she knew better than Alexander Sextus Gillis. And yet she *never* understood what motivated his behaviour. So was it accurate to say she knew him? To truly know someone is to never be surprised. Shouldn't that be the ideal? Then she remembered his manuscript. What had he called it? *Why Men Lie*. Ironic. It was in a drawer somewhere, buried in a confusion of underwear and socks and pantyhose. More lies, perhaps. Or the truth revealed. And were lies so bad? Duncan had a line, a quote from the dead bishop: morality resides in motivation. A well-motivated lie, by that standard, can be okay, maybe even good.

She turned off the air conditioner. She welcomed the sudden silence, found comfort in the instant warmth. *Men are all the same.* That's what Mrs. Gillis used to say. *They're all driven by the same imperatives.* Though Mary Gillis would have used another word: "things." *They're all driven by the same things.* And based on Effie's own personal experience, there was something crudely truthful in that observation. They were all the same. And, if JC's theory was correct, they never change. They pose as individuals, flaunt originality, but were all beset by similar anxieties, the same essential urges, almost all originating in the gut, the palate or the testicles.

The phone rang.

"You're there," he said.

"Yes. Where are you?"

She could hear the sound of traffic, people talking. "I'm on College. Can I come by?"

"Please do."

———

She dressed. Panties, bra, a pale green blouse, buttoned to the throat. A long, slimming skirt, sandals. She considered makeup, then decided there was a certain eloquence in the strain and fatigue around her eyes and mouth. Lies. "I love you"—the biggest lie in the book. She gathered up her hair and clamped it high. How often had she heard those words, said them, meant them? She tried to remember the first time. She could recall the car, a memorable car, a Meteor. Its name appropriately fast and furious, consumed by its own brilliance. "You aren't like any of the others." That was his first lie. What was his name? She had no idea, and realized it didn't matter.

Once she asked Mrs. Gillis, "How do you know when a boy is telling a lie?"

"When there's a sound coming out of the mouth of one of them, that'll be a sign," she said.

"I've never known anybody like you," the nameless boy had whispered. "I love you." And she'd believed it. And the possibility inflamed her—if he loved her, maybe she was someone better than she knew. And so she let him love her. But afterwards she felt a mild embarrassment, as if a stranger had observed her in a toilet, and the boy seemed suddenly morose and distant. She told herself it was because he was so serious, contemplating life. *Love changes everything,* she thought. He was deep, worth the love she had invested in him. He'd used a condom. He had it hidden somewhere in the car seat. Then she realized it could have been for anyone. But it was too late then.

"How do you know if someone really loves someone?" she'd asked Mrs. Gillis.

"They have to know you," she'd replied. "If he doesn't know you and he says it, he's a liar."

And, of course, that boy was a liar.

Who was next? John Gillis. He'd known her from childhood, neighbourhood, school. They were like siblings. When John said he loved her, she believed it—and it was probably true, for a while at least, until she realized that she didn't know him any more than he knew her, and neither knew the darkness in the other.

She poured another glass of wine and realized her hand was trembling.

There was a light knock on her front door. She jumped, the wine splashed, she brushed it from her lap. Then she heard the key turning in the lock.

## 17

"I've always been kind of private," JC said. "Maybe to a fault."

"Maybe?" she said, with no effort to hide her sarcasm. "I respect privacy. I admire privacy. But if someone knows an airplane is going to blow up, privacy might be inappropriate."

"Of course," he said, annoyed. "Everything makes sense in retrospect. Almost everything."

"Why don't you just walk me through it," she said.

He'd flagged a cab on Dundas, where normally he'd have had to wait at least ten minutes. The cab was instantaneous, a miracle, a promising beginning. But at the shelter, the only people he could see were two young European backpackers who'd mistaken it for a hostel. Duncan was giving them directions to a cleaner, safer place.

Duncan told him he had tried to keep Tammy there, but the boyfriend, Robert, seemed jumpy, kept watching passing cars, looking at his wristwatch. Finally he said that he was leaving and she was coming with him. And they struck off down the street, agitated, Duncan thought.

JC wandered around for half an hour before he realized that he was wasting valuable time. Honestly. Why was he so determined to make an effort to locate someone he didn't know when he had no credible reason to believe that she was in Toronto anyway?

The answer, he finally admitted, sitting on a bench in a small parkette next to the family courthouse on Jarvis, was guilt. Guilt, he'd long believed, was fear disguised as empathy, a fear of consequences and, thus, essentially a form of selfishness. He had become the absent man he loathed and feared and longed to know.

"Did you ever find out where your father went?" Effie interrupted.

"No," he said. "I never really tried."

He left the parkette. He walked back to the shelter. Duncan offered a nightcap. It was about ten thirty, give or take. They talked, poured a second nightcap, then a third. The talk was about memory and guilt, the toxicity of violence. Duncan was intrigued that JC had never married, never settled down. And JC explained, more clearly than he'd ever done before, his deepest fears.

Duncan grew quiet then and they just sat. He remembered that it was about two fifteen when he woke up on Duncan's chesterfield, head throbbing, damp face stuck to vinyl.

The outside air refreshed him, the cool dampness and the quiet rumble of the city, the persistent hum of the vast vending machine they call Toronto. He walked in the general direction of Walden, still drunk, savouring the emptiness.

And then the streets, it seemed, were teeming with activity. Flashing lights, pounding feet, darkened figures hurrying around him. He reacted from his long experience in journalism, tried to blend in with all the shadows. But now *he* was the centre of attention, his name proclaimed, his face shoved against a wall. A confusion of voices. Then the back seat of a car. The flat radio commentary mentioned him by name, described him. Caucasian male, middle-aged . . . he suddenly remembered Sam, became Sam. He became an observer from the inside of a crisis. This was a story, he thought. This was *Sam's* story.

"Sam murdered someone," Effie said. "Let's keep that straight."

"Not the Sam I know," he said.

He decided on the spot: let the scene play out. He would study cop tactics, internalize their attitudes, their false aggressive certainties. He would save exculpatory information for later. He wanted to feel the feeling.

"The feeling?" Effie asked.

"Impotence," he said. "The impotence of custody, the debilitating effect of the suspicion and the contempt of strangers wearing uniforms."

But then the cops told him that the Robert he'd been looking for was dead. Someone had told them he'd been hunting Robert. It had to have been Tammy.

"She had my card. She didn't like me. Practically ripped my face off with her nails the first time I confronted her."

"You blamed Sorley."

"I lied. Don't ask me why."

Tammy obviously gave the business card to the police. Told the cops that JC had been acting kind of crazy, a maniac, potentially. They found the utility knife he carried in his pocket, asked him to explain.

He feigned disbelief. It was a household cutting tool, innocuous, forgotten after some domestic chore. It was going to the lab, they told him, for analysis. Did he want a lawyer? No. Okay, then, maybe he'd like to do everybody a favour now by cutting to the chase. Cut your losses. The truth, please and thank you. It was the power of their self-confidence that came closest to unnerving him. He had to remind himself: I didn't do it. I didn't kill anybody. And then he recalled his own—perhaps cynical—belief: it doesn't matter if you did or didn't. If there is evidence that seems persuasive, you will lose what will, in essence, be an argument among disinterested lawyers.

That was a distressing moment.

So they had his little knife. Then a skinny cop came in and sat for a while. Asked the other two to come into the hall with him to talk. And when they came back, they seemed genuinely pissed off. It didn't seem to be an act.

"They asked about you and Duncan, and I realized you had told them I'd been with him and that you had probably told the truth. That I'd headed off at about nine. So I told the truth then too. Even the part about my half-hour search for Robert."

Was he absolutely certain that it had been a half-hour? Maybe it had been a full hour? And he knew that they were looking for "opportunity." Tammy gave them "motive." But there was Duncan. Duncan would have seen him, half-hour or not, and would have seen that he was unruffled, no signs of violence. Duncan was the ace in the hole.

He played the card eventually. He'd been with his friend, the priest, for hours. The priest would verify his innocence.

Okay, so where can we find this Father Duncan? Well, he was out of town. That was another moment of uneasiness. What if something happened to Duncan? Plane crash. Car accident. Sudden heart attack. You hear about these things.

"By the way, when is Duncan due back from Nova Scotia?" he asked.

"I have no idea," Effie said.

"You haven't talked to him?"

"No."

"Well, *hello.*"

"I wasn't sure what to tell him."

Of course the cops also wanted to know about the missing granddaughter, and how JC knew that she was in Toronto.

He didn't, really. Her mother thought so. That was all.

They said they'd check it out. There was a registry of missing persons, nationwide. Then came the first genuine shock.

"The head guy, lead investigator or whatever, comes back and says, 'There's no missing granddaughter.'"

"No missing granddaughter?" Effie said.

"He says, 'What do you have to say to that?'"

"I said, 'Obviously nothing. If that's true, I'm an idiot.' 'Maybe,' he said. 'So maybe you went out and dumped some poor asshole for no good reason. Pretty shitty, eh?'

"I asked what, if anything, they'd found out about the kid, and that was when he told me. Yes, she'd been reported missing over a year ago. But she'd showed up at her mother's place just before Easter. Fit as a fiddle. Never been to Toronto in her life. Never left Nova Scotia. Case closed. And the cops are looking at me as if I was supposed to know."

Effie sighed. "I'm not surprised. I can't believe nobody thought of telling you."

"Why would they?" he said. "You have to remember. For them I'm not real, never have been. It wouldn't occur to them to tell me."

She studied his face and knew that they were at the outset of a conversation that could go on and on and on, perhaps forever.

"I don't even know what she looks like. I saw a picture, from three years ago. Coming back on a plane from somewhere a while back, there was a teenage girl sitting beside me. You know how they all kind of look alike. Pink hair and punctures. I was thinking, *What if that was her?* My own granddaughter and I don't even know what she looks like. We could be sitting together on an airplane and not know. I hadn't even known my own daughter. And that's when I decided to do something."

"We have to find Duncan," she said.

She watched him as he slept. "Just let me rest my eyes for a minute," he'd said. Then he was out. He lay there still and silent, mouth slightly open, a hand resting on his crotch, barely breathing. Even though the room was warm, she fetched a blanket and placed it over him. His hair was damp, face pale.

*How well do you know James Charles Campbell?* How well did anyone know anyone?

She remembered years ago, a night when Sextus brought his buddies home—JC was asleep like this and someone borrowed her lipstick, approached him stealthily, smiling, nudging. But the prankster had barely touched JC when he was on his feet, hand raised to strike, a strange expression on his face. He was a stranger in that disembodied moment. And she was shocked by the instinctive violence and felt a sense of loss until the next time that she saw him and was able to recover the reassuring feeling of familiarity.

Older people would remark, "This one is Angus MacAskill's daughter," their insinuation clear: we know him and therefore we know you. But what did they know of him? Familiarity is not the same as knowledge. But sometimes it's the best we can hope for. We can only love or hate what the other seems to be.

He coughed, then groaned. She thought of Sextus. He could help.

His phone rang six times before Sextus answered it.

"I have to find Duncan," she said. "Have you by any chance seen him?"

There was a silence.

"I'm great," he said at last. "And how about yourself?"

"I'm sorry," she said. "I'm a bit frazzled. There's been a death. Duncan will want to know."

"A death? Anyone I know?"

"You don't know this person."

"Well, I saw Duncan this evening, briefly. He dropped by. He said he was on his way to visit Danny Ban. I can get a number."

She called Danny and he told her Father Duncan had been there a little earlier and they'd had a great visit. A few drinks and lots of reminiscence.

"But he isn't there now?"

"No," said Danny. "He left about two hours ago."

"Did he give any indication of where he might be going?"

"No. But himself and Stella left at about the same time. She might know."

Stella answered on the second ring. "Yes," she said, as if completing a response to someone else. And when Effie asked if Stella had any idea how she might get in touch with Duncan, Stella simply said, "Hang on a minute."

Then it was Duncan on the phone. "What's up?"

She tried to be brief and undramatic. Tammy's boyfriend, the guy named Robert, had turned up dead.

"You're kidding me," said Duncan.

"Unfortunately not."

"When? How?"

"Someone killed him. Friday night."

"Friday night? I saw him Friday night."

"We know. The police have been questioning JC. They think he had something to do with it."

"JC was with me most of Friday night."

"Yes. The police need a statement from you."

"Sure. I'll call them."

"When will you be back?"

"I'm not sure."

"How can we reach you if we need to?"

"Call me here."

Effie said nothing.

"Okay?" Duncan said. "I'll call them in the morning and make some kind of an arrangement. Do you have a number?"

"Yes," she said. She fetched the homicide detective's business card, read off the name and telephone number.

"I'll tell JC," she said.

"How is he?"

"He's asleep."

"Okay. Good night."

"You *are* coming back?"

"Of course."

"So *when* will you be back?"

"I'm not sure."

"Good night, then."

She just stood there, studying the silent telephone. *When or how can we be sure we know another person?* She turned and approached the sleeping form now snoring softly on her sofa. She placed a hand upon a cheek that was rough with bristle. He jerked awake, confused and vulnerable and unfamiliar.

"Let's go to bed," she said.

The phone rang early. The friendly caller asked if JC was there.

"Who's calling?" she asked.

"Tell him Jim, from the office."

He sat on the edge of the bed, rubbing his face and skull. Laughed briefly into the telephone. "What else does it say?"

Then, "Okay. I'll be there shortly."

He stood, stretched, yawned. "The *Sun* has a story, 'TV producer questioned in Borden murder.' I have to go to the office."

"That isn't good," she said.

"Nobody believes what they read in the *Sun*."

"When will you be back?" she asked JC as he was leaving.

"This shouldn't take long," he replied, unconvincingly.

When he was gone, the silence of the house dropped around her like a shroud. It was another hot day with oppressive humidity. She felt a momentary irritation at the thought of Duncan far away in cool Cape Breton. Duncan and Stella. She was mildly disappointed in herself because she found the situation distasteful. Why? What disturbed her? Her brother, the priest, stolid in his certainties, now seemingly adrift on currents that she knew well, the oceanic swells of need and normalcy.

And then she was angry. She had needs. But my needs, she thought, are always . . . subsidiary. I am a subsidiary. And she felt the tears and hated them. Who would notice if she climbed in her car and drove away, never to return? But drive where? She didn't want to think about it.

She called Cassie's cellphone. There was no answer.

She dressed for the hot day outside, but before she left she wrote a note, just in case: "I've gone shopping."

Sweat was trickling down her spine by the time she got to Bay Street. She descended to the underground concourse. It was cooler there, but she was quickly overwhelmed by hordes of aimless shoppers and appalled at being one of them. She found herself at a Starbucks, not sure why, even mildly repelled by the prospect of hot, bitter coffee. But she ordered one anyway.

"Large," she said.

"Grande or Vente?"

"Just give me large. I don't speak Starbucks."

The server rolled his eyes. She glared.

She sat at a small round table, nursing the coffee. Any normal summer she would, by now, be settled in at home. The Long Stretch. How easily she thought of it as home now that she'd reclaimed it. This year she was stranded in Toronto, waiting for JC.

"Just give me a few more days," he'd say. June had disappeared like that, and now July was compromised. For what? To find a runaway granddaughter who wasn't missing after all.

Then Molly was in front of her. "How *are* you?"

Effie mustered a smile. "Fine," she said. "Sit down. Where did you drop from?"

"I was on my way home," Molly said. "How's he bearing up?"

Effie shrugged. "I haven't seen him since this morning."

"You haven't spoken to him?"

"No."

Molly sat. "I was hoping he'd have talked to you by now."

"Has something happened?"

"You haven't heard about the meeting?"

Effie shook her head.

"The word is that they've given him a warning. The complications in his personal life are getting in the way of the job."

"So what does that all mean?"

"It means he could lose his job."

"I'm sure it'll be okay," Effie said.

"He's asked me to look in on the cat. You know what that means."

"He asked you?"

She shrugged. Then she was gone.

Her coffee was now lukewarm.

"May I?"

She looked up. She didn't know him right away. "That was the TV lady, from the news," the man said. He was smiling.

Effie nodded. Then she was afraid.

"Molly something," he said. "I don't watch much television. But I've seen her picture on a bus." He set his coffee on her table. "You don't remember me? It's Paul."

He extended a hand. She stood quickly, spilled her coffee.

"I told you, stay away from me," she said. And she turned and ran.

She closed the drapes and sat in the cool darkness, arms folded tightly. JC called an hour later.

"I've been wondering where you got to," she said. "I have to talk to you."

"I'm at home. I had to check the mail. You won't guess who I just saw on the street."

She waited.

"The dude who put the boots to me at New Year's."

"Oh."

He laughed. "I was going to say something, but I realized that he didn't recognize me. So I just watched where he was going."

"And where was that?"

"The place just a few doors down. Where the gay fellow lives."

"Right."

"I didn't feel anything when I saw him. No resentment, no embarrassment. I must be better."

"Why would there be embarrassment?"

"You know what I mean."

"Not entirely."

"I guess it's a guy thing." He laughed. "What have you been up to?"

"I was out for a while. Look, I really want to talk to you. There's some guy—"

"Him again? Can't it wait till I get back? I have to go away for a couple of days."

"JC, please. I want to go home . . . I just have to get away from this place."

"I'll only be a day or two, and then we'll go. We'll drive, like we planned to do last year. Give me two days."

"Two days . . . what about the police?"

"I'm sorry. I have to go."

"I was talking to Molly."

There was silence.

"You asked her to look after Sorley."

He sighed.

"I wasn't going to tell you I was going," he said finally.

"Molly also told me about your meeting."

"Molly has a big yap."

"Please."

"They're going to execute Sam tomorrow."

"It has nothing to do with you."

"You don't get it."

She heard a sigh, then silence.

The clock said nine. She'd overslept. She showered, let the water pour almost cold, and it was refreshing. But moments afterwards she felt the clamminess again, the sticky forehead. Her hair refused to dry. She decided to go out, find a morning paper. *Take control,* she thought. The paper would have something about Texas. Sam was a Canadian, after all.

The street was loud, the urban sounds amplified somehow by the heat. Turning away from her door, she had the feeling that there was someone out there, waiting. But there was no one she recognized. A man was walking about a hundred feet away. There was something familiar in the set of the shoulders. Or maybe she imagined it. Perhaps JC was right. Maybe she should have called the police. But the thought of facing yet another cop only made her more uneasy. Then she thought, *What am I fretting about? Today is Sam's last day on earth.* Sam who? She'd seen it once, his name, on television but had forgotten.

The paper told her. "The hours are ticking by for Sam Williams, the Canadian who is scheduled to die this evening in Huntsville, Texas, for a brutal murder twenty years ago."

There was a photograph. The face was kind, eyes weary. He had white hair framing features that might once have been striking in their primitive masculinity, especially the chin. The photo was, according to a credit, from the television network JC worked for. She remembered how JC had persuaded Sam to show himself to the public. "You must, because the system doesn't want you to," he'd said. "The system doesn't want the world to see what you've become." The system didn't want the world to see this face, the face of an old, tired man, the violent passions in him long since extirpated.

This is what they would destroy, this shell. "Thanks for the poems," he had written in the Christmas card.

She bought a coffee, extra-large. She was pouring milk when, again, she experienced the sensation of being studied. She looked quickly to her left and almost saw . . . someone. She left her coffee, hurried to the door of the coffee shop, but there was no one she recognized nearby.

She spent an hour at the office, attempting to review some academic studies she was considering for use in her curriculum. But she couldn't get Sam Williams off her mind. His face—the face of resignation or acceptance. *Is there a difference?* She looked up "lethal injection." There was a detailed description of the process, something about a sedative and a muscle relaxant before the fatal shot, administered by some anonymous physician. She stopped reading there, dizzy with the details of what JC had let himself become a part of. She sat for a very long time with her face in her hands. *We are all complicit in this,* she thought. She decided to go home.

On her doorstep, searching for the key, she saw the man's face for one fraction of a fraction of a second before it vanished, wiped out of her sightline by a passing truck. But she was certain. There was no doubt.

And there was no doubt when the phone rang shortly after six o'clock. Instinct told her not to answer it, but reason intervened.

"Fuck you," she said, reaching for the phone. And then said nothing.

"It's me," he said. "Paul. Effie?"

The long pause was broken by a chuckle. "Look, I'm sorry if you think . . . I mean, you don't have to run away from me."

"Please—"

"If you got to know me—"

"I'd appreciate it if you wouldn't call me again."

"I see."

She put the phone down and breathed deeply.

Moments later it rang again. She snatched it up. "Jesus Christ, what did I just say?"

"What?" said JC. "What's wrong?"

She started sobbing.

"It's okay," he said. "It's all over. He's gone. Were you watching the TV?"

"No," she said. "I wasn't. I was on the phone."

"I was wondering," he said. "They interviewed me. Someone from the CBC . . . Anna Maria. She was here, from the news. I wondered what, if anything they used."

"I didn't see it . . . I can't imagine." She fought for breath. "I can't imagine. Are you okay?"

"I'm okay," he said. "Quite pissed, but otherwise fine. Sandra is in rough shape. I'm with her."

"Yes, but you. How did you . . . ?"

There was a long pause. "Sandra was there. I wasn't. I was on the outside, with the media circus. You should have seen it. It was embarrassing."

"You weren't there when they . . . ?"

"They wouldn't let me in."

"They what?"

"They wouldn't let me in, because I'm media." He laughed. He sounded slightly drunk. "I hadn't gone through channels to get on the media list, and they struck me from Sam's personal list because I'm media. Texas. Go figure."

"Oh, God . . . I'm so relieved . . . When will you be home?"

"I don't know, but soon. I have to book something."

"What about the cat?" she said, groping for engagement.

"Right. I told Molly not to bother, you'd look in on him. Okay? Now I have to go. Good night."

She sat staring at the silent phone. She was slow to realize that the message light was blinking.

She slept badly until nearly daybreak, when at last she drifted off. There was a thin halo of daylight around the bedroom window drapes when she awoke again. She sprang out of bed, pulled on jeans, buttoned up a blouse. She brushed her teeth, tried to tame her hair, then finally bound it in a ponytail, found a ball cap. She peered through the front door window from behind the curtain, looking left and right. The street was empty. It was seven thirty.

Hurrying along Bloor, she was alert, alternately nervous and embarrassed by her paranoia. Once she thought she saw him, but realized she was imagining his face on people who were strangers.

The story from Texas was front-page news in all the papers. Sam went quietly, it seemed, no last meal, no final words of protest or remorse. There had been speculation that, at the end, he'd acknowledge his responsibility for what had been a terrible crime. But when asked if he had anything to say, he just smiled and turned his head away. "May God have mercy on his soul," a prison spokesman said.

There was a brief quote from a Canadian television producer, JC Campbell, who had befriended the condemned man and had spent part of the day of execution with him. Campbell said that Williams was "serene" and "noncommittal" in their final conversation, just hours before he died.

"Whatever he did was in the heat of passion," Campbell said. "What we just did to him was in cold blood."

There was a sudden movement in her peripheral vision. She stared toward the door, where she thought someone had stopped quickly, turned and was now hurrying away. She paid her bill but sat staring at the newspaper, her mind in turmoil. She was afraid— illogically, she knew—of going home just then. She remembered the cat.

His indignation was apparent; she'd never heard him yowl so shrilly. When she tried to pick him up, he hissed. And when she started toward the kitchen for the cat food, he dashed ahead of her, tail straight up. For a moment she was smiling, JC, Texas, Sam, dead people from her past and present, all gone. JC's living room was dark, drapes closed against the summer sun. After she'd fed and watered Sorley, who promptly disappeared, she sat in the coolness, feeling safe for what felt like the first time in a long time. And before she knew it, she was fast asleep.

She went home near noon, refreshed. She let herself in, welcomed the familiarity of her own place. She imagined a renewed sense of security as she closed the door behind her, heard the reassuring click of the deadbolt. In her bedroom she stripped, stood briefly in the utter comfort of her nakedness. In the shower, water sensual on skin, she felt a moment of arousal, thinking of JC, and that he'd soon be home. How long since they had showered together? *Time is slipping by,* she thought, emerging.

This she would remember clearly—the flimsy fabric on the floor, beside the dresser, the top drawer opened slightly. Had she opened it before she'd gone out that morning? Or before she'd showered? A dreadful awareness wrapped itself around her. She drew the top dresser drawer toward her carefully until it was fully open, peered inside, felt a momentary reassurance when she saw that everything was there, the pantyhose, the underwear, the socks; a long outdated package of condoms; a tube of lubricating jelly. But it all seemed to have been shoved aside, crushed into one disorganized mass on one side of the drawer. A full minute seemed to pass before she recognized what is most difficult to see: what isn't there.

The manuscript that Sextus gave her was gone.

She sat for a long time on the edge of the bed in a kind of paralysis. She dared not look around her; the closet door was ominously ajar. Now she was cold. She stood and approached the closet. She hesitated at the door, then jerked it open. Dresses, blouses, skirts hung silent, undisturbed. She grabbed a robe, clutched it close. Then sat in limbo.

Time restored some clarity. The intruder had waited until she wasn't there to make his entry. This seemed to tell her that the visit hadn't been to do her harm. But, like all intrusion, it was to take something. He'd come and gone, clutching his newfound treasure. *Knowledge,* she told herself. *He has stolen knowledge about me, something worth much more than property.*

She considered calling the police, but she could easily imagine the response. *Burglary? How do you know? What's missing? What's it worth? How many people have keys to your place?*

She packed a single bag and called an airport limousine. Then she called Sextus and asked if he could meet her at the airport in Halifax. She'd call again when she had precise flight information. Going home was a spur of the moment decision, she said. She was trying to sound cheerful.

"Of course," he said. And then, "Are you okay?"

"I'll explain everything later," she said, even then realizing she had no idea what or how.

## 18

Sextus had always possessed an uncanny ability to read her moods, and he kept the conversation light between the airport and the causeway. There was a brief inquiry about Cassie, some questions about her work, nothing at all about JC. Just before they crossed the strait, he said, "How about some dinner, on me?"

She turned from staring at the ugliness of the gravel quarry at the foot of Cape Porcupine and met his steady gaze, then turned away again. "Watch the road," she said.

"I'm only talking dinner." There was a slight edge of anger in the voice.

She sighed. "I'm sorry."

"How about it?"

She shrugged, but quickly blurted, "Not here," when he slowed as they approached the Skye Motel. "I couldn't."

It was where he'd first confessed his feelings to her, years before, where she'd first yielded to his needs and, as she later realized, her own. "There's a place farther on," he said. "It's actually better."

—

*"You shouldn't have to work here, anyway," Sextus said. "The Skye Motel, for God's sake. I thought you were working on a degree."*

*"Someone has to pay the tuition."*

*"What's wrong with John? I hear the wages at the mill are pretty good."*

*"I don't want him to."*

*"Please stay."*

*"I can't."*

*"Please, I don't think I've ever been so alone."*

*"You don't have to stay at this place," she said. "You could be staying home with——"*

*"There's just death there."*

*"Your father . . ."*

*"He's dying."*

*"I can't——"*

*"I'm in love with you, Effie. I've always loved you."*

———

"I really should go home," she said. "The place will be——"

"You have to eat sooner or later."

"I'm not hungry."

He parked the car. "Let's go."

Walking across the parking lot, he said, "It's a lovely night, for a change . . . July's been shitty. You didn't miss much."

Over dinner, he asked, "What kept you in Toronto, anyway? You're usually home earlier than this."

She put her fork down, pushed the plate away and took a deep breath that almost turned into a silence. "The manuscript," she said at last. "The manuscript is missing."

"What manuscript?"

"The one you gave me. It's missing."

He just stared. "You read it?"

"No."

He looked away. She could see a muscle in his cheek clenching and unclenching. "So you have no idea what's in it?"

She shook her head.

—

*It was embarrassingly late. She had rehearsed the reason: Sextus needed somebody to talk to. She had already cleansed herself of the lingering traces of that comforting. "I love you," Sextus had said. And it caught her by surprise. The surprise obliterated reason. But reason now returned, embittered. What is betrayal anyway, if mitigated by a higher purpose, like generosity or love? Sextus said he loved her. She wanted to believe it, and so she did.*

—

"There's some fairly personal stuff in there," he said quietly.

"I imagine."

"You told me everything, you know."

"Pretty well," she said. "I didn't think you'd write it all down."

He waved toward a lurking waiter. "I need a drink."

—

*It was late, but there was a light on in the old Gillis place. John was waiting, patient John, who loved her as she once loved him. Her explanation was fluent and reasonable. Grieving Sextus. Dying Uncle Jack. "The time just slipped away." But everything unravelled quickly. The accusation, the unexpected strength of his hand jammed between her thighs. The shock of her reaction, her fist swung toward his face and the fluid ease of his avoidance; his raised hand, reconsidered. The violence in his shove. Then the sight of him above her, the grimness in the wrenching of his belt. "John, don't!" She closed her eyes, surrendered to the transformation of her guilt to grievance, the momentary liberating hatred. And she knew that, when he was asleep, she would rise in vindication, move in utter guiltless silence to the door, close it carefully behind her.*

———

"Where did you last see it?"

"When you gave it to me, I put it in a drawer."

"At home or work?"

"Home."

"My God. It couldn't just walk away. Do you have a cleaning lady or something?"

She shook her head. She felt his anger as he looked off toward another table. "I suppose you have a lot of visitors . . ."

"Come on," she said. "Don't be an idiot."

"Well . . . Okay. I'm sorry. But what about JC? You don't think . . . ?" He raised a hand defensively. "I'm only asking. You have to think of all the logical possibilities."

"I have an idea where it is."

"You do? But you're not sure."

She shook her head. "I can get someone to check."

He seemed to relax. "Well, okay. That'll be a start."

"I could stay here with you for the night," Sextus said. The darkened house was almost sinister. "Don't get me wrong. I'll chain myself to the couch. I just think you—"

"I'm okay," she said. "I really am."

"How will you get around? You don't have your car."

"I'll rent something. I'll be fine."

"I'm not going to stick my nose in any further. But I'm going to ask John to check on you in the morning."

"It won't be necessary, really."

"I'm going to anyway," he said. "Let me know when you hear."

She laid a hand on his. "Thanks," she said.

"I meant to ask," he said. "What was your reaction to the baby's name?"

"Baby?"

"John's baby. I assume he told you."

"I'd forgotten."

"Two weeks ago. They called him Jack. He didn't tell you?"

"No," she said. "But that's nice."

"Jack." He chuckled. "I can't remember the last time I said that name out loud."

"It's a good name," she said. "John."

"Jack," he said. "Not John. They baptized him Jack."

She had a sudden thought. "Was it Duncan who baptized him?"

"No. Nobody has seen much of Duncan. The last I heard he was in Creignish. At Stella's, the dog."

"Jack," she said. "I think that's perfect. Your dad was more like a father to poor John. Not to suggest . . ."

"It took me years to admit how much I resented how close they were. John and the old man. I guess because it justified what I did to him."

"What we did to him."

"I suppose." He sighed. "I'm glad it's him keeping the line alive. Whatever goodness there was in any of them—the old man and Uncle Sandy—I think John inherited the most of it. Now maybe this new Jack."

"You have a daughter," she said softly.

"Do you really think so?" he said, then looked away. "It's all in that manuscript, you know. After living with so many lies, I think we're all ready for a dose of truth."

Before he left her, he said, "So you think you might know where it is."

"It's a complicated situation," she said.

He laughed. "I can't imagine any stranger finding that shit interesting."

"Where the hell are you? I've been phoning all evening."

She listened for anger but heard only curiosity, perhaps amusement.

"I'm home," she said.

"Home? I've been—"

"Cape Breton," she said. "I had to come home."

"Cape Breton? Shit, I thought we were going to—"

"Hang on," she said. "I have to sit down."

"Is there something wrong?"

"Yes," she said. "The guy I told you about—"

"The stalker who hands out his business card?"

She fell silent.

"Sorry," he said. "That didn't come out the way I meant it to. Why don't you start at the beginning, how you met this guy."

"It started a while back, in the winter. I was having a coffee. The place was crowded. He sat down at my table, made some small talk. He gave me his card. I left. Then he was calling. And I think he's been following me. And I think he was in my place."

"In your place? How did he get your number? How did he get your address?"

"I don't know. You're the expert at finding people."

"Why in hell didn't you tell me?"

"Tell you? You weren't here. You were in Texas or some damned place."

"Did you call the police?"

"No. But there's something missing. Something personal."

There was a long silence.

"How personal?"

"It was a manuscript. Something Sextus wrote sometime back. Something he decided not to publish but gave to me, because I'm in it."

"I suppose you are."

"I didn't read it. But I can imagine."

"Do you still have that business card?"

"Yes. I have it here."

"Give me his name, and anything else that's written on it."

"What are you going to do?"

"I'm going to try to get your life back."


Through her bedroom window she could see the beginning of a pale sunrise sharpening the outlines of treetops shaped like arrowheads. She felt a deep weariness, craved more sleep, but the silence was distracting, worse than noise. Moments from the days before sluiced through her consciousness. Her uneasiness was full of accusation. Her life was careless. No. On the contrary, it was full of care. *What's another word for "careless"?* She swung her legs over the side of the bed. The floor was cold. She studied feet that suddenly seemed misshapen, bumps and sinews showing. *What if this is all I have ahead of me?* She stood.

The air outside was heavy, moist and fragrant, the tangle of wild rose and evergreen and the musty, muddy smell of broken ground.

She walked along the road toward the Gillis place. There was a light on in an upstairs window. She remembered when it had been her bedroom, and she tried to imagine the new life there, the absence of anxiety, the lack of memory. Jack, they'd called the baby. And she briefly pitied him for the burden of the things he'd learn eventually.

The rising sun burned off the morning mist. She sat on her doorstep with a cup of tea, fighting the urge to call Toronto. She could picture the little house on Walden vividly, more clearly than her own apartment. She'd have to move.

Duncan had told her to bring a bathing suit, and she was trying to find one in the chaos of a dresser drawer. The drawer reminded her of what she'd fled. "Goddammit," she said aloud. "I don't feel like going swimming anyway." She slammed the drawer shut and just stood there.

Then John called out from her kitchen. "Is anybody home?"

They hugged, and it was only afterwards that she found it strange, the hugging.

"I got a call last night, late. Sextus asked me to look in. I hope I didn't . . ."

"I'm fine," she said. "It's good to see you. Would you like a tea or coffee? I could make some."

"No, no," he said. "I was just passing."

"I'm supposed to meet Duncan at his boat in a couple of hours," she said. "I could use a lift to town, to the rental place."

"Sure," he said. "So Duncan's still around?"

"So it seems." She laughed and felt her face flush. John laughed too, but then he seemed uncertain.

"Let's get going," he said.

"You called the baby Jack," she said, as they drove toward town.

"Ah. Yes. I'm sorry I didn't get in touch."

"Don't worry—I know how it is. But Jack . . . not John?"

"Just Jack. Hoping he'll be half the man that Uncle Jack turned into." He studied the road. "You must see big changes since . . . back then."

"Some things never change."

"True," he said. "But we both know why I always found it hard to get in touch."

"It wasn't only you," she said.

"The one thing I worry about, since it turned out to be a boy, is passing on whatever it was . . ."

"Please, John. Don't," she said. "This is a time to be happy. You're a lucky man."

"Yes," he said. "I'm sorry. Raking all that old stuff up."

Then they were at the car rental office.

"Thanks for the lift," she said.

"Where does he keep the boat?"

"Little Harbour," she said.

"I was never much for the water," he said. "Say hello for me."

"I will."

The boat was anchored in a little cove just off Henry Island. Duncan was slouched in a plastic deck chair, picking at the label on a half-empty beer bottle. The sun was stinging.

"The bishop—that must have come as a shock," she said.

"He was getting up there."

"You were close, though."

"He ran my life for nearly thirty years. I suppose you could say that we were close."

"What now?"

"There'll be another bishop. It won't be me."

"You know what I mean," she said.

He sighed deeply, then turned away, staring off toward where Stella was a small disturbance on the still water, swimming away from them with long, slow strokes.

"I always thought that age would bring more clarity."

"And it doesn't?"

He laughed. "I'm learning that men are different in that regard. Women, it seems, mature, accept things. Men just age, grow anxious."

"You learned that from her?" She waved at Stella, who was now floating in the distance.

"Maybe from you."

"Hah," she said.

"How did JC make out, by the way?"

"He seems fine," she said. "Thanks for helping clear up that business with the police."

He shrugged. "I told them he was with me, period. I presume that's all they need."

"We'll see. But tell me about you."

"I met with the archbishop in Halifax yesterday. We had a good talk."

"Are you allowed to tell me what you talked about?"

He laughed. "Bottom line, they don't want to lose me. He wants to know how long I plan to stay in Toronto. He's being decent about it."

"And did you talk about . . ." She nodded toward the swimmer, who was now moving in a wide circle around the boat.

"I didn't feel the need."

He stared at her for a while. Then he reached toward a cooler, rattled among ice cubes. "What about yourself?" he said.

"I think there's vodka in there."

He leaned and looked inside the cooler. "Damned if there isn't."

Stella looked almost matronly in the bathing suit, but her movements expressed a comfortable sensuality. From the moment Effie saw them standing together on the wharf in Little Harbour, she was conscious of an unfamiliar calm about her brother. He was no less serious, but his burdens, she believed, were now mostly from new certainties and all their consequences. There was correspondence in the way they moved together, in their communication. The word "symmetry" came to mind. She'd been apprehensive that Sextus, and the memory of infidelity, would have spoiled the day for all of them.

Now Stella sat with them, rivulets of water running from her hair into the hollows just above the prominence of collarbones. Her shoulders were muscular and brown.

"We've been talking," Effie said.

Stella smiled, raised an eyebrow and looked from one to the other. "Don't mind me."

She lifted the lid of the cooler, produced a beer and handed it to Duncan. He swiftly twisted off the cap and handed it back to her. She held the bottle in both hands against her stomach, tilted back her head and closed her eyes.

"We haven't seen each other since that day in the parking lot, outside the Walmart," Effie said. "Last summer. It seems like such a long time ago."

"It was a long time ago," Stella said, dreamily, eyes shut.

For the first time Effie noticed the impact of the vodka. A tingling warmth, a return of confidence. "Maybe I shouldn't tell you this . . . I don't want to spoil the afternoon. But something happened . . . just before I came."

Effie and Sextus were sitting on her doorstep, drinking tea, the cool of the evening, with its assorted fragrances, gathering around them. The settling sun seemed closer. They both seemed suddenly to notice it, and the silence, as if a threshold had been passed.

"The way the light gets mellower at this time of day," he sighed. "I think it's from the angle of the sun and the rays passing through all the pollution close to the earth. Television people call it magic hour."

"You were always good with words," she said. "I always thought words were your calling."

"I wrote a real novel once. You must remember?"

"I remember. I thought it was good."

"Do you remember what I called it?"

"*The Day They Killed Kennedy.*"

"Very good," he said. "It was about Uncle Sandy and what he did."

"And about the man who lived here," she said. "And why Sandy did what he did—at least what you thought the reason was."

"The missing manuscript is a little closer to reality. Being about us, I suppose. Why we are the way we are. I'm kind of relieved you didn't read it," he said. "It wouldn't mean anything to a stranger. I'm sure of that."

"About me and my father," she said. Then she could say no more.

"It's only based on what you told me."

"It's strange," she said, "how after a while what happened and what you imagined or what you dreamed get all mixed up."

"I guess that's why they have shrinks," he said. "Have you ever?"

"Nah."

"You know that Stella is a kind of shrink," he said.

She placed a hand on his forearm. "It's behind us," she said. "Like everything else. I was with her and Duncan yesterday. On the boat. It all became clear."

His laugh was brief. "They're lucky." And he looked up toward the horizon. "And what's ahead? For us. You and me. Individually, of course."

"We still have that much in common," she said. "Unpredictability."

He stood then and smiled. "I hope so. I always get restless when things are predictable."

"Can I get you something?" she said. "The tea's gone cold. I could make us a drink."

There was a momentary hesitation. "Probably not a good idea."

"Whatever you think yourself," she said. And they laughed together. "I haven't heard anyone use that expression for ages," she said. "Whatever you think yourself," she said again, mimicking an accent from the past.

"It's good to have you home," he said.

As he left, she paid attention to the thump of the car door, the firing of ignition, the brief squeal of a power steering belt protesting a too-tight turn, the crunch of gravel as he drove away and the lingering of engine sound, a sudden whisper from a breeze.

Then her cellphone jumped, and rang.

## 19

The water was dark and flat, the day dull, overcast. They were drifting well offshore, safe from the lurking rocks that girdled the island, out of sight.

"I could try to go in closer, but you can get into a spot of trouble there. I don't have a depth sounder. But I wanted you to see that," Duncan said.

He and JC were standing on the high bow of the boat, and Duncan was pointing toward the land and a large rock fragment in the water, like a section of a wall left after an incomplete demolition. Effie and Stella were sitting on the washboard, legs dangling, bare toes almost touching the water.

"They call it the Door," Duncan said, "because of that hole near the bottom. It's been a marker for fishermen forever. You can spot it as far away as Cape Mabou." He swung his arm leftward, taking in the looming coastline. JC was silent.

"Somebody I know wanted his ashes spread out here because he thought it would be a doorway to eternity or something. Father Mullins vetoed it. He said putting ashes in the sea is a denial of the final Resurrection, the Day of Judgment."

Duncan laughed briefly. "I was thinking of Mullins and the poor fellow's last wish a couple of weeks ago when they were scattering young Kennedy's ashes from a battleship off Martha's Vineyard, with the top brass of the Church officiating. I guess on Judgment Day it'll still matter who you were, just like always. Business as usual."

"Who was it wanted to be put here?" JC asked.

"Some guy who lived away most of his life. Came home when he got sick."

"I'd like that," JC said. "If anything ever happened, this would be the place for me."

"For God's sake," Effie said. "Enough with the being morbid."

The day he arrived, she'd decided to prepare a dinner in advance. In the morning she'd driven to the supermarket. As she passed by the bookstore, it occurred to her to buy a Toronto newspaper, but at the doorway to the shop she realized that she was walking in on something private. The woman she knew to be JC's daughter was speaking loudly to someone Effie couldn't see. "Don't just walk away," she said.

A teenage girl rushed by, her face furious.

"You come back here this minute!" Sylvia shouted from the doorway of the bookstore. Effie was, by now, in full retreat.

She heard a floorboard creak, and when she turned from the stove toward the refrigerator, he was in the kitchen.

"Oh," she said, raising a defensive hand.

"I'm sorry. I didn't mean to sneak up."

In their mutual surprise, they just stood there. Then he came toward her slowly and drew her head to his shoulder. She let her arms hang limply as he stroked her hair.

"It's done," he said. "It's finished."

"What is?" she murmured. "What's finished?"

"So many things," he said.

"I was just preparing supper," she said. "A casserole. I didn't expect you this early."

"I'll bring my stuff in," he said. "I brought enough for a long stay."

"Wonderful," she said. "How long did you have in mind?"

"We can talk about that."

"And what about my cat?"

Suddenly his face was grim.

"What's wrong?" she asked. "What happened?"

He put his arms around her. "He got out again."

"He got out . . ."

"The same way as before, up on the roof. But he didn't come back. I can't tell you how sorry I am."

"It's okay," she said. "It wasn't your—"

"You don't understand," he said. "I wasn't able to go after him this time. I couldn't . . ."

"It's okay."

"No, it isn't okay. I was afraid. That's why I didn't go."

He stepped back, arms outstretched as if in supplication.

They talked late into the night, over dinner and a long walk on the darkened, empty road, beneath the glittering sky, about past and future, how time takes things away and, as we grow aware of loss, anxiety takes over.

"That's why Sam was fascinating to me," he said. "I had to see first-hand what happens when it's all gone, when you become utterly vulnerable."

"So what happens?" she asked.

"I don't know," he replied. "I don't think Sam was typical. He lost everything that we can put a name on, but he managed to hang on to something, and it kept him strong, right up to the end."

"You said that he was religious."

"It was more than that," he said.

They were back at the house then, standing near the gate.

"I want to stay here," he said. "If there's a place that I might be able to figure it out, it's here. What do you think?"

"I like that idea, you being here. How long will it take?"

"Till Christmas. All winter. The rest of my life. I don't know. You don't mind if I stay here?"

She shrugged. "I'd rather have you in Toronto. But I can live with this. I could visit for Thanksgiving, Christmas. Though the old place could be kind of frigid by, say, January."

"I don't mind cold," he said.

"So it'll be a book?"

"Maybe at some point."

"About impotence?"

"About surviving impotence."

"It'll be a blockbuster, I predict," she said.

"Speaking of blockbusters," he said, "come on inside. I have something to show you."

She knew what it would be. "The manuscript," she said. "You didn't."

It was in a folded plastic bag from a No Frills grocery store.

"How did you manage . . . ?"

"I went to his address. Actually, I had to go a couple of times before I found him home. Knocked on the door. Introduced myself and told him that I was there to pick it up. He gave it to me. Case closed."

"Just like that."

"Excused himself, turned on his heel, went somewhere inside his place and came back with it. Not a word out of him."

"You just went and got it. And he handed it over to you, a stranger."

"Exactly."

She was studying his face, particularly the expression in his eyes.

"You don't believe me?" he said, smiling. "Check in the bag. I just looked at the title page to make sure it was there. I didn't read any of it, so maybe he fooled me. Maybe it's just a pile of blank paper."

She reached into the bag and brought out the thick wad of paper, now secured, she noted, by an elastic band. She fanned the pages briefly and saw that it was probably intact.

"The elastic band is new," she said. "It was loose in an envelope when I last saw it."

"Well, that's how I got it."

"And he said nothing."

He shook his head slowly.

"I have to sit," she said. Her legs felt weak.

"I have a better suggestion," he said, reaching for her hand.


She woke to the sound of her cellphone ringing in the kitchen, where she'd left it. She closed the bedroom door behind her. It was Stella, with a dinner invitation. "Duncan wants an evening with you both before he goes."

"Before he goes?"

"Back to Toronto. He can explain it himself. Are you free tonight?"

"Of course," said Effie.

The manuscript was on the kitchen table, near where she'd left the phone, and she was tempted to start reading it. But she resisted. JC's story was all too simple. Why would someone who had risked so much to steal it simply hand it back without a word?

His jacket was hanging on the back of a kitchen chair. She slipped a hand into a pocket. There was a paper that turned out to be a folded boarding pass. Car keys. Then a slim plastic object that she recognized even without seeing it. She removed the little cutting tool and examined it. Extended, then retracted the small pointed blade, sniffed at it then returned it to the pocket. She sat perplexed.

After long minutes she stood and found her purse and, from it, she retrieved the business card and walked outside with her phone. She studied the name: Paul Campion. She entered the numbers and listened as a phone rang somewhere in Toronto. Her thumb was poised to disconnect the moment someone picked up on the other end. But it just rang and rang and rang. Eventually a mechanical voice intruded. The inbox for the party being called was full. Please try your call later, it instructed.

She returned to her place at the kitchen table and sat again, hand resting on the document that she knew recorded so much of her past. Still she couldn't bring herself to read it.

When JC emerged into the kitchen, his face was that of an unsuspecting sleepy child. He rubbed an eye socket with a fist, face contorted.

"You distracted me last night," he said. "I fell asleep with a contact in."

"I didn't know you wore contacts."

"Just one."

"That's odd."

"No. Owww. It stings."

"I was sitting here wondering. About all the things I don't know about you."

He walked toward the chair where his jacket was hanging, fumbled through the pockets.

"I usually keep eye drops handy . . . there should be some in here somewhere."

His hand was now in the side pocket, exploring.

"Oh," he said. "You'll be interested in this." And he was holding up the utility knife. "Look what they returned to me before I left."

"Who?"

"The police. Apparently they sent it to the lab, looking for clues . . ."

"I didn't realize the guy had been stabbed," Effie said.

"He wasn't."

"Oh? What happened to him?"

JC was examining the cutter, extending then retracting the blade.

"Fractured skull," he said. "Apparently."

"So why were they interested in that thing?"

"It was a trick," he said. "If I was to act like I knew how he really died, they'd want to know how I knew something they hadn't made public."

"So how did you know?"

He was now searching her face, expression changed. "Ummm . . . I didn't. Not then." He paused. "You're not thinking what I think you're thinking?"

"I don't know what to think," she said. She studied his face for guile, for all the tics and colouration that betray deception.

"Come here," he said. With his arms tight around her, he said, "We have about a month. How about we try to solve as many mysteries as possible in that time?"

Unexpectedly she wept, but only briefly.

They were approaching Creignish, and Stella's. "It's almost August," she said.

"It's my fault you missed most of July," he said. "I kept you stuck in Toronto. Wondering what I was up to."

"I don't think I missed much. Sextus says the weather sucked."

"Weather isn't what you come here for."

"What, then? Scenery?"

The sun was hanging above the horizon ahead of them, St. George's Bay a vast, dark, dimpled plain.

"Civility," he said, after a long pause. "It's for the civility."

She laughed. "You don't know what you're talking about."

"People need each other in small places. Necessity inspires civility. Trust me."

"You're being sentimental," she said. "You'd better get over that if you're going to stay here. One winter will knock that out of you."

Duncan was loading a large suitcase into the back seat of Stella's car when they arrived. "We want to make an early start," he said. "Crack of dawn. There's a flight at eight."

"What's the plan, then?" Effie asked.

"Stella's driving me to the airport. What did you think?"

She shrugged. "I don't know what to think anymore. So much for your theory about female clarity at middle age."

He slammed the trunk lid and stood, hands on his hips.

"So what does it all mean?" Effie asked her brother. "In plain English."

"In plain English I'm being relieved of my priestly duties, except in dire circumstances. If someone is near death I can hear confession and offer absolution. Otherwise, I go back to doing what I was doing at the shelter. Cook, dishwasher, janitor, bouncer and buddy to the down and out."

"And Stella?"

"She thinks some time apart might be useful for perspective."

Effie laughed. "You've always been apart, except for the past couple of weeks. What perspective?"

"I need time to think."

"But," Effie said, "with this laicization, you're now both free to—"

"I haven't got it yet," said Duncan. "And even when I do, what you're talking about requires a dispensation from the top, from the big fella in Rome. That's if we're even interested in all that."

"Surely just a formality," JC said.

"Forgive me," Duncan said. "I'm old-fashioned."


Over dinner JC asked, "Could you come back, live here?" And he looked from Duncan to Stella.

"Would I want to?" Duncan replied. "I've spent most of my life here already, for all there is to show for it."

JC shrugged. "We mostly never really know what there is to show, which is probably a good thing, on balance."

"So," Duncan said. "I hear you're giving up the TV business."

"Going to stick around here for a while. Reconnect with my roots."

"A fella can't eat those kinds of roots," Duncan said.

"That won't be a problem," JC said. "The TV racket has been good to me."

———

By mid-August they had found compatible routines. She slept late, he rose early. She would feel the bed move, briefly stare toward a window. Dawn was coming later now that summer had begun to wane. She would close her eyes and listen as he moved silently toward the bedroom door. He had the gift of stealth, she noted, the ability to float just above the floor, to pass through doors without a sound. How long, she wondered, would this strangeness last? And she remembered others in her life, men who kept small sectors of their inner selves reserved, the places out of which surprises came.

*Daddy? What's that in your hand?*

She shuddered, drew the blankets tight. And as she slid back into sleep, she could hear the soft thud of the keyboard in her office.

Unlike when she worked, he seemed to carry most of his raw resources in his head. There were two books. She had opened one, *Among the Lowest of the Dead*. She had read the first line on the first page of text: "On Florida's death row, in the bloom time of spring, grimy windows beyond the cell bars glow with the beauty of freedom . . ." She quickly closed it. The second book was very slim—*Four Quartets* by T. S. Eliot. He had underlined "What might have been and what has been / Point to one end, which is always present." There was a reporter's notebook and the small square computer disc that he carried in his pocket any time they left the house. Since he'd explained it, the word "impotence" had lost its dreadful meaning.

"Sam told me once that if you start from the end and work back, everything makes a lot more sense. And a lot of what mattered doesn't anymore," he'd said.

"But we can't know the end," she said.

"That's true. That's why Sam was such a gift, a chance to observe someone at the end. With Sam, everything worked back to a bad

head injury when he was a kid. Nothing about his life was predictable after that. But things made sense in retrospect. Maybe everybody has one, a point from which everything starts to get a little
bit out of control, but you can only know it in the distant future.
I've figured mine out, for the time being."

"Not the head injury on New Year's?" she'd replied.

"No," he scoffed. "That was nothing. It was way before that.
Back in my second year of university. When the word came. Four
words actually: 'I think I'm pregnant.'"

One August morning, as the sun rose high and slowly dried the
silent land, she walked outside. The world felt stationary, emptied
out and motionless except for flimsy contrails in the sky. She
studied them, watched them break apart and fuse with cloud,
and the reality of people up there, chatting, reading, dozing, was
unimaginable. She resumed her study of the land around her, trees
without boundaries, the old road that went nowhere in particular.
Then JC was there beside her. He was holding the manuscript.

"What about this?" he asked. "What do you propose to do with it?"

She shrugged. "I don't know."

"I find it distracting," he said.

"Feel free to read it," she said.

"I only read for what I need to know," he said. "There's nothing
here I need."

"We could burn it. He said he doesn't want it back. We could
have a ceremonial purging of the past."

"Let me know what you decide," he said. And he went back inside.

August melted down. He worked most mornings while she slept.
Late breakfasts flowed into the afternoons. Long dinners occupied

their evenings. They rarely went to town. At some point she finally acknowledged an awareness she'd been resisting. *Stability,* she told herself. *I feel stable in this new arrangement.*

On a morning late in August she found him sitting at the kitchen table, examining a knife. It was a large knife, and he seemed mesmerized and didn't see her in the doorway. Then he looked up.

"What's the matter?"

She found her voice. "What are you doing with that?"

"It's an antique. I found it in Texas, in a junk shop. It's a Bowie knife. Dates back to God knows when. I once heard that Bowie's people originated in Nova Scotia somewhere. Acadians."

"Get it out of my sight," she said.

He slipped the knife into a sheath, placed it in a briefcase. "Come here." He stood, and when she didn't respond, he walked toward her. "Let's go sit outside," he said. "I have coffee on. I'll bring us some."

"I'm not going to pretend I don't know what that was about," he said.

She sipped her coffee, avoiding his eyes.

"I didn't realize you were up," he said. "I'm sorry."

When she knew that she could trust her vocal cords, she said, "I hate fucking knives."

"I know."

"What do you know?" She was staring off into the distance at nothing in particular.

"I read a few pages of that tome," he said, after some thought. "With what you told me, it's fairly clear."

"Oh?"

"About your dad and his obsession with a knife and . . ."

"And what?"

"We don't have to talk about it."

"But I don't know what's not to talk about."

"Okay." And the silence closed in again.

Finally, she asked, "What did Sextus write?"

"What do you remember?"

"I remember that my father had a knife like that, and I remember him just sitting there with that knife, looking at me strangely. Sometimes, at night, standing in my bedroom doorway. And once . . ."

He waited.

"And once he was sitting there with the knife and Sandy Gillis walked in. And Sandy Gillis attacked him. That's all I remember. Except that Sandy Gillis came to me later, asking. And I said that he was wrong."

"Wrong about?"

"Wrong about what he thought he saw."

"And it was after that . . ."

"Yes."

"And was he wrong?"

"I don't know."

"It was more than the knife, wasn't it?"

"It doesn't matter. My father didn't do anything."

"Have you ever discussed this with Duncan?"

"Of course not."

"Did he know?"

"I think so. He hit my father once."

JC laughed briefly. "Seems like your dad got hit a lot."

"What did you read?"

"Just a few pages. Sandy walks in, sees . . . something. Goes after your father. Your father later tries to get even, tells him a story about them raping someone during the war, and then killing her with a knife. It seems that Sandy had no memory of it because of a head injury, from when the girl shot him. And it was after that . . ."

"Does it say what Sandy thought he saw?"

"Yes."

"You don't have to elaborate."

He nodded. "Do you remember when it started?"

"I remember being alone. Duncan went away somewhere, with the Gillises, I think, Sextus and his parents. I didn't go."

"Why not?"

"I don't know."

"But this Sandy intervened at some point."

She nodded.

"I could have prevented it, what Sandy did afterwards," she said. "He was a kind man, down deep. Maybe if I had just thanked him for caring about me. But I blanked it out. And then, when I told him that he was mistaken when he thought he saw . . ."

She stood up. "I want to go inside. I feel cold."

He stood and took her hand. "It's ancient history," he said. "There isn't anything we can do to change it. It's now a part of who we are, and who we are is okay with me."

She examined his face briefly, then squeezed his hand and smiled. "We should go to town," she said. "I don't want to leave you here with empty cupboards."


Effie hated shopping, always had a list, even for the groceries. And so she finished quickly. JC's last known destination was a clothing store—to enhance his country wardrobe, was how he put it. She loaded her bags into the car, then wandered back toward the mall. Her body buzzed with nervous energy. Her mind flitted through compressions of time.

*Please, Daddy, let me go.*

Nothing happened. Something happened. The fatal contradictions fused somehow, somewhere, sometime distant years ago. *Sandy Gillis killed himself because of . . . what? What I said? What he saw? What happened in a war years before that moment?* And for the first time she seemed to understand that questions without the possibility of answers aren't questions at all, just accusations, and that accusations without the evidence of memory are meaningless.

She considered buying coffee for the drive home, but as she approached the coffee shop she saw JC standing near the cash, talking to a girl. Effie recognized the angry teenager from the bookstore. JC was gripping the girl's wrist, and from the expressions on their faces, the encounter was unpleasant. She backed off, but not before she saw the girl roughly yank her arm away. JC's face was dark with anger, the girl's face flushed as she wheeled and hurried off. Then Effie watched the slow transformation in JC's expression, from anger to a helpless kind of grief she'd never seen before.

She went to him. "I saw."

"Great." He exhaled.

"That was . . . her?"

"My flesh and blood," he said. "The peripatetic granddaughter."

"Do you want to talk?" she asked.

"About what, exactly?"

"What happened?"

"She asked for money." He shrugged. "I said sure, but maybe first we should talk about the missing chapter in her life, when she had me running around Toronto like a lunatic. Upon which she told me to do the anatomically impossible."

His expression was impassive. Then he spread his hands, signalling finality.

"You don't owe her anything," Effie said. "You went out of your way—"

"No, don't," he said sharply. "If I thought that . . ." He raised his arms defensively. "There are things you just have to do."

"Let's go home," she said. "I'm in the mood for cooking."

It was a three-hour drive to the Halifax airport, but it seemed to pass in minutes. She realized that she was actually pushing her body backward into the car seat as if to slow the journey down.

"I should have gone to see John's baby," she said. "I know they think it strange that I didn't. I just couldn't bear to."

"Babies," he said. "They make me nervous. Talk about impotence."

"It isn't that," she said miserably. "It's a measure of my character, or lack of it."

JC laughed. "The baby is going to be around a lot longer than we are. There'll be lots of time."

"What if he's Cassie's half-brother?"

"What if he is?" JC said. "What difference would it make? They're either that or they're cousins. It's just a matter of degree."

"You never talk about your family," she said. "You must have cousins."

"Not that I know of."

The countryside around them was green. The light was pale, the sky clear. "It'll be a lovely day," she said. "What will you do?"

"I'll go straight home and get serious about the project," he said.

"I just dread going back to the city. I used to look forward to it, but that business in July changed something."

"There's nothing in the city that you should have to worry about," he said. "Trust me. The business in July was dealt with."

"How do you know he won't . . . ?"

"People like that usually just need a good fright."

"And you frightened him?"

"I think so."

He left her with her bags at the curb. "I'll not go in," he said. "Public farewells aren't my thing. Come here."

They stood there as one, afraid to make eye contact, afraid to speak, until there was the sound of knuckles rapping on the fender of the car. A traffic officer stood there wagging a finger. "Time's up," he said. "Sooner or later, someone has to make a move. Might as well get it over with."

"I'll be back for Thanksgiving," she said.

"I'll be here."

Briefly his lips brushed her cheek as he released her.

Cassie met her at the airport in Toronto. She had what seemed to be an endless store of questions, about JC, about Duncan, about the future. Then, on the expressway through downtown, she told her mother she and Ray were moving. He'd been invited to join a new medical practice in Sudbury. He longed to live closer to his family, and she could sympathize with that. "They're my family now, too," she said.

"I suppose."

Cassie reached a hand across to her. "You know what I mean."

"Yes."

With both hands now gripping the steering wheel, staring straight ahead, Cassie said, "And we're going to have a baby."

Effie said nothing.

"Well?" said Cassie.

"I'm really happy for you."

"You don't sound happy."

"I'm thinking of your father."

"He'll freak, right?"

"I don't know. Maybe not. He seems different. You haven't told him?"

"I was waiting to tell you. Maybe you can help me break the news."

"When the time is right."

"Yes. When the time is right."

"Ray must be over the moon."

"Yes. But . . . you know, his age."

"Come on," she said. "Ray isn't old."

"Ma! He's sixty-three."

"Sixty-three?"

"What did you think?"

"I guess I forgot."

Cassie began manoeuvring the car to take an exit to the Annex, but Effie told her to drive on. "I'm not going there, to Huron," she said. "I'm going to Walden. I'm going to live there for a while."

"Perfect," Cassie said. "Finally."

"JC is staying in Cape Breton for the time being. There have been some changes over the summer."

"What kind of changes?"

"I'll tell you, but not right now. Just take me to Walden."

———

It was September, but the city felt even more oppressive than when she'd left it in July. The sky was a moist grey blanket compressing the accumulated fumes from car exhaust and gases from the rotted produce piled nightly on the sidewalks for collection. Her daily walks through the little Chinatown on Broadview accentuated her feelings of exclusion; on the Danforth, there were women, faces hidden, speaking glottal Arabic where, years ago, she found the Greek romantic. She fought annoyance as she struggled through impassively aggressive little women wearing what appeared to be pyjamas, past the leaking piles of garbage exploding out of plastic bags and bloodstained cartons piled in front of shops that somehow now seemed sinister.

It was no better on St. George, near her office, where the throngs of ageless, timeless students seemed more than ever to be self-absorbed and hyperactive pampered children, products of delusional parental expectations.

During endless meetings with faculty and students, she would drift away on the gentle swell of recent memory, yawning compulsively. She was sleeping badly, partly because of the undiminished nighttime heat, partly thanks to a lingering fear that she was being stared at by a stranger.

Even before she left Cape Breton she had notified her landlord that she would have to break the lease for her apartment. He was sympathetic and, she suspected, not unhappy at the prospect of a rent increase. With Cassie's help, she'd organized her possessions and arranged for storage.

"I wish you'd told us about the creep," Cassie said. "You know it happens all the time. Men preying on women who live alone. Ray could have handled it."

"It's been taken care of," she said. And changed the subject.

"Did you get a name?" her daughter asked.

"I had a name, but I've forgotten it," she said.

But she hadn't. The business card was on her desk. She'd consulted a street guide to locate the address, in a neighbourhood they called the Upper Beach. And one evening, after she had consumed several glasses of wine with her solitary meal, she drove there and sat out front. It was an unusually quiet street, hardly any traffic, no sign of children or family activities.

Maybe if she saw him once again, the bland reality of what he looked and sounded like would neutralize the menacing shapes and sounds that haunted her imagination. Maybe, with the restoration of an accurate impression, she could stop scanning the faces of strangers in the streets and coffee shops.

Eventually she saw a woman approaching from a streetcar stop. She appeared to be in her mid-thirties, and there was a small boy hanging on to one hand. In her other hand she had a bag of groceries. She turned in to the walkway at the address on the business card.

Effie knew by her easy movements that she lived there—the house key slipped without hesitation into the lock, the door swung open, the boy ushered in ahead.

Effie waited for five minutes. Darkness was gathering, and she could see a glow of light inside the house. She opened the car door.

The woman's face was fixed in what seemed to be an expression of permanent caution, eyes full of questions, door not quite open.

"Yes?"

"I'm sorry to bother you," Effie said brightly. "I had a friend who lived here. Paul Campion . . ."

"He isn't here," the woman said.

"He did live here, though?"

"He did, but he doesn't anymore. How did you know him?"

"It was casual. We'd have coffee. I loaned him something. A book . . ."

"He isn't here."

"When do you expect him back?"

"Paul passed away," the woman said. "I don't know about any book."

"He passed away," Effie repeated. "When? What happened?"

"A month or so ago. I'm sorry to tell you he took his own life."

"My God . . . I'm sorry," Effie said.

"The Bloor viaduct," she said. "That's where he did it."

"And you're his . . ."

"I'm his sister."

She drove back to Walden in a daze. She poured a drink but had to put it down to prevent spilling it. It was nearly ten o'clock, time for his nightly call.

The pronunciation was terrible, but the voice was warm and shy: "*Ciamar a tha mo nighean ruadh bhoidheach a-nochd?*"

"You didn't tell me he was fucking dead," she replied. She had not intended to use the F-word or to put such biting emphasis on "dead." But it was out, and everything was changed.

There was a long silence. Suddenly she wished she had simply answered his garbled question, had said, "Your pretty redhead isn't great tonight. In fact, she's feeling pretty rotten."

"Who is fucking dead?"

"Campion," she said. "The stalker."

"No shit."

"Yes shit. You're telling me you didn't know?"

"If I knew something like that, I'd have told you."

"Really?"

"Hey. Why don't I call back in half an hour when you've had time to think this through."

"What on earth did you do to him?"

There was a long sigh on the other end of the line, and it was, to her, more powerful than anything he might have said. "What happened to him?"

"You don't know?"

"I'm asking."

"What if I told you it was a fractured skull?"

"Shit. Really? How did that happen?"

"He went off the viaduct."

There was a laugh, more of a barking sound. "You think I tossed him over. Is that what I'm hearing?"

"I didn't mean to imply that."

"So it was a suicide."

"That's what they think."

"They don't usually report suicides, especially not off the viaduct. Where did you get this?"

She froze for just an instant, then felt an old, familiar grief congealing near her heart. Her voice was a hateful whimper and she knew it. "I don't know. Somewhere, someone." After another long silence, she said simply, "I've got to go now."

*What is it about me?* she wondered. *What draws the damaged and the doomed?* Sandy Gillis in a doorway; Conor in his gym; this stranger, Campion, smiling at her in a coffee shop; men passing through her life, a constancy of needs, of mother-sister-daughter neediness. *When does it end?*

The phone rang. Suddenly, the drink she'd been reaching for was toppling. She grabbed it, licked the splash from her hand, then picked up the phone.

"You're still there," he said.

"Where did you think I'd be?"

"I don't blame you for being shocked," he said. "But I really didn't know."

"I shouldn't have insinuated. It's me who should be sorry. I just wish that you were here."

"Me too," he said. "I'm actually not making much progress. I might be just as well off there."

"You decide," she said.

"I've been going over it in my head. What I might have said to him."

"What exactly did you say?"

"Well, I told him he was a freak and a pervert, and that if he didn't hand over the document he'd swiped from you I was going to put his mug on television, to warn innocent people about him."

"You didn't!"

"I never thought he'd take it seriously. I was only trying to provoke him. I found him pathetic, and I didn't like that. I'd have preferred belligerence."

"And that was all."

"I swear to God almighty."

"Maybe it was the manuscript," she said. "Reading my sordid story just made life not worth living anymore."

"Who knows?" JC said.

"Christ," she said. "Do you really think that's a possibility?"

"Come on," he said. "The guy was a nutcase. Anything's possible."

"I don't know," she said. "Maybe I'm the problem."

He was silent for a while. "I really do think I'm going to have to abandon this thing. At least move it back to Toronto. Life's too short for us to be like this."

"It's your call," she said.

"I'll sleep on it. Tomorrow night? Same time?"

"Please. I promise to be in better cheer."

"I love you," he said. And she repeated the words, and later tried to remember if it was the first time she'd spoken them to him.

It was Thursday night. On Friday night he didn't call.

She woke early on Saturday. She'd slept badly, waiting for the phone to ring. But somehow, in spite of the cascade of speculative reasons for his silence, she drifted off and mercifully slept through till nearly eight o'clock.

She had booked a meeting with a history major for ten o'clock. She got out of bed resolved to activate her dormant optimism. It must be in there somewhere, she told herself, like a long unused article of clothing that suddenly was back in style. In the shower she decided that she'd walk to the office. She needed the exercise.

It was a cool September morning, the eighteenth, she would recall, sky blue, air freshened by a breeze from the northwest. She planned the route, up Broadview, past the jail and through the park, along the pedestrian ramp that crossed the Don Valley Parkway, up through the model farm, where children would already be scampering. *I'll be a grandma soon,* she thought, and there was a ping of pleasure in the memory of Cassie's news. There was a coffee shop on Parliament where, according to JC, the brew was unbeatable. She'd pause there, maybe eat a muffin.

At Bloor and Sherbourne, she could feel a blister starting, so she abandoned the walk for the subway, which she rode to St. George station. Emerging from the subway car, she was startled to remember that it was fewer than two years earlier, on that same platform, that he'd called her name.

The student needed help with sources for a thesis on the influence of myth in history. He had the British Isles in mind, with particular attention to Scotland. He was older than she had expected and unabashedly flirtatious, exuding a cockiness she knew would either serve him well or ruin him in the long run.

She had just checked her wristwatch, and it was ten fifteen when the phone on her desk rang. She excused herself. She didn't recognize the voice at first.

"It's John," the caller said.

"John?"

"John Gillis. I'm sorry to be calling, but it's kind of urgent. I tried calling your other numbers, but thank God I had this one too. Do you think you could come home? Right away?"

"Home?"

"Home. Cape Breton."

"Oh, John," she said. "What . . . ?"

"It's your friend Campbell," he said. "JC. Something happened. You need to come home as soon as you can."

"What happened?"

"I can't talk now. The cops are in the yard. They want to talk to me again."

"For God's sake, what happened, John?"

"Some people tried to rob him. Call me when you know what time your flight arrives. I can meet you at the airport."

She flew out that night, and she would remember how the communities below her looked like the glowing embers of campfires in the darkness. *The light is life,* she thought. She tried to imagine people on the ground, wrapped tightly in their lives, sealed in the particularities of now, mid-sentence, mid-argument, mid-laugh, mid-meal, -drink, -piss, mid-copulation. Everybody, everywhere, engaged, mid-something. And JC, somewhere, in mid-struggle to survive. She tried to pray.

John hadn't told her very much.

"He's in the hospital. It doesn't look good. That's all I know."

She'd forgotten to ask which hospital. She prayed that it was the little hospital near home, that it wasn't one of the larger regional facilities in Antigonish or Sydney. The greater the distance to the hospital, the greater the cause for alarm.

"He's in Halifax," John said as he took the airport exit to the city. "He's in the ICU at whatever they call the old Infirmary these days."

"Halifax?"

"They had to airlift him."

John reached across the car to hold her hand. For the first time, she noticed that his right arm was in a cast from his knuckles to his elbow.

"It's the best place he could be," John said. "He'll get the best of care."

"What happened, John?"

"I can only tell you what I know," he said.


Friday night John went for a run. It was his best time, after the baby was down for the night, or at least part of it. He jogged out past her old place, as far as the main highway, then along the highway to the little airport near Port Hastings. On the way back, he felt a slight twinge in his knee.

"It's an old problem," he said. "Whenever I feel that starting, I back off. You can't mess with the knee."

Near her gate he slowed to a walk. There was a light on in the house, but that was not unusual. There was a light there every night. But that night there was also an unfamiliar car parked near the gate.

"I noticed it was parked kind of crooked, and it wasn't there when I went by the first time."

As he passed behind the car, there was a loud crash from inside the house. He stopped. At that moment the car door opened, and with the inside now illuminated, he could see a woman there, or a girl. He couldn't tell, not right away. She slid out of the car and shut the door, and it was dark again.

There was a shout from inside, someone's name. Obviously hers. She opened the gate and started running toward the house. Now there were sounds of a violent struggle inside, and he followed her.

As he reached the door, it opened suddenly and what was now

clearly a young girl, a teenager, brushed past him. She was carrying something. "It looked to me like one of those portable computers."

"His laptop?" Effie said.

"That's what it looked like."

Inside there was blood, spattered on the refrigerator and smeared on the linoleum. JC was on the floor, and there were two men kicking him. They were young men. JC was curled in a fetal ball, hands covering his head.

"I headed for the closest guy, but he spotted me and turned. I noticed that his left arm was kind of limp, dangling like. So I got him with a hard right. It was a good one, and he went staggering backwards, but my fist caught his forehead mostly . . . so this happened." He held up his injured hand. "The knuckle broke and the wrist got sprained."

At that point the second attacker had grabbed John, but clumsily, shoving him so that he stumbled on JC's body and fell across it.

"That was when I realized it wasn't JC's blood. He wasn't cut. The blood was from the other guy, the one with the bad arm. When I scrambled up, I found one of those little utility knives. That must have been what JC used."

She was now in a state of merciful paralysis.

"I read somewhere that, if you know what you're doing, you can really cripple someone with one of those things and they never see it coming. Cutting the right place in an arm or a leg or a neck. I guess that's what JC did. Crippled the guy's arm when they were grappling."

As he struggled to his feet, John could hear the car speeding away. Afterwards, he wasn't able to remember much—not year or make or model, not even colour. One of those nondescript mid-sized Asian cars that all seem to look the same.

JC stirred and sat up. He seemed dazed. John thought he was fine. But then he vomited, and there was a lot more blood on the floor, and he just kind of rolled over and curled up in it. John knew he couldn't wait for an ambulance. He found JC's car keys, and they were at the local hospital in less than half an hour. "I kept talking to him as I drove. We were flying on those back roads, me talking a blue streak, but he wasn't answering. I was holding on to his hand with my bad hand, and I could feel it getting colder as we drove. But I wasn't sure if the coldness was from him or me."

Clearly at least one of the kicks to JC's head had done serious harm.

"He hurt his head in January," she said. "He was in the hospital, in Toronto."

"You'd better tell them that," said John. They had entered a vast parking lot in front of a hospital glittering with light. For the first time, she was gripped by a nearly suffocating fear.

The doctor was a young woman, still in her twenties, by Effie's estimate. She had an authoritative confidence when she told them that they'd have to wait a bit. There was another assessment of the patient under way.

"Can't you tell us anything?" Effie asked, struggling for poise.

"Are you his . . . ?"

"Wife," Effie said abruptly.

The doctor studied a clipboard. "We have him down as single," she said.

"Well, you're wrong," said John. "I'm her ex-husband. I can vouch for it. And that man inside there is more husband to her than I ever was."

The doctor looked from one to the other. "I'm sorry," she said.

"It isn't important, anyway. You're Dr. Gillis? I think your name is on here somewhere."

"How bad is it?" Effie asked.

"We don't have a clear prognosis yet, but the injuries are serious."

Effie wondered about what she saw as aloofness in the doctor's manner. *Do they disengage when they know the case is hopeless?*

"I'll come back," the doctor said, "when I have something to report. Make yourself comfortable. There's a cafeteria on the second floor, if you want to wait there."

"Can I see him, just for a second?" Effie asked, now barely in control. "I'd just like to see him."

"Not right now," the doctor said. "I'll be back."

"How long have you two known each other?" John asked her.

"I met him when I first moved to Toronto," she said, suddenly aware of how easily she had strayed to the edge of the unspeakable narrative behind those simple words: "when I first moved to Toronto." She searched his face, but there was no reaction there.

"That's a long time ago," John said.

"He was part of the crowd Sextus knew. Then he went away. Years went by. Decades. He resurfaced two years ago."

"What a shame," said John. "For this to happen."

They were silent then, the sounds around them—muted conversations, the clatter of mugs and plates and cutlery, bland voices calling doctors over unseen speakers—accelerating a slide into a weary sense of helplessness.

John sighed, studying his coffee mug. "Funny they'd pick your place, and him a stranger there. When these things happen, it's usually to someone everybody knows. Some old fellow living by himself. And sad to say, more often than not the culprit is a neighbour or a relative. But he has no connections there. So you have to wonder. Just the luck of the draw, I guess."

She felt cold. "What did she look like, that girl sitting in the car?"

"I couldn't say. Everything happened so fast. I might have got a look at her when I met her in the doorway, but there was so much going on inside . . ." He shrugged.

The doctor reappeared. "There you are," she said. She smiled, and Effie read it as a sign of hope.

"You can see him, but only for a moment. You'll find him very groggy, and he can't speak."

He was propped up in a high bed, a thin blanket covering his lower body. His mouth was distorted by a plastic hose that ran from a chugging ventilator. There were transparent lines taped to his arms and abdomen. His head was bandaged. On a stand beside the bed, an electronic line of light lurched erratically.

She felt wobbly, clamped to John's good arm.

JC's eyes unexpectedly flipped open, and she saw what looked like panic in his glance.

"Who did this?" she whispered.

He closed his eyes and turned away, limply raised an arm, moved a hand toward hers. She caught it briefly. His hand seemed small and dry, diminished, and at the touch of it, she felt time stop.

She was there for only seconds, but the images would last a lifetime. And then there was a sudden urgent sound from the monitor beside the bed. The young doctor quickly reappeared. "You'll have to leave," she said.

Effie could feel the pressure of John's hand as he gently drew her back and away. She could already hear raised voices and hurried footsteps in the corridor. The doctor swiftly drew a curtain.

## 22

The city was an hour behind them before she felt the confidence to speak aloud. "There's a curse on the place," she said quietly. "What place?" said John.

"My place. Home. Maybe the Long Stretch. Maybe the whole wretched island. We're all cursed."

"I wouldn't go that far," John said. And the silence fell upon them once again.

The formalities were over. JC, in a moment of clarity, had legally designated Effie as his next of kin when he was admitted to the hospital. They advised her that it would be up to her to notify the other members of his family. She said she would, even though she knew of only two and she had no idea what, if anything, she'd ever say to them. The doctor told her there would have to be an autopsy because of the circumstances, and she agreed.

"Ever since your father," Effie said. "Since that day. The day Kennedy was assassinated. Everything seems to lead back to that day. And what happened that day colours my memory of everything before it."

John was nodding. "You aren't the only one felt that way," he said, eyes fixed on the road ahead of them.

"Nothing's been normal since then."

*We become bystanders,* she thought. *In all the large, life-altering moments, we are on the margins.* The outcome of the crisis happening behind the curtain in that sterile room would redefine her as she had once been redefined by an unseen act of violence in the forest and, before that, a single unknown outrage in a war of inconceivable ferocity. There was nothing she could say or do, not then, not now. JC's word came back to her. "Impotence."

After what had seemed to be an hour, the doctor said the words Effie had prepared herself to hear: "I'm sorry. We did everything we could."

"You never get over it," John now said. "You cope the best you can. You try to manage with what you have. But you never get over it."

She reached across the car and touched his broken hand. "How long will you have to leave the cast on?"

"Months," he said. "No big deal. It'll get me out of doing housework."

The young doctor had telephoned a downtown hotel. There was one awkward moment as she cupped the telephone receiver and asked, "One room or two?"

"Two," John said quickly.

Outside her door, he hesitated, then wrapped his arms around her and held her firmly, as if to save their bodies from the sudden explosion of her grief. It lasted for perhaps a minute, and then he relaxed, released her and stepped back. "Life's awful flimsy," he said.

She nodded and turned toward the door. He was still standing there when she closed it gently.

———

After the first call from Toronto, she decided to turn off her cellphone and put it away for good—forever, if such a blessing could be arranged. The voice had been impersonal. "I'm calling from the newsroom. The wires are reporting what happened. I got your number from Molly Blue. She didn't think you'd mind . . ."

She'd mumbled something briefly. Maybe, "We really don't know anything. I'm sorry." Which was very, very true.

Just before the causeway, she said, "You can take me to a motel in town. I know one with a car rental agency. I'll need a car while I'm here."

"I figured you'd be staying at the house. And there's JC's car."

"No, John, please. I couldn't . . ."

"My house. You'll be staying with me. Janice is expecting us."

It was late afternoon when they turned up the country road known as the Long Stretch, where their common life began, evolved and ended. She wished that she'd insisted on staying somewhere else, even at the apartment Sextus rented in town.

"I haven't heard from Sextus," she said.

"You will," John said. "He called first thing Saturday. We decided it should be me contacting you. Since I was there when it happened, in a way. But I think he's pretty shook up about it. Himself and JC go back a way, I understand."

"Way, way back," she said.

"He said he wants to get himself together before he sees you. Says he wouldn't be much help to you the way he is now. Okay?"

She nodded.

———

The old house had the tidy, well-maintained appearance of a year-round dwelling. The grass was cut, firewood neatly stacked on the little deck that ran along the front. There was a car—a second-hand Toyota JC had purchased when he'd first arrived. This visible reminder of his recent presence was almost more than she could bear. She remembered how he'd used the word "civility," and she suppressed a bitter laugh.

A yellow plastic ribbon fluttered in the gateway. "The Mounties put that there," John said. "People were coming out all morning, just to look. This kind of thing is still pretty rare around here."

She turned her face away.

Janice was holding the baby in her arms, pacing, when they entered the kitchen. Little Jack was squawking loudly, his mother shushing. John set his backpack on the floor and took the baby from her. "Hey," he said. "Come and meet the visitor. This here's Effie." He turned the child to show his face. "What do you think? A Gillis or what?"

"He's got the Gillis lungs," his mother said.

Effie turned toward her. "Janice, we haven't met," she said. They shook hands.

"I wish the circumstances were happier," Janice said.

Effie nodded.

John had walked away with the child, chatting to him with an intimacy that seemed to register, for the crying had stopped.

"You must be hungry," Janice said, and Effie demurred. "Maybe a drink?"

Effie declined that too.

She sat on the bedside in the unfamiliar room. This had been her home, thirty years before. It was a place in the memory without features, just a sensation of time passing. Two years, perhaps. Could it have been just two years? It had been not quite two years since her first encounter with JC Campbell on the St. George subway platform. She curled her body on the bed, hands clasped between her knees, trying to remember details of the two years she had lived in this place, but they were lost in the overwhelming immediacy of the time just gone, the two years that would define tomorrow and the unimaginable march of time beyond tomorrow.

Janice was speaking softly at the bedroom door. Effie had somehow unpacked, undressed and slept, and now she was confused. The word "police" brought clarity. An officer had called and would like to meet with her in an hour at her house. They were hoping she might be able to help them ascertain what, if anything, was missing.

"I asked if it could wait, but they said it was important to the investigation. They let me clean up the place yesterday, after they took their pictures and went over everything for fingerprints. It was a mess, but it's okay now. I could go with you. Or John could."

"It's okay," Effie said. "I have to face it sooner or later."


The officer seemed young, his manner awkward. He explained much of what she already knew. John was their only source of information, other than the speculative recreation they had sketched out on a large yellow notepad. He explained a theory, referring to a floor plan of the kitchen/living area, the two small bedrooms, once hers and Duncan's, one of which was now an office. There were dotted lines, showing the presumed entrance and subsequent movements of the attackers.

"We figure they didn't get beyond the kitchen right away, or at least not far," the policeman said. "There was a wallet, with money and credit cards here." He was pointing to the bedroom in the sketch. "We figure if anything was missing, it came from here." Now he was indicating the office.

"There should have been a laptop," she said. "Before I went away, he had it here."

She walked slowly toward the office doorway. The table that had served as a desk was littered with scraps of paper, notepads and pens. There were books.

"The witness, from up the road, said he saw a young female carrying something," the policeman said.

"I believe that would have been the laptop."

And suddenly the scene was clear to her.

"He would have fought them for the laptop," she said. "He wouldn't have allowed them to take that without a struggle. Money wouldn't have mattered, or if they tried to take his car. But the laptop . . ."

"Do you know what was so important about the computer?"

"Yes," she said. "He was writing something."

"Do you know what he was writing? It'll be important if we find it. Unless, of course, they deleted everything."

"Yes," she said. "He was writing about something that happened to someone he knew."

"I see. Like a book?"

"Like a book."

The policeman walked past her to the desk, and when he turned, he was holding the manuscript that Sextus had written.

"Would this be the hard copy?"

"No," she said. "That's something else. Something different."

"Do you know the make of the laptop?"

"No," she said. "I never really paid attention. It didn't seem important."

"I'm sorry to be dragging you through all this," the policeman said. "But every little bit of information helps."

"You have no idea who did this?" she said.

"No," he said. "This sort of thing doesn't happen much around here, though there have been a few recent cases. Some old folks don't trust banks and don't lock doors. It's usually about drugs."

"What are the chances you'll find out?"

"Oh, chances are better than good," he said. "It's still pretty shocking when this happens here. Even the perpetrators are kind of disturbed by it. They have to talk about it; word gets around."

The policeman returned the manuscript to the desk. "I guess that'll be all for now," he said. "Do you need a lift home?"

"This is home," she said.

"Yes, I suppose. Sorry about that. I meant, to where you're staying."

"I can walk," she said. "I need fresh air. May I take that with me?" She gestured toward the manuscript.

"I suppose so," he said. "It belongs to you?"

"Yes," she said. "It's mine."

He picked it up again, examined it briefly. "*Why Men Lie,*" he said. "Sounds interesting." He handed it to her.

"There was a plastic bag," she said. "A No Frills bag."

"No frills," he said, and smiled, and looked around him, taking in the bare wooden walls, the modest furnishings. "You could do a lot with this place."

"That's the bag over there," she said.


Duncan arrived Monday evening. On the telephone he'd inquired about a funeral. She gave the phone to John and left the room. John told her later that Duncan felt he had to be here. Now he held her briefly, and it felt odd, the comforting of this familiar stranger. She realized that he was wearing his priest's collar and black suit.

"The collar," she said.

"I had to go standby," he said. "I thought I'd use all my assets."

She forced herself to listen as John again recounted what he knew, the scene inside the house, the fleeing girl.

"It wasn't anyone you recognized?" Duncan asked.

"I never really got a good look at her face," John replied. "The light was behind her. I was distracted by what was going on inside."

"So what's next?" Duncan asked.

"They told us it might be days before they release the body," John said.

"I can stick around," said Duncan.

After John and Janice had gone to bed, they sat in silence in the living room. "Do you remember how we'd come over here on Christmas Day and they'd always have a tree decorated? Over there, in that corner. We weren't much for Christmas trees at our place."

He laughed. "John always got things from Santa. We did too, but his stuff was always better. I remember once he got a train set. I had a cap gun and was pretty thrilled until I saw that thing."

"There was always something here for us too. Under their tree. Do you remember?"

"Yes," he said. "And it always felt queer. Like they felt sorry for us."

"They meant well."

"We should be home," he said.

"I don't think the police want us staying there yet," she said.

"They told you that?"

"No."

"He was happy here," she said eventually. "He liked the quiet."

"He had it tough growing up."

"He never talked much about it."

"He'd get beaten up a lot as a boy," Duncan said. "Once he asked his dad if he could join a gym so he could learn to box. His dad said, 'You don't need to learn to box, you need to learn to fight. Boxing's a game. Fighting isn't.' So his dad taught him how to fight. I guess he remembered."

"But not enough," she said.

Duncan produced a bottle. "A little splash?" he offered. She declined. "It might help you sleep."

She stood. "I don't think so." She yawned. "I'm tired," she said, then leaned and kissed her brother's forehead.

Later she heard the outside door closing behind him.

Awaiting sleep, she fought the urge to speculate. The safest place, she realized, was memory, where there were no longer any questions of importance. But memories were painful. She left the bed, stood by a window that overlooked the lane. It was a bright night, illuminated by the rising moon. She could see the road, but looming poplars blocked the sightline to the house where she'd grown up. She raised the window, felt the instant breath of cool, moist air and shivered. Then she donned jeans, a T-shirt, a sweater, running shoes, and followed her brother into the revealing night.

Duncan was leaning on the gate, elbows resting on top of it, one foot on the bottom rail. He had the whisky bottle in his hand. "A crime scene," he said. "Who'd have thought?"

She took the bottle from his hand. The cork squeaked as she twisted. "Depends on what you mean by 'crime.'"

He was staring at her, but she resisted the implicit invitation. "You were right," she said. "We should have just moved in here. Move in and move on, I say."

She sipped straight from the bottle and handed it back.

"I was thinking, walking over, that we should just get rid of the place," he said. "Bulldoze it. But that would be pointless."

"What's your plan?" she asked.

"It hasn't changed," he said. "One day at a time until I hear the call."

"Could you be alone, for the duration? I mean, knowing solitude as well as you do, in every sense."

"I don't know. Maybe I can join the Anglicans."

"That's one solution," Effie said.

"There was a fellow in the seminary, Aloysius Ball, his name was. Used to say that he was going to join the Anglicans just so he could be called Canon Ball."

"You're ducking the issue," she said.

"Who knows what I'll do? Everyone has needs," he said. "Including me."

"JC didn't," she said. "He was self-contained. It was what attracted me and scared me at the same time."

"What scared you?"

"I needed him to need something from me, something that would hold him."

She heard the plunk of the extracted cork, and a gurgle as he swallowed. "Let's walk back," he said, disengaging from the gate.

He draped a heavy arm over her shoulder, and she caught his hand as they walked. "Would it make you feel any better," he said, "if I was to tell you that he so badly needed something you have that he once did something almost . . . unforgivable to get it?"

"I wouldn't believe it, anyway," she said. "So . . ."

They walked in silence for the remaining distance to the Gillis driveway. Then he stopped and seemed to study the ground at their feet. "Well," he said. "I'll tell you anyway. JC needed to have you in his life. And he needed it badly enough to make up a big bad lie to get you."

"A lie?"

"He lied to both of us about Stella and Sextus."

After she had listened and understood, she said, "He didn't really lie, did he? He never said it in so many words."

"That's true. But he intended to make something happen, and he did so by creating false impressions. I told him so."

"You told him?"

Duncan hadn't really expected to see JC again that July night in Toronto. And it was late when he reappeared, maybe just past eleven. He seemed preoccupied, lost in thought. He asked if Duncan had anything to drink and, while it was strictly against the shelter's rules, Duncan was able to produce a bottle from somewhere deep in his personal belongings. "It's medicinal," he said. "I keep it for emergencies."

He poured two drinks. "So you didn't find your fugitive?"

JC shook his head. "But that isn't why I'm here. I didn't come to tell you that." After a pause, he said, "I owe you an apology."

And he explained how Sextus, distraught, had been in touch with him just before Easter—Palm Sunday, in fact. He asked JC to intervene with Effie and her brother, to explain a situation. Duncan had misunderstood something Stella had attempted to communicate, then Duncan had compounded the damage by telling Effie. JC had history with everyone, and yet, because he'd been away so long, he had the appearance of neutrality. Sextus wanted him to set the record straight—to tell them that he and Stella were just friends.

Except that JC was anything but neutral. For decades, Effie had represented, in his mind, an ideal that no other woman could ever hope to meet. "At some deep level he was a Platonist."

"A Platonist?"

"An idealist. They tend to be extreme in their expectations. They aren't afraid to lie for a good cause."

"Why did he tell you?"

"He wanted me to get back in touch with Stella. He felt bad about her. And, I suppose, me."

"And Sextus?"

"He figured Sextus had his chance, years ago. And blew it."

"It sounds so simple, like that."

"He wasn't entirely wrong, about Sextus."

"So he was asking for your forgiveness."

"No. He understood that for absolution there has to be contrition. And he wasn't sorry for anything. They can be like that, Platonists. Kind of rigid."

"You're not one?

"Far from it."

"So this is what he gets for lying. If it wasn't for that lie, he wouldn't have been here."

Duncan hesitated. "I wouldn't go too far down that avenue. I think you've punished yourself quite enough for one lifetime."

"What about the next lifetime?"

"We'll cross that bridge when we come to it," he said.

The night had darkened. Clouds had appeared, and now the damp breeze was gusting gently. Duncan sighed. "There was a time when we knew this place so well that you could make precise predictions based upon the smallest things. The weather, the old man's mood. You'd see the gulls on a garbage pile and know right away that there was a storm coming from the southeast. The old man would come in the door, half-skiffed, with a certain look in his eye, and it was batten down the hatches. It's something, to know people and a place that well. Then there are the moments that take you by surprise, no matter how well you know a person or a place."

"I don't care how many lies there were," she said, after what felt like a long time. "They don't change anything."

"I didn't think they would."

The wind rustled in the trees. "Love and faith," said Duncan, after a long silence. "Human impulses that have nothing to do with knowing anyone or anything."

She studied her brother's face as he stared off into nothingness.

"Don't ask," he said.

"You can't last."

"I have lasted," he replied. "More than thirty years I've lasted."

"But it can't go on."

He sighed. "We'll see."

## 23

She woke to the battering of wind, the whoosh of trees. The keys to memory are in the subtle senses, the otic and the olfactory, the ear, the nose. She listened to the timeless, unalterable sounds, felt the shifting air around her as the old house creaked and gave up its musty memories of past lives, memories inert as attic dust. Silently she vowed, *He'll never be like that, nor the part of life he occupied and energized for all the time to come. Never dust. And he must never be nostalgia, which is, like dust, the wasted memory of loss.*

She rose, stretched. Her suitcase was open on the bedroom floor. She rummaged for a warmer sweater, brushed plastic. She picked up the No Frills bag and removed the manuscript, then the title page. She began to read.

## PROLOGUE

Jack Gillis had the moral advantage of having come to terms with personal extinction. "There isn't much to be said for where I am right now," he declared. "But you get to know what matters. And it doesn't matter why my brother shot himself. So if there's nothing else to talk about, just go away."

"You're going to listen," Sextus said. "Maybe then you'll under-stand why I'm the way I am."

"What does it matter the way you are . . . the way anybody is?"

"Truth matters."

"Truth isn't all that it's cracked up to be."

She stood, then squatted to return the manuscript to the yellow No Frills bag.

She entered a busy kitchen. Janice was at the stove, stirring a pot. Duncan had accepted the offer of porridge and was on the phone. John was in a rocking chair near the sandstone fireplace that dominated the kitchen, balancing the baby on his knee. Then Duncan was saying, "You can courier the ashes? Great."

When he'd put the phone down, Effie said, "I think I could have handled that."

"I'm sure you could have," he replied. "But why would you?"

"When?" she asked.

"They think Friday."

"I haven't thought it through," she said. "I suppose there has to be a funeral."

"A little service," Duncan said. "Maybe on the boat?"

Then John said, "That Mountie phoned a little while ago. They want to talk to you again."

"Oh God."

"I'll go with you," Duncan said. "They want to see you at the office as soon as possible. I think they've made some progress."

Driving by the old house in daylight, she was reminded of her brother's words the night before. "I was thinking about what you said, about getting rid of it. Maybe not bulldozing it. But maybe passing it on to someone else."

"Who would want it?"

"I don't know."

"The old Gillis place has come a long way," he said. "Nothing like new blood to bring an old place back."

"Maybe Ray and Cassie," she said. "Maybe they'd want it." Then she remembered: "Did I tell you they're expecting?"

Duncan laughed. "That old Ray." Then laughed again.

"And they're moving to Sudbury," she said. "He's joining a new practice there."

"It would take quite a bit of work," Duncan said. "It should be jacked up, and a proper basement dug."

"I doubt they'd want it," Effie said. "Even if we could forget what happened, it's ugly here. Nothing you'd want to look at. No vistas."

"You never know what people see in a place," Duncan said. "Have you ever been to Sudbury?"

At first the name meant nothing to them. Marguerite Bourgeoys. "There was a famous nun," Duncan ventured. "That's the only one I ever heard of."

"Nun?" the Mountie said, perplexed.

"Founder of the CND," said Duncan. "The Congrégation de Notre-Dame. Long, long time ago."

Then Effie said, "I think I know who you mean."

"She showed up here yesterday with her mother," the Mountie said. "She gave us the whole story. Then they said they wanted to tell you, face to face. Can I bring them in?"

She might not have recognized the girl, and realized it was because on both previous occasions the face now before her had been contorted by fury. The fury was gone, replaced by fear and what Effie would later realize was hopelessness. The mother's face was damp and swollen. *She's his daughter,* Effie thought, with a sensation resembling distaste. *Sylvia.* Then she wondered, *Should I commiserate? Say, "Sorry for your loss?"*

She struggled to contain her anger. *Trash,* she thought. *These people are trash, a blight upon society.*

"I want to tell you again," the policeman said. "You can have a lawyer here if you wish. Anything you say can and will become evidence. You understand?" His tone revealed that he shared her attitude.

The mother shrugged. "What's the good of a lawyer now?"

"As long as you understand your rights," the policeman said.

Sylvia ignored him, faced her daughter and said, "Tell them how it happened."

The girl began to cry, and everybody waited awkwardly as the raw emotion rippled through her.

Their names were Steve and Jason. She'd met them at the rink. She knew them from school, though they were older. They were already high, and she shared a joint with them. They needed money. Someone they knew had a fresh supply of Oxycontin pills, potent oxy-40s. She called it "oxycotton." She told them that she thought she knew someone who would help them. Her grandfather, actually.

They'd laughed at her and made mean jokes: "We didn't know you had a grandfather," they said. "You never even had a fuckin' father."

And she had told them that, actually, her grandfather was a famous man, a writer who was also big in television, had been everywhere in the world, been in all the wars, knew important people everywhere. And that he was obviously well to do.

"You don't even know him," they mocked.

"I do too," she replied. "He told me if I ever needed anything, just to look him up."

"And where does this grandpa live?"

"Out the Long Stretch," she replied. "My mom showed me where. We went out there to see him one day, but she got cold feet at the last minute and we didn't go in."

"That's true," JC's daughter said now. "I thought maybe he could make an impression on her. He really tried to help when she went missing that time."

"I saw you together, you and your grandfather," Effie said.

"Maybe," the girl said. "He tracked me down once. That was when he said if I ever needed anything."

"That's crap," Effie said. "I saw you run away from him."

The girl went still and stared at her, blinking rapidly.

"It's okay," Duncan said. He took Effie's hand in his. "Just keep on with your story."

So they drove to the Long Stretch Friday night. It was between nine and ten. They sent her to the door. He opened it and seemed pleased to see her. The guys had told her to ask him for a small loan. They'd pay it back. They had money coming. But before she got a chance to ask him anything, they came charging in and ordered her to go to the car and wait.

"And what was he doing at this point, JC—your grandfather— when these guys barged in?" Duncan asked.

"Nothing," she said. "Just standing there, quiet like. He didn't seem to be concerned. I think he said something like, 'So what can I do for you guys?' He even sounded friendly."

"So you went out?" said Duncan.

"Yes. And then there was a big noise. And I heard one of them calling me back in. So I went."

"And what did you see?"

"They were fighting. There was blood. Jason, I think, handed me the laptop and told me to run. So I did. Then the other guy came, an older man. I don't know who he was."

"So you went to the car."

"Tell them about the laptop," her mother instructed.

"It was broke. They hit him with it, and it must have broke something. Steve knows about computers, and he said afterwards that it was ruined and told me to get rid of it."

"They hit him?" Effie said.

"Yes. They told me afterwards that when Jason came out of the room with the computer, the guy freaked."

"You mean your grandfather," Effie said.

The girl put her fist to her mouth and began to weep again. They watched and listened. "Steve tackled him, and they were struggling, and Steve got cut somehow. And that was when Jason hit him on the head."

"And where's the laptop now?" said Effie.

The girl turned to her mother.

"Tell them," Sylvia instructed.

"I threw it off the end of the government wharf. Where the tugboats are."

The policeman shook his head. "I know what you're thinking, and we can try. But there's nothing but muck out there. It'll be lost in the ooze. We don't really need it, anyway."

"I want it back," said Effie. "Whatever it takes."

"I'm sorry," the Mountie said. "It would be a waste of time."

Then the girl said, "This fell out of it." She was holding up a disc.

"You didn't tell us about that," the Mountie said sharply as he reached to take it from her hand.

"I forgot," the girl said. "I just realized now . . . I had it in my pocket."

"Do you recognize this?" the Mountie asked Effie, holding it up.

"Yes," she said quietly. "It's his."

The policeman wrote something on a notepad, then opened a desk drawer and took out an envelope, sealed the disc inside.

"I'd like to have that," Effie said.

"I'm afraid it's evidence," the Mountie said.

"At least a copy," Effie said. "Please. It's all that's left."

"I'll speak to the Crown," the Mountie said. "It shouldn't be a problem to make a copy. You know what's on this?"

"Yes," she said. "I'm pretty sure I know."

When they returned to the Long Stretch, Sextus was in the kitchen with Janice. They were seated at the table, teacups before them, and Effie realized that of all the people in the room, Sextus was the one to whom she felt the closest, the one whose life had most consistently intersected with her own. He came to her slowly, reaching for her hands. She put her arms around him, closed her eyes, felt his arms encircle her, a hand stroke her back and then her hair.

"You don't have to say anything," he whispered. "I know."

Later Janice lit a fire in the vast fireplace. "There's a chill tonight. It'll warm the place."

"It was probably once the centre of the house," Duncan said. "You'd spend the winter pretty close to this thing."

"I didn't know it existed when I lived here," Effie said. "It must have been walled in." Her voice must have inadvertently revealed regret at having once again stirred the embers of a long forgotten past.

"How long was it, that you were here?" Janice asked.

"Off and on for years," Effie said. "I practically grew up here. Mr. and Mrs. Gillis were like my parents."

And they all just sat there for a while, memories retracting into private places.

"Did you ever find that manuscript?" Sextus asked after the long silence.

"Yes," Effie said. "JC found it for me. It's upstairs, actually."

"So it wasn't lost after all."

"No. It wasn't lost. I had an idea all along where it was."

"Go get it," Sextus said.

"I think we all could use a drink," said John. "Even me. What do you think, Jan?"

She squeezed his hand, and he stood. Then the door opened, and it was Stella. Duncan went to her.

"I hope I'm not . . ."

"Thanks for coming," Duncan said quietly, and took her hand in his.

When Effie returned with the No Frills bag, John was balancing a tray of drinks, and eager hands were claiming tinkling glasses. Then he fetched the bottle and a jug of water and placed them on the floor within easy reach. "Next round, you're on your own," he said. They sat, chairs hauled up close to the fire.

Sextus took the manuscript from the bag and studied it, flipped through some pages, then sighed. He removed his reading glasses and slipped them into a shirt pocket. He tossed some pages into the fireplace, almost carelessly, and watched them flutter and land separately just beyond the flames. Nobody moved or spoke. The title page sat there for what seemed like many seconds. Sextus sipped his drink, then threw in more pages. These landed closer to the blaze and caught, curled, flared and blackened.

And he continued feeding paper to the insatiable fire until the manuscript was gone.

He drained his glass. "That felt good," he said.

A sudden draught from the chimney caught the remnants of a blackened page, and it flaked into tiny fragments.

"Now we'll never know," said Janice.

"Know what?" said John.

"Why men lie," she said.

Nobody spoke. Duncan seemed to be asleep, chin resting on his chest, eyes shut. Then he opened his eyes and sat up. "Don't look at me," he said. "Sextus wrote the book."

Sextus raised his hands in a gesture of helplessness.

When she awoke on Saturday, a dense fog seemed to hold the morning back. It lingered in the trees and hollows like the smoky aftermath of devastation. Grief wears many disguises, but today it would arrive as naked sorrow. Silently she prayed for rain and wind. The air outside was motionless, flattened and subdued by the weight of moisture, and by nine o'clock she saw the clear blue sky briefly, as if through a small tear in a dreary canopy. By ten the day was shimmering with sunshine and warmth that only added to her pain because it brought back memories of summer.

Duncan had spent most of Friday at his boat. There were obscure marine functions he had to check: battery, starter, various fluids and pumps. Effie suspected that there were other reasons for Duncan's absence, but she welcomed the solitude. She slept a lot, aware that a compulsive urge to stay in bed could be a symptom of depression. She didn't care where the urge came from. She indulged it.

When she heard her brother's voice late Friday afternoon, she rose and dressed and started down. Approaching the kitchen through the living room, she overheard him telling John he'd left "it" at the old house.

"What's 'it'?" she asked, and Duncan answered with a brief, uncomfortable glance. Finally he said, "The urn."

"The urn," she said.

"His ashes," Duncan said. "I picked them up at the funeral home in town. They arrived by courier from Halifax today. I left them on the little table in his room."

"His room."

"Your room," Duncan said.

They sat with drinks while supper was prepared. She said, "It must have cost something, the cremation and the shipping. The urn."

"I took care of it," Duncan said.

"I'll settle with you after, when we're back in Toronto."

"Sure," he said. "And I'll give you a hand with the formalities."

"What formalities?" she asked.

"The estate. He made you his executor," Duncan said. "He didn't tell you?"

"No," she said. "When did that happen?"

"Back in the winter. The little encounter on New Year's Day seemed to make him conscious of mortality."

"How do you know this?"

"He told me."

"You two talked a lot."

"We did. I think he considered me his . . . like his brother."

And she noticed the tiny catch in her brother's voice, the briefest hint of vulnerability. She couldn't see his face, for he was staring at the opposite wall, but she could see the tension in his shoulders and his neck, a tiny ripple just below his jaw.

She put down her drink and returned to the bedroom.

And now it was Saturday morning and sunshine had defeated fog and summer had returned. She sat up, willed her legs to move, to rise and shove aside the heavy blankets, to swing to the bedside; her back to stiffen; her arms to move her body upward. And then she studied the floor and her bare feet. And suddenly it came to her, as if in his voice. *Get up,* the voice said. *Move on. You are the custodian of hope.*

She dressed quickly. The washing and the brushing and the makeup could come later.

Duncan was in the living room with a mug of coffee and a newspaper.

"They've caught them," he said. "They found one of them in the hospital in Sydney. Seems JC made quite a mess of him. The other one was holed up in Halifax. They've been charged with murder."

"What will happen?"

"Nothing much. They're still under eighteen."

"What about the girl?"

"She's in just as deep as they are. She made it happen."

"I want to help her."

Duncan put the paper down.

"Last night you told me I'm his executor. He'd want that. He cared about her. I have to do something."

"The courts take victim statements seriously. If you were to ask for compassion . . ."

"Not just that," she said. "I want to use whatever money there might be in his estate to try and help that girl build a life for herself. Do you think it's possible?"

"It's worth a try," he said. "Stella said she knows the kid. Had a lot of dealings with her through the school. She's badly messed up, but basically decent, down deep."

"JC said once that there are no bad people . . ." Effie said.

"Just people," Duncan continued, "who do bad things for complex reasons. I believe that too."

"I think he discovered that talking to that murderer in Texas. Sam."

Duncan nodded. "Have I ever told you, sister, how much I've always lo—" His voice caught. He cleared his throat. "How much I've always looked up to you?"

She studied the sky and saw that puffy clouds were invading the vast blue emptiness. The sea had been still and dark as cobalt when they first left the harbour, boat moving slowly, sombre as a hearse. But now the warmed land radiated heat upward, and as the air began to move, the sea responded lazily. The boat had turned broadside to the swell, rocking gently, drifting closer to the shore.

"That's an interesting rock formation," Sextus said.

"Duncan said it's called the Door," Effie said. "Because of the shape of the hole in it."

"More like a very dramatic tombstone," Sextus said. "Maybe we could put a little plaque on it, with his name and who he was."

"Who he was," she said.

Duncan and Stella were moving carefully along the washboard, Duncan cradling the brass urn in his arms. "We might as well do this," he said. "I think it's going to start to blow."

Duncan studied his sister's face. She nodded.

"Why don't I?" he said.

Nobody spoke.

"I was trying to think of something appropriate to say," Duncan said. "Maybe read something from Scripture. But I drew a blank. Somehow 'dust to dust' doesn't seem right. We are so much more than dust. Ecclesiastes didn't do it for me either."

He handed the urn to Stella and from a back pocket produced a slim book with a pale yellow cover. Effie recognized it. *Four Quartets* by T. S. Eliot.

"When I was at the house yesterday, I saw this on the bedside table. It was open. I suspect he might have been reading it when . . . last Friday night. I'd like to read what it says, where he had it open, because it seems to sum things up."

He cleared his throat:

In my beginning is my end. In succession
Houses rise and fall, crumble, are extended,
Are removed, destroyed, restored, or in their place
Is an open field, or a factory, or a by-pass.
Old stone to new building, old timber to new fires,
Old fires to ashes, and ashes to the earth
Which is already flesh, fur and feces,
Bone of man and beast, cornstalk and leaf.

When he'd finished, he took the urn from Stella and, with some difficulty, pried the lid off.

"Dear friend and brother, I now commend your ashes to the sea, your spirit to the stars."

He began to pour the grey ash and sandy minerals into the water, and they watched it drift away, the lighter, dusty material lingering like lace upon the surface.

Then Duncan made a brief announcement. "I'm going to open a very special bottle—a seventeen-year-old single malt—so we can properly reflect upon the passing of a good man. To JC Campbell, who brought us to this place this day, together in so many ways."

Sextus came to where she was seated, touched her glass with his.

"I'd like to finish what he started," he said. "I heard they found a disc, that they've salvaged a lot of what he had written."

She studied his face until he blushed. "Don't get me wrong," he said.

"I understand. You're being kind. I'm going to need time. Maybe a lot of time."

"You'll never be alone," he said. "Unless you want to be."

She looked away, and as she did something moved along the washboard, near the emptied urn. It was a fine film of ash and dust, and it drifted briefly on an air current then eddied upward, becoming suddenly a tiny cyclone, turning then stalling. Then, finally stilled, it sank to the surface of the throbbing water and disappeared. The sun dimmed briefly as if by a passing cloud, and the wind, awakened, rocked and turned the boat away.

"Goodbye," she whispered.

# Acknowledgements

A woman friend recently asked me where I got the nerve, never mind the insight, to write a novel from a woman's point of view. I didn't have to think long to find the answer. I grew up among women, a houseful of them, in a family and a community that seemed to be defined and dominated by the women. Almost all my teachers were women. Many of the most impressive people I have known and worked with in journalism are women. I have been blessed by close friendship and frequent collaboration with articulate, insightful women. The women I have known have been, for the most part, more interesting than the men—maybe only because they excited greater curiosity on my part, I not being one of them.

This, then, is the product of long observation and close association with women, all of whom I've respected, some of whom I've loved. I'll mention only a few: my mother, Alice Donohue MacIntyre; my aunt, Veronica Donohue MacNeil; my wife, Carol Off; my friend-editor-publisher, Anne Collins; my friend and agent, Shaun Bradley.

A special *tapadh leat* to my friend and Gaelic "editor," John (Seonaidh Ailig) Macpherson.

www.vintage-books.co.uk